Photo by Five Petals Photography

Abigail Owen is an award-winning author who writes romantasy and paranormal romance. She is obsessed with big worlds, fast plots, couples that spark, a dash of snark and oodles of HEAs! Other titles include: wife, mother, Star Wars geek, ex–competitive skydiver, AuDHD, spreadsheet lover, Jeopardy! fanatic, organizational guru, true classic movie buff, linguaphile, wishful world traveller and chocoholic. Abigail currently resides in Austin, Texas, with her own swoon-worthy hero, their (mostly) angelic teenagers, and two adorable fur babies.

abigailowen.com

FICTION
HQ

ALSO BY ABIGAIL OWEN

THE
BLOOD
KING

INFERNO
RISING

ABIGAIL OWEN

The Blood King
© 2020 by Abigail Owen
ISBN 9781038945006

First published in the USA by Entangled Publishing, LLC.
First Australian edition published 2024 by HQ Fiction
an imprint of HQBooks (ABN 47 001 180 918), a subsidiary of HarperCollins
Publishers Australia Pty Limited (ABN 36 009 913 517).

HarperCollins acknowledges the Traditional Custodians of the lands upon which
we live and work, and pays respect to Elders past and present.

Edited by Heather Howland
Cover art and design by LJ Anderson, Mayhem Cover Creations and Bree Archer
Stock art by ppart/GettyImages, getgg/Depositphotos, PHOTOGraphicss/
GettyImages, draco77/GettyImages
Interior design by Britt Marczak

A catalogue record for this book is available from the National Library of Australia
www.librariesaustralia.nla.gov.au

Printed and bound in Australia by McPherson's Printing Group

MIX
Paper | Supporting
responsible forestry
FSC
www.fsc.org   FSC® C001695

The Blood King is a high-heat fantasy romance—and not just from the dragon fire. As such, the story contains elements that might not be suitable for all readers, including war, battle, blood and gore, violence, death, gang violence, murder, injury, hospitalization, perilous situations, graphic language, alcohol use, loss of family, grief, and sex on the page—on *a lot* of pages. Readers who may be sensitive to these elements, please take note and get ready to enter a spicy new world of dragon shifters!

THE DRAGON CLANS

GOLD
King: Uther Hagan
Location: North Europe
Based in: Store Skagastølstind, Norway

BLUE
King: Ladon Ormarr
Location: Western Europe
Based in: Ben Nevis, Scotland

BLACK
King: Gorgon Ejderha
Location: Western Asia/Northern Africa
Based in: Mount Ararat, Turkey

GREEN
King: Fraener Luu
Location: Eastern/Southern Asia
Based in: Yulong Xueshan, China

WHITE
King: Volos Ajdaho
Location: Eastern Europe/Northern Asia
Based in: Kamen, Russia

RED
King: Pytheios Chandali
Location: Central Asia
Based in: Everest, Nepal/China

PROLOGUE

"*The time has come.*"

At the sound of her mother's voice, Skylar Amon jerked her head up from the computer screen she'd been staring at. She'd been studying for her next-level pilot's exam, having completed her final hours needed. But everything in front of her faded as she focused on those words in her mind, a telepathic communication.

Mom is afraid.

That alone petrified Skylar, freezing every thought, every muscle. Their mother was never afraid, always knew what to do. Skylar's heart stopped cold, then slammed against her chest in an attempt to leave her to deal with this alone.

She knew what her mother's words meant, what she had to do. Since the moment she and her three sisters were born, their mother had been preparing them for this day.

"Skylar!" So much fear filled her sister Meira's call, Skylar's body clenched against the sound of it.

"In here," she shouted back.

I can't let the fear in. Fear had no place here. Right now, all she had to do was act.

The screen door banged as Kasia ran into the kitchen from outside. Her pale skin had a greenish tint to it, probably made worse given the contrast to her deep red hair. Her pale blue eyes were wide and wild. "Did you hear that?"

"Yes."

A second later their other sisters, Meira and Angelika, sprinted into the room and they stared at one another. They all knew what those words meant.

"He's come for us," Skylar spat through lips almost frozen.

Pytheios.

The Rotting King of the Red Dragon Clan. The man who had once deluded himself into thinking he could mate their mother, Serefina, because mating a phoenix would make him the High King, legitimize his reign, and grant him incomprehensible blessings. A tyrant whose every decision, every choice, ended with the exact consequences he wanted.

But Serefina had chosen another—Zilant Amon, the King of the White Clan of dragon shifters. For her sins, Pytheios had murdered Zilant.

Terrified, Serefina had escaped.

What the mad king would do if he discovered their mother was pregnant at all, let alone with four babies, had kept them in constant, vigilant fear.

Four possible phoenixes when there had only ever been one born to any previous phoenix in history? The most likely scenario to enter Skylar's nightmares, when she allowed it, would be Pytheios using the sisters against one another. Maybe even force one of them to mate him.

Not that it would end well for him.

Nor for whichever sister he forced after his followers found out he was dead.

Running was all they'd ever known. Five centuries of it. Ages of training, preparing, and hiding.

Was it all to end this night?

The shock that had held her immobile, if only for moments, disappeared. She was the strong one of the four of them. She was the fighter.

Kasia was the courageous one. Meira the brains. And Angelika the heart.

But Skylar was the protector. Ever since they were tiny, she'd been the one to pluck her sisters off the ground when they fell down, or take out the bullies, or speak the hard truths.

She could protect them from this, too.

Gods above I hope I can.

"Let's go." She ran back out through the same screen door Kasia had just come in, her sisters right behind her.

They sprinted through the small backyard of their unassuming house—rickety white siding that needed replacing, dirt-covered screens, and white sheets drying on the line out back. A house in nowhere, Kansas, USA, where they'd lived quietly for the last twenty years. Out through the gate in the chain-link fence and into the clearing beyond. Skylar stopped in the middle of a field with tall, dry grass almost silver in the light of the full moon—the location her mother had told them to meet if they ever heard those words.

The time *had* come.

Death, in the form of a red-winged monster determined to claim the phoenix as his own, was upon them.

"Where's Mom?" Skylar whispered, searching the fields with a desperate gaze. *She should be here by now.*

No sooner had the words passed her lips than a woman suddenly appeared in the field. She hit hard, crumpling to the ground. Skylar gasped as she immediately recognized the long silver handle of a knife illuminated by the moonlight. The blade was buried in their mother's back.

No. Oh, gods, no.

Pytheios had already attacked? He must've caught their mother alone at the diner where they all took shifts. Where Skylar should've been working tonight.

This is my fault.

"Get up. Get up. Get up," Skylar chanted under her breath.

Only her mother continued to lie there, unmoving.

"Mother!" Kasia's voice pierced the sweltering night air.

Serefina Amon raised her head, her black curls, so like Skylar's own, matted to the sweat on her forehead at the effort that small movement took, her expression a mask of dread and determination.

Could she even get them out of here with that injury? She needed to, quickly. The house where they lived was located only ten miles from the diner. Pytheios would be here any second.

Skylar took a step forward but jerked to a stop when her mother gave a miniscule shake of her head. That's all it took. That one tiny movement, and Skylar knew what was coming.

Their mother—their immortal mother who always had time on her side—was dying. This night, one phoenix would turn to ash, and another would rise to take her place. The only question was, would one rise? Or would all four of them?

Before that moment, though, Skylar knew her mother would send them away. Without her. That was the plan. Had always been the plan.

No. I'm not ready. I'm not strong enough to keep us all safe without you.

Serefina focused on her children—each as different from the other as the moon from the sun, all a reflection of both their darkly beautiful mother and her ancestry, born of the red dragon king and the previous phoenix, and their blond-haired, pale-blue-eyed white dragon king father.

A cry of agony burst from Serefina's lips as she forced the crackling energy inside her to manifest into flames spilling over her body, igniting the source of her powers. All around her, the grass burned, tinder to her flames, catching quickly. Her body began to shift—long, glorious feathers bursting from her arms for the first time in her life. A sight Skylar had never wanted to witness. The one time a phoenix ever turned into the bird was when she passed her powers to her daughter, either in death or by choice to willingly give them up.

Serefina seemed to heave a breath into her body, then her voice sounded in Skylar's mind...all their minds. *"I love you all, and I am so proud of you. You are women worthy of our phoenix legacy, but don't let history control you. Find your own way in this world."*

A colossal roar reverberated across the land. Pytheios, in his true form, lured by the flames, was coming for them.

Kasia, Meira, and Angelika all ducked, covering their ears. Skylar didn't duck. She crouched, assuming a fighting position, then looked to her mother.

Her face a mask of anguish, Serefina directed her gaze to the youngest of her quadruplets.

Skylar turned her head to look at Angelika, too. Tears streamed down her sister's face. Her pale blond hair whipped in the wind. "I love you," Angelika mouthed. Skylar had to close her eyes, torn apart. Torn every which way. When she opened them again, her sister was gone. Sent to another place, a safer place, by her mother's will alone.

The flames covering her mother's body ebbed slightly, but she pushed through, focusing next on Meira. More angular and serious, with her bouncy strawberry-blond curls at odds with her personality, she held her body rigidly, dark eyes closed as though unable to watch their mother's last moments.

Just like Angelika, in a silent instant, Meira was gone, too.

Breath coming in panting bursts Skylar could hear even above the crackling roar of flames, her mother had almost completed the shift, her features turning more delicate and yet sharper. At the same time, her feathers had already taken on a gray hue, turning to ash before Skylar's eyes.

Serefina shook her head, as if clearing it, then looked up.

At Skylar.

Skylar stared back, trying to will strength into her mother's body. She knew what came next, but she silently sent her mother a promise. *I'll make sure my sisters never come to harm, and, by the fates, I will destroy Pytheios for doing this to us.*

In an instant, Skylar disappeared into that space, the in-between. Every sense shut down, and she was surrounded by pressure and darkness and utter silence.

But only for moments.

With a whoosh of returning sound, her feet suddenly stood not in the brown grassy field but on solid rock. All around her was granite, mighty columns framing what appeared to be a doorway.

A cave. Where had her mother sent her?

"No. It can't be possible."

Skylar whirled at the sound of a man's voice, crouching into a defensive posture once more, her hands up. Ready to fight.

Before her stood a man with hair so white, it almost glowed even in the dim light of the cavern, cropped close to his head, almost military-style, and eyes a glacial blue. Eyes she and her sisters shared. Her father's eyes. The hallmark of a white dragon shifter.

Only this wasn't her father. Zilant Amon was dead.

"Who are you?" she asked through stiff lips, her voice harsh. Even now, the scents of fire and ash clung to her skin and her clothes.

"I'm your uncle, Tyrek." He took a step forward but stopped when she scooted back. He held up both hands. "You must be Skylar. Serefina made me promise—"

"My father's brother?" Skylar scoffed. "Try again, asshole. He's dead. Pytheios took out the entire royal family of both the Red and White Clans."

"Not dead," the man said. "In hiding these five centuries. Just like you."

She refused to let up, her posture stiff. "Show me."

Without hesitation, he turned. He wore a loose outfit, almost like a *gi*, but with buttons instead of belted, and collarless. She had a clear view of his neck. Sure enough, the intricate design of the Amon crest marked the skin at the nape. A design her mother had made her memorize.

For this day?

"Show me your hand," she snapped.

Every dragon shifter bore two marks. That of their family on their neck, and that of their king on the back of their hand. If any brand showed—an indication he was loyal to the current reigning king of his clan—she'd kill him where he stood.

Tyrek held up his hand, and Skylar sucked in a breath. No mark, which meant... "You're rogue?" she asked.

At the same time, she relaxed her posture, dropping her hands. To be rogue was anathema to dragon shifters, which could only mean he was telling the truth. When Pytheios murdered their father, Tyrek must've run, the danger of being rogue a lesser evil than facing that red bastard.

The man before her gave a sad smile. "You're so like your mother."

Mom.

She'd sent her here to a man Skylar could trust to protect her. To a dragon shifter, a creature she'd learned to hate. To family.

"Mom," Skylar choked.

She dropped to her knees as sorrow grabbed hold of her heart and twisted, squeezing until she couldn't breathe even as sobs wracked her body.

Immediately, Tyrek was there, taking one of her hands in his. He waited through the storm of her tears, an unexpected source of comfort.

"Was it Pytheios?" he asked softly once she quieted.

Skylar nodded, then took a shuddering breath and raised her head, cold determination filling her veins with ice. "I'm going to make him pay. Whatever it takes."

She had to. Her sisters, wherever their mother had sent them, would never be safe until he was dead.

CHAPTER ONE

W*hy the hell did I come here?*
Oh, right. Kasia needs me.

Skylar stayed close to the smoothly curved rock wall as she eased herself down the long, human-sized tunnel the dragon shifters of the Blue Clan used only when in that form. Most of them seemed to prefer flying to their rooms via a massive, hollow center to the mountain fortress inside Ben Nevis, Scotland, where they lived. So the likelihood of being caught was minimal.

After all, she'd been here days without incident.

Still, she remained vigilant, moving slowly, cautiously, the skintight combat-ready gear she wore designed to slide noiselessly, every sense acutely attuned to her surroundings. Any sign she wasn't alone, any hint of a sound or twitch of her instincts, and she'd make herself scarce, ducking into one of the many rooms—mostly small meeting rooms used for clan business—that lined this hallway.

Helpful that a subtle smoky scent hovered around these shifters, preceding them and warning her with plenty of time to spare. In fact, unless she missed her guess, a group had come through here shortly before her. One man in particular. That underlying note of bourbon and blood surrounding Ladon Ormarr, the new king of this clan, was unmistakable. After only a short while hiding here, she'd recognize his scent anywhere.

Skylar gritted her teeth at the admission. She shouldn't be paying attention to any of those blue bastards other than playing keep-away.

"Dammit, Kasia," Skylar muttered under her breath. "This is all your fault."

Her sister was the only reason she'd set a toe anywhere near this place. How Kasia managed to get herself captured by dragon shifters—clan dragons no less—and brought to one of their strongholds was beyond Skylar.

Their mother had taught them a hell of a lot better than that, and now Skylar had to come out of hiding to fix it.

Getting into the citadel of Ben Nevis had been easy. The Blue Clan had been under attack by other clans of dragons at the time, distracting the sentinels. No one had paid the slightest notice to a woman with dark hair and pale blue eyes—not unlike many of the blue shifters here—amid the rush of battle. While gold and green and blue dragons fought over the lair like starved jackals fighting over a carcass, she'd snuck inside and hidden herself away in one of the abandoned living quarters on the upper levels where royalty should be. From there, she'd searched the mountain, trying to find her sister.

When the gold dragons had taken over the place, she'd almost left. Before she could, the blue dragons returned, taking their mountain back—something to do with the death of Uther Hagan, the King of the Gold Clan. Good riddance to the man who'd helped Pytheios murder her father. Skylar had managed to stay hidden through all that, still waiting for her sister.

All her intelligence said Kasia was here.

However, even after Kasia had finally shown her face, Skylar'd had no luck trying to get her on her own, thanks to the damn dragon shifter her sister had mated.

Fucking mated. *What the hell, Kasia?*

Still couldn't get over that one. Disgust curled through her, entwining with deep-seated concern. Had they broken Kasia's mind? Her will? Except, by the glimpses she'd had, her sister didn't act broken. Either way, this had gone on long enough. Skylar was done with patience and waiting. She needed to get both of them out of here to safety. Time to try a different tactic.

Shock and awe.

Maybe more shock than awe. The likelihood of the dragon shifters being awed by her was low, arrogant bastards that they were. They considered themselves top of the supernatural food chain and untouchable. Wrong. Shock, however, she could work with. She needed only seconds once she got close enough to Kasia.

With careful steps and years of being the best pickpocket in her family—stealthy and quick with small hands that made light work—she made her way to where she knew Kasia and her mate would be meeting with the king and his personal guard.

Skylar tucked herself by the door and peeked inside a room set in the natural formation of the cave. A small meeting room with a nondescript conference table and uncomfortable-looking chairs. Sure enough, Kasia and her "mate" sat at one end with Maul, their faithful hellhound, behind her.

Skylar hadn't been the least surprised to see the massive black dog with her sister. Her mother had arranged for Skylar to go to Tyrek. No doubt she'd taken the same protective steps for Kasia, Meira, and Angelika, wherever she'd sent them. Kasia apparently with Maul. The hellhound had been protecting their family ever since they'd found him as a puppy, so it made sense.

The king's sister, who Skylar'd heard called Arden, sat beside Kasia, seemingly fast friends. Skylar shook her head at that. The woman was part of the king's personal guard. A rare female-born, and even more rare female warrior. What was Kasia thinking, befriending the woman?

Around the table sat the rest of the king's personal guard. Seven of them—she catalogued their faces. She'd figure out their names and roles later.

Despite herself, Skylar's attention was drawn to the king. The tall man sat with his back to her, but she recognized him regardless. Black hair, worn cropped close to his head, broad shoulders that held perpetual tension, the sleeves of his dark blue shirt rolled up, as though he couldn't quite submit to the bindings of kinghood.

The Blood King of the Blue Clan didn't scare her.

Even with that long scar running down one side of his face, off to the left of his eye. A wound that had to be terrible not to have gone away with a dragon's accelerated healing. Ladon Ormarr's appearance was as brutal as his reputation.

That damned enticingly dark scent of his wended its way to her. She fisted her hands, irritation with herself spiking.

Focus.

Skylar refused to admit to a certain fascination with the king. Yes, he was striking in a brooding, scary-mother-fucker sort of way, but that should be exactly what turned her off. This was the closest she'd allowed herself to come to him since she'd arrived, and she could practically feel the power vibrating from him. A power that didn't come from the title, but from the man himself, though she had no idea how she recognized that fact. Gut instinct told her that this was a man who could go toe-to-toe with any threat. Unwanted respect stirred but sat uncomfortably.

Could he handle me, *though?*

She had a suspicion that he could, and the idea insidiously settled within her as a point of…interest. Another mental shake was needed. She had yet to meet a man who could keep up.

He's a fucking dragon king. Like Pytheios. Not to be trusted. Definitely not for you.

Skylar pressed her lips together and ignored that stirring of awareness warming her blood, as seemed to happen any time she caught his scent, frustrated as hell that she had to deal with the bothersome sensation at all.

Ladon gazed down the table at the man seated beside Kasia, her sister's mate, Brand Astarot—a gold dragon, made obvious by his golden-hued eyes and his size. All dragons were big, even in human form, but gold dragons tended to be even taller and broader than the others.

"Brock Hagan is your biggest roadblock to the throne," Ladon was advising in a voice that put her in mind of smoky bars and back alleys. She hadn't been close enough to hear him speak yet. Damned if that voice didn't echo the beast living inside him—a low snarl of sound.

Skylar shivered, then frowned and buried any hint of fear under what she had to do. Fear had no place here. Or had that not been fear? She scrunched her nose in distaste at the alternatives… interest, or, gods forbid, attraction.

I'd almost rather it be fear.

"But?" Brand asked.

Ladon didn't move, and she couldn't see his face to gauge his expression. "I would rather not lose my only allied king, or the phoenix, or both. It's too dangerous. You're too valuable."

Anger tightened inside her, and Skylar clenched her fists. He was *using* Kasia, just like their mother had warned. Just like Uncle Tyrek warned before she'd left the safety of her hiding place among a band of rogue dragon shifters holed up in the Andes Mountains to come here.

Damn dragon shifters. Power hungry. Assuming they were the pinnacle of the supernatural food chain. Sneering down on any other paranormal creatures apparently wasn't enough. Any and every man who took the throne of one of the six dragon clans was not to be trusted when it came to what she and her sisters were. They would want a phoenix for their own selfish purposes, do or say anything to claim one.

"What do you suggest, then?" Brand demanded.

"We take the throne," Ladon said.

Take the Gold Clan with only a handful of gold dragons as backup? As far as she could tell, most of that clan's fighters were either dead or currently in a dungeon cell in this mountain.

Skylar rolled her eyes. Did these shifters think of nothing but who sat on a throne and who and what they had to use or kill or fuck to get them there?

"Killing more of my people?" Brand asked. "Why would they accept me as king after that?"

"There has to be a middle ground," Kasia insisted.

Everything inside Skylar slowed and stilled. Why did her sister even care? Wasn't she a captive in this situation?

"Such as?" Ladon asked.

This was as good an opportunity as any. Shock and awe time.

Skylar stepped into full view inside the door. "I'd love to hear this myself."

In her periphery, she was vaguely aware of the king jerking around to face her, but Skylar was too busy glaring at Kasia and her new mate to pay him much heed. The men around Ladon's table all jumped to their feet, low reverberations of warning filling the room, echoing off the rock walls.

"Skylar?" Kasia choked as she rose unsteadily to her feet, her skin leaching color, leaving her now-pale face in stark contrast to her dark red hair.

"Holy shit." Kasia's mate had to reach out to keep his chair from tipping over as he stood as well.

Maul raised his massive head from his paws and whined, a sound Skylar recognized as both a warning and a reprimand. He didn't want her here? Too damn bad. Her sister *needed* her.

Ladon Ormarr stood as well, his gaze intent, penetrating even, though he said nothing. This close, she realized he had a cleft in his chin, which only added to his brutal looks. She shook off her strange awareness of him above all the others in the room.

A dragon king. So freaking wrong.

Arden was the only person to calmly remain seated, looking back and forth between Skylar and Kasia. "Who's Skylar?"

Meanwhile, Ladon raised his head, sniffing the air. Phoenix smelled of smoke, like dragons, but with a sweeter underlying note. Would he scent the difference?

"Who are you?" He reiterated his sister's question, but softly. Again, that shiver skated over her at the deep tumble of his voice, the command there.

"What are you doing here?" Kasia overrode his question before Skylar could answer.

"I'm here to save you from yourself." She flung the accusation at Kasia more harshly than she intended.

Kasia scowled. "Dammit, Sky. I mated Brand by choice."

"Not what I heard." No way that could be true. They'd blackmailed her or brainwashed her. No other explanation made sense.

Granted, the year since her mother's death had shown Skylar a different side to dragon shifters. Living with them after over five hundred years of running from their kind and despising all dragons would not have been her choice of hidey-hole, but that had been different. Those shifters had been in the American colonies, loners fighting against the laws and traditions of the clans—fighting the rule of the dragons in this very room.

Kasia flung out an arm. "I don't give a shit what you heard. We're supposed to stay apart—"

Skylar cut her off. "We were supposed to stay apart so we could be safe from dragon kings and the clans. You went and *mated* one."

Another growled warning filled the space as Ladon's warriors and advisors took offense to her words and the venom in her voice. She didn't give a flying leap about their delicate sensibilities. Skylar advanced into the room. If she could get close enough, she could send Kasia away, somewhere safe. Her own escape would be more difficult, but they could hash that out later.

Ladon stepped into her path.

Incredible blue eyes gave her pause—deep blue and so intense they stole the thoughts from her mind. She hadn't been close enough to see them like this, or to be under his direct influence.

What am I doing? So what, his eyeballs are pretty?

With a sneer, she ran her gaze down him, sizing him up. Then she lifted a single eyebrow, in deliberate insult, making her finding him wanting obvious.

"You're not going near her," he said.

She crossed her arms, unimpressed. She had abilities she was about to rely on to get Kasia out of here. All he could do was shift, and that was doubtful in a room this size. He'd need more space. "You're not going to stop me."

"Who the hell are you?" His lips flattened.

Awwww…the poor king didn't like repeating himself if his frustration was any indication.

Skylar smiled in grim delight. "I'm Kasia's sister."

"Fuck me," Dopey exclaimed, his bald head shiny under the lights.

The rest of Ladon's guard stirred, but she kept her gaze on the king, who focused on her in a way that made everything else shrink into insignificance, fading into the background like white noise, leaving only the two of them to face off.

Mimicking her posture, he crossed his arms and smiled back. "You shouldn't have revealed your presence to me, little firebird."

Those blue eyes took on a hungry expression that sent an answering, inappropriate, inexplicable heat rushing through her, both the look and her reaction resulting in a reverberation of shock that pounded through her like an avalanche.

She returned his watchful stare with a narrow-eyed glare of her own, trying to cover her reaction. "And why not?" she challenged.

"Because now you're *mine*."

Silence settled over the room so thickly it turned deafening. Skylar snorted to cover her sharp inhale. "Like hell." She leaned around him to address Kasia directly. "I'm getting you out of here."

The corner of the eye close to the scar twitched. "I can't let you do that." Ladon clamped a hand down on her arm.

"Bad idea, Ladon—" Kasia's warning came too late—a warning for the king, not Skylar.

Before Kasia finished talking, Skylar rotated her hand in his grasp to grab his wrist in return. At the same time, she turned her hips, a move that shifted both his grip and his angle in relation to her, pulling him off-center and sideways. Needing him down fast, she followed up with a kick to the back of his knee. That should've put him on the floor, except his knee wasn't there when she struck.

Ladon released his hold and spun out of her reach. She backed up quickly, needing to reset and reassess. Damn, he was fast for such a big man.

Ladon held out a hand to stay the men around the table who all appeared ready to step in and help subdue her. "I've got this."

"Keep telling yourself that." Good. He was still underestimating her.

"I don't want to force you," he said, circling her slowly. "But I can't let you leave."

"You don't have a choice." Skylar prowled to the left, studying the way he moved, determined not to admire the powerful grace of his body, anticipating his attack.

Ladon lunged for her, and she blocked, then followed with a knee to his ribs. His grunt at the contact was music to her ears, but she'd gotten too close. He flipped her around and got an arm around her neck.

Luckily, he held her up against his body. Using his grip as leverage, she slammed her head backward, right into his nose.

"Fuck." His grip loosened.

She shot a hand straight up in the air, then stepped back in to him, spun, and brought that arm down over both of his, breaking his hold and trapping his arms under hers. At the same time, she brought her other elbow across, intending to smash it into his face.

But he bodily lifted her with both limbs still stuck under her own. He tossed her back, away from him, then glared across the space between them. Ladon wiped his elbow under his nose, leaving a crimson streak of blood on the sleeve of his otherwise pristine button-down shirt, as well as across his face. "You've been trained."

"No shit." Dragon shifters were bigger, stronger, and faster. Her mother had been no dummy.

He shot across the space, using the speed most shifters could claim, and she jumped back, blocking his hand. Then struck for his face, only to have him block her in return.

They went at it, setting up a rhythm, almost a dance, as they struck, blocked, and parried, trying different moves on each other in rapid succession. Ten moves in, Skylar knew she couldn't beat him. The man had incredible strength on his side, but he was also fast and a phenomenal fighter, one who'd obviously spent a lot of time perfecting his abilities. His technique was flawless, whereas she relied more on instinct and the element of surprise, an advantage she'd lost by now.

He wasn't striking to disable her; he was merely trying to capture her. That meant he wasn't bringing his A game. Worse, the skill he displayed was a big freaking turn-on. How her traitorous body could be reacting to him right that instant infuriated Skylar. Lust was the last thing she should be dealing with.

Frustration roiled inside her, causing her moves to turn more erratic, less precise. The more frustrated she got, the more he seemed to settle into a cold control.

After he tapped her cheek, as if to say he could put her down if he wanted, she let loose a low hiss. "If you're going to hit me, then do it, asshole."

Ladon grinned, a dark predator playing with his prey. "I don't want to hit my future mate."

That did it. Skylar went up in flames, her entire body alight with brilliant red-gold fire that lived and danced across her skin, casting beguiling shadows over the walls. Ladon dropped his hands at the sight, his gaze traveling down her body in a way that had her heart skipping a couple beats.

Focus.

She took advantage of his distraction and lunged, brought forth her fire in a flash of light, and shoved hard with both hands against his chest as she applied the only supernatural gift she'd appeared to inherit from her mother—teleportation. In a blink, he disappeared, leaving a hole of silence in the room.

Ha. Turned out the lame ability to teleport other people— everyone except herself—*could* come in handy after all.

She didn't wait to gloat, and the fates were on her side for once. Kasia had stepped in front of her own mate to watch the fight.

Skylar ran at her hard and pushed her sister the same way she'd done Ladon. "Wait for me," she ordered.

On a gasp, Kasia vanished as well.

Unfortunately, Skylar couldn't go with her. If she could get to Maul, though, he'd get them both out.

As she pivoted to sprint to the hellhound, Brand flipped her around with a heavy hand on her shoulder, then wrapped his other hand around her neck and lifted her off her feet. "What did you do to Kasia?" he demanded through clenched teeth.

Maul lunged to his feet, letting loose a threatening rumble, but Brand ignored the hellhound.

Skylar clawed at his fingers even as spots appeared in her vision at the immediate lack of oxygen. Her fire doused itself as every part of her fixated on the need to breathe, to survive.

He brought her closer to snarl in her face. "I don't give a shit if you are her sister. She'd better be alive and close by."

Maul's growls filled the room as he prowled forward. Even with her own eyes bugging out, she could see the dog's red eyes glowing brighter.

"Get your hands off her." Ladon's voice cracked through the room, lightning in a bottle, making the hairs on her arms stand up even as she flailed.

Damn. I'll never get out of here now. The thought pushed through the blackness trying to take over. She should've sent the king farther away than one room over.

Kasia suddenly reappeared beside them with zero warning she was coming, not even a disturbance of the air around them. Maul's growls immediately ceased, leaving only silence. Kasia laid a hand on her mate's arm. "I'm here, Brand."

Instantly, he dropped Skylar, and not carefully, as he yanked Kasia into his arms, burying his face in her hair. "You're going to be the death of me, princess."

Skylar dropped hard; her disorientation from lack of oxygen had her collapsing to the ground. She rubbed at her neck as she sucked air in, trying to reorient. "Dammit, Kasia," she wheezed through a painful throat. "Control the mongrel you mated, will you?"

Kasia kissed her mate before she dropped to her knees and put her hands on either side of Skylar's face. "When are you going to learn to listen first and act second?"

Skylar glared. "I thought that's what I was doing."

With their mother gone, if she didn't protect her sisters, who else would?

"I should take a look at her neck," a male voice said. Probably Ladon's Healer.

"I'm fine," Skylar insisted. Unfortunately, the strong words were ruined by hoarse vocal cords. She added a glare for good measure, and the man approaching her held up both hands in surrender.

Kasia shook her head and raised her gaze to Ladon, who stood at Skylar's back. She could feel him there and tried to convince herself that her sense of him was more like that of a spider lying in wait in its web, rather than what it actually was.

Awareness.

That term was about to join "moist" on her list of most hated words at this rate.

"I'd like to talk to my sister alone," Kasia said.

Just talk? Skylar probably would've protested, but she was too distracted by a sudden, stark realization that sucked the air out of her lungs a second time, leaving her dazed.

She'd always been able to read people easily. Especially her sisters. For the first time, she was close enough to really take stock of Kasia. Concern bunched her eyebrows together, but that was directed at Skylar. Otherwise, she exhibited no fear. No desperate need to run away. No secret sign that she did, indeed, need help.

"You really mated him of your own free will?" Skylar whispered.

Kasia's lips curved up in a soft smile. The only confirmation Skylar needed.

"Why would you do that?" she demanded now, louder.

CHAPTER TWO

At the derisive tone in Skylar's question, Ladon's eyebrows shot up. Granted, with what he'd learned from Kasia about their family history, he couldn't blame her for hating dragon shifters. Except that was going to cause serious problems with his plan.

Claiming her as he had was the wrong damn move. He could see that now.

Kasia didn't answer Skylar's question, instead looking to Ladon. "I'm serious. I need to talk to her alone."

"No way." The denial punched out of him.

After Skylar had shoved him literally out of the room, it had taken a second to figure out where the hell he was and realize she'd somehow managed to send him next door.

Another teleporting phoenix.

Finding himself in another room in an instant had been a new experience, one that left him bewildered and slightly seasick. As soon as he'd figured out where she'd sent him, he sprinted back to the conference room only to find Kasia gone and Brand holding Skylar aloft by the throat, her feet thrashing in the air as she struggled to find leverage, and none of his men rushing to help.

Immediate and fierce need to rip his friend and only ally's throat out had Ladon starting across the room. Thank the gods Kasia had arrived and stopped Brand before Ladon could give in to that urge.

No way in all the realms of hell was he letting this phoenix out of his sight until she was bound to him—not only to claim her for his people, but to keep her out of the clutches of every other king. He needed her to be his. He'd have to work around her hating dragon shifters issue.

The shock of there being more than one phoenix still shook him to his core. Legend had it only one phoenix ever existed at a time, each mother passing her powers on to her only daughter either through death or with the conscious choice to let those powers go.

There was supposed to be more… Whispers of some kind of blessing, or good fortune, an inability to make a wrong decision. No one was quite sure exactly what. But that *more* had guaranteed the man mated to the phoenix took the position of High King.

Except that hadn't happened for Brand. No bolt of lightning or spotlight from the heavens.

Granted, Kasia brought other assets to the table: teleportation and her visions. And now that there were multiple phoenixes? The other kings wouldn't know what to make of that development. Not that it'd stop them from trying to take one of the phoenixes for themselves.

Ladon gritted his teeth. Too many unknowns. He didn't like it. But they'd have to figure out the High King business and what more than one phoenix meant later. After they killed Pytheios and took down the other old kings.

"I'm not leaving you with her," Brand barked at his mate. "She's clearly dangerous."

Kasia sat back on her heels and rolled her eyes. "She's my sister."

"I wouldn't *hurt* her," Skylar mumbled, still rubbing at her neck.

Ladon scowled as his gaze lit on a pale white line just under the red markings left by Brand's grip. Friend or no friend, if he'd hurt Skylar…except the mark appeared permanent. Like an old scar.

Brand didn't relent, jaw and fists clenching.

"Fine," Kasia conceded. "Brand and Ladon may stay but sit

over there and keep quiet." She pointed across the room at the table. "Everyone else out."

Skylar remained where she was on the floor, rubbing at her throat and glaring at the others with those bright, watercolor blue eyes. At least her skin had turned less sallow. Seconds ago, her pallor had him…concerned.

Ladon did his best to push adrenaline, along with the burning need to claim her immediately, down deep in his gut, though it tested the limits of his control. He gave the members of his guard— his closest friends—as well as the advisors who made up his Curia Regis, a sharp nod and waited in silence while they filed out.

"This is a bad idea," Asher, his Beta, muttered as he passed, but he left just the same.

"Don't do anything foolish," Arden grumbled on her way out the door. "Not that you'll tell me."

Reid, the captain of his guard, followed her out the door with a shake of his head. "I'm sure you'll wheedle him out of any information you want."

He ignored his sister and Reid and took a seat.

Maul returned to his corner, making his intention to remain in the room more than obvious when he dropped to his haunches and leveled them all with the hellhound equivalent of a glare. No one dared argue with the creature. Brand was probably lucky that he'd mated Kasia, or he might not be alive.

Brand sat, too, saying nothing, probably sensing the dangerous edge on which Ladon's emotions balanced.

"Damage my future mate like that again, and I'll rip your arms out of their sockets." The warning slid from Ladon. He couldn't have held it back even if he wanted to. Not that he wanted to.

Still on the floor, Skylar's back stiffened. "I'm not your future anything, asshole."

"Not helping," Kasia said pointedly, adding a glare at him for effect.

Shit. Where'd his control go? He'd just been telling himself to cool it with the claiming language. Ladon clamped down on more words.

Kasia held out her hands and pulled Skylar to her feet, allowing Ladon a view of Skylar's face. His body tensed in reaction. Now that he had a chance to study her, he couldn't deny her beauty. Darker and sharper than her sister, those glacial eyes a striking contrast to her midnight hair, her skin a darker shade than Kasia's paleness, and those lips…

Kasia focused on her sister, her gaze settling. "I love you, but you got this totally wrong."

Given her attitude so far, Ladon waited for an immediate rejection, but Skylar didn't speak for a long beat, searching Kasia's eyes. "My sources informed me that a rogue dragon kidnapped you and dragged you here to mate you to a king. Brand *is* the rightful King of the Gold Throne, right? He killed Uther, and apparently at least some gold dragons now bear Brand's mark on their hands, which makes him king. A king you're mated to. Am I wrong?"

Kasia sent a smiling glance at Brand. "You got it mostly right, but what you missed was that I didn't mate the king I was intended to."

Skylar turned those ice-blue eyes on Ladon. As realization dawned, her lips quirked. "What happened, big boy? Couldn't close the deal?"

Ladon held her glance with an unaffected stare, hiding his reaction. Why the hell was her insulting him so amusing?

"Stop that." Kasia shook her head. "I wasn't aware of Brand's claim to the Gold Throne until after. So, I sort of mated a king, but not on purpose. Ladon stepped aside and is now our strongest ally."

"How sweet," Skylar drawled.

Again, Ladon had to bite back a laugh at the sarcasm glazing her words like a poisoned candy coating. Nothing made him laugh these days. And really, he *should* be offended.

Skylar crossed her arms. "Do you hear yourself? Why are you helping dragon kings?" She spat the last word.

Yeah. She really hated them. Which meant him. This was going to be harder than he had time for.

Kasia scowled. "Are you so blinded by hatred that you can't hear me or see what's in front of your face? I *love* him. Brand is my destined mate."

Kasia turned and lifted the heavy fall of her hair to reveal a symbol branded into her skin at the nape—an insignia that combined the sisters' family crest and Brand's own family mark. Their mating bond had solidified quickly, tethering them to each other for life.

The fight went out of Skylar, her shoulders drooping. She studied her sister's face, then tossed a glance at Brand before returning her focus to Kasia. "You must love him if you'd believe that crap," she said softly.

Given how passionately determined she'd been that Kasia couldn't be here on purpose, that had been fast.

"Our mother mated a dragon king." Kasia's voice was low, and Ladon caught it only because of his enhanced hearing.

Maul lumbered over from where he'd settled in the back corner. He padded to stand in front of Skylar, nuzzling her. She softened, reaching up to scratch the massive hellhound behind his ear, her lips even tipping up as he leaned into her hand. Ladon had to clamp down on the strangest dark emotion. Not used to anything along those lines, it took him a second to place it as jealously.

Of a damn dog.

No.

No way should he be this possessive this fast. He needed her for what she was. That was all.

His ruthless reputation might discourage challenges to his throne from within his own clan, but not impending war with the old kings still ruling the other clans. White, red, black, and green—all the other dragon shifters were gunning for him. To keep the throne and protect his people, what he needed was a miracle, and a phoenix in his corner counted. Luck or no luck. Brand didn't have his clan behind him yet, and Kasia was his.

That left Skylar.

Suddenly both women tensed and focused on the pitch-black

dog who stood more than a head over them both, the scent of a forest fire with an underlying rancid odor of death trailing him everywhere he went in the mountain.

"You were there when our father was killed?" Skylar demanded.

Maul communicated with telepathic images, like a picture book. But telling them about their father's death? How was that possible? Why would he have been there?

Hellhounds were thought to be warriors who had unfinished business, killed before their rightful time, reincarnated to finish what they'd left behind. Legends abounded that their arrival portended death. Not that that had proved true with Maul. How the Amon sisters even had a hellhound as a loyal pet was still a big question mark.

"What's he saying?" Ladon asked.

But neither woman answered, absorbed by whatever Maul was showing them. A few times Skylar shook her head, as if she was denying the images, rejecting them. "No. I don't believe it."

Maul gave a low growl, the sound rousing the dragon inside Ladon. He and Brand were up and out of their chairs in a heartbeat, except that sound turned more menacing as Maul directed his bottomless, red glowing gaze at them and bared his teeth in a snarl.

At the same time, an image of Maul playing with Kasia and Skylar as toddlers flashed through Ladon's mind.

Brand held up both hands. "Okay, boy. You won't hurt them. I get it."

"Do you?" Ladon asked.

Because, despite that image, Maul didn't back down, appearing as though he was about to rip into the two precious phoenixes standing before him at the smallest provocation.

"Hey." Skylar pulled Maul's focus back to herself. "If we were supposed to help dragon kings, then why did Mom hide us from them all our lives?"

Again, the sisters held still, gazing into space, almost trancelike, eyes moving back and forth with whatever the hellhound was showing them.

"You're saying that a *new* king makes a difference?" Kasia asked slowly.

The dog shook his massive head, jowls slapping.

Skylar wiped a spray of drool off her arm. "New kings?"

Maul let out a short huff. An affirmative, if Ladon hazarded a guess.

Hands on her hips, Skylar stepped back, blowing out a long, low breath. "I don't know Kas. This isn't what Mom taught us."

Kasia put a hand on her sister's shoulders. "She taught us to survive. We'll do that better with them than without them."

"Meaning dragon shifters?" Ladon asked. Had the damn dog just helped his cause?

Both women faced him, eyebrows raised.

He stepped closer. "You know, being spoken of like a virus is getting old fast."

Kasia grimaced. "Sorry."

But he hardly noticed, intent on Skylar, who flicked the thick braid of her raven hair over her shoulder. She crossed the room and stepped right in to him, invading his space in a way most didn't dare. Kasia tried to pull her back, and even Brand winced.

But Skylar didn't hesitate even a second, practically chest-bumping him. "I'm so sorry *your* feelings are hurt. Silly me." She smacked her forehead. "I sometimes forget to ignore the fact that your kind *murdered* my entire family. In the name of…what would you call it…" She mimed thinking hard, then snapped her fingers. "Oh yeah. In the name of all-consuming, selfish fucking greed and a throne."

The woman was on a roll, so Ladon crossed his arms and waited for her to run out of steam…and tried his best not to chuckle. Again. Why was this his reaction to her? He also did his best to ignore the way his body hardened as her cloves-tinted smoky scent tantalized his senses.

What would she do if he kissed her right now to shut her up?

Probably slit his throat.

She swung back to Kasia, effectively dismissing him. "You

were saying?"

"You're right," Ladon said.

Slowly, she turned to face him. "Excuse me?"

He dropped his arms and stepped closer, fully aware of how her pupils dilated and those amazing eyes darkened, more of the blue coming out. "I said you're right. My kind, as you put it, wronged your mother and her line. A horror that should never have happened, breaking generations of trust. But, before that, your ancestors ruled beside our kings."

She scowled. "What's that supposed to mean? That we're obligated to continue the tradition or something?"

He shook his head. Gods she was prickly. "No. I'm saying a good relationship is possible."

Skylar snorted her opinion of that.

"It starts with taking down Pytheios, the *false* High King, and his regime of puppet kings. Something I'd think you would want, too."

She narrowed her eyes. "You, a dragon king, want to take him down?"

Ladon couldn't help the way his lips flattened. "These centuries haven't been kind to most dragon shifters, either."

"You're telling me you've suffered?" she scoffed.

He didn't back down. "My people? Yes. After centuries under Thanatos, the king Pytheios made sure was placed on the Blue Throne, all the wealth of the Blue Clan was gone, and most of my people lived in poverty. You said you've been here a while. Did you not notice how...shabby...things are?"

Her gaze flicked around the room. A nondescript meeting room, but the air of neglect and age was unmistakable.

"Worse, the kings in power took those thrones from decent men. Not just your family. Brand's family was killed, too, and Thanatos did nothing to help Brand when he survived and came here asking for asylum as a child. Even though I didn't know who he was at the time, I helped him. I hid him away."

Skylar glanced at Kasia, who nodded a confirmation. She

returned her gaze to him. "And you think you'll do better than those kings?"

Ladon stood straighter, despite the weight of his own self-doubts. He'd be a king for his people, of that he was confident. Protect them, build them back up. Unfortunately, ruling was politics, and he didn't have the temperament for that crap. No tolerance for bullshit, grandstanding, backstabbing, or any of the rest of it. Still...he didn't have a choice, and she didn't need to know any of that right now. "I do."

She cocked her head. "Really?"

Huh. Maybe he wasn't getting through to her.

"Because you are called the *Blood* King for a reason, I understand."

Dammit. For the first time, his reputation reared its ugly head and bit him in the ass.

"And..." she continued, "as soon as you found out what I was, your immediate reaction was to claim me." She took a step back. "Sounds like the same old shit to me. Different justification."

I can't let her leave. A reverberation of shock followed that blink of panic at the idea of her disappearing.

Ladon didn't panic. Ever.

Not when his parents disappeared. Not when he'd taken the throne. Not when the mountain was attacked. Not ever.

"Are you so brainwashed you'll make assumptions on outdated and inaccurate data?" Ladon tossed the words between them and waited for her to pick them up. No way would Skylar, with her obvious fire, be able to ignore a challenge like that.

Except she raised a single eyebrow in an unimpressed smirk. "I stopped taking dares centuries ago."

He spread his hands wide and forced the next words out, no matter how they grated. "Not a dare. More like a challenge, or a proposal if you like. Kasia believes in our vision for the future. Give me the chance to show you."

And now he was back to wooing a phoenix, using time he didn't have. Fuck.

She considered that, considered him. "Why?"

"I won't lie. I can't risk a phoenix falling into the hands of one of the other clans. I'm also not an idiot. I know I can't mate you without you choosing me."

Or he'd definitely burn up in her fire. With dragons, the fates determined who were destined couples. But phoenixes were different. Skylar's own magic would add a whole level of complication and uncertainty to the process. As he understood it, she had to choose him.

Ladon groaned inwardly. Gaining Skylar's approval would likely be the most challenging thing he'd ever tried to accomplish, taking the Blue Throne included. Forget wooing and forget comfort levels. He'd tried that with Kasia before Brand claimed her and look where that got him. She fell for the wrong guy. Not that Ladon's heart had been affected. With Skylar, he'd have to be unrelenting. In his world, he only had time for black and white. Shades of gray were excuses. Until she was his, Skylar Amon was all kinds of gray.

"I can take care of myself." Skylar's chin went up in a gesture so like her sister's the similarity finally showed. "And I don't trust you."

"If she stays, Skylar chooses who to mate and when."

Kasia's statement dropped into a vat of silence.

Skylar swung around to glare at her sister. "Excuse me?"

Ladon narrowed his eyes as he assessed the words and Kasia's hard expression. "I'm not that kind of man. As you know."

Skylar scowled, and he held up a hand. "I don't force women... even for the greater good."

Even if he already wanted Skylar more than he'd wanted a woman in a long damn time. A physical reaction he wouldn't bother to deny.

Skylar snapped her mouth shut.

But Ladon remained focused on Kasia. She obviously had something in mind. For her part, she stared at him long and hard before switching her gaze to her mate. Out of the corner of his eye,

Ladon caught Brand's nod, as if he was agreeing with whatever Kasia was thinking. Their bond as mates must be strengthening if they were already able to communicate wordlessly like that.

Kasia let out a long breath. "I trust him, Sky. I think you should, too."

Those amazing lips pinched. "Nothing you do or say could convince me. He tried to mate you, and now he's just moving on to the next phoenix in line."

"It wasn't like that," Kasia insisted. "I trust him with *our* lives."

The emphasis on "our" snagged at Ladon's attention like a spark catching fire. Something about the way she'd said that meant more than what he could discern. He had no doubt of it. But what?

Skylar jerked back a step, only to bump into him and hastily hop to the side as if he were radioactive. "You *wouldn't*," she hissed at Kasia.

The tension between the sisters was way too high for the surface words. What was Kasia threatening?

Kasia glowered back. "Do you think I would risk it if I didn't believe a thousand percent that he could be trusted? Do you?"

"No..." Skylar conceded slowly. "But—"

Kasia turned sharply to Ladon. "There are four of us."

Skylar sucked in sharply.

Ladon frowned, glancing between them. "Four of who?"

Kasia pulled back her shoulders. "I have three sisters. Skylar, and two others—Meira and Angelika—who are still in hiding."

Her revelation slammed through him, impaling him like the spike of a dragon tail.

Four... Four phoenixes.

How was such a thing even possible? And what the hell did it mean? Dragons believed for millennia that mating *the* phoenix—as in only one—designated which of the kings would be High King. Ladon had naturally assumed Brand, his friend and ally, would one day be High King because of it and was fine with that. Two of the firebirds in existence already called that belief into question.

But *four*?

Skylar threw up both hands, and Kasia would be a puddle on the ground if looks were laser beams. "I can't believe you did that. I am out of here. Hopefully I can get to our sisters before your mate and his goons."

With that, she slammed out of the room.

"Shit." Kasia took a shuddering breath. "I'll go talk to her."

"No." Ladon stepped in front of her before she could follow Skylar out the door. "Let me."

Kasia snorted. "She's not going to listen to *you*. That's for damn sure."

"I can be persuasive." Before she or Brand could say any more, Ladon turned to Maul. "I need to get outside quick, buddy."

The hellhound cocked his head. Kasia could teleport, but so could her pet, and Ladon needed to convince Skylar without an audience.

"I won't hurt her," he promised. He'd merely kidnap her if he had to, because she was damn well not leaving yet.

Maul gave a low bark Ladon took to mean "yes." He put one hand on the animal's spiky-furred shoulder, and they disappeared.

CHAPTER THREE

I can't believe Kasia did that.
Incredulity vied with dark fury in a toxic mash-up that wanted to spark the fire inside her and had Skylar prowling through the massive mountain the Blue Clan called home. She kept to the human-sized hallways, not bothering to watch out for the shifters she might come across. Not that any crossed her path. Though in the mood she was in, they'd be better off staying out of her fucking way.

With every step, she churned through the implications of what Kasia had just revealed.

Their sisters. Their family. How could she put them in danger like that?

Was Kasia that sure these kings could be trusted? Despite seeing her sister and that Brand character together, Skylar had thought, until today, that Kasia had been forced to mate the unsmiling brute of a man.

Apparently, she'd got her wires crossed.

The shock of what Kasia had shared ebbed, and Skylar's steps slowed. Kasia wouldn't easily give that information—she would *never* play with her sisters' lives—unless she was beyond sure. Hell, even Maul wanted Skylar to stay, if those images he'd shown her meant anything.

Stay and be a part of taking down the regime of dragon kings who'd been responsible for so much pain. Her own included.

An actual purpose to her life—not just running and surviving—stirred inside her like a cauldron of insidious, seductive potion.

But she wasn't an idiot. No way would Ladon allow her to choose another shifter to mate, or allow her to stay here indefinitely, without binding her to him. He couldn't risk her power, such as it was, falling to his enemies. Even she got that.

Based on his instant claiming of her as his, she'd bet dollars to doughnuts he'd want that binding sooner rather than later.

The alternative was to go back to where she'd been. Hiding like a coward with her uncle in the mountain of misfit toys. For what?

Or she could seek out Meira and Angelika. To take them where, exactly?

Kasia trusts these men.

Could she, though? Mate a dragon?

A mental image of mating Ladon Ormarr—the two of them wrapped in a tumble of sheets and limbs and fire—came unbidden to her mind, and a throb of instinctual wanting pulsed through her. From a simple physical perspective, mating the man wouldn't be a hardship.

Shit. Why am I even considering this?

Her steps sped back up as she tried to outrun her body's ridiculous reaction to Ladon as well as the wild ideas banging around in her head. Better to leave now. Survive to fight another day, so to speak.

Exactly how their mother had taught them.

Skylar came to a thick dragonsteel door that she knew led outside. After checking that the way was clear, she punched a code into a keypad that she'd managed to witness one of Ladon's people enter a while back. The door beeped, the panel lighting up green, and she burst through a side door onto a wide landing platform that faced out over a natural canyon formed by the mountains of western Scotland. This was where she'd teleported Kasia to wait for her earlier.

As Skylar scanned the craggy mountainside above her, she idly wondered what Angelika and Meira had inherited. What would the dragons do with them when they found out? The thought could be paralyzing if she let it, so she focused on getting away. One thing at a time. Teleporting herself would be nice about now, because without that, she had to climb her ass out of this place, the same way she'd arrived.

Only this time the sentinels weren't distracted by a battle.

With teeth gritted, she grabbed a handhold and got started up the rock face. She'd made it twenty feet up or so when a massive shadow passed overhead, blocking out the watery light of the late autumn sun. Only one thing could make a shadow like that—dragon. Skylar stilled and made like a hole in the wall, slowing her heartrate and hushing her breathing so as to not make a sound.

"You didn't think I'd let you run away that easily, did you?" Ladon's gravel-laden voice penetrated her mind.

Wind whipped, tugging at the loose tendrils of her hair, and a massive blue talon plucked her from the side of the mountain. The action gouged marks into the rock, boulders tumbling out of sight into the canyon below. His grip on her, however, was like being hoisted over a shoulder, knocking the wind from her.

"Ouch," she protested, more for him than because it'd hurt. She could tell he'd attempted to be gentle.

With a powerful downward push of indigo-colored wings, Ladon shot them up the mountain. Skylar didn't bother to fight. She didn't feel like being dropped, and no way would she make a dent against him anyway, not without a weapon. Instead, she waited. He'd have to put her down eventually. Dragons couldn't stay aloft indefinitely. Even the greatest of all the shifters—according to them—needed to rest every now and then.

Stone facing flew past her in a rush, close enough to touch if she reached out. With Ladon's bulk above her, as they continued to fly upward, she couldn't get a view of where they were headed. Until, with almost jarring suddenness, the mountain ended, and they burst into the sky. Ladon leveled out above the ground, his momentum slowing until he hovered before touching down, carefully releasing her and letting her move out from beneath him before putting down his back leg.

She started in on him even as he backed away. "If you think you can force me to stay—"

"*I don't.*"

Skylar paused, both at the words and the sight of him in full dragon.

She had to give it to the bastard—dragons were nothing short of terrifyingly magnificent. Ladon stood at least thirty-five feet high. Wicked spikes rose from the back of his neck and trailed down his spine to a tail that was a weapon all by itself, like a mace. Long and lean, every ridge of his muscled body stood in stark relief. His scales were a striking shade of indigo lightening to slate blue in the centers like his eyes. Under the sunlight, he'd shone like the living waves of a stormy ocean, a swirl of blue in motion as his body rippled with each move, each thrash of his tail, each heave of his lungs.

Whoa.

She shouldn't be impressed, but reluctantly, she couldn't ignore the spark of wonder that ignited inside her. To counteract the effect, she went on the attack. "You don't want to force me to stay? What do you call kidnapping me?"

The massive creature snorted, a blue flame slipping out the side of his maw. *"I call it saving you from stupidity. That fall would've killed you."*

So weird hearing his thoughts while his mouth stayed shut. Most shifters could project their thoughts when in creature form. She should be used to it, especially after the last year, but she had tried to stay scarce when the people she'd lived with shifted.

"So, this was for my benefit?" She waved her hand, like doffing her cap to him. "Thank you, sir. I can take it from here."

She marched off in the direction she knew would take her over the easiest path off the mountain.

Instead of answering, he said nothing. Skylar frowned and tossed a glance over her shoulder, only to catch the faint shimmer around him, like seeing water in a desert when none was there.

He's shifting.

She sped up, though even once he was in human form, she'd never outrun him.

Another series of glances showed his shift as she increased the distance. In silence and a smooth motion that appeared to blur before her eyes, his body changed. Scales morphed into skin and clothing and hair, towering beast became six foot plus, his spine realigned as he pulled upright to stand on two feet, and suddenly standing behind her was a man.

Skylar whipped her head around and kept walking, muttering to herself. "Stubborn dragon shifter. Just leave me alone. Pretty damn obvious that I have no intention—"

The faint rustle of footfall against the stone warned her of his approach. Probably deliberately loud, because no shifter made that much noise by accident.

"Go away." She tossed the words over her shoulder.

Silence.

A quick glance showed him only five feet behind her. She faced front and kept marching. Only he made it obvious that he continued to follow her.

With a *grrrr* of frustration, she lit her hands and spun, lunging for him. Only he hopped out of her way before she could touch him.

"I'm not falling for that twice," he said with a grin guaranteed to raise her ire.

Skylar doused her fire, her fingers taking a second to stop glowing, and kept walking. "How long are you going to be back there?" she asked after another minute of being ridiculously conscious of her ass and the fact that he was probably watching it right now.

"Until you listen to me."

"I have no interest in listening to someone like you."

"No shit."

She braced herself for another round of arguments, not to mention the impact he seemed to have on her. She refused to give way to idiotic, ill-timed attraction—he was too rough for her, too rugged…and way too dragon.

But hearing him out was obviously the only way to get him to leave her alone. She jerked to a halt. "Fine. Say what you have to say."

In a blink, he stood before her. Skylar eyed the man in front of her and tried to filter through conflicting information. Ladon Ormarr was a mass of contradictions—murderer and protector, king and pauper, dragon and man… Destroyer or savior? All growl, that low rumbling voice was a reflection of the creature inside him, but what was his bite like?

Kasia trusts him. Skylar batted that thought aside. Kasia could be too quick to trust.

Except she'd put all four of their lives in the hands of this king. Kasia trusting her mate was one thing, but trusting Ladon… Could she? Could they? Could new kings alter the course of so many fates?

Maul thought so. What did the hellhound see in Ladon Ormarr?

Again, the elusive pull of purpose tugged at her. Skylar crossed her arms against its sway and waited him out.

He held up both hands. "I'm not your enemy." But she didn't miss how he glanced over his shoulder. Searching for what? Backup from other dragons coming to help him capture her?

Skylar tipped up her chin. "Yeah?"

He leveled a look on her that dared her to ask that question again. She'd bet no one questioned this man, but that was not her style.

"Don't leave. Stay and at least see how things are here."

"And I'd be free to go anytime?" she scoffed.

He lowered his hands, moving closer, slowly like she was a trapped animal he didn't want to fly away. "Yes."

She had no reason to trust him, but something in his eyes— hard but resolute—told her he meant that.

Am I even considering this? If she stayed, ultimately that would mean mating.

"I'll be honest. I don't have time to court you," he said.

See. Right to the mating. "Mating is not on the table."

His jaw worked, as though whatever problems he shouldered were piling on him right that instant. "I need to make you mine. I won't deny that."

Who knew intensity, when focused solely on her, could shoot heat through her body like lava in her veins?

"But…" Ladon continued. "I won't force you. Even if I could without being burned to a crisp, I refuse to build my kingdom that way."

A dragon king not just taking anything his greedy hands could grasp? Was such a thing possible? A small voice whispered that her grandfather and her father had been good men, and her uncle still was. "As a phoenix, I could be the difference between your success or failure as a king. You're saying you'd pass that up if I choose to leave?"

Ladon's gaze didn't waver, rock steady. "I'm trying to save my people. I'd do anything for them. *Anything.*"

She believed him.

Ladon rolled his shoulders. "*Except* be like the kings who've ruled these five centuries."

Skylar eyed him dubiously. "The Blood King has a moral center?"

He took a step closer, crowding her—leashed power and determination. "Stay and find out."

For a long beat, Skylar searched his face. She'd always trusted her instincts about people. But, in this case, she was having trouble wading through her own prejudices and a growing attraction that was fucking with her senses. She needed more time. "Prove it to me."

He frowned. "Prove what?"

"Prove to me that I can trust you," she said.

He considered that, his gaze never leaving hers. Did he ever blink? "How?" he asked.

Skylar shrugged. "That's up to you. Just know that I'm not Kasia. I don't trust anyone."

"Is that a challenge?" His eyes glowed with an inner flame. Damn, the man's dragon was still close to the surface.

And that is not sexy.

Who was she kidding?

"Consider it a warning," Skylar said.

"I accept."

That sense of purpose settled inside her more fully. Centuries of running...wandering, and for what? To stay safe? She'd never seen the point, but her mother had been obsessed, and Skylar had her sisters to think about.

She had no intention of jumping into anything without the proof she'd asked for. But... What if helping these new kings could liberate her sisters still in hiding? Angelika and Meira were... softer, sweeter. They wouldn't fight for themselves. They'd stay hidden as long as they could.

If Ladon convinced her that dragons were worthy, she'd stay, even knowing what that ultimately meant for her. If not, she'd kill the Blood King and every other dragon in here on her way out the fucking door. Maybe trigger an avalanche for good measure.

· · ·

That was too easy.

For a woman who'd just tried to climb her way off the mountain, she'd given in faster than he'd expected.

The cold, logical part of him whispered that two other phoenixes existed who could fulfill his needs, and this one was clearly going to be a pain in his ass. He should wait for one of the other sisters and pursue her instead.

But he'd laid a claim the second he'd clapped eyes on Skylar, and a part of him usually frozen deep in his core wanted this woman. Hell, the dragon half of him stirred restlessly inside, eager to claim her now. It made no sense, so he shut it down.

Ignored it in favor of logic. He couldn't risk any of the other kings getting her. He'd have to pray to the gods that Skylar would choose him, and then, if by some miracle she decided in his favor, that *this* phoenix was the one. The fates couldn't be so cruel as to muddy the waters with four. The High King was needed to bring all dragon shifters together. The *right* High King. He needed that if his people were going to survive this war. That was all. "I have a few conditions."

Her dark eyebrows winged high. "You think you have leverage to insist on conditions?"

Ladon shrugged. "I could kick you out while Kasia stays here and we find your other two sisters and bring them under our protection."

Her scowl came fast and fierce. "I wouldn't let you find them—"

"You're one woman against a legion of dragon shifters." He uttered those cold words with no regret or remorse and watched them hit the mark, her eyes widening, though no fear flashed in those icy depths, only anger.

She opened her mouth to argue, but he held up a hand. "I'd rather convince you to help bring them here."

She settled back, glaring at him. He'd be a human Popsicle if looks could freeze. "What conditions?"

Now he was getting somewhere.

He held up a hand, ticking them off on his fingers. "One, you accompany me everywhere, observing how things are, how I lead, meeting my people and my warriors."

"Okay."

"And you don't interfere. Not until you are my mate."

Lips flat, she nodded.

"Two, you sleep in *my* suite."

Her rejection came immediately as she took a jerky step back. "Fuck that—"

He slashed a hand through the air. "I didn't say in my bed. I have another room in which you can sleep."

That slowed her backward progress, though suspicion

continued to spark back at him. "Why?"

"Partly because I am interrupted with business and information at all hours, and I don't want to have to track you down every time you need to be there."

Her shoulders dropped a hair. "You said partly. What else?"

"This." Ladon took three steps until he was close enough to feel the warmth of her body, despite the mist-laden chill in the air humans would probably find freezing. He ran the back of his fingers down the side of her face. Damn, her skin was incredibly soft against his battle-rough hands. This close, the urge to taste those lips rose inside him, dragging at him like a riptide.

How could she have this kind of pull on him already?

Skylar froze, her lips parting in what he wanted to interpret as an unconscious invitation. His body, hard with need, pushed him to take, claim, and plunder, but that needed to come later.

She didn't pull back. Too stubborn, he'd bet. The woman didn't know how to back down. Neither did he.

"Condition three," he murmured, his gaze on those fantasy-inducing lips. What would they look like wrapped around him? "Only stay if becoming my mate is on the table."

He was taking a huge risk. She could walk away, and he'd be fucked.

Slowly she pulled back, a steel wall slamming down behind her eyes. Not that there'd been much give in her a second ago. "I figured mating was the endgame. But you should know, even if we mated, I'm not the type of woman to be claimed like property. I won't be a figurehead, trotted out for special occasions."

Just like Kasia. He should've seen that one coming. Ladon dropped his hand to his side as an answering determination settled deep in his gut. "I don't blame you."

Her chin lifted a fraction. "No?"

"No. I'll earn your trust. When I do that, you mate me. We figure it out from there."

She eyed him warily, and he held his breath. Had he read her wrong? He got the impression this woman didn't back down from a challenge. "*If* you earn my trust."

Her words shouldn't have his blood pumping, but he couldn't deny they did. What would it take to get the firebird to submit to him? His body was eager to find out, had been since she'd walked into the conference room with that smoke and cloves scent of hers.

He stepped back, needing space between them before he did something reckless, and held out a hand instead. "Do you agree to *all* my conditions?"

"Do I have a choice?" she flung at him.

"You could walk away. I won't stop you." An outright lie. Not that he'd meant to lie to her, but the sudden image of Pytheios anywhere near her slammed a black rage through him that took every ounce of his control to subdue.

"I'll find your sisters, though," he continued. No way would a woman who broke into a dragon lair to rescue one sister walk away when all three were in play.

Skylar's lips pulled back in a snarl this side of feral. "*Not* the best way to gain my trust," she observed, almost idly. But he recognized the anger sparking in her eyes anyway.

"Only if you force my hand. I want *you*." The hard truth of those words settled under his skin like shards of glass.

Skylar's eyes flared wide, and, for a brief flash, he thought an answering heat glittered back at him before she shifted her wary gaze to his outstretched hand. "I'm totally going to regret this," she muttered, more to herself. Slowly she reached out to shake, and triumph lit fire through his blood. "Agreed," she said.

"Excellent." He tightened his grip as she tried to extricate her hand. "Let's get started. I'll fly us back down."

She spun on one booted heel and headed toward the edge. "I'll climb down on my own, thanks."

"With me at all times." He let the reminder hang in the air between them.

She paused, and he got the distinct impression that she was arguing with herself right then, though his enhanced hearing didn't pick up any mutterings.

Then her shoulders lifted in a sigh. "Fine," she capitulated. "Go ahead and shift. I'll wait."

With her toe tapping in impatience.

Ladon started his shift to hide another shaft of amusement, an emotion that had been foreign to him for a long time. He hadn't found much to smile about in decades. Centuries. He shouldn't find her in-your-face personality amusing. That damn sure wasn't *her* intention.

But no one challenged him like she did. Not even before he took the throne. Maybe getting his little phoenix to find him worthy would be more fun than he'd thought.

CHAPTER FOUR

Pytheios commandeered the Gold Throne—a gilded, carved masterpiece of beauty—deep in the heart of Store Skagastølstind, the mountain stronghold of the Gold Clan in Norway. Fingers steepled in front of his mouth, he pretended to listen to the previous king's lame-duck heir.

Brock Hagan should be king, yet the Gold Clan remained divided. Half bore the mark of Brand Astarot on the space between their thumb and forefinger. The other half, possibly those still loyal to the Hagan name, bore no mark at all, technically setting them as rogues.

But why? He might be young, but Brock was confident, intelligent, a leader.

Pytheios allowed his gaze to drift to his own son, Merikh. His slighter body, slouched shoulders, and fancy suit stood in stark contrast to Brock's utilitarian gear worn with the air of a fighter. Brock was ready for battle, Merikh a day at the office.

And I thought to make him my heir, put him on the Blue Throne.

Although that had partly been to control his son's mother. He needed his powerful witch to remain loyal. Needed her to continue draining paranormal creatures' power and syphoning it into his body, to keep him alive. At least until she could do so with a phoenix.

Phoenixes were rumored to be immortal. If Rhiamon transferred the powers of one—just one—he would live forever. Rule forever.

No need for an heir.

His gaze slid back to Brock. Though perhaps alternatives to a blood heir should be considered. Immortality wasn't his yet. Even once it was, he would need strong men ruling the clans under him. Uther had been ruthless, and his participation in taking out Zilant Amon had also given the gold dragon reason to remain faithful. Pytheios didn't have that axe to hang over the son's head. Plus, he got the impression that Brock was more unpredictable, which could make him more dangerous. Not necessarily a bad thing.

But will he be loyal?

"If we attack now," Brock was saying, "with the might of the Gold, Green, and Red Clans, we'll topple Ormarr from his throne, kill Astarot, and crush this rebellion before it's truly started." Brock slammed a fist on the large glass tabletop, currently in screen mode, showing thermal imaging of Ben Nevis, the Scottish mountain that housed the Blue Clan.

"The rebellion is already started," Pytheios pointed out in bored tones that brought a flush to the younger man's skin.

Uther had been almost amber in coloring, but his offspring could possibly pass for a black dragon if, true to form, his scales reflected the darker coloring of his eyes.

"Then we finish it." Brock's hands formed into fists.

Pytheios locked gazes with the impudent pup still yapping for scraps and waited. After a long tension-filled silence, Brock sneered and glanced away, stuffing his hands in his pockets.

Ah, there it is. The flash of fear in the younger man's eyes that told Pytheios everything he needed to know. Like Uther, Brock could be loyal. Could be controlled. Perchance, more.

"Do you have a better idea?" Brock asked.

Pytheios rose slowly to disguise the stiffness that had invaded his aging joints of late. He did better in the thinner air of his own mountain stronghold in the Himalayas and should return there posthaste.

"Your father already tried attacking Ormarr directly. Tried…" He deliberately glanced at Brock's hand where the brand of a king should show. "And failed."

Brock's eyes flared with gold flame, casting his face in a surreal glow. Good. He'd need that anger to see this through. Ormarr had proven himself a difficult opponent. With Astarot at his side, and mated to that fucking phoenix…

"I'm not my father," Brock spat.

"No?"

Brock loosed a low rumble that bounced off the rock walls. Before he could do more, Pytheios shot across the room, though his bones protested. He wrapped one gnarled hand around the younger man's neck and used their combined momentum to slam him into the stone, leaving a human-sized imprint.

Pytheios held him there, suspended and choking. "Growl at me again, and I'll rip out your jugular. Understand?"

Deliberately, he'd pitched his voice in casual tones, as though he wasn't choking the life out of the man twisting in his grasp.

Brock clawed at his arms, legs thrashing in the air but finding no purchase. Still, he managed to nod.

Pytheios released him and deliberately turned his back to return to the map displayed on the black glass of the table in the center.

"What do you suggest, my lord?" The voice behind him came out strangled, and satisfaction settled over Pytheios's shoulders like a cloak.

"We don't attack them. We give them a reason to come to you."

Brock stepped up to the table, where his own Beta and several advisors stood in silent anticipation. "How does that help? I can't defend this place. Most of my warriors are still prisoners in Ormarr's godsforsaken fortress. I run this place with women who have never been trained to fight, children too young for their first shifts, and a council of blithering old fools."

A glance at the group of men who looked to be sucking on

lemons at Brock's words didn't change Pytheios's opinion any. Brock's father, Uther, had surrounded himself with men easy to control. Not fighters or leaders.

"We give them what they need most." Pytheios gave a grim smile of anticipation.

"What does that mean?" Brock demanded. At a single glance from Pytheios, he cleared his throat. "I mean, I don't understand."

"Brand Astarot believes all he must do is put down a small contingency of followers loyal to you, and the rest of the clan will fall in with him as their king."

Their sources had reported that Astarot held Brock's men within the bowels of Ben Nevis's dungeons. Only those whose hands had shown the mark of house Astarot had been allowed to live. The same had happened here. Those *with* the mark of Astarot gathered and held. However, the numbers of branded were greater than expected.

Damn that phoenix. Her existence was already having an impact.

In the end, it wouldn't matter. No dragon shifter wanted to follow a rogue. A true rogue, as Brand had been most of his life. The dregs of their society, rogues were usually hunted down and killed by their own. As soon as Brand was killed, his mate would die, too, and loyalty would return to the rightful king.

Ormarr was the bigger concern.

That traitor had taken his throne by force with the support of people who already knew him. There was no question of his rule as every blue dragon shifter bore his mark. And Ormarr had proven he'd kill anyone and anything that got in his way.

However, Ormarr would have to help his friend. He needed allies, too.

"They have no choice but to risk coming here," Brock said slowly. "They must take this throne to legitimize his reign."

Pytheios ran a hand over the smooth screen with the warm bodies glowing red. "They will take their time and attack only when they have the numbers."

Brock shook his head. "They could wait me out, pick off those loyal to me a few at a time."

Pytheios smiled, ignoring the way the expression pulled painfully at his skin, and enjoyed the way Brock's face blanched. With the way his flesh hung from his bones these days, he was well aware how...grotesque...his smiles could be. "So, we give them incentive to come sooner. *Before* they are ready."

To give the man credit, Brock quickly collected himself. "I will not be able to defend this mountain with my depleted numbers. Will the red army be at my disposal?"

"Not the red army, but green."

King Fraener, who stood silently among those listening, gave an eager nod. "You know you have our support."

The King of the Green Clan had already lost men in the attack on Ben Nevis, but Fraener had always been a loyal dog. He would sacrifice more before this was over.

"We'll need a large number of forces," Brock insisted, hands curling into fists on the glass top, the touchscreen responding and scrolling the map, though that fact went unnoticed by the man. "This must be a decisive victory."

"I agree," Pytheios murmured. "Which is why I have called in the services of one of the other kings."

Brock lifted his head at that, a suddenly eager expression turning his yellow-tinted eyes even lighter. "Who?"

A door nearby banged and every head in the room turned to face the massive carved doors that led into the throne room. Within seconds, those slammed open as well and a man with skin the hue of an ancient gold coin entered. He ran into the room with the harried expression of someone on a mission.

"My kings," he paused to bow first to Pytheios, then Brock, then Fraener. "My commander sent me directly to you with a message."

Pytheios slashed a hand through the air. "Speak."

"Another phoenix has been located, sir."

The very air in the room seemed to still as the words echoed off the high ceilings of the chamber.

Pytheios hid a building rage behind a blank expression. He'd hoped to have more time before any other kings discovered that secret.

No one else had known Serefina survived after Zilant was gone, believing she'd died with her mate. Pytheios had always known he'd eventually hunt her down. He'd planned to keep her ashes in his personal chambers—right beside the urns carrying the ashes of her lover, her mother, and her father. The constant cold had preserved their charred remains nicely.

Too late now.

Pytheios aimed a glare at the tall, bony man lurking in the shadows of the room, his pale red hair pulled back in a ponytail that draped over one black silk-clad arm. How had Jakkobah, one of his most trusted advisors, not known already? The man called the Stoat behind his back—thanks to his weasel-like appearance and time-tested ability to be everywhere and know everything—should have been the first to know.

Pytheios narrowed his eyes, allowing his fire to fill the sockets, and still Jakkobah didn't even flinch. This was going nowhere. With a snarl, Pytheios returned his attention to the man in front of him.

"Impossible," Brock snapped.

"I scented her myself, sir," the shifter spy declared in no uncertain terms.

"Then you scented the woman named Kasia," Blake stated.

"No, my lord," the soldier denied, though he lowered his gaze. "The red-haired phoenix smells of chocolate. This woman had black hair, and her scent was of cloves. I am sure."

"Where?" Fraener demanded. "Where did you see her?"

Pytheios did not miss the avaricious light that entered both the other kings' eyes.

"At the top of Ben Nevis in discussion with Ladon Ormarr," the soldier answered.

Rage threatened to boil up and spill out of Pytheios as buzzing took over his hearing for a brief instant. Damn the eyes of the fates. Ormarr had his hands on *two* of the sisters?

The Stoat wasn't the only one who'd failed him. Pytheios would also have words with Rhiamon when he returned. She had found a phoenix for him once before. It had taken her centuries, but she'd tracked down Serefina Amon. Eventually.

He didn't have centuries to wait. Not this time.

The legacy of dragons, tens of thousands of years, was something he'd sworn to protect and grow at all costs. He alone had shown he could make the hard choices for his people—like ensuring the leaders mated before lower-level dragons got the chance, like pooling the wealth to ensure it could be applied in the most appropriate ways, like eliminating those who dissented.

He needed a phoenix. Now.

"I must return to my home and investigate this further," Pytheios managed softly.

If he'd tried to speak in a normal voice, it would have come out as a thundering roar. His skin stretched and itched with the leashed fury of the creature inside him.

He turned to Brock. "This is rumor at worst, truth at best. I will deal with it. You enact the plan."

"But my lord, if Ormarr has a—"

Pytheios held up a hand and Brock cut himself off with a snap of his teeth. "There has only ever been one. Two is not possible, which tells you what?"

Brock's high brow furrowed. "Ormarr and Astarot are lying and neither is a phoenix?" He paused, considering. "Makes sense. If they start a rumor like that, more dragons will support them."

Pytheios gave a grim smile. "Lies we will not give credence to." He paused, letting that sink in. "I will handle it."

He'd get to that phoenix *before* she mated and suck her dry of any power she held. Before the kings supposedly loyal to him got to her first. He was tempted to capture a mated phoenix so that when she died, so did her mate, ridding him of a traitor king. But a mated dragon—especially a king—was a dangerous fucking thing.

A lesser protected target would be easier.

Eventually, he'd take all four. He could only rely on rumors for so long. The existence of phoenixes would test those limits.

Brock's lips pulled into a sneer, but the words that came out of his mouth were what Pytheios needed to hear. "Yes, my king."

He waved to Jakkobah and Merikh who accompanied him to the small chamber where Rhiamon waited in secret. Her eyes widened as she encountered the fury in Pytheios's gaze, but she said nothing. With a nod, Rhiamon's magic whipped through them, skating over his skin like static electricity as she teleported them to a chamber within the Red Clan's stronghold, inside the most colossal mountain on the planet. Everest.

"Get me intelligence," he ordered both Rhiamon and Jakkobah. "We will take that phoenix, now."

CHAPTER FIVE

Ladon stood in the doorway and stared at the woman out cold on his worn leather couch. Dawn had only just started its slow takeover of the skies, and the strip of lighting, set to mimic daylight, illuminated the mountain's interior, barely cast a soft glow over her.

A mate had always been a vague idea that grew into a political idea. That had even been true when he'd thought of mating Kasia. But something about Skylar Amon...

Ladon frowned at the thought.

Like every room, his personal suite was built into the natural configuration of the caverns, all rock formations and rough, rounded walls and a constant soothing sound of water. Laid out in a free-flowing way, he lived in a space the size of a three thousand square foot house, with all the accompanying rooms. In his living area, dead to the world, inky hair cascading over the leather like a waterfall in the darkness, Skylar had slept hard all night.

She and Kasia had asked for time, just the two of them.

Reluctantly he and Brand had granted them that, though they hadn't gone far, staying in the suite. Hours later, they'd found both sisters asleep on the couch, curled around each other. Brand had pried Kasia out of Skylar's grasp and carried her away to their rooms. Ladon had tucked a blanket around his own phoenix and settled in the armchair across the way to keep watch over her, strangely reluctant to let her out of his sight.

The not-so-subtle stomp of feet coming down the hallway leading to his suite reached his ears. Arden. No doubt about it. His sister, like all his warriors, usually tread too softly to be heard, but she was probably being obvious to deliberately warn him.

Not wanting to disturb Skylar, Ladon stepped out into the hall, closing the thick wooden door behind him.

At the sight of him, Arden pulled up short from what appeared to be a walk of determination, the purple glitter on her T-shirt catching in the dim light of the hall. "Good. You're still alive."

"Nothing happened."

She ignored him. "I heard Kasia's sister is still here?"

"She has a name." He knew where Arden was going with this but didn't feel like arguing about it.

Arden eyed him narrowly. "You're going to try to mate her, aren't you?"

"Yes."

"Dammit, Ladon. Kasia was one thing, but this one seems to want blood. *Dragon* blood." His sister beat one hand against the veins at her wrist.

"No shit," Ladon commented. "And here I thought she was all sunshine and light."

That only earned him a glare. "This is not funny."

"Am I laughing?"

Arden clenched her teeth, muttering through them. "You can be such an asshole."

He softened. Only for his sister, and only a smidge. "I know," he said softly. "But you love me for it."

She stared at him, most likely searching his eyes for any kind of give about his decision. She'd find none. Not this time.

"You're going to do this no matter what."

"Yes." The risk to himself was well worth keeping her away from Pytheios, let alone any other benefits that came from mating a phoenix.

Arden plunked her hands on her hips, her head dropping forward as she stared at the rock flooring worn smooth over the

ages. After a long, mute moment—rare for his opinionated sister—
she lifted her head and pinned him with a commanding stare that
he suspected she'd learned from him.

"Don't you dare die on me," she whispered.

Damn. Ladon pulled Arden into a hug, though she remained
stiff in his arms. "I'd never leave you uncared for," he murmured
into her hair. "You know that, don't you?"

"It's not the same," she grumbled into his chest.

"No."

His only remaining blood relative, his baby sister had been
born over a century after him. Her mother had called Arden her
miracle child. He'd watched over her since she was an infant, even
more so after their parents were killed. As a female-born dragon,
she was sterile. At best, she'd be an aunty to his offspring. At
worst, since she was the king's sister, she could end up mated to
help him politically. Most female-born never mated. However, his
becoming king had put her in more danger, because he was facing
off against most of the other clans. Plus, she insisted on fighting
at his side, becoming one of his personal guard.

Ladon finally pulled back. "I need to go wake up Skylar."
Giving her that time with Kasia last night had delayed discussions
that couldn't wait any longer.

"Oh, it's Skylar now, is it?"

"You'll give her a chance." A command.

Arden wrinkled her nose. "Only because she's important, and
she's Kasia's sister. Can't be all bad, right?"

Ladon ruffled her hair, like he used to do when she was little.
Only she jerked out from under his touch, her hands flying to fix
her perfectly styled ponytail. With a shake of his head, he punched
his code on the keypad beside his door to let himself back into
his rooms.

Kasia and Brand would return soon. Last night, the sisters
had spent their time together, but plans hadn't been discussed for
next steps. Ladon crossed the room on silent feet and leaned over
Skylar's sleeping form. His entire suite smelled of her cloves and

smoke scent, but he wanted it on his sheets, on his body.

Fuck. Twenty-four hours with this woman, and he was already on the edge of obsessed. Ladon chose to see that as a good sign for their mating. He couldn't worry about any other implications right now.

"Skylar."

Not even a twitch.

"Skylar, wake up."

He reached out to shake her arm. The second he connected, Skylar moved. Before he knew it, she swept his feet out from under him, landing him on his back, and she was straddling him with a knife at his throat.

Not about to let himself be gutted by a woman obviously acting on instinct, Ladon rolled them, pinning her to the ground and knocking the knife from her hand. Only, by the time he got there, she'd stopped struggling.

She stared at him, breasts heaving, eyes locked to his. Damn, she was incredible—all fire and ice with a fight that wouldn't quit. Respect coated the strong desire lancing through him.

Mine, the dragon half of him whispered.

That growing urge to claim, to plunder, had him leaning toward her, needing to taste her. Except a sudden flash of light, a second of silence, then he was outside in the hallway about to kiss the fucking floor.

Shit.

She'd done it again. Teleported his ass outside the room. With a growl of frustration, Ladon was off the floor and back through the door to find her standing and waiting.

She held up both hands in surrender, but her words conveyed anything but. "Your fault, not mine."

Ladon studied her and tried his damnedest not to drag her back to his bedroom and establish once and for all who was boss here. Except he'd vowed to win her trust. "You can't keep—"

"I know. I know. I was half asleep and going on instinct."

He lifted one skeptical eyebrow, and her gaze tracked what the movement did to the scar that ran down that side of his face.

Did she find him grotesque? "Are you going to do that when we mate?" he demanded.

Skylar crossed her arms, lush lips drawing up into a smile that had his groin tightening. "It would sure make for an interesting story."

Ladon grunted by way of response, choosing not to join her in seeing the funny side. Her comment about being not fully awake, combined with how hard she'd been sleeping had him examining her more closely. Purple shadows under her eyes and a pallor to her skin had him wondering. "How long has it been since you slept?"

"Slept? Last night. Slept well?" She shrugged. "I had to get here. That required traveling off the radar—a lot of walking and sleeping where I could find a place, a few stolen planes to get across land, and an ocean voyage stowed away on a container ship. Once I got in here, I didn't want to be found."

Stolen planes and stowing away followed by hiding from dragons here. In other words, all that time, she'd allowed herself to drift, but only half asleep, ready to act. An image that sat like a lead weight in his gut.

"You growl a lot. You know that, right?"

He hadn't realized that he had until she called him on it. "How far did you have to travel?"

"Far."

Stubborn woman. Ladon stepped past her and dropped to the couch. Maybe she'd loosen up if they weren't squaring off against each other. "Let me phrase it a different way. Where did you come from? I assume your mother also sent you to safety."

Skylar eyed him warily, like she was debating what she could trust him with. "She did."

"With anyone in particular?"

"A bunch of rogue dragon shifters."

Ladon straightened in his seat. "Why the hell would your mother send you there?"

Even through her visible exhaustion, her mouth still pulled up at the corners. "Dragons who are anti-clans and anti-kings? Who could be more perfect?"

Then she finally followed suit and sat at the other end of the couch, angling her body to face him.

Ladon considered her description. In the colonies that could mean only one group. "You're talking about Rune Abaddon's people?"

"You've heard of them?" She tucked her feet under her like a fastidious little cat. Getting more comfortable? Or deceptively so? He still couldn't tell with her.

"Of course I've heard of them, though I didn't know they were in the Andes."

She blinked, then winced. "Don't... Don't use that against them. Please?" Except she knew she didn't need to ask.

"I have bigger worries right now. But let me get this straight. Dragon kings you can't stand, but you want to protect feral dragons who've been attacking our Enforcer teams and stealing mates?" That made no fucking sense.

Apparently, she caught that mental tag in his tone, because Skylar scowled. "Yes. Anyone fighting the current regime is worth a second chance." She gave him a significant look that he had no trouble interpreting. Skylar included him in that bunch. Barely.

Then she glanced away, as though considering her next words. If he hadn't been watching her so closely, he would've missed the deep breath she snuck. "Also, one of them was family."

Family. Pytheios and his kings had taken out the old ruling families. One had survived? Which side? The Amons? Or the Hanyus? The questions piled up in his mind, but, despite her cozy position on the couch, he could see the wariness in the lines of Skylar's body.

Time chased him like a hound on the scent, but he put aside his questions. He needed her trust more than he needed answers. "I'm glad you had someone there you trusted."

After a long pause, during which she studied him just as closely as he did her, Skylar nodded. "Me too."

"What about your other sisters?" he asked. "Where do you think your mother sent them?"

She pursed her lips in thought. "Hard to say. Maul was logical. But where I went was a huge shock. Who knows what other allies Mom relied on."

"Powerful allies are important."

Her eyes narrowed. "Like a phoenix?"

"I was thinking about Brand, actually." Not that his assurance made the suspicion in her eyes go away. "Do your other sisters look more like you or Kasia?"

That question didn't help.

"Neither," she said slowly.

"Quadruplets who don't look alike? How is that possible?"

That at least made the shadows pull back in her eyes. "Who knows? Angelika has white blond hair, though she's shorter. Meira is tall like me, but more willowy, and is a strawberry blonde with curls."

"Same eyes, all of you?"

"Same eyes. Our father's eyes. Though Meira's go darker blue when she gets upset."

"Where'd all the different coloring come from?"

Skylar glanced at the dark braid across her shoulder. "Mother was the daughter of a phoenix and the red dragon king. Grandfather had dark red hair, like happens with some of that clan. I got my grandmother's dark hair. So did Mom. Father was a white dragon king. As far as we can tell, that combo of parents and grandparents resulted in an...eclectic mix."

She chuckled, the raspy sound skating right over his skin and waking up parts of his anatomy he'd rather keep out of the mix for now.

"Mom claimed it helped her keep us straight as babies," she said, unaware of his sudden tension.

"Are Meira and Angelika as...feisty as you and Kasia?"

Skylar smiled. Actually *smiled*, and Ladon got a shot of the same exhilaration as when he won a skirmish.

"Awwww. You think I'm feisty, booboo?" She batted her eyes. When he didn't smile, she stopped and shrugged. "Meira is quiet, super smart, but more of an observer with emotions that run deep and quiet. Angelika is the kind one, the outgoing one. Like sunshine in a bottle. The one everyone loves."

"And you're…?"

"The wild one," she popped off.

He didn't like that. Not the "wild," but the way she said it. Like she didn't like it about herself.

Ladon shook his head. "Bold, decisive, maybe a little on the rash side, but I don't believe there's such a thing as too wild."

Skylar stilled across from him, searching his eyes as if deciding whether or not he meant that. "Don't give me too much credit. My mother died because of me."

As if that wasn't meant to slip out, she snapped her mouth shut with an audible clack of her teeth. No doubt she regretted that comment.

But Ladon wasn't going to let it slide. He moved closer to her on the couch, intent on her face. "You can't say something like that and not keep going."

She opened her mouth, probably to put him off, but paused, then frowned, closing it again. Then she licked her bottom lip and seemed to come to a decision. "We were living in Kansas at the time, working at a diner down the road. It was supposed to be my shift, but I wanted to get more flight hours in. I'm a pilot. Mother took the shift for me."

She paused, swallowing around words that appeared to lodge in her throat. "Pytheios found her there, alone. He didn't know about us yet, I think. Mother was barely pregnant when she fled… after he murdered our father."

Ladon stayed quiet, listening, attuned to her in a way he rarely experienced with anyone.

"The day he found us, he got to her first. Lodged a knife in her back just as she managed to teleport to where we waited for her. She turned to ash before our eyes. Her last act as she died was to teleport us each to safety."

The fact that she was sharing this at all was like a gift he hadn't expected to receive. He should just listen and be grateful. But he couldn't ignore the tone in her voice. "And you blame yourself?"

She looked away. "Who else? It should have been me."

"So Pytheios could kill you instead and possibly find your mother and sisters anyway?" An element of anger filtered into his voice, but she didn't look at him. "Even if he didn't find them, I doubt there is much worse pain than that of a mother losing her child. Do you think she would have wanted that?"

Still she didn't look his way. "The logical side of me figured that out a long time ago."

"But you still blame yourself." A statement, not a question.

"If I hadn't been so selfish, so focused on what I wanted—"

"He would've killed you."

"Better me than Mom. I can't—" She swallowed hard.

"Can't what?"

She winced.

"Skylar?" he prodded when she didn't speak.

"I can't keep my sisters safe," she threw at him, still looking away. "I'm not strong enough. Not like Mom."

"Skylar, look at me." He waited, tempted to make her. But if he knew anything about this woman, it was that forcing her wouldn't work.

Finally she turned that glacial gaze his way, a wall up behind her eyes that he had a feeling she always kept raised. He understood because he did the same thing himself. Emotions, especially strong ones, weren't helpful as a king.

"I think you're putting too much pressure on yourself," he said.

Skylar sat up straighter, away from him. "I can't even teleport myself," she pointed out. "Mom could send anyone anywhere with a thought."

"And you think you should be able to do that?" How many times had he said the same to himself about a hundred different things? Especially since he'd become king.

"Yes."

"Bullshit." That kind of pressure wasn't good for anyone. A lesson learned the hard way, every damn day.

"Excuse me?"

"You heard me. That is total bullshit. Your mother had centuries to hone her skills. You've had what? A year?"

"I don't have centuries. I need to keep my sisters safe *now*."

A low growl reverberated from him. "Stubborn woman."

She scowled. "Damn straight. Stubborn women keep the world from falling to shit."

Ladon snorted and leaned forward, taking her chin in his fingers, needing her to hear this. "Do you even realize what you've managed to do in just a year? Learned your powers, found Kasia and tried to rescue her, and agreed to give a king a chance. All to protect your family."

She didn't pull away, if anything pushing into his hold as she stared him down. "My mother survived Pytheios and managed to hide herself and four children for ages," she shot back. "Hell, she used the last of her strength to send each of us away to safety."

"Exactly," he shot back. "To safety. So, stop kicking yourself for no good reason. Instead, how about you use the resources you have… me, Kasia, Brand, an entire clan of dragon shifters…and figure it out?"

Harsh, but maybe words she was supposed to hear.

Skylar's scowl eased. Had his words scored a direct hit? Found a way over those walls of hers? Blame didn't solve anything. Neither did self-pity.

"I'm not used to asking for help," she grumbled.

The look in her eyes told him that maybe, just maybe, she wanted to. And suddenly, he wanted to be the man who took that weight she'd been lugging around and shoulder it for her.

Why, he had no damn clue.

But he found himself leaning toward her, his gaze held by her hypnotic eyes. Wounded eyes. Fuck, she was like gravity, drawing him in. Or a black hole, about to crush him.

Closer, her heat warming his skin, her lips and eyes drawing him in. So damn close.

Before he could claim those lips, and whatever the hell came next, a knock sounded at his door, shattering a tension that had taken hold of them both.

CHAPTER SIX

"I'll go clean up a bit," Skylar blurted and disappeared into the spare bedroom with an en suite bathroom that he'd shown her last night.

With a frustrated sigh, Ladon answered the door, letting Kasia and Brand inside. A whine outside the window had Kasia crossing the room to let Maul in. The hellhound had trouble fitting through the human-sized doors and preferred to teleport to the beams the dragons used, rather than directly inside. Some kind of hellhound honor system was Ladon's best guess.

Maul lumbered inside, bringing his smoky scent of rotting with him, the glow of his red eyes brighter than usual in the dim morning sunshine manifested by their lighting system.

Kasia gave him an absentminded pat.

"I hope you and Skylar got all caught up, because we have a lot to talk about," Ladon said.

She grinned. "I figured."

"Breakfast would be nice, though," Skylar said from behind him.

He turned to find that she'd changed into clothes Kasia had had brought up last night. Another black outfit more suitable for fighting than any activity she'd be engaged in today—skintight pants and top, zippered pockets, sleek toolbelt, her black hair back in a long braid that he could picture wrapping around a fist as he pounded into her body.

Where the hell did she hide the knife?

He scanned her form for any possible location and came up empty. He had no doubt she had it on her somewhere. Probably a good idea to figure out where before he tried anything with her.

"I ordered food to be delivered in a half hour," he said with a glance at the clock in his kitchen.

"Wait," Skylar said. "What kind of breakfast?"

The rank suspicion in her voice had Ladon's lips twitching. Again. He managed to stuff the reaction back where it belonged. "Don't worry. Not a full Scottish breakfast. A proper American one. I've been around Kasia long enough to know that."

Kasia patted his arm on the way to a chair at the rough wood dining table tucked to the side of the kitchen.

Skylar sat beside her sister, beating Brand to it. On purpose if the way she stared down the gold dragon shifter was any indication. For his part, Brand grunted, grabbed the chair at the end of the table, and plopped it down at an angle to Kasia's so that she sat between his legs.

Skylar rolled her eyes and turned to Ladon, still standing. "You wanted to talk. So, talk."

Challenging woman.

He took the seat opposite her, but his first question was for Kasia. "Why didn't you tell me about your sisters earlier?"

Deliberately he lowered his voice, speaking softly, and Skylar turned a look his way that he couldn't quite interpret.

Kasia shrugged, unrepentant and apparently unconcerned. "There was no need as long as they remained hidden and safe."

No need? When their mere existence was inexplicable with far-reaching implications he had yet to fathom? "Do you know where the other two are?"

"Why?" Skylar taunted. "You need more than one to pick from for your fuck buddy?"

He flicked her an impatient glance and didn't reply.

Kasia sighed. "I know where Angelika is. She's safe there,

for now."

That was apparently news to Skylar, whose lips parted in a silent gasp. "Where did Mother send her?" she asked. Then held up a hand, sliding Ladon and Brand looks ripe with distrust. "Never mind. Tell me later."

"No," Kasia said slowly. "They can hear this."

Skylar's lips went white she clamped them so hard. "I'm not ready to go that far."

Kasia considered that, then nodded. "Where did she send you?"

"Somewhere safer than you, apparently," came Skylar's dry reply.

Maul let out a wheeze that came off like a grumpy grumble, and Kasia chuckled. "Brand didn't find me where I was sent. I left to go to that clinic Mom told us about."

"The one in Wyoming that treats paranormal illnesses?" Skylar scooted forward. "Why?" Urgency laced the word, and she sat up straighter. "Are you sick?"

Again, Kasia chuckled. "I get visions, but at first they came with migraines, and I'd sort of explode when it happened, lighting everything on fire. I couldn't control it until recently, after I mated Brand."

"Visions?" Skylar burst out. "Wait. You can teleport yourself *and* you have visions? Damn."

At her disgruntled expression, Kasia raised her eyebrows. "Is that a problem?"

Skylar flopped back in her chair. "No. My gift just sucks in comparison."

Ladon sat forward in his own seat, his hands on the table between them as though reaching for her in a gesture unconsciously made, but one that immediately had him frowning. This need to be near her, as though a string attached them, tugging him along in her wake, was growing. Way too quickly. He didn't have space for weaknesses like that. "What *did* you get?"

She waved a hand. "The teleporting thing, except I can only send others, not myself, and I have to touch them to do it. Not exactly awesome."

"I don't know," Ladon grumbled. "Seemed to work well for you earlier."

She visibly brightened, releasing a low chuckle that shot straight through him, arrowing to his groin. Only this time, Ladon didn't push the response down as it dawned on him that he should be using it against her, to convince her their mating was the right move.

He couldn't be the only one feeling this. He'd seen that flash of awareness in her eyes before she'd tossed him out of the room. And, before Brand and Kasia had shown up, when he'd wanted to claim those lips, she'd leaned toward him, too. Was she drawn to him the same way?

He leaned forward and brushed his fingers over the back of her hand, studying her reaction. Her smile faded, but otherwise she didn't move, except her pupils dilated. With what? Fear? Interest? "Any other skills?" he prodded.

She scrunched her nose, refusing to pull her gaze away. "Not that I know of."

Her stare held a significance he could easily guess at before she slid her gaze to her sister, eyebrows raised in question.

Kasia shifted in her seat. "I can't tell yet if one of us or all four of us will be *the phoenix*. Mother's stories made me think the…effect…would be immediate, though, so…I don't think I am."

Both women stared at each other, depths of pain in their gazes, though their eyes remained dry. Still, heavy emotions swamped the room—a sadness so deep neither seemed able to voice it.

Was this the first time they'd seen each other since their mother died?

Kasia covered Skylar's hand where it lay on top of the table and squeezed. They both took a deep breath.

Kasia cleared her throat and continued. "If I was, Brand wouldn't still be fighting for his throne, right?"

"Who knows?" Skylar answered. "There have never been four before. Maybe we all have to mate for it to work? Or maybe only one of us will inherit that power? Even Mom didn't know for sure. We seem to be splitting things up."

Maybe they should secure the other two then.

"What kinds of other powers does a phoenix have?" Ladon asked.

Both women turned his way. Skylar frowned. "You don't know?"

Ladon shrugged. "I was young when the last one died." He paused, realizing that was no longer correct. "Or we *thought* the last one did." He'd have to get used to history rewriting itself. "It seems only those in direct contact knew most of the details. In five hundred years, facts have turned to rumors and become myth."

"I see." He could practically see the wheels turning in Skylar's mind.

Before they could discuss more, his cell phone rang. Ladon yanked it out of his pocket, intending to silence it and call whoever it was back later. Until he saw the number on the screen. "I have to take this."

As he walked toward the door, planning to go somewhere more private for this call, he hit the button to answer. "Yes?"

"You found another phoenix." The nasal voice on the other end stopped him in his tracks.

Ladon didn't speak.

"I take it by your silence that I'm correct," his informant from among Pytheios's clan murmured.

After ten years working the back channels together, this man was familiar with Ladon's silences.

"How did you know?" Ladon demanded.

"Pytheios knows. You were seen with her by one of the Gold Clan's spies watching your mountain. You really should keep a prize like that out of plain sight."

Ladon turned slowly back to the room to find both women on their feet. "How the hell did they know what she was?" he asked.

"Her scent."

Ladon closed his eyes. Of course. Phoenixes smelled of smoke, like dragons, but with a sweeter undercurrent.

He'd been a complete fucking fool to take her up to the top like that. Once he plucked her off that mountainside, he should've flown her back inside immediately, but he'd suspected she would've fought that, and it wouldn't have earned the miniscule amount of trust she'd placed in him. She'd already be long gone.

"Have you mated her yet?"

Ladon snapped his eyes open. Rather than answer, he rapped out his own question. "Did *you* know more than one existed?"

"No. I would've shared that with you."

"Of course you would." While his informant had been critical to Ladon's success in taking the throne, and keeping it, he was still a red dragon. One of the false High King Pytheios's Curia Regis, his king's council, the shifters who were his closest advisors and held positions that helped him run his kingdom. Ladon would never entirely trust this man.

No need to tell him two more phoenixes were out there. He wouldn't betray Skylar that way.

"Anything else?" he asked instead.

"I'd let her know that Pytheios is aware of where she had been hiding."

Did he truly know? Or was this a ploy to try to find out?

"His witch had tracked her to South America, but then she disappeared, presumably to go to your mountain. She can't return to Abaddon's people."

So they *did* know. Shit. "What about the other kings? Do they know?"

"Brock and Fraener were there when Pytheios received the report." Gold and Green, the two clans that had banded together to attack his mountain. And almost won, if Brand hadn't taken out Uther.

"I don't know about Volos or Gorgon," his informant said of the Kings of the White and Black Clans. "But if Brock's spies saw you, most likely we aren't the only ones with spies circling that mountain."

Pytheios sure as hell wouldn't share that tidbit with more men who could benefit from mating a phoenix. In fact, Brock and Fraener's knowledge would likely drive the red king to act faster in trying to get to Skylar. It didn't take a strategic genius to figure that one out.

"Thanks for the heads-up." Ladon gripped the phone harder. "When is he coming for her?"

"Two hours. Tops. He's gathering his warriors—all of them—to protect him. His witch will teleport them to you."

Fuck. Ladon wanted to hurl the phone at the wall.

Just one break. One day without something going horribly wrong. Apparently even that was too much to ask.

His gaze landed on Skylar, who stared back with wary curiosity. "Inform Pytheios that she's already mated," he said.

"What the hell?" Skylar jumped to her feet.

"Is she?" his informant asked, almost idly.

"She will be before he gets here."

Ladon hung up the phone. For a long beat, he stared at the three people in the room watching him with combinations of concern and determination and fury.

"We need to move up our timetable," he said. "Pytheios knows. He's coming for Skylar."

"I am not mating you just to save my ass." The words almost jerked from her body. "Or yours."

Ladon shook his head. "He'll be here tonight."

"Then let's kill him," Skylar said. "Set a trap."

Tempting. That had been his initial thought as well. Except that was short-term thinking. As king, he had to think beyond the immediate. See the entire board.

"He's bringing his warriors. All of them." The Red Clan were tough sons of bitches, basically tanks with their heavily armored bodies. Hardest to kill of all dragon shifters. Deadly fighters. "We're still recovering from our recent battle, and to win this war, we need the gold dragons as allies. Which means we need that throne. If we mate now, it could buy us more time."

"Could?" Skylar demanded.

"If he would've risked this kind of attack for a mated phoenix, he'd have come for Kasia sooner. As it stands, that was only ever just a matter of time. Pytheios doesn't take risks like that unless his back is to the wall."

The fact that he was willing to come get Skylar himself, with an army at his back, said a lot about the frame of mind of the false High King.

"The green and gold kings were there when he found out. If the others don't already, they'll know soon. Which means every dragon king will be after you until you are claimed," Ladon said. Maybe even then, especially once their bond solidified. Kill one mate and take out both a phoenix and an enemy king at the same time.

A risk he was willing to take to keep her.

Ladon didn't need to see how Skylar's jaw clenched, or the flush that ran up her neck, or Kasia's wince to know he'd used the wrong word. She'd already said she wasn't a woman who could be claimed.

Though begging went against everything in him, chafing like sandpaper against his skin, he moved to squat in front of her. "You aren't safe anymore. I can keep you safe only if no one else can have you."

"Especially Pytheios," Kasia said.

Skylar sat forward, getting in his face. "I'll keep myself safe. Thanks. I damn well won't be rushed into mating."

"It's not just about you, Sky," Kasia reminded her, a world of regret in her voice. "If Pytheios gets you, it's about all of us. The dragon shifters caught in the middle of these kings…and our family."

"You want me to mate a man I barely know?" Skylar flung an arm out at him, smacking him in the chest, her tone implying that to do so was a fate worse than death.

Kasia grabbed her hand, clasping it in her own. "I want you to find your destined mate, like I did," she said, her eyes wide. "But I want you to live more."

. . .

Skylar put every emotion, every thought, on pause as she stared at her sister. Kasia was terrified in a way Skylar had never seen before. Just because *Pytheios* was coming for Skylar...

He'd been smart enough to attack her phoenix grandmother as she'd willingly passed her powers to their mother, killing both her and their grandfather with one blow when they were most vulnerable. He'd managed to best their father, a king in his own right. Eventually he'd murdered their mother.

Underestimating Pytheios would be the height of stupidity.

This was not how Skylar had pictured saving Kasia would end up.

She knew with lead-lined certainty her sister was right to be frightened. If the other kings knew, they'd come for her, track her down. She couldn't leave. At the same time, her unmated presence made things more dangerous for everyone here. Including her sister.

She didn't dare glance at Ladon. Looking at him would only cloud her thinking with his eyes, and that sexy cleft in his chin, and the rough voice. He'd surprised the hell out of her with that conversation about earning her trust, and she'd been dumb enough to almost kiss him for it. One little genuine offer of help and she was a goner. What was wrong with her? She and Kasia were the strong ones, but Skylar knew down deep that she was supposed to keep her family safe. Instinct or a calling. Whatever. But that's who she was.

Mating a king seemed like the only way now.

"Do you see anything, Kas?" Brand prompted Kasia, slipping a hand up under the heavy fall of her hair.

That's right. Kasia had visions.

Her sister's lips flattened, turning white. "No," she said. "Nothing." She turned eyes heavy with worry to her mate. "What does that mean?"

"It doesn't mean anything," Skylar declared. Not that she was truly certain, but worrying about it wouldn't solve a damn thing. "It means I have to make a decision as blindly as I did before."

Could she mate a man she didn't know? One she still wasn't sure she trusted? One who was the kind of creature she'd been running from her entire life? Sure, she'd already chosen to give him a chance at convincing her, but that was still a thousand leagues away from doing the deed right this second.

He sees you, a small voice whispered.

He saw through the wildness, calling her bold and decisive. No one had ever believed in her like that. Sometimes not even her mother. Most of the time, her family assumed she was irresponsible when the exact opposite was what she was trying to be. Protect her family, the only people in the world who mattered to her, even when they couldn't do it for themselves. Did Ladon truly understand that? She got the feeling that, of any dragon shifter in the world, he did. A king who took his throne to help his people.

There could be worse things.

An image of deep red dragon scales and molten eyes flashed in her mind's eye. Pytheios. If he got to her first, gut instinct warned her that her fate wouldn't be as simple as killing him with her fire when he attempted to mate her. He'd lived too long and taken out too many powerful players to not know that was coming. No doubt he had a plan, even if she couldn't see it yet.

Skylar shuddered, then took a breath and reached for calm.

She cast her gaze over the man still squatting in front of her with way more patience than she'd ever give him credit for. Strength radiated back at her. Determination. An iron will reflected in that jagged scar that gave him a fearsome permanent scowl.

Can I trust you?

In her mind she cataloged what she knew of him. Fierce warrior. Ruthless. Would do anything for his people. He'd given her the opportunity to get to know him before choosing him.

Respect.

She could respect him. He'd offered to be a resource.

When it had been her mother and sisters, only their mother had the abilities. So Skylar had been the one determined to do everything else she could—become the best fighter, learn to fly a plane so she could help with escapes, stay up at night, watching over them.

The mere concept of Ladon and his clan being a resource. Something big and dangerous to help her protect her family...

He remained still, waiting for her, not touching, but in her space in a way she couldn't ignore. In a way that her body responded to even as she willed it to stop. She could definitely have sex with Ladon. The odd appeal he held for her was undeniable.

But mating meant the rest of her extremely long life tied to the man. What if he was a total dick? What if all that understanding and ruthless good guy was an act?

"Trust me, Skylar," Ladon murmured in that rough voice.

And a small, illogical part of her suddenly wanted that. Which made no sense.

Okay. Look at this logically.

Mating didn't mean she had to stay here forever.

There was an idea worth examining. Say they managed to take down the old kings and bring peace not only to the shifters but freedom for her and her sisters. She could safely leave him then, if she wished.

Win-win.

She either earned her eventual freedom—that was the long game—or she fried a dragon king as they mated.

A result that brought its own set of issues worth shoring up.

"What if I kill you?" she asked.

He stilled, and she could see his mind whirring. "I'm willing to risk it."

"That's not what I meant, and you know it."

He crossed his arms. "If you choose me, I won't—"

"I could be choosing you for the wrong reasons, and it all goes tits up. No one can say how this works for sure."

He narrowed his eyes, a brooding cocktail of command and

determination reflected in eyes she could drown in. "So, choose me for the right reasons."

"There's not enough time, according to you."

His lips flattened at the implication that she didn't trust him, but she ignored his irritation. "Rush a mating, and you might burn to ash instead of getting a phoenix. So...what happens to me if I kill you?"

The chilly expression that stared back at her should've had her quivering in her boots.

"You're like a fucking brick wall, you know that?" she said. "Immovable." Granted, she wasn't any better, but she was giving up a lifetime of hatred to mate him.

"I've had to be," Ladon snarled.

That gave Skylar pause. Everything this man had said or done so far told her Ladon Ormarr was a reluctant ruler. Meira was usually the one to see both sides of a situation, but Skylar couldn't deny that she wasn't the only one being forced into an untenable situation. Still... What was he giving up?

Everything, a small voice whispered inside her. He'd put his life on the line just to take his throne and defy the regime in power. He'd risk it again trying to mate her.

The insight broke over her almost gently. Ladon's motive was to help his people. This wasn't about power or greed but survival.

That she could trust.

She studied his face, the rigid set of his shoulders, the way his jaw clenched. She sensed a restlessness, as though his life had caged him. Or kept beating him down in a barrage of shit events.

That she could relate to as well, suddenly making him more... real to her. More human. Less monster.

How had the trajectory of her life changed so drastically, so inalterably, so fast?

"I wouldn't try to hurt you on purpose. I promise." The words were out of her mouth before the conscious thought even formed, and she had to hold herself still to keep from jerking back. Not kill a dragon when she had the chance. What kind of power did this man hold over her that she'd willingly promise such a thing? It had come out more easily than she liked to admit, even to herself.

A brief flicker in his eyes was gone before she could interpret the emotion. "I'll leave orders that you are to be protected if the mating fails and I die," Ladon said. "Brand will enforce them."

The silent mountain of a man sitting beside Kasia gave a sharp nod of affirmation.

Skylar stared at Ladon. Hell. She'd been going for *not executed outright for killing the king*, but protected? He'd do that for her?

Skylar refused to acknowledge the shard of rejection the thought of accidentally killing him wanted to push through her chest. Ladon Ormarr meant nothing to her beyond another layer between her and her family's murderer. Plus, potentially good sex.

She eyed him—all muscle and menacing force. Make that damn hot sex.

"Fine. I'll give it a shot."

Ladon scowled, as if he didn't like that answer, then reached out, taking her face in his hands. Staring at her with a look that sent a shiver skittering down her spine. "Was that a yes?"

Skylar swallowed, then hated herself for the weakness. All that intensity focused on her, and they weren't even in bed yet. "Yes. I'll mate you."

Giving in didn't sting like she expected. Instead, a sense of anticipation fizzed inside her like bubbles and butterflies. That couldn't be because of Ladon, though. She didn't know the guy. Maybe because of the possibilities this presented, the change to the course of her life? The purpose it gave her? Or maybe because her traitorous body was already heating at the thought of what was about to happen.

Ladon released her and stood, and she had to stop herself from shaking her head to clear it.

What is wrong with me?

No light of victory entered Ladon's eyes, no smirk. All he did was nod and turn to Brand. "We need to inform my men, and then my Curia Regis."

Brand stood, towering over them, and crossed his arms. "I don't think this is a good idea."

"I didn't ask."

Brand paused, as though he wanted to argue the point, his gaze moving to Skylar. She stared back, unmoved. After a minute, his expression turned disgruntled. "Gods save us from stubborn phoenixes."

Kasia snorted a laugh, but Brand finally nodded and left the room.

"Ready for this?" His lips pulled up in the first full smile she'd seen, reminding her more of a jaguar about to lunge for her jugular.

I'm the prey. The idea sat about as well with her as the hot pink dress Kasia made her try on for a formal event at one of their schools. She lifted her chin. "Maybe I'm hoping I kill you."

CHAPTER SEVEN

Even before his smile disappeared behind a scowl, that twitch near his bad eye going off, Skylar wished she could take it back.

I don't mean it.

She slammed into a wall of realization. A short time in Ladon's presence and she wasn't ready to rip the head off this particular dragon king.

What did that mean?

"You said you'd choose me," he growled. The man actually *growled*. "Even if it's only about survival."

"Calm down. I was kidding." Which was still a shock.

Ladon grunted, though his glower eased. "We need to work on your teasing."

She harrumphed. "Yeah, well, if you want the funny one, Angelika's your girl. If you want the nice one, you should wait for Meira."

"Skylar," Kasia groaned, a hand covering her face. "Can you be serious for five seconds?"

"I am." Granted, she wasn't being entirely fair. That had been a horrible thing to try to tease about. Way too soon.

Ladon cocked his head, eyeing her closely. "Did I hit a nerve?"

Maybe. "Of course not."

He grunted his disbelief. "Do you think you can act smitten

in front of an audience?"

The change in subject left her spinning. "Smitten is not my thing. Why?"

"If I'm going to ask my people to protect you—should you incinerate me—they need to believe you didn't kill me on purpose. Destined mates have been known to share an instant connection." He looked to Kasia. "Not love, from what I understand, but they're drawn to each other."

Skylar snorted. "Who told you that big fat whopper?"

"Hey!" Kasia protested. They both ignored her.

"My mother," he said. "She said that's how it worked for her and my father. Instant, insatiable need that grew to...more."

She tried to figure out how to pry her foot out of her mouth. Maybe with a crowbar? She went for humor instead. "Your mother said the word insatiable? To her son?"

He gave a small shrug. "I filled in the spaces she left unsaid. Love, connection, devotion, those all came later. According to my father, he was barely able to get her out of the room before mating her, he was so desperate to make her his forever." His gaze dropped to her lips, and she had to force herself not to go all girly and lick them.

Her mother's own rarely shared story had been much the same. So had Kasia's, apparently. *Lust and hormones.* At least, Skylar had always dismissed it as such. "Sounds intense. Are they here? I'd like to ask—"

"They're dead."

The way he said it sent a chill skating over her skin and sinking deeper. Not because he didn't care, but because she could see that underneath the control was a devastation that ran too deep for him to allow it free rein. Skylar knew that kind of devastation.

Her mother. She may not have entirely believed the love at first sight, soul mates part, but her mother's desolation and yearning for her lost mate had been real enough.

"I'm sorry," she murmured softly.

Behind him, Kasia raised her eyebrows. Skylar gave a slight

shake to her head. Her sympathy for him wasn't fake. Not about this.

Brand popped his head into the room. "They'll be gathered in ten minutes."

"Can you do this?" Ladon asked. "Convince them that you can't keep your hands off me?"

"The things I have to do for my sisters." The bigger problem was, she didn't think she'd have any trouble at all.

"I'm serious."

"Can *you*?" she demanded.

His jaw tightened, and he stepped into her—warm, solid, and forceful. "Are you attracted to me?"

His smoke and bourbon scent swirled around her, and those blue eyes wouldn't release her gaze. Skylar tried to keep a handle on her body, though her control was slipping. Attracted didn't begin to cover it. She wanted him in a highly inappropriate, idiotic, delicious way.

"Are you attracted to me?" she fired back. No way was she admitting anything. That would give him too much power in this dynamic of theirs.

"Yes."

Holy shit. She had not anticipated that stark, completely honest response.

"That's cute." She crossed her arms.

"You don't believe me?"

"Sure I believe you. I think hormones have a lot to answer for," she said. A huge fucking lot.

His blue eyes lit again with that inner flame, appearing to glow, and she stared, fascinated, while her body leapt with a heat of its own in direct response. He trailed a finger down her cheek, and she couldn't control the shiver or the irritation when satisfaction joined the fire in his gaze.

"So you feel it, too," he murmured. Not a question. "I can work with that. To start with."

This was wrong on so many levels. Her mother's words came

back to her. *When you are backed into a corner, take one step forward and reassess. Then another. Then another. Until you're out of the corner. Step one…* "Let's go convince your people."

"Good girl."

His approval should mean jack squat, so why did part of her warm under praise that edged on patronizing?

Skylar turned to her sister. "Can you keep your bad poker face to a minimum?"

"Are you sure about this? It's rushed—"

"Now *you're* questioning things?" Skylar shook her head. "I'm sure." For now. "You know I never did like to wait to make decisions, and it's worked out so far."

Kasia surprised her by stepping in and wrapping her arms around Skylar's neck, squeezing hard. "At least we'll get to be together again."

The burn of unexpected tears pushed behind her eyelids, and Skylar took a step back, forcing her sister to let go. "Yes, we will."

Ladon took her by the hand to lead her down the hall, not letting go. Conscious of how small her hand was in his, Skylar didn't pull away. She'd never show weakness, perceived or otherwise.

The walk through the tunnels from his rooms to where his men waited didn't take long. She figured he'd take her inside, but instead, Ladon stopped outside the door that she already knew from exploring led to the largest of the conference rooms and tugged her around to face him.

His pupils narrowed to slits and the blue irises expanded, consuming the whites—dragon's eyes. Like a predator stalking its prey, he moved closer, crowding her. He backed her into the wall, then stopped, staring down into her eyes. With the softest touch, he trailed the back of his hand down the side of her face, like he had on the top of the mountain, and just now in his suite, leaving a trail of heated, tingling nerves in his wake.

"What are you doing?" she whispered.

"Setting the stage." The fire in his eyes glittered back at her. "Don't push me into another room for this."

She opened her mouth to answer only to have him claim her lips. Her heart stopped, so did her mind as her body took over, responding with sheer carnal hunger. Damn, the man could kiss—demanding yet sinfully soft in stark contrast to the man he presented to the world—possessing her lips in a way that had her hot and needy in record time. Or maybe she'd already been on the edge of this precipice and that kiss simply pushed her into free fall.

Ladon was so large and so damn hard against her, the rod of his cock pushing into the softness of her belly through their clothing. He wanted her, and that knowledge only spurred her own desire. Skylar nipped at his lower lip and barely kept herself from rubbing against him to increase the friction. With a low grunt, almost as though it pained him to do it, Ladon pulled back, slapping a hand on the wall beside her head to push away.

"Damn."

Damn? What? He didn't want her now? "Hey, you started it."

He scowled. "I didn't mean…" He stopped himself and ran a hand through his hair. "I just didn't expect…" He blew out a long, low breath then held out a hand. "I don't think chemistry is going to be our problem."

. . .

Usually Ladon preferred to conduct his business in the large open main hall, not wanting secrets like his predecessor. But until he secured Skylar as his mate, he had no choice. Her hand in his, he led her into the bigger room where Brand had assembled his warriors.

Demonstrative was not an adjective most would apply to Ladon, but the question was, how did a destined mate act when he'd found his match? Like his parents who apparently couldn't keep their hands off each other? Or something else?

Pulse-pounding attraction to the woman holding his hand as they entered the conference room would help convince his guards. Would a mate be super touchy with her in front of his men? Ladon had no fucking clue.

Brand and Kasia hadn't been that way. But who the hell knew?

At least Skylar looked well kissed. Though he had to ignore the possessive satisfaction snaking through him at the sight of her pink lips swollen from his touch.

Ladon stopped in front of his personal guard and pulled Skylar in close to his side. After stiffening slightly, she deliberately relaxed and snuggled into him, her small hand resting against his chest.

Given the scowls descending over his men's faces, this was going to be interesting.

"Skylar Amon, allow me to officially present my personal guard and closest friends. I trust these men with my soul."

"Howdy, fellas."

Arden cleared her throat.

Skylar grinned. "My bad. Howdy, all."

Yeah. Interesting didn't begin to cover it.

Going around the room, he introduced them in quick succession, though he got the feeling Skylar already had a good idea who each were. "As you've probably guessed, Arden is my sister."

"Yeah. I picked that up." Skylar nodded at Arden, who stared back with narrowed eyes.

He turned to the two men standing off to the side, one with dark hair, the other a dirty blond, but with the same bone structure to their faces along with identical grins and bright blue eyes. "Ivar and Rainier are brothers."

"Guess it's a good thing I dubbed them Sleepy and Sneezy, then," Skylar murmured.

The seven dwarves? Ladon closed his eyes to hide a wince. That was going to go down like a balloon built of bricks.

"You named us after a damn fairy tale?" That was no doubt Asher's dark tone.

Ladon opened his eyes in time to see Skylar shrug. "I had to label you something until I figured out your names."

She turned to blink up at him with an angelic smile saints

would be jealous of. "In fact, you don't need to continue the intros. I think I've got it."

"Ho, ho," Duncan boomed in his rough burr. "Káthor, no way could she have gotten *that* close."

"Want to bet?" Skylar smirked.

A growing dark anger took root in his gut. She'd gotten close enough to figure details of who they were without at least one of them discovering her? He hadn't even told his men the plan yet. This was not going well. He waved a hand. "By all means."

She patted his arm. "Well, after Sleepy and Sneezy over there—"

Ivar, the youngest and prettiest of the group, sporting a slightly fussy goatee, grinned even as Rainier crossed his arms with a glare.

Skylar ignored them. "The gentle giant over there I called Bashful for a while, because he's the quietest." Actually, more like the steadiest. "Wyot, right?"

Wyot flicked Ladon a glance, then gave her a nod.

"The bloke in the corner with an American edge to his accent has to be Fallon. I know of your brother and his Enforcer team."

Fallon had been with Ladon's guard only a short while. He came off the wall he was propping up. "You know Finn?"

"No." She shook her head. "Just of him through a...friend."

"I see." Though, based on the confusion tugging his lips down, Fallon clearly didn't.

"What'd you call him?" Duncan demanded.

"Doc of course," Skylar said. "Because he's a Healer. And you were Dopey."

Ivar snorted, and Duncan smacked the back of the man's head. Ladon, meanwhile, held in a snort of his own, because Duncan was a bald, brash brute of a man, who happened to be missing a tooth, which made the nickname pretty damn hilarious.

"Mostly because I'd run out of dwarves." Skylar bent enough in her needling of his guard to own up. "But, since your name is Duncan, and they both start with D, I guess it works."

She turned to Reid, who'd watched all this with a fairly neutral expression, though he continuously flipped a butterfly knife in one hand, a sure sign he didn't like what was happening. His blue eyes sparked with the beginnings of cerulean blue flames, made even more blue against his ebony skin. "You, handsome, I dubbed Happy, since you smile a lot. I know better than to not take you seriously, though. A badass fighter. Captain of this guard, and Ladon's Viceroy of Security. Right?"

The knife stopped its movement. "Got it in one," Reid acknowledged. "You'll have to share with me how you got in and where you hid. Looks like someone should kick my ass for not doing my job right."

He wasn't wrong. Ladon and Reid would be having a serious talk about this soon.

Skylar waved that away. "Don't beat yourself up too hard. I got in while the mountain was under attack, and you've been dealing with all that since."

"She's also been practicing for years," Kasia commented. Based on the put-upon tone in her voice, Ladon would bet her practice had been against her own family.

Skylar merely chuckled. "And finally, we have Grumpy, which is self-explanatory." She tipped her chin at Asher's grim countenance, and Ivar had to hold in another laugh or get smacked again.

"Asher. Beta and serves as Viceroy of Defense on the council," Skylar said. "Correct?"

"Yes," Asher acknowledged through clenched teeth.

As if determined to poke deeper, Skylar canted her head to regard his Beta more closely. "And the best friend?"

Damn, she had them pegged. Brand and Asher were his closest friends, the only men he allowed remotely into his head. He'd better get this over with before she could antagonize them further.

"Skylar is my mate," he announced. "And we'll be consummating our union immediately."

Beside him, his soon-to-be mate practically cackled. "Wow. Way to ease into it."

"The hell you say," Asher hissed. His Beta flung a hand at her. "She tried to take off with Kasia, hates dragon shifters, and now you want to trust her enough not to *kill* you?"

"I don't hate *all* dragon shifters, Grumps," Skylar pointed out sweetly.

"Not helping," Ladon whispered.

Zero remorse stared back at him, then a devilish grin lit her face. "So sorry, my love." Skylar went up on her toes and proceeded to trail her tongue up his neck, practically purring as she tasted his skin, to nibble at his earlobe.

Ladon's cock, already on high alert, jerked to rigid attention and he grunted, which pulled a chuckle from the woman at his side, who lowered to her feet, batting those big, unusual eyes at him in what he was sure was entirely fake innocence. The minx had done that on purpose, just to fuck with him. He should not have admitted his attraction.

Still, two could play at that game. He slid his hand, which had been innocently resting against her hip, up to cup her ribs, brushing his fingertips against the side of her breast. She sucked in a breath, but he focused on his men. "The Blue Clan is more than their king. You'll survive without me if this goes wrong."

Skylar stiffened under his touch and tipped her head back, studying him closely, her brows furrowed. What about that statement bothered her?

Asher's scowl only deepened, his navy eyes turning almost black. He crossed the room to stand directly in front of Ladon. "Who will lead if you go? They won't follow a gold dragon. Especially one who doesn't even have his own clan under control. No offense, Brand." He tossed the last comment over his shoulder.

Brand remained passive beside Kasia. "None taken, dickhead."

Kasia rolled her eyes.

Ladon clapped a hand on Asher's shoulder. "They'll follow you."

"Fuck," Asher muttered, looking away. Tension vibrated from him. "Most see me as a man who could betray his king."

Grim anger settled over Ladon like a cloak of death. Every single day, something would happen that rammed the weight of his past, present, and future down his damn throat. Apparently, today, this was that moment. "*I* asked you to infiltrate Thanatos's inner circle. Everyone knows you did that for the clan."

"Do they?" Asher scoffed. "I'd rather not test the theory."

"What'd you do?" Skylar asked. "Help kill the king?" Only the tone of her voice had gone softer, easier. She wasn't poking, merely curious.

Rather than snap at her, Asher canted his head. "I became one of his most trusted guards and reported everything I could back to Ladon. *He* killed the king. But yes, I helped."

Skylar's lips twisted as she thought that through. "Why?"

No one ever questioned his Beta so directly. His mate apparently had no instinct for self-preservation. That might be a problem.

Asher stepped forward, and pure, protective instinct ripped a growl from Ladon's throat.

Immediately, Skylar smacked him on the chest. "Quit that. Asher understands why I'm asking."

Ladon looked up to find his Beta staring with eyebrows practically in his hairline. After a small shake of his head, Asher looked directly at Skylar. "I did what I did because Thanatos was killing our clan—fewer mates granted to us than other clans, our wealth gone, starvation creeping in—all for his own power."

She nodded slowly. "Okay. You and I will be fine then, Grumps, as soon as you get over yourself."

Asher glowered at her before shooting a glare at Ladon. "You'd better be right. I don't want to be king."

Ladon had felt exactly the same when his men had come to him and asked him to take the throne. To be their king. Still did most days. "Let's hope it doesn't come to that, my friend."

"Yeah." Asher glanced from Ladon back to Skylar, and his jaw clenched. "Still, what if she's playing you? What if she only intends to kill you?"

"Brand was right about that dickhead label." Skylar glared at Asher. "I thought we understood each other, then you had to go and ruin it." She shook her head with a *tsk*. "Not that killing a dragon shifter didn't cross my mind. Even better, a king."

Seriously? His mate was worse at politics than he was.

Before he could intervene, she tipped up her chin, suddenly serious. "I gave Ladon my word. I choose him as my mate."

Her words punched through him like an iron fist to the gut. He had no doubt she'd meant them completely. She had chosen him, in the space of hours. Why, he had no idea, but he wasn't going to look a gift horse in the mouth, either. If the horse ended up containing the entire Trojan army, then so be it.

Ladon pulled her closer and kissed her, hard but swift. He lifted his head to gaze down into those eyes—ice and fire. Kasia had the same eyes, but the way Skylar watched him... Without meaning to, he got tangled up in her gaze and a low sound he couldn't control poured from him.

His dragon was close to the surface, which had him tensing in shock. Usually the animal side of his nature remained under his steely control, coming out only when Ladon demanded it.

"Maybe you two should go take care of things right now," Reid suggested with a wink.

Arden, who stood beside Reid, punched him in the arm. "Gross. That's my brother."

Then she crossed to Ladon, going up on tiptoe—despite being tall herself—to wrap her arms around his neck. "I hope you know what you're doing, big brother."

"Reid will take care of you if something happens," he said into her hair.

Arden pulled back and aimed a scowl at Skylar. "You better be worth it, or you'll have me to deal with."

Skylar eyed his sister up and down. "I believe you."

Arden drew her shoulders back and gave a sharp nod. "I'll welcome you to the family after it works."

That brought a slow blink from Skylar before she wrinkled

her nose. "I always wanted a littler sister."

While he didn't know their birth order, Ladon suspected Skylar wasn't the youngest of the quadruplets. Her tone indicated that she had plans to mess with said little sister. Ladon silently wished his mate good luck with that. Arden and his soon-to-be mate were similar in more ways than one, both having ride-or-die attitudes, and being well trained in hand-to-hand combat.

"This is the right thing to do," Wyot said in his quiet way. He crossed his arms, an indication that he'd say no more.

"Two phoenixes on our side may be worth the risk," Rainier added.

The others in the room shifted on their feet. Brand and Kasia hadn't been the only ones wondering about all that luck that was supposed to be raining down around them.

Ivar, more sober now, ran a hand over his goatee, visibly less inclined to agree. "Even if it kills our king?"

"I don't think it will," Duncan commented in his thick brogue. "Destined mates would explain his odd behavior earlier."

Ladon frowned. Had he acted oddly? No. The discovery of a phoenix would do that to any dragon king who needed every advantage he could find. And yet, Ladon couldn't rip his gaze from his soon-to-be mate as he battled the raging need to bend her over a chair and claim her here and now. In front of his guard and friends. That would definitely count as odd behavior for him.

It would also get him fried by the woman.

Skylar raised her eyebrows, dark amusement dancing in her gaze, and indicated the room full of people watching with a tip of her chin as though reminding him of their audience.

Lifting his head with more effort than he cared to admit, even to himself, Ladon addressed the group. "Much as your support is appreciated, in this instance I didn't fucking ask for it."

Silence crackled among his men and they all straightened.

"You wanted a king, you got one. This is *my* decision."

"Is that why the rest of your Curia Regis aren't here?" Arden asked, though the serious light in her eyes belied her casual tone.

"As my Beta and Viceroy of War, Asher will inform the rest of the council for me. Before that, though, I want a promise from my guard. If this goes wrong, I want Skylar protected."

"Fuck," Asher spat.

But Ladon bent a glare on him that left no doubt as to choices. That was an order, and his Beta knew it.

"We'll protect her with our lives, either way it goes," Asher agreed, reluctant obedience in every syllable.

Ladon directed that hard gaze to every man in the room.

"Aye," Duncan added.

One by one, each of his men voiced their agreement. Leaving only his sister. Ladon raised his eyebrows.

Arden crossed her arms. "No way. Don't expect *me* to help the woman who killed my only remaining family."

Reid gave her a shove in the arm. "What are we, duchess? Chopped liver?"

Arden didn't let up. "You're not blood."

Reid's skin pulled tight over his cheekbones at that, any teasing dying a swift death as his eyes went dark and serious. Not that Arden caught it. She was too busy glaring at Ladon.

"You would hurt my sister?" Kasia questioned.

Arden glanced at the redhead who'd been silent until now and grimaced. In the short time Kasia had been here, the two had grown close. "I won't hurt her," Arden finally conceded. "But I'm not protecting her, either. That's the best I can offer."

"Good enough for me." Skylar held out a hand to shake.

After staring at each other a long, silent moment, Arden shook.

"Good," Ladon said.

Business handled, he took Skylar by the hand and left the room without another word. Thankfully, Skylar remained quiet as she walked beside him. Hell, practically glued to him, because he didn't let go of her.

They'd made it halfway to his suite in silence before she spoke. "So...you'd choose Asher to leave in charge, huh?"

For once, he didn't hear censure in her voice, more like idle curiosity. "Asher's role with Thanatos was discussed long before he took it. He would *never* betray me."

"I can see that," Skylar murmured, and he gave her a sideways look. Maybe she did.

"Still, I'd rather not have to try to mate him next," she continued. "That would go down faster than the Hindenburg. This mating thing had better work and you better not die on me, Ladon Ormarr."

A pang of something dangerously close to jealousy—he was starting to get familiar with it—shot through him at the thought of her with Asher. Hot on the heels of that thought came another, scorching away the jealousy. That was the closest to a compliment she'd given him since they met.

Skylar walked along quietly for a while. Her silences were starting to make him nervous. "Did you mean what you said?" she asked.

He flicked a glance her way. "About what?"

"About the clan being more than their king, more than one person."

So that was why she'd looked at him funny? "Yes."

"But *you're* the king." She couldn't seem to help digging at the issue. He had a sudden image of her as a child, blithely and willfully running into danger just to test out how dangerous it was. A handful, he'd bet.

My handful, now.

He shook off the possessive thought and the pinch of worry that came with it. Maybe she truly needed to know.

Except explaining himself sat about as easily with him as Thanatos's mark had on his hand. He'd scratched that brand raw for years.

Cold logic came to his aid now. More trust would only help him survive what was soon to come. "The last king did nothing for our people, selling us down the river in deference to stronger, more power-hungry kings. In the meantime, dragon shifters as a race haven't evolved much since Pytheios claimed the Red Throne and the title of High King."

Suspicion pinched her lips and narrowed her eyes. "So, you're going to take it away from him?"

He frowned, not quite following. "High King?"

"Yes."

Ladon shrugged. "I'm going to kill him and any others who try to take us down. What follows will be up to all those who remain. Technically, I'd say High King should go to Brand, as the first to mate a phoenix. We need to get him that Gold Throne either way, though."

Skylar stopped dead in the middle of the corridor, her braid swinging behind her back. "No way can you be for real."

Ladon couldn't help it. Everything about her challenged him in a way too visceral to ignore. He reached out and yanked her up against him, watching with satisfaction as she registered the hard ridge of him pressing into her, her eyes widening.

But then that stubborn chin lifted as she refused to give an inch. "So, you'd help another dragon shifter become High King?"

"Will you ever believe anything I say?" Ladon snapped, then released her, turning to walk down the hall, though his throbbing dick made that process damned uncomfortable.

She caught up with him. "Surprisingly, I might."

The incredulity in her voice made him want to laugh. Again.

Ladon stopped at his door and ushered her into the room. Skylar stopped just inside, staring at the king-size bed beyond the main living space the doors opened into, visible between the natural arches formed by the cavern.

Quietly, he moved in behind her, not quite touching, but enough to feel her heat, to inhale that sweetly smoky scent.

"We're going to have sex," she said, more to herself than anything.

A laugh punched from him, and she spun around with a glare, only to gasp at finding him standing so close. Skylar tilted her head back, refusing to step away or show any sign of weakness, as he'd come to expect. Damned if that part of her personality wasn't a huge turn-on.

He didn't want a mate who cowered.

Her gaze narrowed. "Yeah. Laugh it up, Chuckles. Pissing me off probably isn't your best play right now."

Only her reaction, instead of angering him, reminded him of an orphan dragon he'd met once. The child lashed out when afraid, which was most of the time. No wonder, since the majority of orphans in their society were abandoned or killed. Without blood family to anchor their humanity, they turned feral the first time they shifted into a dragon, causing untold destruction. Most human legends about dragons originated because of rogues and orphans.

Where was this coming from? "I'm not laughing at you."

"No?"

He wanted to touch her but didn't think she'd let him. "This isn't exactly easy for me, either, you know."

"Don't mistake this for nerves." Skylar crossed her arms, pushing her generous breasts up in a way he couldn't fail to notice. Nor did he miss the way her nipples beaded beneath the thin black material of her shirt.

Angry *and* turned on—a cocktail he was becoming intimately familiar with since she stormed into his life.

Ladon slowly moved closer, trying not to spook her. "Nerves aren't necessarily a bad thing."

Only because he was intently studying her did he catch the way she swallowed.

"I wish I could have taken this slower, take my time winning you over." He was close enough now to catch how her chest moved with a deep breath.

A spark of surprise ignited in his chest as the depth of those words struck him. He wanted to win her over. For a man who'd looked on mating as only a political maneuver, this felt...deeper.

"You didn't strike me as a patient man," she said on a snort.

"I'm not." He wouldn't insult her intelligence by denying it. "But I would have tried to be patient if it meant earning you."

He reached for her braid, pulling the elastic band off the end and slowly undoing it, the long blue-black tresses falling around her face and down her back in soft waves, raven-black against the pale oval of her face.

Damn, she was gorgeous.

"So, in your version of slow, how long would it have taken to get here?" she asked. Stalling?

"Are you attracted to me?" he asked, smoke in his voice now, his dragon close to the surface. She still hadn't answered him from earlier.

She slow-blinked. "What?"

"I asked if you're attracted to me. I already told you I want you. Do you want me?" He moved a hand around the back of her neck, under the heavy fall of her hair. At the same time, he got caught in the vortex of her pale blue gaze, but he didn't want to look away now, too intent on her answer.

"Well, I do like this." She ran a fingertip over the indent on his chin.

"Not an answer."

Again, that stubborn jaw tilted up. "You don't disgust me."

Blunt honesty, though not an answer. He could work with that. "Then let's start there."

Her lips parted, and he took advantage, bending to take a quick taste before pulling back.

"To answer your question," he said, "I couldn't have waited too long anyway. I want you too much."

She tipped her head, eyeing him closely. "You mean you need me too much."

"I do need you." Ladon slowly pulled his hand from her neck, brushing it across her collarbone and down to graze an eager nipple begging for his touch. "But that has nothing to do with how badly I crave you."

Skylar sucked in a shuddering breath.

"If you want me to stop, I'll stop," he murmured. He circled that tantalizing finger around her puckered nipple, barely brushing.

Her eyes darkened as he watched, more of the blue swirling

in those icy depths. "How do you want to do this?" she asked.

Triumph lit a fire in his blood. She wasn't going to stop this. "If I'm going to die, I'd rather my last moments be ones of pleasure."

He cupped her breast, testing the weight in his hand, loving how she leaned into the touch with a small whimper.

"Sounds reasonable," she breathed.

He dropped his gaze to those berry-ripe lips. He wanted to possess them, claim them, see them wrapped around his cock. His voice dropped low and harsh. "How about we just enjoy each other?"

Skylar shivered against him. "Sex for the sake of sex?"

Not exactly what he was thinking, but her shoulders dropped when she'd said it. She seemed to like that idea. "Pleasure, because it feels damn good," he reworded.

"I can do that," she whispered.

CHAPTER EIGHT

Taking things back to the most basic—for the sake of the pleasure they could give each other—relaxed Skylar in a way she realized logically it shouldn't. Somehow that took the pressure off, like she gave herself permission to give in to an attraction that had been grasping at her like a riptide since she'd laid eyes on Ladon Ormarr.

"Good," he murmured, lowering his mouth to hers way too slowly.

Any other time, she would've smacked him upside the head for the smug satisfaction in his voice, but she was too busy waiting for him to kiss her.

When he hovered, just out of reach, she speared her hands through his thick hair and tugged. "Kiss me, dammit."

His kiss was immediate, possessive and demanding, taking over her body as he wrapped his arms around her, pulling her flush against his hard length.

He grunted, the sound annoyed. "Damn, you're shorter than I thought."

"That's a first," she snarked back through panting breaths. "Human men find me too tall."

He didn't respond. Instead, he cupped her by the ass and hauled her up so that her mouth was level with his. Skylar didn't hesitate to wrap her legs around him, grinding against the thick rod of his erection in a move showing him exactly what she wanted.

"Fuck," he grunted against her lips.

"That's the idea," she teased as she licked her way down his neck.

He huffed a half laugh, half groan. "If that's the idea, this is not going to be gentle or slow."

Even through the need tightening his voice, she still caught a lilt of concern. For her? She'd expected him to claim and be done with it.

She brushed aside the thought. Instinctual hunger possessed her, driving her actions. Needing to mark him, to drive him to take what he wanted, she pulled his shirt off, the first couple of buttons popping off, and bit his shoulder. Not hard enough to draw blood, but hard.

Ladon sucked in a breath and shuddered. "Like that, is it?"

He clamped his lips down on hers, dominating her mouth, demanding her submission, which, for once, Skylar willingly gave because what he was doing just felt so damn good.

Vaguely she was aware he walked them back to the bed.

With an abrupt move that had her gasping, he tumbled her to the bed, then grabbed her shirt and yanked it, none too gently, over her head. Her own driving need pumping through her, Skylar whipped off her sports bra before he could get to it.

That intent gaze zeroed in on her half-naked body, and heat flushed through her, turning her skin pink under his greedy stare.

"This is wild," Ladon muttered. "Why do I want you so much?"

He was going to pause *now* to debate their loss of sanity? Skylar rolled her eyes. "Get moving, or I'll keep going on my own."

She inched her fingers down her stomach and under the band of her pants.

A low growl ripped from him, an obvious protest, and Ladon dropped forward, hands fisted on either side of her head, to pull a straining nipple into his mouth, every suck zinging pleasure straight to the juncture of her thighs.

"Harder," she commanded, pressing her body up into him.

He released her with a pop to give her an evil grin. "Demanding little thing, aren't you?"

"We'll talk about size-ism and sexism another time. For now..." Skylar bucked, trying to rub herself against him, but he leaned over her, just out of reach.

Instead of grinding into her like she hoped he might do, Ladon snagged her wrists, pulling them above her head where he held them with one hand as he lay down on top of her, pinning her with the weight of his body. She should be fighting back, or frightened by the submissive position in which he held her. Only, being caged by this man evolved into an unbelievable turn-on. Wet heat soaked her panties as she trembled beneath him.

Ladon buried his face in her neck and inhaled. "Gods, you smell amazing."

"It's just shampoo," she panted as he sucked on the juncture of her neck and shoulder.

"It's you," he said. "Cloves and smoke." He drew back and traced his fingers over her neck. "What happened here?"

She knew exactly what he was asking about, the thin white scar had been with her forever. "The umbilical cord was wrapped around my neck in the womb."

Even then, the fates, if they did exist, were trying to take her out of the picture.

"A fighter," Ladon murmured, a light in his eyes that went beyond need. If she had her full wits about her, she might've said pride. In her.

But he distracted her, trailing his lips over the scar back to her shoulder. Was he going to bite her in that spot like she had him?

Not all shifters were rough when it came to sex, but many could be, incorporating biting and scratching into their play. Skylar never had. Until today. She found herself holding her breath in anticipation.

Did she want him to?

He kissed his way to the upper swell of her breast, and conflicting needs buffeted her—disappointment that he hadn't bitten her, and a new anticipation that he'd tease her nipples again.

"Fuck." He abruptly returned to that spot at her neck, where he sank his teeth in. Like her, not hard enough to break skin, but enough to have her clit throbbing in response.

Skylar let out a long moan.

"You like that." Satisfaction permeated the words.

"Shut up," she said.

Ladon stilled and pulled his head up, putting a halt to the touching, though he still gripped both her wrists. "If this is going to work, we need total honesty."

He said the words quite seriously, but a challenging light in those flaming blue eyes managed to ratchet up her breathing another notch. She knew what he wanted—her to admit she'd liked his bite—but Skylar wasn't into voicing emotions. "Your point?"

His stare turned hard and cunning.

And damn hot.

"Are you just going to lie there glaring, or are you going to fuck me?"

Surprise lit his eyes. On a huffed laugh, he levered off her. "Definitely fuck you." Swiftly, he divested himself of his clothes.

Ha. She'd won that round. Meanwhile, her clamoring body was loving every inch of lean, hard flesh and rippling muscles he exposed. Battle tested, warrior trained, she'd explore the scars and ridges and planes of him later. Right now, she needed him inside her.

Keeping her gaze trained on Ladon, she shimmied out of the rest of her own gear. She kicked off the last leg of her black body-clinging pants only to have him snag her by the ankle.

He grasped the other ankle as well and spread her legs wide, pulling her ass to the end of the bed.

Every nerve in her body pulsed in anticipation as he lined his cock up with her entrance. He pushed the tip in, then paused and speared her with a blazing look. "Did you like me biting you or not?"

Fuck. She hadn't won that round after all. Skylar scowled and bucked her hips, trying to force the matter, but he grasped her by the waist and shook his head. "Did you?"

He wasn't letting this go, and she needed him inside her. Hell, she was crawling out of her skin with the tension, the need to have him fill her.

Now. Shit. "Yes, dammit."

Using his grip on her as leverage, Ladon slammed into her body, seating himself balls deep inside her. "Good. Because I fucking *loved* you biting me."

Her entire body flushed with a new kind of pleasure that joined the rest of the pounding as Ladon set up a driving rhythm, pumping into her hard—the slap of his body against hers joining his grunts and her own moans.

With her ass off the bed where he held her through sheer animal strength, Skylar had no leverage. She flattened her hands on either side of her, gripping the sheets as she tried to meet him, thrust for thrust. Sensation piled on more sensation, building inside her body until everything thrummed, pressure building.

"Fuck, you feel so damn good," Ladon groaned.

For a guy who kept to a minimum of words in general, he sure liked to talk in the bedroom. Which only managed to add to her own pleasure in the strangest, hottest way.

"Skylar?" He grunted between thrusts.

She knew what he was asking. Was she ready to trigger the flames that would bind them in mating?

Skylar didn't allow herself to think beyond the pleasure and a confidence in the logic of her decision—a confidence that she had no idea, until this moment, she truly possessed, or what it even meant, but she wouldn't question it.

At the flick of her will, her body lit on fire, glowing from the inside as red flames, which were now tipped in startling blue sparked all over her, flaming cinders rising around them in a dance of light. Another heat joined her own, and she realized Ladon was blowing fire over her skin. His blue flames joined hers and curled through them, turning the inferno around them violet.

Immediately, Skylar's skin started to glow, as if lit from within by his flames. Delicate lines of illuminated fire appeared across her neck and down her arms, over her chest, and probably her back. Lines that connected to form feathers. Then the fire rose from her skin, surrounding her, forming intricate shapes, like flaming wings, joined to the lines across her skin.

The mark of a phoenix.

"Damn, that's beautiful." His gaze traveled over her with awe bordering on worship, even as he waited to die in her flames.

That look and his fire only added to the heat consuming her body as Ladon filled her with glorious pressure at each thrust. He paused, rearing back as the combined flames poured over him, and they both held their breath.

Would this work? Suddenly she wanted this to work. Wanted him to live through it.

Heart pounding and chest heaving she waited, watching his face for any indication. If he had mated a human woman, they'd be worried about his fire. But with a phoenix, hers was deadly if they'd chosen wrong.

Suddenly, Ladon grinned. "I guess we're meant to be," he said, then dipped his head and claimed her lips. At the same time, he resumed what he'd been doing, pumping into her slowly at first, then faster.

Relief stirred through her. He wasn't burning to death. This was going to work.

The feverish need inside her reached a screaming pitch. Ladon pushing her back on the bed to join her there, never stopping his hammering into her for a second as he did. He adjusted their positions so that he lay over her, taking his weight on his elbows.

Then he sucked in, a sound like a bellows surrounding her as he built his own flames inside his body. He leaned over her and took her lips in a hungry kiss. Warmth filled her from the inside as he pushed his fire into her.

The mating kiss of a dragon shifter.

A flurry of thoughts pinged against the sexual haze she found herself in. Wait. What if his fire killed her instead? What if the legends were wrong and she was about to burn?

Too late now.

The fire inside her spread out, flowing through her blood and over her nerves to increase the heat and tension already built to the tipping point.

Skylar flung her head back. "I'm going to..."

A second fire pushed inside her from the juncture at her thighs and Skylar arched her back, clawing at Ladon as she screamed through an orgasm that ripped through her body, slamming into her and through her and out of her.

Ladon tipped his head back and roared his own release, a feral sound that took hold of her soul, echoing her own screams, his face harsh and beautiful above her. He didn't stop his pumping hips until the waves of ecstasy ebbed.

Finally, he slowed, then stilled, though he remained seated deep inside her. Chest heaving, he dropped his head so that his forehead rested against hers, eyes closed as he caught his breath.

For her part, Skylar sank into the afterglow of that incredible orgasm. She'd never experienced pleasure like that before, and damn if her body wasn't completely sated. Part of her wanted to stretch beneath him, reveling in the lovely sensations filling her. Skylar tried to listen to that part of herself, because the other part—the real world, logical part—niggled at the back of her mind.

Unfortunately, despite her resistance, logic won. "Holy shit," she gasped as realization crashed through her. "That worked."

They were...*mated*? Was it truly that easy? Because she'd sort of, deep down inside, expected him to die in the process. Regardless of her sudden, intense desire for him not to.

Ladon grunted. Amusement, or concern, or agreement—she wasn't sure which. Then he lifted his head to gaze down at her, his eyes no longer lit with an inner fire, serious as hell. "Yes, it did."

What the hell am I supposed to do now?

Immediately her own snarky inner voice answered her. *Keep fucking him until this is over and you walk away, because damn that was good.*

The more reasonable voice in her head latched on to her half-baked plan—help take down the old regime of kings, then go on her merry way a free woman.

"Are you sure?" she asked. "Maybe we did it wrong?"

Wicked amusement gleamed back at her. "I don't think it gets much more right than what we just did."

She grinned and traced the cleft of his chin. "Arrogant ass." But the words held no conviction because she couldn't deny the power of what he'd made her body feel.

"Is your brand on my neck?" She reached back to feel, but only smooth skin met her touch.

Ladon leaned over to peer at the spot. "I don't see one, but that can take months to form. Something to do with the connection, the bond solidifying, and we only just met."

Said the man still buried inside her, half erect.

He tucked a strand of hair behind her ear, his eyes darkening. "Did I hurt you? I know I was rough. Maybe too rough—"

She held a finger to his lips, shushing him. "Don't go getting all gooey on me, Blood King. You didn't hurt me. I..." Dammit. Voicing feelings again. "I liked it."

A flash of an emotion she couldn't quite identify, relief maybe, sparked in those blue eyes. "Good."

. . .

Shit. He'd never come so hard in his life, and he'd damn sure never bitten a woman, let alone during sex, though, to be fair, she started that business. He finished it. And he liked the look of his mark on her skin. He suspected seeing his family crest, combined with the Amon insignia, on her neck would hit him even harder.

Part of him expected her to start flinging names like Neanderthal at him, but strangely, she seemed contented to remain lying beneath him.

My mate.

A strange sort of satisfaction welled up inside him at the thought. Not satisfaction that he'd claimed a phoenix, though a certain relief floated around in the emotions he sifted through. This was more a satisfaction that *she* was his. He'd survived, and now Skylar Amon was his.

Mine.

The intensity of his emotions in this moment sent shock slicing though him. His dragon loosed a rumble of pure possessiveness, and Skylar's eyebrows shot up.

Ladon didn't bother apologizing. The animal was part of him, was him, and she'd have to get used to that side of his nature.

She was his. That was all that mattered. He stuffed the roiling emotions in a dark hole and focused on the practical. One massive step closer to winning this war he'd started the day he'd killed Thanatos and claimed the crown.

"So, what happens next?" she asked. "Because I'll be honest, I sort of thought I'd be informing your people that a funeral needed to be happening for your pile of ash."

"That's definitely honest." He lifted one eyebrow. "And descriptive."

She shrugged. "I'm not the sentimental type."

"Or the squeamish type, apparently."

"Nope."

Neither was he. Maybe the fates knew what they were doing after all. "Hmm. Next, we inform the rest of the clan that I have a mate and that there are two phoenixes in existence?"

"Not four?" she asked.

He shook his head. "Not until we have your other sisters safe." This was a weird conversation to be having in this position, but he was oddly reluctant to move, and she'd made no indication she wanted him to. "Then I get down to the business of getting Brand on his throne. I need all the allies I can get."

Skylar tilted her head, eyes narrowed. "You mean *we*, right?"

He didn't follow. "Me and Brand?"

"No, stupid." She smacked him on the arm. "We. You and *I*. Your *mate*."

Mated less than ten minutes and already he'd been called stupid and been hit, two things that hadn't happened to him in centuries. Not since he honed his fighting skills with deadly intent, and his clanmates decided fucking with him was a bad idea. "Maybe we should work on your self-preservation instincts."

She rolled her eyes. "Don't avoid the topic. I am not going to be a puppet. I have skills and a brain—"

"And opinions," he said.

"You'd better believe it."

Ladon blew out a heavy breath. "I get it. Kasia asked for pretty much the same thing."

That pulled a scowl from the woman in his arms. "You mean when you intended to mate her."

Damn. Bringing that up right at this second hadn't been the best idea. The strategic move would be to avoid answering and redirect. "How do *you* want to contribute?"

"Do you really want to know?" Skylar shifted under him, not to move away, but to get more comfortable.

Only her wriggling served to remind his still semi-hard cock that they were naked, and he was inside her.

Her eyes widened as he thickened. Fuck, she was going to think he had zero control, like a callow youth, all ready to go again so soon.

"Yes. I want to know," he managed to grit as he fought for command over himself.

Rather than telling him, Skylar tipped her head, then wriggled some more, and Ladon grunted as his body responded.

She looped her arms around his neck. "We can talk after."

Shock reverberated through him. "Are you sure?"

She lifted her legs to wrap them around his waist and he slid deeper, pulling a low groan from him.

"I'm sure," she murmured.

CHAPTER NINE

The glass moonhole and walls that made up the dungeon chamber in which Airk Azdaja had spent most of his life usually showed a sky he could never get to, but not tonight. Tonight, a snowstorm raged outside, obscuring his view of the Himalayas.

A blast of sound seemed to rock the very mountain beneath his feet as the blizzard hammered them, producing a lightning strike they called thundersnow. Only, underlying the rolling tumble of sound, Airk swore he caught a sound not of nature.

Dragon.

"That was a bad one," Nathair commented, glancing nervously overhead, not that he could see anything through the whiteout blasting outside.

"Do we need to be concerned?" a raspy male voice, almost more of a hiss, questioned from the cell directly across the way.

Airk ignored the man—a blue dragon shifter who'd identified himself as Chante. Posh accent, clear assumption that he should not be here, and lots of whining. Probably one of Pytheios's lackeys or spies who hadn't done his job right. The only reason he would end up in the dungeons with Airk. That type came and went with monotonous regularity, and all met the same end.

Airk nodded at Nathair and reached through the bars of his cell to move a chess piece.

He had not been surprised when Pytheios's younger brother

appeared this morning. Even as a child, Nathair had never liked the storms that could slam into Everest with no warning. He had taken to coming up here to watch, his thought being that if the hollowed-out mountain home of the Red Clan collapsed, he would rather be on the top of the rubble, not underneath it.

The chessboard sat on the floor between them, only those damn bars an indication that, of the two of them, Airk was the prisoner.

As a child, before Pytheios, Airk and his parents used to visit this mountain. Airk would come up here, to the top of the world, just to marvel at how big the sky was.

A sky he would never touch.

That had been before. Before the phoenix had foreseen that any man who dared to kill Airk would die not long after.

Now he sat imprisoned in the most fortified dragon stronghold in existence in a room with walls turned to glass and then magically warded to act like a one-way mirror, allowing those inside an unimpeded view, even through the ice and snow coating the rock, and preventing those outside from perceiving that anything but rock and ice and snow lay there in the first place.

He studied the chessboard.

Airk knew why his ancestors had put the dungeons at the top— to torture the captives with what they could never have. Dragons *needed* to fly, their souls craving the sky like the body needed the blood in its veins.

Nathair's dark hair flopped over one eye as he stared up at the fury of the storm overhead. The man rarely sat. After years of these visits, Airk figured Nathair's mind, which never stopped calculating, on a constant churn, would not allow him to be still.

Airk made his move. "Your turn."

Nathair turned and barely glanced at the board, making his move with quick confidence.

Airk held in a sigh of frustration, taking his time to consider his next. He never beat Nathair, but these visits were one of the few breaks in the monotony of his life. He didn't count Chante or the others like him who'd come to stay as "guests" before.

Nathair was the only reason Airk knew what had developed in the outside world, telling him stories, and eventually bringing books and pictures of technology and cities and wars, marvels and discoveries. Even with that information, Airk still couldn't wrap his head around what awaited him if he ever escaped this hell.

Another blast of thundersnow, carrying with it another sound. Airk was sure now. A dragon fought the storm outside. A dragon in a rage, unless he missed his guess. A roar Airk was painfully familiar with. "The lord and master is not happy this night."

Nathair flinched and turned away from the view. "No."

"Bad news?"

Nathair said nothing. He never did when it came to Pytheios. His loyalty to his older brother had never broken in all these centuries, but that did not mean Airk wouldn't keep nudging.

"Not there," Nathair said, referring to where Airk was hovering his piece over the board.

"I need to liberate my queen, or you have me in two."

"Yes, but—"

Airk cocked his head as Nathair stuttered to a halt and stared at the board while his mind seemed a million leagues away. "Liberate the queen," he murmured to himself.

"What?" Airk asked.

"I have to go." It spoke to the red dragon shifter's distraction that he failed to collect his board as he all but ran from the chamber.

. . .

For once, the freezing temperatures of the air at this altitude did nothing to assuage Pytheios's roiling fury. Instead, a storm raged around the mountain, bringing with it a barrage of ice and snow, obscuring his vision.

But he didn't need to see to know where he was. He'd grown up on this mountain. Everest was *his* mountain. And right now, he needed to fly, to bleed off his rage out of the view of others, even if his body's haggard state meant he shouldn't.

If he didn't, he'd lose control and unleash this frenzy on his people, something he couldn't afford. Not now.

He prided himself, above all, on his self-control. Control was what had kept him on his throne all these centuries. Control, and no fucking phoenix to get in his way. Now he had four to contend with, if all of Serefina's spawn inherited her abilities. If the reports were to be believed, the new one recently found had already mated the traitor king.

"My love, come down."

The soft call of his witch barely reached him over the howl of the storm. He caught it only because he'd passed close to the entrance. She must be inside, because no way could she handle Everest on a good day, let alone in this blizzard.

He didn't bother to soften the volume of his mental words, knowing they would pierce Rhiamon's fragile human mind and cause her pain. *"Have you found either of the two missing phoenixes?"*

"No." Even from this distance, her frustration with that fact screamed through that single word.

Pytheios didn't give a shit. She *should* be frustrated. Rhiamon had found Serefina for him.She could damn well find her daughters. These phoenix women were young, only five centuries old, and only having just come into their powers upon their mother's death. They should be easy to find and capture.

"We have nothing to talk about," he barked and hoped Rhiamon lay on the ground writhing in pain with the volume of his words.

Yes, she'd located the phoenix in South America. However, her information came too late for him to do anything about it. By the time they discovered her location, Skylar Amon had already made her way to the Blue Clan. To Ladon Ormarr.

He'd lost two phoenixes to that fucker. All Pytheios's power, his network of spies, the other clans, even his witch, had done nothing to stop it.

Pytheios snarled as he bobbed in the air. The holes in the

membranes of his wings, now more like tattered rags than flesh, made flying more difficult. Already the task was draining his reserves of power. Impotent fury poured out of him, and Pytheios loosed a torrent of red fire from his maw as he roared his wrath.

Rhiamon's voice whispered on the winds. "I know this appears to be a setback, but we can turn the situation to our advantage."

"My king, the witch is right." The Stoat's nasal intonation found him now. Like Rhiamon, not as a dragon, but in human form, trusting Pytheios's sense of hearing would catch the words. "We have several plans in place we can use to find the others, now that we know of them, and possibly take out the two already in play. Your brother has also made a suggestion."

Nathair had an idea? His brother's brilliance couldn't be relied on regularly, working only if left to his own devices. If Nathair had an idea, it would be worth listening to.

Pytheios tipped his wings, shooting back to the mountain, battling the elements and his own feebleness. He flared his wings only at the last second, as he began his shift, human feet touching the ground. He completed the transition as he stalked toward the entrance, where he knew his people would be waiting. Despite his usual finesse, red flames surrounded his body as he moved.

He didn't bother to suck them back inside. Let his people see how angry he was. Maybe fear would spur their actions to get this fixed. Immediately.

Pytheios passed through the security measures allowing him entrance to the mountain. Rhiamon flinched at the sight of him. In this state, she couldn't go near him, or she'd risk burning to death. Fire and witches did not mix, regardless of his control over the flames. She lowered her gaze and backed away from him.

Beside her, Jakkobah displayed his usual lack of reaction, a wall of blank nothingness, which only served to increase Pytheios's ire. Someday he'd put fear in that man's eyes. Not today, though. Not if he was involved in this plan.

Slender and pale to the point of albinism, only the slight tint of color in Jakkobah's hair showed him to be anything related to a red dragon shifter. Even his dark eyes showed no red. A rare thing. As children, Pytheios had protected Jakkobah from the taunts and bullying of others who'd deemed him an outsider. That action had paid off. Now the most well-informed man in the kingdom was loyal only to him.

"Where's my brother?" Pytheios demanded.

Jakkobah extended a hand, indicating they should move down the hall to the right. "Let us discuss this in a more private location. Nathair is waiting for us in his chambers."

Pytheios frowned, ignoring the pain that small action caused as it dragged at his hanging skin, and turned to walk in that direction. "Go on, Jakkobah. I need to speak with Rhiamon alone."

With a birdlike bob of his head, Jakkobah walked ahead of them, the tail of his white, ornately decorated suit flapping around his skinny legs.

Rhiamon moved to his side, though she gave him a wide berth as he hadn't entirely doused the flames pouring from his body.

"My king?" Rarely had he seen the woman so tentative. He must be projecting a more fearsome image than even he was aware.

Pytheios twitched his shoulders and sucked the remaining fire into his body. "You have nothing to fear from me...my love."

Tension bled from her, lowering her shoulders and lightening her vibrant green eyes. "I know that."

But she didn't, or she wouldn't fear him. Pytheios let it go. He covered her hand with his own. "I'll need another influx of power soon."

She slipped her hand through the crook of his arm. "You shouldn't have risked flying tonight," she admonished.

"Either that or kill every living soul in this mountain."

His witch caught his meaning. She, and their son, would both be included in that. With a barely audible gasp, she went to pull her hand from his arm, but he clamped his own down, manacling her to him. Her lips pinched at the pain of his grip. "I have no other creatures to tap. I will need to find something suitable."

The last had been a hellhound. That should've lasted longer, but she was right. He'd wasted it tonight.

He wouldn't make that mistake again. "Our newest guest in the dungeon should work admirably," he murmured.

He didn't miss the glance she sent him. "We haven't drained a dragon shifter before."

The implication that the shifters he ruled over wouldn't like it wasn't lost on him. "He's a prisoner and from the Blue Clan. What better way to deal with him?"

"An…inspired conclusion." She walked quietly at his side after that.

Without knocking, Pytheios ushered both of them into Nathair's chambers. He hadn't been in this chamber in some time but was not surprised at the state of it. An entire room dedicated to dozens of computer screens, monitors, gaming systems, and such took up his brother's entire living room. Half-eaten meals crusted over on plates piled all around the kitchen. Disgust had Pytheios's lip curling.

Meanwhile Nathair's bedroom appeared untouched, the bed pristinely made and not a single personal item to be seen. At a guess, given the rumpled pillow and blanket there, Nathair slept on the couch between manic bouts on the systems at which he'd become so adept. His brother's extraordinary mind plugged into those devices in a way that both calmed him and benefited Pytheios on a regular basis.

He said nothing about the disarray. He cared only about results. "You have a plan for me?"

Nathair nodded rapidly, making no eye contact, as usual. In his hands, he held a child's toy—his fingers flying through patterns on the Rubik's Cube at a dizzying rate, keeping up with his mind. "We need to liberate our queen."

"What…exactly…does that mean? We don't have a queen."

"They don't know that."

Pytheios sucked air in through his nose as the implications struck. "We put it out there that we have one of the other phoenixes?"

And risk other clans learning sooner that more than two existed?

The Rubik's Cube picked up speed. "We position multiple pieces, so they can't see our strategy. The board is still too cluttered, so we need patience."

Chess. His brother was talking about chess strategy. "Which pieces?"

Clack. Clack. Clack. The toy was moving now. "First, we have two of the other clans attack."

"Rather than wait for Ormarr to attack the Gold Clan?"

"Use that as part of the strategy."

"Gold and White," Jakkobah suggested.

Volos, the King of the White Clan, would do as Pytheios bid. The White Clan was based out of Russia, which made them vulnerable to the Gold Clan if Astarot took over as king. That put Volos in a position to want to help Brock keep a hold on the Gold Clan, which was based out of the Scandinavian countries.

"A distraction?" Pytheios asked.

Nathair nodded. "Meanwhile, we start a rumor of another phoenix being located with Rune Abaddon's rogues in the Andes."

Pytheios cocked his head. "Why? We already know that particular phoenix is now with the Blue Clan."

"*We* do."

Pytheios cocked his head. "I still don't see—"

"One of several things happen with this move. We know there are more, but the other kings don't. A secret that won't stay kept for long. By providing a false trail, we buy ourselves more time."

Allowing Pytheios to hunt for the remaining two.

Clack. Clack. Clack. "The two phoenixes currently with the Ormarr people may think a sister went to find the one who had been there originally."

Possibly drawing one or both out to a vulnerable position.

Nathair's hands stilled, telling Pytheios what the man was about to say was likely the critical part of the plan.

"We allow our fake phoenix, our poison pawn if you will, to

be taken to her 'sisters,' who will deny her. However, her presence will throw doubt as to their own validity, which you've already started rumors to hurt," Nathair said.

Cold satisfaction settled in his gut. *Yes. This could work.*

With one phoenix mated to a man who had yet to claim the Gold Throne, Pytheios could instill doubt in the other clans and kings that any of the women were a true phoenix. Claim the rogue had no throne and kill him before more could come of it. According to his sources, the phoenix bore her mate's mark, so she would die, too.

There had never been more than one before. Never. Cast doubt on their legitimacy, and the other kings would rally behind him, rather than become another point of threat.

Another thought occurred, one he did not deign to speak aloud. Once he'd killed all four true phoenixes, their imposter would come to him. He'd mate her, making Pytheios the only remaining king with a phoenix, as far as anyone knew. If she died in his fire, then so be it.

A false phoenix... Brilliant.

Pytheios turned to Rhiamon to find a smile curving her lips.

She cocked her head, her white curls flowing over one shoulder.

"Can you do it?" he asked.

"Make you a phoenix?" She nodded slowly. "Yes. I can do that."

CHAPTER TEN

A rhythmic thudding noise combined with soft grunts of effort had Skylar peeling her eyes open. *What in the—*

She sat up in bed and froze as a combination of facts assailed her all at once. She was naked. That came with being pleasantly sore in all the right places. And the man responsible for that was visible in a room across the way from the bedroom, half naked with sweatpants hanging low on his hips and punching the living daylights out of the black bag hanging from the ceiling.

My mate.

How long would it take to get used to *that* situation?

Skylar slowly pulled the sheets up to cover herself as she watched Ladon move, fascinated. She already knew, intimately, how leanly muscled his body was, but getting her own personal peep show while he punished himself physically was a morning treat she couldn't pass up. A burn of wanting fast becoming familiar spread through her, gathering and tightening and warming everything.

At the same time, though, something about the determination that radiated from him, obvious in each precise, violent strike, more obvious in the hard blue of his eyes, told her more about the man. This wasn't physical activity to keep up a perfect physique or even bolster his reputation as a vicious fighter. This was determination to be at the top of his game in order to achieve his one goal.

Protect his people.

How the hell she knew that was beyond Skylar. But, not for the first time in the last twenty-four hours, respect spiked through the heat watching his skill had brought her.

Only one way to deal with that.

Ignore it.

Getting attached sexually was already a bad idea. Getting attached emotionally would be the height of idiocy.

Quietly, she slipped from the bed and dressed in her clothes from the day before—clothing easy to move and fight in. She'd go grab the rest of her things before she showered. On silent, bare feet, she padded across the living area to the open gym where Ladon was working out and leaned against the door, arms crossed.

"Do you need something?" he asked, not breaking his rhythm or even glancing her way.

Of course he knew she was there. All those shifter senses. Skylar didn't take offense at his rather abrupt manner of addressing her. She tended to be the same way when she was in the zone. "Want to work with someone who fights back?"

That slowed him down. But then he shook his head and kept going. "I'm faster than you."

"What makes you say that?" She knew exactly why he'd come to that conclusion, because she'd realized the same thing herself when she'd fought him before.

But her question had the desired effect. He executed an impressive round kick that set the bag swaying, the chains from which it hung rattling with the impact, then stopped to stare at her with a hard light in his eyes. "I was holding back when we fought."

Her serious king was back, replacing the sexy, lust-driven man in her bed. Too bad.

Skylar gave herself a mental shake. Not too bad. Exactly what she needed. Whatever explosive thing had happened between them was a distraction.

"I wondered." She hopped down the steps leading into the slightly sunken room. "So, when I went at you like this—" She punched in a jab-hook combo.

Sure enough, rather than allowing her to land the second punch, as he had before, Ladon moved and blocked with a technique she hadn't seen from him. She ended up spun around by the hand she'd used for the hook and pinned with her back against his chest.

He could bend her over and...

Shit. Stop that, Sky.

"Who taught you to fight?" His rough voice rumbled in one ear, his lips brushing her skin.

"My mother."

"I'm surprised she learned those skills."

If any other man had said that, Skylar would've taken it as an implication that women didn't or couldn't fight and bristled. Except the tone of his voice said that wasn't Ladon's point. "Every phoenix teaches her daughter survival skills. We all learned hand-to-hand combat, among other things. Kasia's a mechanical engineer. I fly planes."

Silence greeted that statement, though he kept his hold on her. "I'm sorry that has to be true."

Skylar frowned. Because she believed him.

"Show me how you did that." Her voice came out a bit strangled, but hopefully he'd put that down to how tightly he was holding her and not weird emotion clogging her throat.

Ladon immediately released his grip, and she hid her small intake of breath, trying to loosen up and focus on the moves and not the man.

She turned to face him, and he waved her forward anyway. "Here. As you come across with the hook, I take you by the wrist with the opposite hand and pull you through, using your momentum against you." He demonstrated the rest of the move. "Want to try it?"

"Yeah."

They worked through the move slowly a couple of times, until she had it, then sped up until she could take the full force of his punch and use it against him.

"Not bad." She grinned as she bounced lightly on her toes. "I think I have a defense against that move, if I'm the one punching."

The wariness from when she'd first come into the room had left his eyes, but now a light of interest had him cocking his head. "Okay. Try it."

In slow motion, they played through it, but with her punching, until he had her pinned. "Right. From here, if I grasp your arm with my free hand and throw my hips back, bending forward suddenly, that gives me leverage. Then I step out and—" Still holding his arm, she twisted in a way that put him on the ground.

"Yup," he grunted, his face in the floor. "That's effective. But then I can—"

Before she had a chance to step back, he rolled, taking her down, her breath whooshing out of her at the contact with the ground. He didn't stop moving until he had her pinned underneath him, her wrists in each of his hands up by her head, and the rest of her held still by his body weight.

They stared at each other, both panting from the struggle. Unbidden, a sexual tension she still couldn't quite fathom filled all the space between them, clotting the air and tingling through her body, bringing her achingly alive. "I'll...have to give that one some thought," she said.

"Yeah." Only he didn't get up.

No way was she giving in to this thing again. Mating was one thing. Bonding was entirely different. With deliberate insouciance, she tugged her wrists free of his grip and brought her hands up behind her head to lay there casually. "Take your time. Oxygen isn't all that important."

"I'd like to kiss you." Damn that voice. A purring rumble at the best of times, it had dropped lower, smokier...sexier.

Skylar froze. "Oh. Well... That's..." What did a girl say when her brand new mate, who she barely knew except carnally, made a statement like that? *That's nice? Go for it, big boy?*

"Good for you." As soon as the words were out of her mouth, she bit down on her lips, trying to contain a slightly hysterical giggle. What a lame comeback.

Ladon shook against her in a silent laugh. "Good for me?"

"Best I could come up with on short notice." Damned if she was going to acknowledge it more than that.

"You'll have to translate for me, as I don't speak Skylar...yet. Is that a 'yes, kiss me'? Or is that an 'I'll knee you in the balls if you try it'?"

"I don't think kissing is a good idea," she murmured. And now she sounded like a schoolmarm she'd once had in the mid-1800s in Minnesota.

Prudish. Priggish. Boring.

Except Ladon didn't appear bored. The amusement faded from his expression, replaced with that intensity that had her breathing going all wonky. "I think it's a fucking fantastic idea," he said, almost casually, gaze dropping to her lips as he leaned closer. "In fact, I think *fucking* is a fantastic idea."

Holy hell. And I thought the comment about kissing was bad. A needy ache took up immediate, throbbing residence at her core. Maybe... Just to bleed off some of this tension...

His cell phone chose that moment to ring.

Skylar did her best to not appear relieved or, for that matter, disappointed, but based on the cockeyed look he gave her as he helped her up, she guessed she didn't succeed. "Saved by the ringtone," he said before answering the phone.

A glance at the clock told her it was only five in the morning. What could be that important to wake the king?

"Ormarr," he barked into the phone.

Pause.

"When?" he asked.

The scowl that descended over his face left her in no doubt that he wasn't happy about whatever the person on the other end was saying. "Fine. Call the council and my guard. We'll meet them in"—he glanced at the clock—"one hour."

We. She didn't miss that he'd included her in that statement.

He dropped the phone on his bedside table. "Gorgon Ejderha,

King of the Black Clan, is here with a contingency of his people."

Skylar got to her feet with a frown. "The timing seems…"

"Wrong?" he finished.

"Suspicious."

"Yeah. I think so, too. Although he was set to arrive before the Gold and Green Clans attacked."

Did that spin things differently or not? Was this Gorgon guy only resuming plans already in place?

She cocked her head. "Want to play good cop/bad cop?"

He crossed his arms, muscles straining in an entirely distracting way she had to consciously ignore. "I'm not sure what that means."

Dragons and their isolationist tendencies. "It's an American expression, sort of." She sighed. "It means *you* come across reasonable, someone to negotiate with. And *I* come across the exact opposite."

"*I'm* the reasonable one?" He looked to the ceiling, seeming to roll that around in his head for a minute. "To what end?"

"I'm an unknown element, and already out of control according to Brand and your men."

"True. Not that I believe it."

Skylar blinked at him and the small warm spot those words created in her chest, then shook it off.

Focus, woman. "As bad cop, I either antagonize them into revealing something, or, if that doesn't happen, you appear the reasonable one, gaining their trust and approaching them from a different position."

Ladon nodded slowly. "That could work. Except one thing."

"Oh?"

"I'm not exactly known for being reasonable. Blood King, remember?"

She waved away the concern. "That doesn't mean you can't be now that you're the king. Or, even better, they'll worry if they think you're the sane one of the two of us. Especially now that we're mated. Mates are supposed to have a strong influence over each other. Right?"

"Hmm…" Those blue eyes narrowed, training on her in that total way of his. "I get the feeling you play bad cop often."

In other words, the day they met? Skylar grinned. "You think so?"

He took a few steps closer. "From what I can tell, you're a woman who will do anything for the people she loves. And the 'out of control' thing is your way of keeping people on their back foot."

Well, damn. She should be irritated that he read her so easily. Most people didn't see past the act. The fact that she might *like* being seen for herself was disturbing. On many levels.

She refused to step back and turned that same insight on him. "That's an interesting theory. I might say the same about you, *Blood* King."

His lips twitched, and he closed the gap with another few steps. "As long as you don't play a part with me…"

Skylar lifted a single eyebrow. "I may be your mate, but I still don't know you," she pointed out with brutal honesty.

The next few steps brought him directly into her personal space, his heat, his bourbon and smoke scent curling around her, the scar marring his face less and less what she saw. "I guess we'd better work on getting to know each other, then."

"What?" she challenged. "Starting in the bedroom?" The heat flushing through her indicated her body would totally be on board with that.

Ladon ran the back of his hand softly down the side of her face. "I did give us an hour to get ready."

She stiffened her resolve. Token modesty, innate wariness, and lifelong contrariness insisted she put up some kind of protest. "We're mated. It worked. Isn't that enough?"

It would have to be. She was leaving him as soon as all this was over. Granted, that could be years yet, but she wouldn't let herself sign up for more.

Twin flames of indigo ignited in his eyes. "Not for me." He stepped closer, the tips of her breasts brushing against his chest in the most torturous way, even with clothing separating skin from skin. "I want my scent all over you."

Everything in her wanted to reach for him, plans and emotions in direct opposition. Skylar fought with herself another second… and lost. The wanting was too much. Too demanding. Too tempting. Too everything.

She sighed. "It appears I mated a Tarzan."

"I've been wondering when you'd get around to calling me that." He dipped his head, bringing his lips to her ear, his hands to her hips. "So long as I get to play with Jane, you can call me anything you want."

Skylar shivered, even as she smoothed her palms over his pecs, unable to keep from touching him for another minute. "You're going to regret that offer."

"Maybe," he murmured, just before he claimed her lips.

. . .

"Don't warn your men about good cop/bad cop."

Ladon paused in the hall, the louder clack of his dress shoes noticeably pausing as he looked at his mate. Honestly, he couldn't *stop* looking at her. Partly because looking at her gave him pleasure. But a growing part of him was enjoying how her mind worked and seeing her in action. Either way, this was becoming a compulsion. Plus, she kept making him laugh.

What the hell is wrong with me? Where'd all that "scare the shit out of people" go around her? She was just supposed to be a mate. A figurehead. Plus, all the good things a phoenix brought.

He'd start questioning if that whole mates-rubbing-off-on-each-other thing was worth a closer look, but Skylar was even less reasonable and patient than he typically was.

After another tussle in bed that left him content in a way that dropped lead boulders into his gut, and yet still aching for her, she'd disappeared to return with a suitcase. A freaking suitcase. Only she wouldn't tell him where she'd been hiding, or how she'd managed to sneak that in here with her, saying something about how a girl had to have *some* secrets. After commandeering a small section of his dresser and closet to unpack her things, she'd disappeared again, into the bathroom...only to emerge a completely different woman.

Gone were the black tactical clothes and long braid. Instead, she'd morphed into a sophisticated woman wearing a sleek white pantsuit, all one piece, with a demurely high neckline in the front, but no back to it. Red, fuck-me-please heels, a perfectly made-up face with matching red lipstick, and her black hair arranged in a sleek knot at the nape of her neck.

The previous time in bed disappeared as far as his dick was concerned, and he hardened painfully, pulling a grunt from him. Not even Kasia dressed this way. Somehow, he hadn't expected it from Skylar, who seemed even less traditionally-feminine-inclined.

She sent him a sweet smile from the mirror over his...their... dresser. "Being underestimated is always an advantage."

How often had she been forced to play a part? Because his gut told him this woman, as confidently glamorous as she appeared, wasn't who his mate was. Not really.

And I want to know who she is. The realization had him frowning, because a relationship wasn't what he signed up for. A partnership. A political advantage. Yes. Bonus of great sex. But no more.

So where was this new urge coming from?

With effort, Ladon dragged his gaze from her to finish buttoning a suit jacket that sat on his shoulders about as comfortably as using sandpaper to wipe his ass. The suit was an unfortunately necessary torture when meeting other clans.

"Why shouldn't I warn them?" he asked now, when they were almost to the room where their guests waited.

"Because their honest reaction will make it seem more real."

"They'll be pissed at you," he warned.

She snorted, clearly unconcerned. "And?"

The thought of teaching that sassy mouth a lesson later held more appeal than it should. Hell, he was about to walk into a room full of dragon shifters. Male dragon shifters. With her looking like that. With a growl, and his dragon driving, he leaned forward and placed his lips over the cords of her slender neck, right where that white scar marred her skin, and sucked. Hard.

Rather than push him away, Skylar leaned into his touch with a soft moan. Then came the shove he'd half been expecting.

"What was that for?" she demanded.

"You don't bear my mark on your neck yet."

She glared. "So?"

Ladon grinned, unable to help himself, even if the possessiveness underlying the action was entirely against his character. "So…now you *do* bear my mark. Of a sort."

Her jaw worked, even as an answering heat bloomed in those pale blue eyes. "We really need to work on your Tarzan instincts," she grumbled.

Probably. But no dragon among his men, or Gorgon's, would mistake her as available now.

They walked into the same conference room where he'd met her for the first time. A sense of déjà vu fell over him as the council members of his Curia Regis and the warriors of his guard all got to their feet.

Kasia, meanwhile, threw her arms around her sister. "Thank the fates," she whispered in Skylar's ear. "It worked."

"Fate had nothing to do with this," Skylar whispered back, low enough that most likely only Ladon and Brand, standing closest to them, caught it. Ladon didn't examine too closely what about those words bothered him, working their way under his skin faster than a bloodsucking tick.

He had a dragon king to host, or to confront. "You're all up to speed?" he asked.

Both Brand and Asher nodded.

"Good. Follow me."

"Wait," Kasia called out. Every person stopped. "I had a vision," she said.

"Really?" Interest lit Skylar up as she took a step toward her sister. "How does that work?"

"What did you see?" Ladon asked, overriding his new mate.

To give her credit, Skylar merely sighed her impatience.

Kasia closed her eyes, as if accessing the images of the vision the fates had given her. "Blue and black dragons fighting together. To win the Gold Throne, we must ally ourselves with them."

"So, it's war?" Ladon asked. More innocent blood shed to rid themselves of these obsolete old men clinging to power?

"No…" Though Kasia hesitated over the word. She gave her head a shake, her red tresses falling over her shoulders. "I'm not sure."

"Which is it?" Ladon demanded.

A warning grunt from Brand had him checking he wasn't about to be gutted. The man had become even more possessive since mating the firebird.

"I see Brand inside the mountain of the Gold Clan with Uther's Curia Regis. I see him taking the mountain. But I don't see Brock. I do see fighting, but not inside the gold mountain."

Ladon did his best to sift through all that.

At least her vision didn't involve more sitting and waiting. That shit was getting old.

"Right. First things first. We feel out Gorgon and his people. Then develop a plan that involves bringing the fight to Brock."

He didn't need the nods of agreement around the room, but he got them. Bonus, Skylar didn't argue. Was she starting to trust him?

"Good. Let's go meet a king."

As a group, they filed their way to the next level where receiving rooms, more welcoming with comfortable seating, lovely art, the last of what had once been a valuable collection before the previous king sold most of it, and soft lighting, held their guests. One of the few places in the mountain that Thanatos had kept nice, for the sake of appearances.

Ladon paused outside the door to the reception room where his people had brought King Gorgon and his entourage. Skylar slipped a hand in his as naturally as though they'd always touched this way. She paused beside him, watching but silent. Behind them, Ladon's own entourage waited for their king to make his move.

He looked down at the woman, who until a few days ago, he'd had no idea existed, and today was his mate, and raised his eyebrows in question. She gave a small nod. She was ready.

Let's do this.

With a twist of his hand, he led the way into the room. Gorgon stood at the center, ten men gathered behind him, the captain of his guard, Samael Veles, to his right.

Tall and lanky, with a face all angles, black hair peppered with gray and slicked back, and the fathomless black eyes of a black dragon shifter, Gorgon bore himself with a regal authority that, after so long on the throne, was probably as natural as blinking.

As a child, Ladon had found this man intimidating. But he was no longer a child.

Ladon stopped in the center of the room and dipped his head in acknowledgment. "King Gorgon. To what do we owe the honor?"

Only the dragon king's gaze slid to Skylar and remained there. The man raised his head, sniffing the air, no doubt checking her scent. Primitive satisfaction oozed through Ladon; he'd made damn sure Skylar carried his scent.

For her part, Skylar narrowed her eyes. "Staring is rude, you know. So is sniffing."

Apparently, she was going straight for bad cop. Behind him, Asher let loose a low sound of warning, or protest, at the same time that Samael growled beside Gorgon, and the tension in the room ratcheted up a notch on both sides.

Ladon snapped a quelling look their way, and both men blinked in obvious surprise but stopped. Turning back, he moved his gaze to the king before him.

After a long, pregnant pause, Gorgon smiled. "My apologies. It's been too long since I've been in the presence of a phoenix."

Skylar tossed Gorgon a look that clearly said she was unimpressed—a single raised eyebrow and those cold eyes gone glacial—a look now familiar since she treated him to the same look the day they met. "How'd you guess?"

Gorgon cocked his head. "Based on your scent, you are King Ladon's mate."

Skylar managed to appear bored. "And?"

"And you smell of smoke."

"So do most dragon mates," she shot back.

Gorgon finally glanced at Ladon, who said nothing. He was having too much fun watching the fearless woman beside him walk all over one of the strongest of the six kings—the only one to retain his throne when Pytheios purged the other clans of their original kings.

"Perhaps we should take some time for introductions," Gorgon finally murmured.

"You think?" Skylar muttered, but under her breath. Which of course, every shifter in the otherwise quiet room could hear, and she knew that.

Again, Asher's displeasure with her came out as a *tsk* of a sound, and Reid cleared his throat.

Ladon leveled a glare on them that had the scar on his face twitching. "One more sound and you can leave."

Both men paled slightly, then lowered their eyes. A sign of submission.

"Of course." Ladon returned his attention to the black king and moved forward, Skylar's hand in his. "May I present my mate, Skylar Amon Ormarr."

Her new name slipped from his lips like he'd said it a thousand times. He liked the sound of it.

"Amon." The whisper moved through Gorgon's men as they recognized the name of the previous lineage of white kings.

"And this"—Ladon turned to Brand, who stood to his left—"is Braneck Astarot Dagrun, newly branded King of the Gold Clan... and his mate, Kasia Amon Astarot."

Only a twitch at the corner of his mouth indicated that the revelation had thrown him. Otherwise, Gorgon's eyes tightened with patent curiosity about both Brand and the sisters, but Ladon continued around the room, introducing the rest of his people. Gorgon did the same.

Formalities over, Ladon took a seat on one of the leather couches situated across from each other, crossing his ankle over his knee in a deliberately relaxed pose. Skylar took the seat beside him, and he rested his hand on her knee. That move wasn't deliberate… more like compulsion.

Gorgon settled in the wingback chair at an angle to Ladon, the captain of his guard standing at his back. "May I speak plainly?"

"Please." Ladon waved him on.

"We came because of rumors that you have a phoenix." He flicked a glance at Skylar and Kasia, who stood with Brand behind the couch. "But you appear to have…two."

Ladon couldn't get a handle on what the king thought of there being more than one. The presence of a phoenix could potentially turn some of the clans in his favor. Gorgon in particular. Of the old kings, he seemed the most likely to be turned. He knew what it was to reign under a true High King.

"We do." Ladon's words hung heavy in the room.

Again, Gorgon's gaze flicked to Skylar, who returned his stare with a bored one of her own. "Two is not possible. It's never happened before."

Ladon opened his mouth to reply, but Skylar beat him to it. "What is your interest in phoenixes?"

Gorgon gave her a condescending smile, and Ladon was surprised he didn't hear popping sounds from Skylar's jaw as she gritted her teeth.

"I should think that obvious," the black king replied. "Our kind base our leadership on who mates the phoenix. In fact, I would have liked to have her consider me."

Given there were four of them, that made Gorgon's comment even more interesting than the old king was aware.

"And now that you know *both* are already mated?" Ladon asked.

Gorgon cleared his throat. "I would owe my allegiance to the rightful High King. But, again, we have the problem of two."

"You would go against Pytheios?" Brand demanded softly, dangerously.

A wealth of implication lay in that one question. Gorgon would have to word his reply carefully.

Only the King of the Black Clan appeared perfectly relaxed. Crossing his legs, mirroring Ladon's posture, he gave Brand a direct look. "I've been king of my clan since before any of you were born. I held that position by giving Pytheios no reason to take it away, but I remember a time when peace reigned among our people. I've been waiting over five hundred years for a phoenix to appear, choose a king, and allow us to take down that red-winged bastard."

Damn. New respect sifted through Ladon at the king's extremely non-politic answer.

"If you're so eager to see Pytheios gone, why not come forward sooner?" Skylar asked. "Like when Ladon took the Blue Throne?"

"I've tried. Several times. The last time, we were on our way here when this mountain was attacked."

Skylar lifted a single eyebrow, showing her visible doubt.

"I have no proof other than my word." A smile transformed the man's face, turning those angles into something both charming and compelling. "You have the look of your grandmother," he said softly. Gently.

Behind him, Kasia's soft gasp dropped into the silence. Skylar, meanwhile, tensed, but he knew that only because she sat beside him.

When none of them said anything, Gorgon continued. "I was around during a time when the High King was named Hanyu. That king was mated to a phoenix who willingly gave up her powers to her daughter, Serefina, who was mated to Zilant…Amon. The King of the White Clan."

Gorgon rose to his feet. "Your grandmother was a beautiful woman, and, other than your father's eyes, you are her spitting image." His gaze slowly slid to Kasia. "While you have more of your grandfather in you, red hair being more common among red dragon shifters. I'll tell you what I remember of them sometime, if you wish."

Kasia nodded, but Skylar remained unresponsive, stiff beside Ladon on the couch. He had the strangest urge to put a hand to her back in a show of...what? Comfort? Support? Except he knew she wouldn't appreciate it right now.

Gorgon clasped his hands behind his back, observing both women. "I've never heard of a phoenix having more than one child. Which of you inherited her powers?"

The old king glanced at Brand and Ladon, no doubt wondering which of them he'd have to contend with as High King, as they'd already introduced both women as their mates. No way would he assume that both women had inherited their mother's powers, not when there'd only ever been one phoenix.

Would he join them if he thought the power of the phoenix had been split or reduced? The appearance of more than one certainly brought into question the idea of a High King at all.

Beyond taking down the current regime of kings and attempting to find a peaceful coexistence between the clans, Ladon had no interest in it. After centuries of being hunted by his own kind, Brand didn't, either.

But Gorgon already said he was in search of a legitimate High King to follow. So, what would he do? This was the first true test of the entire situation.

"Kasia is the phoenix." Skylar dropped that bomb of words into the conversation.

Ladon had to physically stop himself from whipping his head down to stare at her. What was she doing? Castrating his power position was what she was doing, dammit.

"I didn't get anything." She curled into Ladon, batting her eyes at him with a smitten smile he'd never thought to see cross her face. "But he fell for me anyway."

Her hand caressed his thigh up near his groin, and Ladon lost himself in those eyes for a heartbeat, only to be harshly jerked back when she gripped him harder, digging her nails in like a cat. "Isn't that right?"

Obviously, she wanted him to go along with her. She'd better have a fucking good reason. "I took one look and knew she was mine," he agreed.

He held in a grunt as she tightened her grip. Damn, the woman hated being claimed like that, but pushing her buttons was half the fun. She pushed his enough. Turnabout was fair play.

"I see," Gorgon murmured. He turned to Kasia and Brand, not dismissively, though. "I hate to ask, but would you mind showing me?"

Kasia spoke up. "You just claimed to know our parents, but you doubt I am what I say I am?"

Gorgon held up both hands. "I mean no offense, but another rumor reached me only this morning, shortly before I arrived."

Ladon shot a look at Asher, who gave a shake of his head. "What rumor is that?" he asked.

"A woman identified as a phoenix has shown up with a small group of rogue dragons who've banded together in the colonies."

Skylar's hand stilled against Ladon's leg. "Where?" she asked.

"In the Andes mountains in Argentina."

Skylar made no outward reaction, but somehow Ladon knew that information had shaken her deeply. "That had to be me," she said. "Their intelligence is old."

Keeping his expression neutral in the face of that information was a damn miracle.

"You were staying in the Andes?" Gorgon asked.

She nodded. "With a group led by a man named Rune Abaddon."

Behind Ladon, a small noise from Fallon was no surprise. Rune had once been part of his Enforcer team over in the Americas but had turned traitor.

At the same time, Gorgon nodded, as though that information confirmed his intel. "That must be it then. Old information."

Ladon stood, dislodging her hand, which had gone limp. "Will you join with us, regardless?"

Gorgon considered his face and Brand's hard expression. "Against Pytheios?"

Ladon and Brand nodded in unison. "Your clan evens the odds significantly."

"I *could* be playing you falsely." Gorgon's voice was laden with irony.

"That's a risk we're willing to take," Brand said.

Every man in the room nodded.

Ladon held out his hand and willed the other man to shake it. "If you mean what you say about waiting to take Pytheios out, this is your best opportunity, phoenix or no phoenix."

CHAPTER ELEVEN

Skylar glanced at Ladon as they walked through the same small hallway she'd used to try to leave him the day she'd confronted her sister. The man was exhausted. Not that anyone else seemed to notice. Outwardly he gave no sign, walking with his usual focused intent, not a hint of slowing steps. But that didn't fool her.

Apparently, once you had allies, things moved damn fast. In order to take advantage of their increased numbers and not give Brock or his allies time to organize, Ladon, Brand, and Gorgon had put a plan in place within days. One involving a bit of sleight of hand with the players on the board.

The plan, as far as anyone not in their inner circle was aware, would look as though they'd chosen to leave both the blue and black mountains minimally guarded while the bulk of their forces traveled north to the gold mountain, stopping short of invasion. Brand had come up with the perfect location to hole up. One most likely forgotten by his people. The idea was to draw Brock out rather than risk lives attacking on his home turf.

Hopefully the younger shifter's inexperience would skew his thinking and he'd go for the bait they'd set under his nose.

But if Brock were smart, he'd go where the true threat really was.

They'd be ready either way.

A solid plan. Even Skylar had thought so.

Preparing for it in days, however, trying to keep ahead of the spies and traitors, had been a mad rush involving nonstop work—developing a strategy, training, communicating, coordinating, meeting. It never ended.

Ladon had hardly spent more than an hour in their suite. Even with a dragon's ability to recover physically, he'd dropped into heavy sleep beside her any time he actually made it to bed.

"I can feel you watching me," he suddenly said. "What?"

She had to hold in a snort, because no way would he guess that concern for his wellbeing had been top of mind. "Nothing."

He stopped in the middle of the hall to look down at her with barely concealed impatience. "I'm starting to learn your expressions, Skylar. That's not a nothing look."

Stubborn man. "Just thinking through what's about to come."

Ladon crossed his arms and waited.

Skylar made a little huffy sound of frustration. "Fine. You won't believe me anyway."

"Try me."

"I'm…concerned."

"The plan will work."

She shook her head. "No. About you."

Gods, she felt like a fool even saying the damn words. How he managed to get her to say this shit was beyond her. This wasn't the first time he'd made her speak her emotions.

Ladon's eyebrows inched upward. "About me?" he said slowly.

Yup. He didn't believe her.

She shifted on her feet and glanced away. "You're about to lead a major offensive, but you've hardly slept."

"I'm fine."

With a roll of her eyes, she stalked in the direction they'd been headed. "I know that. But don't tell me you're not exhausted."

Silence greeted that statement, and she dared a glance his way to find him walking with flat-lipped determination. But he didn't deny it.

"Don't treat me like a child," he finally said. "That's the last thing I want from you."

What did he want from her? Because she'd gone into this assuming he just wanted a figurehead queen, but he'd insisted she share his bed, and he watched her with a possessiveness that seemed to go beyond being a new mate.

Or she was seeing things.

"If I were treating you like a child, I would've made you come to bed at night. But that's not who you are. I've never seen someone so relentless—"

Ladon snorted. "Have you looked in the mirror?"

She ignored him. "Just remember that you may be a king, but you're also mortal." She grimaced. "Even with a phoenix for a mate."

Ladon paused at the door that led to the training room. He frowned at her upturned face, searching her expression for who knew what. "And you're concerned."

She couldn't pinpoint the tone in his voice. Confused, if she had to guess. Skylar shrugged and tried to brush this entire conversation off. "Just pointing things out."

Ladon's eyes narrowed. "I see."

She doubted that. Honesty, even with herself, was something she'd been trying to avoid since mating this man.

Entering a new code in the key panel—a code now changed daily after Skylar shared how she'd gotten it—Ladon opened the door. Skylar followed him into the massive training arena situated between two dragon-sized doors. One led deeper into the heart of the mountain where the city was located, the other outside to the canyons. While she'd been hiding, Skylar had avoided coming anywhere near this room, which always seemed to be full.

Even more so now with blue, black, and a handful of gold dragon shifters gathered inside.

A man from the Blue Clan, if his watery blue eyes were any indication, stood at the sight of them and nodded at Ladon. "Káthor."

Ladon returned the nod and kept walking.

Another man stood and nodded, obviously some sign of respect. "Káthor."

Then, almost as they lined up, every man they passed stopped what they were doing and came to a sort of attention, saying the same word. Káthor.

This wasn't the first time she'd seen this behavior, but with so many in the space, this was the most obvious. Before she could ask Ladon about it, they reached his men. Men she'd come to realize more and more were beyond bodyguards, more than his best warriors. They were his friends, those closest to his heart.

She only had to spend one day with the man to pick that up.

As they approached, Skylar observed their training with curiosity. All seven men and Arden sparred in a large ring, though no one seemed to be for or against another, each fighting only for himself. They moved almost faster than she could track, trading blows. It quickly became apparent that each was skilled, though in different ways.

The brothers, Rainier and Ivar, worked together, back to back or tag-team style. They didn't seem to need to see each other to know what the other was doing. Fallon, meanwhile, tended to change up his moves, switching fighting styles depending on who he faced off against. Smart. Duncan charged, bringing the full weight of his size to bear in each strike, the crack of his fists against the others making Skylar wince. Wyot, however, circled from the outside, picking off anyone Duncan pushed his way. Arden was easily the fastest, dodging the men like a viper and striking just as quickly.

But Reid and Asher were undoubtedly the most skilled. A long scar down Asher's back made total sense now. She'd seen him in dragon form, missing an entire half of the barbed spike on the end of his tail. Most likely lost in battle. He fought with a directness that should've telegraphed his intentions, but moving with such speed, his opponent couldn't see it coming. He also kept a knife at his belt, which he produced practically out of thin air.

On the flip side, Reid—who apparently had a diamond tattoo

over his heart now that she saw him with his shirt off—fought with cunning, studying his opponent and using weaknesses against him or her. The third time Reid took the legs out from Ivar, Duncan's rusty laugh filled the space. "Reid. How do you do that?"

Breathing hard, Reid held out a hand to Ivar, still on the floor. "I aim for the legs."

"So do I," Ivar muttered, though he grinned around the words.

Reid grinned back. "Move faster."

"You are a slow bastard," Rainier said. Only to have Ivar take out his legs with the same move Reid had used.

"What do you know?" Ivar chuckled. "Moving faster *does* work."

Maul suddenly appeared out of nowhere. As soon as he spied Rainier still on the floor, he gave a yip Skylar hadn't heard since he was a puppy and gave the man a slobbery lick up his face.

Rather than gag at the putrid-smelling rotting breath—a smell Skylar was intimately familiar with—Rainier got to his feet with a laugh. "I'm okay, mutt. Is this what you want?"

He reached up and scratched Maul behind the ear. He definitely knew the spot, because the massive black dog started to kick his back leg.

Ladon stepped forward, and all his men quieted, their focus entirely on their leader.

"Maul. Go to Kasia," Ladon ordered.

Without even a huff, the hound disappeared.

"Men. Arden." His sister nodded at the acknowledgment. "Today we must separate."

Duncan scowled, even as Rainier and Ivar exchanged confused glances.

"Separate?" Asher asked.

"Fallon will stay here. We're bringing Gorgon's Healer with us."

Fallon nodded an acknowledgment. Despite his previous role as an Enforcer in the Americas, as a Healer, he was most likely to be left behind frequently, too important to risk in direct battle.

"Ivar, Rainier. You will also stay." He gave them a significant look, because this part of the plan had been worked out ahead of time. This speech was for any spies within the mountain. "If the mountain is attacked while the bulk of our warriors are away, I need you here to lead."

"Ivar?" Ladon demanded.

"I am with you, Káthor." He glanced at his brother, whose glower needed no interpretation. "Rainier as well."

"Good." Ladon looked to the others. "We will be splitting into three separate groups to travel to the Gold Clan's stronghold in Norway. Duncan, Wyot. You will lead one group. Reid. Arden. You take the second."

His men nodded.

Skylar blinked her surprise at that. He must truly trust Reid if he was sending his sister with the man.

"Asher, you're with me."

"Káthor."

There it was again.

As if a sixth sense called to her, Skylar turned to find Kasia standing near the far wall, waiting there while Brand and Gorgon, along with Gorgon's man, Samael, crossed to where Ladon stood.

Skylar went to her sister. Ladon had already discussed all the plans with her. She didn't need to be there for this. She'd spent a lot of time with Kasia in between, touring the mountain, discovering for herself the people Ladon was working so tirelessly to defend.

My people now. She still couldn't quite wrap her head around that idea. After all, she'd intended to leave them when this was over. Except now she had faces and names to put with her new clan. So many faces. People who needed what she could bring them as the phoenix. Dragon mates turned from their human lives to the lives the fates had set for them. Children who'd known only hunger and a constant state of apprehension. Elder dragons with far-flung memories of her mother and father. Though fewer of them existed, having been purged by the old kings or died when a mate was killed. Ladon's parents had gone that way, though she didn't have details.

Still, leaving would be easier if she didn't have those faces in her head. Or a certain face with blue eyes and a ragged scar…

"What does Káthor mean?" She blurted the question at Kasia.

"It's an ancient dragon shifter word. It literally means 'fire king' and is a term of—"

"Respect," Skyler finished for her. Yeah. She'd picked that up, but she was no longer surprised when it came to him.

She shook that thought off and tried instead to think of what was coming next.

The forces would've departed sooner, except Gorgon's men had to fly up from Turkey where they were based. Now a tornado of blue and black dragons swirled through the chamber. A handful of the gold dragons who'd been part of the attack on Ladon's clan, but who had since sworn allegiance to Brand, his mark starkly black against paler primarily Scandinavian skin, glittered like stars in an inky night sky against their blue and black allies.

Ladon stood, still human, in the center of the activity—the eye of the hurricane—with Brand and Gorgon.

A small tug on the sleeve of her shirt had Skylar looking down to find a small child regarding her. A little girl with blue eyes this side of violet, starkly beautiful against teak skin, and adorable with a head full of curls.

Skylar dropped to one knee. "Hi."

The girl's small face remained solemn. "You're the phoenix, right?"

Skylar shared a smiling glance with Kasia. "One of them. Yes."

Confusion pleated the child's brow. "Where are your feathers?"

"Feathers?" Skylar chuckled to hide an abyss of sadness that innocent question inadvertently had her hovering over. "You know how you don't see a dragon's wings or scales until he or she shifts?"

A nod.

"Well…my feathers come out when there's fire." The real ones would manifest the day she died, right before she turned to ash.

Like her mother.

She didn't dare glance at Kasia. Neither of them could afford to be emotional. Not now. Not with everything else happening. They'd mourn their shared loss one day.

Today was not that day.

"Are you going to fix everything?" the girl asked.

The question knocked through Skylar like a punch to the gut. Other than being handy in a fight, what could *she* do? Being a phoenix, so far at least, hadn't brought good fortune. Only pain. "Is that what your mother told you?" she hedged.

The girl shook her head. "My baba."

"Rukiya."

The girl jumped as someone called her name. Someone with a thick Scottish accent. She turned, her serious expression dissolving into childish delight. "Baba."

Duncan, all six foot four of him, bent down to scoop her up, earning a childish squeal for his efforts. He settled her in the crook of one arm. "Sorry if she was bothering you."

Finding it difficult to reconcile the crude, bald brute of a dragon shifter—one missing a tooth that hadn't grown back after a fight—with the total teddy bear snuggling his daughter, Skylar couldn't hold back a grin. "No worries, Dopey. We were just getting acquainted."

"What does quainted mean?" Rukiya asked in her tiny voice.

Given how long shifters and phoenixes lived, the phase of life spent that small was relatively short. Skylar had forgotten how precious, how vulnerable, a child could be. How had her mother gotten all four of them through it while still dealing with her own grief and learning her own powers? "It means we're getting to know each other."

"Oh. Should we shake hands?"

Duncan grinned, the gap in his teeth even more obvious. At the same time, Skylar laughed and held out her hand. "I think that's an excellent idea."

Only Rukiya didn't shake. Instead, she placed her other hand over their clasped hands. "Mama says the longer you shake, the more you want to be friends."

"My mate is from Tanzania. Or Zanzibar when she lived there," Duncan explained. "That's a tradition of her people."

Brought to weak-ass emotions like sentimental tears by a mite of a dragon shifter. Skylar had to clear her throat. "I like that. People I lived with a long time ago tended to use food as a greeting. The first thing they said wasn't 'hello' or 'how are you.' Instead they'd say, 'Would you like something to eat?'" She exchanged a grin with Kasia. "Remember?"

"I do," Kasia murmured. For once the memories didn't bring a pang of bittersweet sorrow.

"Where did you live?"

"With a few tribes in North America."

As expected, Rukiya's eyes rounded with awe. "Wow," she whispered. "Did they shoot things with bows and arrows?"

Kasia and Skylar chuckled. "Some did. Not all."

Duncan shook his head. "Let's go find Mama."

"Okay," Rukiya said, though with obvious reluctance.

Skylar waved at the child as Duncan carried her away.

"You'd better pray for boys when you and my brother have children," Arden said as she joined them, her gaze fixed on the departing father and child.

Skylar'd had a little time to get to know Arden. Kasia and the other girl had apparently become close, and Skylar found she couldn't not like Arden. She respected her spunky determination to join her brother's guard as a warrior, despite the bias she fought against as well as her size. Not to mention Ladon's protective instincts.

Anyone who did her own thing and be damned to the obstacles like that deserved respect.

"Is it difficult?" Skylar asked. "Being a female-born?"

Arden made a face, though she only shrugged. "It's not easy. Only one in a hundred births result in a female-born. My parents were lovely...supportive, never making me feel less than. Being schooled with chauvinistic little princes wasn't exactly fun. Plus, it was made clear from an early age that I was expected to do little more with my life than be a very involved auntie to whatever offspring Ladon whelped."

Even the idea of that chaffed at Skylar like rough wool over her skin.

"Knowing I'll never have a child is awful in a way I can't even put into words," Arden continued, her voice softer. "Knowing I can't mate for love…" The she-dragon's gaze drifted toward the group of men gathered around Ladon. "That's even harder."

It'd taken less than a day for Skylar to see the connection between Arden and Reid. She gave Arden's arm a squeeze. "I say, if you love him, then fates and traditions be damned. Mate the man."

Arden cast a furtive glance his way, but Skylar knew they weren't paying them any attention, because Ladon wasn't paying her attention. She could feel his focus, like a physical touch almost, even when she couldn't see him.

"I can't," Arden whispered. "Other than being the sister of the king, which gives me a little political leverage, I wouldn't contribute to his career or his life. I'd take away any chance at children and continuing his line. He's an only child. No brothers."

"But he'd get a woman who loves him," Kasia pointed out.

Skylar wasn't nearly so sentimental. "He'd get you. Period. Why don't you give him the respect of deciding what that means to him?"

Arden frowned. "You think not letting it happen is disrespect-ful?"

"I think he knows all the implications. Not letting him have a say in the matter is not respecting the strong person he is. Wouldn't you want to be involved in a decision that impacts your life in a huge way?"

Before Arden could answer, the men stirred, a low murmur pulsing through the room.

"Won't be long now," Kasia murmured, then made a face.

"What?" Skylar prodded.

"I'm not a huge fan of flying on dragons. It's easier now, but…" Kasia gave another grimace.

Right, that whole falling off and slicing her hands on the tips of Brand's spikes thing. Skylar had seen the crisscrossing scars on Kasia's palms. She didn't blame her sister. "How can you tell it won't be long?"

Kasia smiled. "I can feel Brand."

Skylar made a silent vow to avoid acting anywhere near that sappy. Not that she and Ladon had a relationship remotely like her sister's. But still… "Feel him?"

"Like he's inside me, part of me."

"Mr. No Emotions?" Arden snickered, and a pair of dimples showed as she allowed what might be her first real smile around Skylar. "What's that feel like?"

"Brand has emotions," Kasia defended her mate. "He just doesn't like others to know."

Skylar shivered at the thought. Having someone in your head like that sounded disturbing. "Isn't that weird? And intrusive?"

Kasia turned to face her, taking her hands, as if this was important. "Not when you love that person. I like knowing that any time I need him, I have access to him. When we fight in battle together, I'll be able to know he's okay, or try to help him if I can, and vice versa."

Skylar snorted. "Will he even let you near the fighting?"

"He will if he knows what's good for him."

Skylar's gaze slid to Ladon—serious, intense, and in total control—across the room. Would he take over if he could tune in to her like that? She pulled her gaze back to her sister. "Can you hear his thoughts?"

Kasia shook her head. "Only here and there, and not on purpose. Maybe later down the road. This will happen to you, too." She waggled her eyebrows.

Doubtful. "Let's not even go there."

Kasia held onto her hands as she tried to turn away. "How *is* it going?"

Skylar shrugged. "We mated. He didn't die. So far so good."

"That is my brother you're talking about," Arden commented drily.

"Oops?" Skylar winked to show Arden she harbored no hard feelings.

Meanwhile, Kasia huffed a laugh. "Only you could be so blasé about mating a dragon king."

"I've hardly had time to think, honestly. When this merry-go-round quits spinning, I'll tell you what I think."

Kasia leaned forward to put her forehead against Skylar's—quiet understanding passing between them—something their mother had started, and which all four girls had done since childhood.

When they stepped back from each other, Skylar bonked into a wall of male muscle at her back. On pure instinct, she spun, already moving into a defensive crouch, only to find Ladon standing there. He raised his eyebrows as she paused and straightened.

"You okay?" he asked.

"I don't like to be snuck up on."

He ignored that. "I meant with the whole forehead thing." He waved at Kasia.

Skylar peered at his face more closely. Was he concerned? "That's something we do to say we understand each other." The explanation spilled from her unbidden.

"Ah." Only his frown said he didn't get it at all. That was okay. He didn't have to. At least he dropped it. "We leave in twenty minutes."

Brand appeared beside Kasia, snaking an arm around her waist. Always with the touching, like he had to assure himself she was there and his for the taking.

He's your brother by blood now. Give the guy a chance.

The voice in her head had to be her projecting Meira. Skylar could easily picture her sister saying something like that. Born third of the four of them, she was the peacemaker.

The opposite of Skylar.

Still, Skylar managed not to glare or roll her eyes at Brand and considered that progress.

"We're ready," Kasia said to Ladon.

Brand's perpetual glower deepened. "I still don't think—"

Kasia turned into him and lifted her chin. "Your people need to see me. With you. I fight at your side. Got it."

Brand stared at her sister, his golden eyes glittering with flame. "If something happened to you—"

"If something happens to me, we're both dead, but at least we'll be dead together." Kasia's lips tipped up.

"Not. Fucking. Funny," Brand snapped.

"Yeah," Skylar interjected. "For once I agree with Barney Rubble."

"Barney Rubble?" Ladon asked. Was that contained laughter in his voice?

"An American cartoon about cavemen," Skylar explained. Then grinned. "Guess that makes you Fred Flintstone."

"I think I like Tarzan better," he muttered.

Behind them, Maul's unmistakable odor preceded a low whine.

Kasia turned to her pet, reaching above her head to scratch him behind the ear, which he leaned into. How the gruesome animal could appear adorable was anyone's guess, but he did.

"We talked about this, buddy," Skylar said. "You refuse to ride on Brand's back, and you'll exhaust yourself teleporting that far, that fast. Stay here and help keep the mountain secure."

He let out a harrumph.

The beast had never liked to be far from them, even though he'd often gone off on his own, sometimes for months at a time. They had no idea where, or what he did when he was away. He'd never shown them.

Kasia patted the leathery hump of his shoulder. "We'll be okay."

Then Kasia's hand stilled mid-pat, her gaze suddenly going all vague and distant a split second before her body erupted in golden flames.

CHAPTER TWELVE

"Kas?" Skylar yelled. What the hell was happening?

Before she could get to her sister, Brand wrapped his arms around Kasia and held on tight. At the same time, Ladon stepped into Skylar to stop her. "She's having a vision."

Cool relief battled with raging concern as the vision seemed to go on and on, whatever Kasia was seeing in her mind causing her eyes to move in the strangest way. Then Kasia sucked in a rasping breath that rattled in her lungs, and her face transfigured in slow motion from concentration to terror, her mouth opening in a gaping hole. *"No."*

This couldn't be good.

As quickly as the vision came, the flames snuffed out, leaving smoke to rise to the heights of the cavern ceiling. The entire room had gone as silent as a tomb as they watched the phoenix in the throes of seeing. But seeing what? Kasia pitched forward, her hands on her knees as she breathed hard. Brand was right there, hand on her back. He knelt to whisper in her ear, calm her.

"Oh gods," Kasia choked as she straightened with a jerk, her eyes wild. "He's found—" She broke off, glancing around the large chamber filled with dragon shifters.

The bright copper flavor of blood bloomed in her mouth, and Skylar realized she'd bit down on her lip hard as dread had filled her to overflowing. Only one thing would put that much fear in her sister.

Pytheios had discovered one of their sisters.

"No," Skylar whispered.

Dammit. With sheer will, she shoved away any demons of fear. "No," she said, her voice stronger.

Ladon loosed a heavy breath and glanced at Brand, who nodded. "Let's go somewhere more private."

The four of them and Maul moved into one of the smaller rooms just off the larger chamber used for private training sessions.

"Who?" Skylar demanded.

"Angelika." Kasia was shaking so hard, she had to sit down.

Needing her sister to focus, Skylar knelt in front of her and put her hands on her knees, her sister's trembling telegraphing through the touch.

Gradually, Kasia's breathing slowed, her eyes clearing. "Pytheios knows where Angelika is. He's not coming for you anymore. He gave that up as soon as you mated. But he is going for her."

Kasia unfocused, her eyes seeing something none of them could, as though she was replaying the scene in her mind. "Two days. Maybe three."

"Why not sooner?" Ladon asked.

Kasia concentrated, still watching her vision, then shook her head. "I'm not sure. Something about sucking power. He seems... weak."

Skylar stood and paced the room. "We need to get her out of there."

Ladon stepped in her path. "We can't call, or we risk the attack against Brock."

They'd shut down all communication until this assault was finished. After the fiasco with the gold and green attack on the mountain, and the traitor who'd let them in, Ladon was taking no chances. Like going back to the Stone Age.

"Dammit. This is more important—"

He grabbed her by the arms, giving her a little shake, though not harshly. "Don't say it," he snapped.

Anger sparked at her from behind his eyes, and suddenly the dangerous predator that lurked inside the man became more evident. Except, at that moment, his cold fire was exactly what she needed. Skylar straightened, purpose grafting steel to her spine. "We have to get her out of there."

"I agree."

An image flashed in Skylar's mind. One of a woman their age with the same ice-blue eyes, but with pale blond hair closer to white.

Angelika.

Skylar whipped her head around to find Maul. "*You* want to go to her?"

The dog cocked his head, ears perked, those red eyes eating up the blackness in the sockets around them. *I'll take that as a yes.* If Kasia knew where the youngest of the quadruplets was, then so would Maul. "Sounds like a good idea to me."

But Kasia was shaking her head. "It'll take him more than two days to get to her at his rate. We don't have time."

"Fuck," Ladon muttered beside her, echoing her own thought.

"Send two of your warriors…" She trailed off as he was already shaking his head. Realization struck before he voiced the reason. "Right. Gorgon will realize something big is going down."

"Gorgon could be the distraction allowing Pytheios to get to Angelika," Brand said.

"I thought of that," Ladon said, his voice practically smoke now. "We weren't planning to attack Brock this soon. Not until Gorgon showed."

Gods, what if they were walking their people into a trap? There had to be a way to—

An idea sparked. What if…

She lifted her gaze to Kasia and tipped her head, a question in her eyes.

"What?" Kasia asked slowly.

"There might be a way…"

Kasia blinked, then scowled. "No. No way, Sky. I know that look and you're thinking something illogical."

"Illogical?" Ladon asked, glancing between them. "Of the dangerous variety? Or something else?"

Skylar waved her hand. "Don't worry. On the bad-idea scale, it's maybe a level two. Three tops. Somewhere between unwise and trouble."

"I don't like trouble," he said.

"No," Brand snapped.

She ignored Brand and gripped Ladon's forearm, trying to make him see. "This is important. Just hear me out."

As soon as she said those words, Skylar paused. When had mating turned into asking for his...not permission...but understanding? Like he was becoming important to her. "I'm doing this. With or without you."

Maul let out a small growl. What, even the dog was against her plan?

Ladon's eyes narrowed. Suddenly he leaned closer, lips to her ear. "I'm not *dictating*, we're *partners*."

Partners. An insidiously seductive idea the more time she spent with him. Only she already had partners. Her sisters. Skylar scowled at him as he straightened. "You can't hear my thoughts yet or anything, right?"

He stared back, waiting for her to tell him the idea.

Right. Focus. Angelika. "I can teleport others long distances," she said. "But I can't go myself."

He nodded.

"So, I teleport Kasia, and she pulls me with her. That way we can get there, inform Angelika so she can get away, and return quickly."

Ladon smoothed a hand over his jaw, fingering the smoother skin of his wicked scar. "Do you even know if that would work?"

No. "We could try it over a short distance here. Then a little farther, just to be sure."

He stared at her for a long, silent minute, considering, and, for first time in days, given he was preparing for war, she had his total focus. Her body tingled under that stare, something Skylar shut down with a mental snap of irritation.

What is wrong with me?

"Kasia?" he asked, not taking his gaze from Skylar.

Skylar harrumphed. "My word's not good enough for you?" she butted in before her sister could respond.

"Until I get to know all levels of your kind of trouble...no."

Disappointment tried to choke off her air, constricting her lungs. That lack of faith shouldn't be a surprise but still hurt more than she would've expected.

Kasia shrugged. "It's worth a try."

Brand stepped between Skylar and Kasia. "I said no."

Skylar lifted an eyebrow at him as if to say, "Like that would keep me away."

Based on his scowl, Brand got the message.

Ladon crossed his arms and set his feet wide, a stance she was already recognizing as, "I'm the fucking king."

"What happens if this goes wrong?" he demanded.

Skylar gave him a pointed look. She'd meant what she'd said. For Angelika, any risk to herself was moot. At the same time, out of the corner of her eye, she caught the way Kasia put her hand on Brand's arm. Were they communicating with each other through that link of theirs?

"Try going into the other room and back," Ladon said. He glanced at Brand. "Agreed?"

"Shit." Brand shook his head. Obviously not happy. "Do it."

Skylar's breath punched out of her as both men gave in, though just a little.

Before he could change his mind, Skylar turned to Kasia. "When I shove you, try to grab my wrists and pull me with you."

Kasia set her feet and held up her hands. "Ready."

Brand clamped a hand on Skylar's shoulder, bringing a harsh growl from Ladon, which the gold shifter ignored. "You'd better bring my mate back with you."

Rather than snap off a witty retort guaranteed to irk the man, Skylar caught the emotion in his eyes, tightening his jaw to the breaking point, almost like being punched in the face with it. This massive shifter who was both dragon and king, who had survived being rogue and years as a mercenary for hire, was terrified.

Soul-deep terror—like falling into a bottomless chasm of blackness—emotion that could never be faked.

The depth of that fear, and the fact that he even allowed her to see it, had Skylar rethinking her opinion of him.

Eating her words, she covered his hand with hers. "I'll keep her safe."

Leonine eyes stared at her hard for another couple of heartbeats before Brand nodded.

Skylar turned back to her sister, who watched the byplay silently and now raised her eyebrows.

"He really does love you," Skylar said as she stepped in closer.

"Duh." Kasia grinned.

Skylar let the snark slide. She sort of deserved it. "Ready?"

Kasia smirked. "Already said I was."

"Maul. We're going next door." The hound would understand. Reaching for calm, Skylar called to the fire inside her.

Flames sparked to life, manifesting on her skin and clothes. Whites and reds cast shadows over Kasia's face as the fire flowed over Skylar and onto her sister in a flickering dance. She didn't burn, rather, her fire was like wrapping herself in a sleeping bag in front of an open fire on a chilly night—comforting, friendly even.

A shower of sparks, and Kasia did the same, her red hair lifting around her with the blaze.

"Ready?" Skylar asked.

Kasia nodded. "Bring it."

Skylar didn't need to picture the destination exactly, more like she felt where she wanted them to go—a vague, imprecise method but it worked for her. "On three... One. Two. Three."

She shoved her sister at the shoulders. As Kasia disappeared from view, her hands wrapped around Skylar's wrists, and the strangest tugging sensation pulled at her. A blink of familiar darkness and silence, like when their mother used to move them using this ability, pulling her through a portal between space and time. Unlike with their mother, though, it felt as though icy fingers reached out, grasping but not getting purchase of her. Suddenly they were standing in the next room and the sensation disappeared. The momentum of Skylar's shove had Kasia stumbling back, taking Skylar with her, but they managed to stay upright.

Skylar grinned. "It worked!"

It had. Except that odd sensation... Skylar brushed it off. This was just a different way.

In a blink, Maul appeared beside them and gave a gruff yip— his version, at least, which came off more like a snarl. Probably saying "good job."

Her sister grinned back. "We've gotta work on your need to shove, because it makes the landings a bit rough. The first time you did that to me, I ended up outside on the landing platform and tumbled over the edge."

Skylar grimaced. "Sorry about that. How Mom did this without even touching..." She shook her head.

"We were in our second centuries before she mastered that trick," Kasia reminded her.

A nice thought, but not helpful. "We don't have two hundred years to master our skills."

"Neither did she," Kasia said. Then, as if she knew Skylar wouldn't agree anyway, she switched subjects, a mischievous light entering her eyes.

"Did it feel different to you?" Skylar asked.

"Different?" Kasia frowned. "No. You?"

Skylar just shrugged, and luckily, Kasia let it go.

"Want to try to go farther?" Kasia asked.

"What about Brand and Ladon?"

"You mean overprotective and uber-overprotective?" Kasia waved a hand, casually dismissing their mates. "Better to tell them after the fact. Brand wasn't happy about us just going next door."

Part of her wanted to say yes, but a bigger part pinched with guilt at not telling Ladon.

What the hell?

Days. It had only been days. This mating thing was getting to her more than she'd anticipated.

Skylar shook her head. "Let's go."

. . .

Waiting like an asshole was not where Ladon expected to be right now.

Not when most of his men were about to fly to a fight that would determine if this rebellion of his took a step forward or turned to ash in the wind.

Brand stood like a silent fucking statue beside him, staring at the spot where their mates had been standing. Ten minutes.

Where the hell were they? It shouldn't take this long to come back from one room over.

Panic was not a luxury he permitted himself. So the fact that the emotion was trying to slice its way into his heart served only to amp his growing anger.

In a flash, the two women reappeared, stumbling into each other, and that knife of panic turned into relief, which was swiftly swept aside by a tide of anger.

Without a word, he grabbed her hand and dragged Skylar out of the room and into the one next door.

"What the fuck, Kasia?" he vaguely heard Brand say as they left.

"Calm down, lizard man," her sister's reply followed.

Ladon ignored them, still grappling with the fear that had reached inside him and hammered at his heart when she hadn't returned immediately. Fear that had little to do with losing a phoenix. Fear with a personal edge to it that he wasn't willing to examine too closely yet. The mating bond taking effect, perhaps. A potentially deadly distraction if he let it become one.

For both of them.

As soon as the door closed, he turned on Skylar. "You want to explain yourself?" he demanded.

His mate didn't even flinch. "It worked."

"It worked?" Was she fucking kidding him?

With a huff, Skylar crossed her arms, pushing her breasts up. "Yes," she said. "It worked. We made it to the room, then to the top of the mountain, then came back here."

"We expected you to come right back. *Immediately*," he pointed out in what was a remarkably calm voice given how much he wanted to shake his mate right now.

"You would've argued us out of it," she said. Not a lick of remorse in the words or tone.

"Aren't mates supposed to discuss and..." He flung out an arm. "I don't know, compromise, and be on the same page, and shit?"

Skylar shrugged. "How would I know? Pytheios killed my father before we were born. I never witnessed mates interact until Kasia."

Ladon opened his mouth to snap back at her, only something in her voice, a vulnerability in those incredible eyes had him pausing, looking closer in the half light. That soft spot inside her, a part of her he doubted she revealed very often, if ever, tugged at something inside him. Ladon chalked it up to seeing such a strong woman, one who seemingly felt no fear, hurting.

He glanced away, rethinking his own response, then returned his gaze to her. "Good news. My parents showed me that mates work together. Not against each other or separate from each other. A team."

"A team..." she echoed slowly.

Ladon gave in to the urge, stepped in to her, needing the physical contact, because dammit, she had scared him more than any fight he'd ever been in. "A team. A partnership. I thought that's what we agreed on. We've been doing pretty well so far, given everything."

"We've been a little too occupied with taking the Gold Throne to do much partnering."

Ladon scowled, eye twitching in a slow tick. "Are you saying I've neglected you?"

Skylar rolled her eyes, which only stoked his irritation more. "Of course not," she said. "I can take care of myself."

He knew that what she meant had nothing to do with sex, but damned if that wasn't what he pictured. "That's my job."

"Listen here, Tarzan." She poked him in the chest with the tip of her finger. "I can get on board with trying out this team idea. Only if you rein in that urge to go all 'me dragon king, you lowly woman' crap."

"Crap?" he barked. "You scared the shit out of me, disappearing like that." Even now his heart clenched to the point of pain.

Her eyes widened at those telling words. He fully expected her jaw to tighten stubbornly. But she bit her lip, the first show of doubt he'd ever seen from her. "You didn't have to worry—"

"I did." His voice went quieter, and she flinched. Good. She needed to get this. "You're my mate."

Impossibly, that was coming to mean more than just the phoenix being bound to him. The fates had sent him maybe the only woman alive as stubborn as he was. And as dedicated to what she believed in.

Gods, even through his anger, he wanted to run his fingers over the silky skin of her face, bury his nose in her hair, and breathe her in. Now that he knew she was safe, and the anger was, if not fading, at least worked through, need was kicking in hard.

She fidgeted again, a vulnerable sign he'd yet to see from her. "You should know I'm not the obedient mate type."

Ladon groaned. She was definitely not getting it. "It's not about obedience, Skylar. Dammit."

She put her hands on her hips. "Then explain it to me."

"Would you have done that alone and left Kasia behind wondering?"

She traced the back of a chair with one finger. "If I thought she'd stand in the way of what I knew to be the right decision…"

"Fuck, you're stubborn."

"You'll learn to love me for it." Skylar paused, eyes going wide as she realized what she'd said. "I mean, my sisters do. Not that…"

Ladon's lips gave a reluctant twitch. She was damn cute in a panic.

Her lips twisted as she regarded him with something akin to regret. "I'm sorry," she said. "For scaring you."

Shock immobilized him for a beat. Had he heard right? "What?"

That earned him a glare for making her repeat it. "I said, I'm sorry," she muttered through clenched teeth. "At least I came back. Kasia wanted to keep going."

And give him a fucking heart attack if they'd done that.

"But I couldn't."

Something in her expression sent a new kind of tension through him. "Why couldn't you?"

She wrinkled her nose, as though arguing with herself what to reveal. "Because of you."

Before he could process the implications of what she was admitting, a soft moan floated through the walls. Kasia. Brand had the right idea. Ladon shifted his gaze to the woman at his side, everything in him going hard in anticipation.

Skylar lowered her lashes so he couldn't discern her thoughts. Lips tilting slightly, she raised a hand and drew a pattern across his chest with the tip of her finger, her touch branding him, leaving a trail of fire in its wake, even through his clothing.

"There is one area in which I wouldn't mind trying that whole obedience thing out," she murmured.

The animal inside him roared his approval. "Is that so?"

Already he was thinking of all the decadent, dirty things he wanted to do to and with her.

She flirted outrageously with those eyes. "I'm not saying that our mating has been on my mind way too much these last few days, or that I've had to take care of myself more than a couple times just to alleviate the tension."

"You're not saying that, huh?" Ladon put his hands in his pockets, faking any sort of relaxed pose while tension gripped him. "I have definitely not been constantly hard since then, either."

Her chuckle, full of sin in that husky voice of hers, shot straight to his dick, already straining against his zipper.

The timing was shit, but if he was sending her to her death, then dammit…

"Strip for me."

CHAPTER THIRTEEN

Blushing was not her thing, but if ever there was a time for it, being on the receiving end of a knowing look from her sister after she'd been up to all sorts of no good with her mate in the other room was it. Skylar lifted an eyebrow and Kasia's smirk faded. After all, she and Brand had been pretty loud.

"I don't like this fuckery," Brand said in his snarling way.

"You're not the only one," Ladon muttered under his breath, though she caught it.

She'd held back any mention of those icy fingers reaching for her in the dark silence of the in-between as she and Kasia teleported together. Kasia obviously wasn't feeling it, so she wasn't in danger. But their mates would never allow them to go if she revealed it.

It would be fine. Worth the risk.

Before Skylar could go back into her argument about the energy it took to teleport this way—for both her and Kasia—and needing to save that in case Angelika needed help, Ladon held up a hand. "I get it. We'll wait for you here."

Skylar paused, mouth open, which pulled that small quirk of his lips from her new mate. The closest he got to amusement as far as she could tell. "I can be reasonable," he said.

Brand's dubious snort didn't give her much confidence in that statement.

"Who knew someone called the 'Blood King' leans toward reasonable?" Skylar said drily. Except she already knew that about him. The dichotomy was…annoyingly intriguing.

All she got was a grunt in return.

"We'd better get going," Kasia said.

"If you need to contact us, get in touch with Hershel," Brand said to Kasia.

"Who's Hershel?" Skylar asked. Not Kasia, but Ladon.

"The ancient who practically raised Brand while he was hiding in a back system of caves in Ben Nevis. He lives near Manchester… And he's a demon."

She had no trouble interpreting that tone. "Not happy about that?"

Ladon's lips flattened. "The fact that we might have to involve a demon at all only heaps onto the steaming pile of shit I'm dealing with here."

He took Skylar's face in his hands, staring at her with that intent way he had. "You'd better fucking come back to me."

As if he cared. Really cared. Her heart pulled in tight before giving a hard thump.

The level of her reluctance to leave him was…concerning. Too soon. Too much. And with no chance for her to sit back and figure it out.

Time was against them. Angelika, and whoever she was with, needed to be able to clear out before that red asshole showed his raggedy ass.

She should step back. Go. Instead, the fear in his eyes held her fast. Fear. From the Blood King. Ladon struck her as a man who was never afraid, but he was now. For her. Skylar stepped in closer, speared her hands through his hair, and tugged his head down so she could kiss him. Gods he tasted good—like man, and dragon, and…hers.

"Was that supposed to make me feel better?" he whispered against her lips.

She hid a smile. "A little."

Taking a deep breath, she forced herself to step back. Then Skylar threw her arms wide, allowing her flames out to play, red glowing embers lifting into the air all around her.

"Skylar." Ladon's gruff voice had her looking over her shoulder. "Stay safe…"

An order, she had no doubt. But this time it didn't rub her wrong. "You, too." Her gut clenched on the realization that she meant it. "Don't wait for us. Go take that throne."

His jaw hardened, but Ladon gave a single, sharp nod.

I'd better see him again.

The thought came unbidden, and dread dropped into her stomach like a weighted body in the ocean, sinking fast. She couldn't be falling for her mate. Her stubborn, bossy as hell, dragon king mate. Her tenacious, principled, fighter. That was *not* the plan.

Skylar shook it off and counted down, picturing the area Kasia described in the Pyrenees Mountains separating France and Spain. Specifically, the abandoned town where Angelika was staying.

With a shove, she and Kasia disappeared into the nothing. Only this time, she could feel Kasia's grip slipping, and those icy fingers dug deeper into her flesh.

Blind and deaf, trying her damndest to not panic, Skylar tried to bend her wrists in a way that allowed her to hold on to her sister without accidentally twisting out of her grip. If Kasia lost her, and she couldn't get herself out, she was screwed. She suspected it meant ending up in the in-between limbo. Forever. Fear scraped at her nerves like a cheese grater the longer it lasted.

With a sudden bright light and rushing *whoosh* as sound returned, they reappeared, tumbling over each other to end up in a heap on stone floors so old they'd been worn smooth and uneven. Again, Kasia caught the brunt of it, the dull crack of her head against the stone making Skylar wince.

"What the fuck?" a masculine voice barked.

Instantly, Skylar levered off her sister, jumping to her feet in a defensive position to find three men crouched low, eyes glittering dangerously, ready to attack.

A quick inventory told her she'd managed to teleport into one of the buildings in the village, a grocer's shop, perhaps, given the long wooden countertop with built-in shelves behind it stocked with various canned goods. And scorch marks on the walls beside patches of new wood or stone.

A view of narrow streets out the single, thick-glassed window showed more dilapidated buildings, including a few burned to cinders. Hard to tell through all the grime covering the glass, though.

The man at the center of the trio was stocky, all muscle, with a white streak through his rust-colored hair. The one to his right was younger, mid-twenties maybe, and pretty except for a nose that had clearly been broken once. To his left a deeply black man, bald, and with eyes so dark she could drown in them, snarled.

The stocky guy in front pulled back his lips to reveal teeth elongating to sharp edges. *Wolf shifters. Holy shit.*

Kasia hadn't told her what to expect, just where to go. With a groan, her sister got to her feet as well.

"Kasia?" The man in front scowled. "You've got to give us warning before you pull that shit."

Rubbing her head with one hand, Kasia aimed a glare at Skylar. "That's twice. How about I shove *you* next time?" Not giving Skylar a chance to answer, she held up her other hand in apology and addressed the shifter. "We couldn't, Rafe. Too risky. Ben Nevis has spies everywhere."

The three men straightened, the man named Rafe retracting his teeth with a sick slide of bone and flesh. "Please tell me dragons aren't coming again. We're still rebuilding from the last time you brought them down on us."

Kasia clamped her lips so tight, they turned white. "I can't tell you that."

"Fuck."

Kasia closed her eyes, then opened them. "I'm sorry. I need to see Angelika."

Not taking his eyes from them, he canted his head to address the dark man to his left. "Hunter."

Without a word, the man prowled from the room. Hell, they even moved like wolves when in human form. Wolf shifters were supposed to be notoriously closed off to outsiders, and unpredictable with how they treated anyone not of their kind. Especially anyone associated with dragon shifters. Why had their mother sent Angelika to them?

Then again, she'd sent Skylar to live with a colony of organized rogue dragon shifters, most of whom were liable to go feral any time they shifted. Not exactly the safest place. Granted, her uncle had been among them, but still…

Hiding her daughters with the exact creatures least likely to help had been damn smart of her mother.

The question was, how had she worked it out?

"Kasia Astarot," a deep voice boomed, preceding an older gentleman into the room.

"So weird to hear that instead of Amon," Skylar muttered at Kasia, who raised her eyebrows.

As lean and muscled as his younger compatriots, the man addressing Kasia only showed his age via two gray stripes in his pointed beard. This had to be the alpha of the pack.

"Bleidd." Kasia moved forward to embrace him.

Skylar watched in silent contemplation. Apparently, her sister had spent enough time here to develop some relationships. Kasia turned, ushering Skylar forward. "This is my sister, Skylar Ormarr."

Even weirder. Her new name.

No doubt Kasia introduced her that way on purpose, to make a point. They would both always be Amons and Hanyus. Their parents' legacies lived on in the sisters. But something about Ormarr sat easily with her name.

What if—

She stopped the thought dead. This was not the time or place to be thinking about her mate or her life with him. She'd figure that out later.

"A third little dove to protect," Bleidd murmured.

"There's another one?" Rafe exclaimed at the same time. "Fuck. No wonder those scaly bastards keep coming at us."

For his part, Bleidd paused in holding out his hand to shake, his dark gray eyes flicking back and forth between the two. "I see the resemblance."

Skylar shook his hand with a grin. "You're one of the few. None of us looks anything alike."

"Except for the shape of the face and the eyes," he said.

Observant. Most couldn't see past their wide range of coloring and difference in body types.

Already, she liked this Bleidd guy.

"Where's Angelika?" Kasia asked. "I hate to ambush you, but this is urgent."

Skylar studied her sister. *Would* Kasia be able to teleport again before nightfall? She'd barely held on that time.

"She's coming," Bleidd said. Then he lifted a single eyebrow at Skylar. "Ormarr? As in the Blood—"

"Yeah," she cut him off.

"Interesting."

You're telling me.

Rather than bother with idle chitchat, the room fell silent as they waited. The patter of rapid footsteps heralded Angelika's arrival. "Where is she?" she called up the stairs before bursting into the room.

Angelika stopped at seeing them both there, her lips parting in a gasp, before she squealed her delight and barreled into them, wrapping an arm around each sister.

Behind her a tall man with his dark hair cropped short, military style, and an air that shouted warrior, appeared at the top of the stairs, watching Angelika with a proprietary light in his hazel eyes.

"You're both here. I can't believe it. Have you come to get me?" she babbled while clutching them both tightly.

"No," Skylar said. "We came to warn you."

Angelika pulled back, her brows, darker than her white-blond hair, drawing down in a fierce frown. "Warn me? Why aren't you coming to get me? You're obviously together now."

"No one knows about you except our mates."

"Mates," Angelika echoed glancing rapidly between them. "Both of you now?"

Skylar grimaced. "I sort of expected to kill mine, but..." She shrugged.

Behind her, one of the men snorted a laugh. "Would've loved to see that," a male voice muttered. Rafe again, she'd guess, based on the rough voice.

Bleidd gave a miniscule shake of his head at whoever had spoken.

"We can't stay," Kasia said.

Angelika's expression fell momentarily, but then she took a deep breath and pulled her shoulders back. "What warning?"

Skylar squeezed her arm. "Pytheios knows you're here. He's coming for you."

"Gods be damned. We barely survived the Gold Clan hitting us. Pytheios—" Bleidd shook his head, visage grim.

"Based on my vision, he doesn't come until tonight," Kasia said. "Run. Hide."

"Excuse me if we don't entirely trust your visions," Rafe snapped. For the second time his canines elongated, giving him a fierce scowl.

Skylar glanced at her sister, eyebrows raised in question. Kasia twitched a shoulder. "When they were attacked last time, I saw it at a different time of day. So, we got ready based on that and were ambushed."

"Oh."

"Yeah. Oh." Rafe turned to his pack leader. "We could call up the Federation of Packs."

Bleidd shook his head. "No time."

Kasia cleared her throat. "You should also know that Ladon and Brand have joined forces with Gorgon, King of the Black

Clan, and we are going to take the Gold Throne for Brand. They are on the way there now."

The tall dude still standing by the stairs stepped forward. "That leaves Ben Nevis vulnerable."

"As well as Mount Ararat to the southeast," Bleidd agreed.

"And we're right fucking between them, with three phoenixes to bring Pytheios down on top of us," Rafe grumbled. "Perfect."

Angelika's eyes darkened. She turned to Bleidd. "You've already risked enough for me. Your vow to my mother is fulfilled."

"Vow?" Kasia asked.

"Mother saved his life," Angelika tossed at them distractedly, her gaze on Bleidd, who was shaking his head.

"No," Bleidd shook his head. "I promised to keep you safe."

"Enough wolves have died for me. My sisters' mates can keep me safe now. You can't stop me from going with them."

"Uh…Houston, we have a problem. You can't come with us," Skylar piped up, thinking fast.

"What?" Angelika swung around, snapping the word in a way the youngest of the four of them had never done in the past.

Skylar went glare for glare. "Hear me out. King Gorgon isn't mated. So, unless you want to end up hitched, or a target for black dragons if you try and it goes badly, I suggest you stay with the wolves. Is there anywhere safe you can go?"

Angelika, stubbornness written all over her, opened her mouth to protest, then paused, speculation entering her gaze. "Does Gorgon seem like a good king? A good man?" she asked tentatively.

"No." The tall, possessive guy jerked forward with the word.

"You're not mating anyone you don't want to." This from Rafe.

Skylar raised her eyebrows, reassessing the brash shifter. Though she shouldn't be surprised. Everyone who knew her loved Angelika.

"He might not want me," Angelika said slowly.

Skylar scoffed. "Of course he will—"

"I didn't inherit any powers." Angelika's words dropped into a moat of silence.

Kasia blinked. "Wait. Are you sure?"

Angelika nodded and put on the brave smile she'd always used as a kid when she couldn't do something Kasia or Skylar could. Meira was the quiet one who never cared if she could do the same things, finding her own way. Despite the smile, Angelika had always cared.

"Maybe it's subtle? Or you'll find it later?" Kasia tried.

Angelika crossed her arms, a sure sign she was done with the conversation. "I don't want to talk about it. Anyway, I doubt Gorgon will want me when he finds out I'm not useful to him."

"Perhaps," Skylar said slowly. "But let's not add that complication to the mix. Wait until they've fought this battle to the finish?"

"That doesn't solve the Pytheios issue," Bleidd said. "Dragons took out most of our town. They know we've allied with Ladon and Brand. We're still rebuilding, and we can get only so far in twelve hours."

Damn.

If she'd known that, Skylar would've dragged Angelika's whereabouts from Kasia and come even without the threat of the red king. How could the dragon shifters have not considered the impact on anyone but themselves? How could she not have asked? Was their myopic focus on only themselves rubbing off?

"Come to Ben Nevis," Skylar offered.

Kasia swung sharply around to stare at her. "Skylar..."

She ignored her sister. "I'm the queen there now." Technically. "As our allies, we owe you our protection if our actions endanger you and your people."

"But if Angelika goes there, people will find out," Kasia pointed out through a forced smile.

Skylar waved that away. "Gorgon's already departed with all of his men, so he won't hear until later."

"What if we disguise her as one of ours?" Military Man said.

"Jedd—" Angelika went to protest but stopped when he held up a hand.

"You don't smell like your sisters…like smoke. We dress you in clothes worn by wolf shifters. Keep one of us with you any time you're among the dragons. They don't need to see you shift to assume you're one of us."

"That could work," Skylar said. Was it selfish that an eager buzz ran through her? The need to have all four of them together again was a powerful draw.

"We'll have to pretend like we don't know each other," Kasia said. "But we'll be at the battle, so that shouldn't be hard at first."

Bleidd crossed his arms, contemplating the logistics. "Except we'd still have to go by foot. That will leave us vulnerable for several days' journey with Pytheios on our trail."

"Actually…" Skylar grinned. "I can help with that."

. . .

"Your mate is a bad influence on mine," Brand grumbled beside Ladon as they stood inside the large, hangar-like space inside Ben Nevis.

The message relayed via Kasia through Hershel informing them of a unilateral decision, this one to offer the wolves sanctuary, had meant turning the fuck around and returning to Ben Nevis while his warriors moved ahead with the plan to fly to Norway, so he could be here for the arrival of the wolves. The opposite fucking direction of his army.

The bustle inside the main city beyond the large opening into that space remained about the same as any day, except with a different intent. Getting ready for their plan—both parts of it.

So many of his own people to protect. Bringing wolf shifters to his mountain—creatures most dragon shifters considered about as trustworthy as cobras—plus another phoenix they intended to hide put him in an untenable position.

Not that he had any choice.

Ladon contained a growl. "They *both* have minds of their own."

"That's for damn sure, but Kasia is swayed by Skylar in a way I haven't felt from her before. Not that we've been mated long, but..."

"Skylar's decisions aren't bad ones," Ladon pointed out with a thread of warning in the tone. Not that she needed him to stick up for her. "*We* should've offered the wolves sanctuary. They are allies now, and our actions put them in direct danger."

Except the idea had been to continue to allow Angelika to hide with the shifters. A dumb idea as it turned out.

"Yeah," Brand muttered. "But what about the other thing?"

The abrupt appearance of two men fifty feet from them put an end to the conversation. Ladon recognized Rafe, the russet-colored wolf shifter with a sarcastic, bitter attitude that rivaled Brand's. The other wolf shifter with him was Cairn, the one with a major chip on his shoulder when it came to dragons.

"Over here," he called.

Rafe shook hands. Cairn did not. "Thanks for the offer to put us up," Rafe said.

"Not exactly our offer," Brand pointed out.

They all ignored him. "You are welcome in Ben Nevis any time," Ladon said.

"She's going to try to send five through on this one. We'll know Kasia and Skylar are on their way when Bleidd shows. He'll be last."

They nodded and waited.

Sure enough, seconds later a larger group appeared, linked by their hands, only they stumbled a bit, twisting up in one another to fall over.

Immediately he went to help, taking a young woman's hand as she struggled to her feet. With a flick, she tossed her white blond hair back and turned to face him. "Thanks."

Holy shit. No way could he mistake that heart-shaped face or those frozen eyes. This had to be Angelika. Skylar and Kasia had actually risked exposing their sister to dragons, especially with an unmated king on the loose.

What the hell was his mate thinking? He respected her need to protect everyone around her, but that meant she made no goddamn sense sometimes. At this rate, he'd be an old man well before his time.

Angelika's scent reached him, swirling around him, and he paused. Wolf, human, but no smoke. Not a phoenix?

"You must be Ladon," she murmured. "My name is…Angel. I'm—"

"My mate. I'm Jedd." A tall man, leanly muscled with hard hazel eyes that reminded Ladon of his most battle-tested warriors stepped forward, clamping an arm around her waist.

Except the woman calling herself Angel cringed. Barely, but Ladon caught it just the same.

Had she mated this wolf? Unlike dragons, wolf mates didn't carry a brand. Instead, part of their mating involved mutual bites that turned into a permanent marking. Usually at the neck, and he didn't see any such mark on either of them.

Regardless, he couldn't ask them about it here.

The unmistakable howl of a hellhound—part high-pitched scream and part full-bodied roar— cut the air, bloodcurdling enough to have every shifter in the place crouching, ready for attack. Ladon included. Except suddenly Maul poofed right in front of his eyes and pounced on the blonde, knocking her to the ground and making little whining sounds as he attempted to give her a bath with that rancid tongue while making a sound like a cackle, which Ladon was pretty sure was the dog's version of a laugh.

From the ground, Angel, or Angelika, put a trembling hand to Maul's face and whispered something that Ladon, even as close as he was, didn't quite catch.

The dog did, though. He gave a snort of acknowledgment and poofed away again.

With a wary gaze, checking those around her, Angelika got to her feet and brushed off her clothes. "Interesting welcoming committee you've got here," she said a little overloudly.

Ladon played along. "Welcome to Ben Nevis."

Next, a group of five appeared in the same discombobulated state. Over the next twenty minutes, that continued until his training room was filled with wolf shifters. The entire town was being sent here, apparently.

Bleidd was the last to come through, his lips compressed in a grim line. "She's losing steam," he said to Ladon. "And I don't think Kasia is confident Skylar can get them both this far."

Beside him, Brand's hands tightened into fists, but the Rogue King said nothing, merely stood staring at the space where each group had arrived.

Five minutes stretched to ten. Ladon was reaching for the sat phone when a woman appeared. Except only half of her showed. Her legs appeared to float in midair as the rest of her seemed to be trapped by an invisible tunnel. She thrashed and kicked, her feet too high to find purchase on the rock floor.

At the same time, Brand and Ladon sprinted forward, each grabbing a leg and pulling. Every powerful muscle in Ladon's body screamed with the effort until deep red hair cleared whatever kind of portal they made, her arms still invisible.

Kasia.

"I can't hold onto her," she panted.

A knife's edge of panic split him in two, pain and fear Ladon had to push down deep. "You got her?" he asked Brand.

The gold king nodded.

Bleidd showed up beside him, taking Kasia by the legs. "We've got her, too."

Carefully, Ladon moved to her head and skimmed his hand down her arms, hoping that by touch he could access wherever Skylar was at the end of Kasia's fingertips.

He had no fucking clue if this would work, but his mate was on the other end.

Shock scissored through him as, before his eyes, his hands disappeared. He could still feel Kasia, but Skylar wasn't there. He pushed farther, heart rate jacking up as he made it to Kasia's hands and still couldn't feel his mate.

Only now, the strangest sucking sensation, as though the vortex was trying to yank him in, dragged at his body. Icy fingers clamped around his fists, the chill of death permeating his entire body.

Hurry. He had no idea how he knew he was losing time, but he wouldn't ignore the instinct.

Finally, at the very tip of Kasia's fingers, he felt her. Terrified that if he stopped touching Kasia he'd lose the connection, or if he jiggled either one, Kasia would lose her grip, Ladon moved with a slowness that felt as though time itself had crawled to a stop. With deliberate movements, despite urgency riding him hard, he inched forward, careful to keep in touch with Kasia.

The dragging sensation started to pull his feet across the floor, the cold going deeper into his body. Two men grabbed him, grunting at the effort to keep him still, the vibration against his skin noticeable.

Finally, he got his hands wrapped around Skylar's wrists. He sucked in a sharp drag of relief. But this wasn't over. "Pull," he gritted. "Slowly."

Working as a single unit, everyone took measured steps back. His shoulders, elbows, then hands reappeared, and the chill released his body from its grip as the first part of Skylar showed. The tunnel still had her caught, though. Shaking with the strain of the effort, he pulled until his mate's head appeared, flopping forward, her dark braid dangling toward the ground.

Oh gods, have I lost her already?

Only he couldn't stop to assess her state, needing to pull her from the grip of whatever had her. With agonizing slowness, they pulled the rest of her free. The second her feet appeared, the force turned off. She and everyone pulling at her flew back and hit the ground hard.

Ladon crawled over to his mate, pulling her into his lap, turning her so he could see her face. He checked her pulse, and a small part of his fear dissipated as a thready beat fluttered against his fingertips. "She's weak, but still with us." He brushed her hair back from her face. "Come on, Sky, open your eyes."

Gods, she was like a block of ice.

Brand helped an exhausted Kasia to her sister's side and she took Skylar's hand, rubbing it between hers.

For the second instance in as many minutes, time seemed to slow as he waited for his mate to show some signs of life. "Come on," he whispered, giving her a little shake.

Finally, her eyelids fluttered.

"That's it, Skylar. Open your eyes."

Gradually, she managed to lift her lashes, her blue eyes groggy, confused. "What...happened?" she whispered, as if even talking drained her.

"I told you that was too far." Kasia pinched her sister's arm.

"Ow." Skylar frowned, obviously trying to remember how she ended up here. Then her eyes widened, focusing on Ladon. "You..."

"I pulled you out."

"I could feel you there with me."

Having traveled in that void himself before, with Kasia, Ladon knew she'd been cut off from sound and sight in there. "Barely. It took a lot of us."

Even still half out of it, he could see the spark of recognition about what that meant. Shifters even in human form were still incredibly strong. If it took a lot of them, that nothingness could easily have taken her.

Damned if he ever let her teleport again if that result was on the table.

"Right. Well..." She rolled to sitting, though he had to help keep her from wobbling all over the place. "Let's not do that again for a while."

Kasia snorted. "You think?"

"We couldn't stay there alone, Kas," Skylar grumbled as she rubbed at her eyes.

He wanted to carry her back to their suite and just hold her, make sure her lips turned back to pink, rather than the tint of blue still bruising them. But he couldn't. He'd already lost so much time. "Do you think you can fly today?"

"Are you kidding me?" Brand's shoulders flexed with tension. "They're both exhausted."

Ladon lifted a hard gaze to his friend. "And we're already a full day behind our people."

"Strap me on in case I fall asleep. It'll be fine." Skylar waved a weary hand, slurring her words.

Dammit.

Kasia straightened. "Me too."

"You've got to be kidding me," Brand snarled. But he let it go.

It took another hour to get the wolf shifters settled and introduce them to Ivar and Rainier. Having already fought side by side with the wolves when Uther had attacked their town to get to Kasia, they accepted the new additions to their arsenal more easily than they might've not all that long ago.

"Glad to have you here to help defend this place," Rainier said as he nodded at Bleidd. "We have an entire floor of rooms where we can house you together." He sent a significant look to Ladon, who nodded. Rainier would inform Bleidd about the full plan later and find a way to incorporate the wolves.

"You have our thanks," Bleidd answered.

"We should go," Brand said.

Ladon backed up and shifted, worry about his mate threatening to override the urgency driving him to get to his people. Using thick ropes, Ivar and Rainier lashed Skylar to the large spikes at his shoulders behind which she sat. They did the same with Brand and Kasia and, together—way the fuck more vulnerable to attack than he wanted to be—they launched out the wide door and into the canyon. Ladon remembered to stoke the fire in his belly as they quickly gained altitude, warming his mate's delicate human form as the icy air buffeted them.

He and Brand set a punishing pace.

An hour into the journey—taking a different route from Kasia and Brand, both men deeming it safer to split up two kings and two phoenixes in case of attack—Skylar shifted positions, his first indication she was even still lucid.

"You okay?" he asked.

"Yeah. You mad?"

He had to strain to hear her soft answer as the wind snatched the sounds in the opposite direction. His mate was clearly still recovering. *"You scared the shit out of me…"*

"Sorry." She shifted against him again. "I thought we could make it."

"I'm not mad."

Silence greeted that.

"Don't believe me?"

"You yelled at me about doing reckless stuff without consulting you first only yesterday."

"We'd already agreed to a plan. You made a call as part of that. One that involved trying to keep you and Kasia and Angelika safe. I'm not going to blow up over that."

Shake her. Fuck her. Lock her in a cell. All things he'd considered.

"It was almost the wrong call."

Ladon tensed at the anger in those words. She was beating herself up over this. He could tell by the tone in her voice. As king, even if for a short time, he knew going down the path of what-ifs was an exercise in futility that only made you doubt yourself down the line. *"Don't do that."*

"What?"

"Don't second-guess yourself. You're better than that."

Silence greeted his words. Had she fallen asleep again?

CHAPTER FOURTEEN

Skylar couldn't figure her mate out. One second, he was pissed about her making life-and-death decisions without him, and the next he was telling her not to second-guess herself. Only she was too damn tired to argue about it. "Whatever."

Silence greeted her grumpy, if somewhat garbled, comeback.

Skylar leaned against the spike in front of her, eyes closed, as she battled with the fear swirling in her gut and the questions whipping through her mind. All the different ways that last jump with Kasia could've ended beat at her. Forget herself, what if she'd killed Kasia?

Skylar blew out a long, low breath.

"Was the blonde claiming to be mated to a wolf your sister?"

Was he deliberately changing the subject? "Yes."

"Are they really mated?"

"No." She would've said more, but her speaking out loud meant others could listen in to her side. "Can anyone else hear us?"

"They'd have to get damn close, as softly as you're speaking. Close enough that I'd know."

I'm speaking softly? The effort to do that much was enough of a struggle.

While she'd been sitting here in a silent half sleep, her mind had finally had time to turn over some facts.

The largest of which was, despite his bloody reputation,

Ladon Ormarr was a decent man who'd done nothing but offer her patience she suspected didn't come naturally, support, and partnership in how they went after the men who'd threatened her family and his people.

Maybe it was time to add trust—gods that was a terrifying word—in what they could do together. Which meant sharing a few things.

"Did you know a phoenix is immortal?"

The muscles under her shifted, as though he'd tensed and then forced himself to relax. *"I've heard the legends, of course. But where are you going with this?"*

"Once we mate, we give that up."

Silence spread over them as he continued to fly. A silence that just got longer and more awkward with every beat of his wings. Even the wind seemed to thicken, pushing on her harder. Or maybe he was going faster. Hard to tell up here.

"You're telling me you gave up your immortality for me?" he finally rumbled. Her indomitable mate sounded...thrown.

"Yes and no. Mother never was sure how things would work once she passed her powers on." She was trying to make him feel better. "There's more..."

"Terrific. What other good tidings do you bring me?"

Did he not get what she was trying to tell him? Skylar bit her lip. "The oldest among dragon shifters remembers only my grandmother and mother. Maybe my great-grandmother. But each phoenix passes down our history to the next, so it won't be lost."

"Each?"

"A phoenix has mated a dragon for the last ten thousand years. When she senses her mate is nearing the end of his life, she willingly gives up her powers to her daughter so that when her mate dies, the bond between them will take her with him."

Only her mother had to live with the hell of continuing on without her mate. Their bond had not solidified when their father had been murdered. *"Is that what your grandmother did?"*

"For my mother? Yes. That was when Pytheios struck. When

they were at their most vulnerable. According to Mom, he was under the false impression that only the Red Clan had claimed phoenix queens before and assumed he'd be next, with her. They underestimated his obsession with power and perished because of it. Mom didn't die with our father because their bond hadn't solidified, and she didn't bear his mark yet."

There was more. Lots more. Including the fact that the Blue Clan might not be next up for High King. The White Clan was, in theory, though her mother had mated the White King, so who the hell knew what was next? But she wasn't allowed to tell him the rest. Not until he'd captured her heart, her mother had always said. Dead serious about it. The trouble was, Skylar suspected Ladon might be the only one who *could* capture hers. A thought that scared her more than the void.

Another beat of silence. *"Why didn't you tell me before we mated?"*

Damn. Did he regret mating her now that he had this information?

Skylar leaned her forehead against him, exhaustion washing back through her. "Mother always warned us not to. A man can fake love if he thought it would win him the gifts we give." She paused, not sure she wanted to ask the question looming. "Would it have made a difference in your decision to mate me?"

"No." No hesitation, which warmed her insides for reasons having nothing to do with fire.

But then the following silence dragged out even longer. What was he thinking?

"Why tell me now?"

A fair question. One Skylar took her time answering. "We're partners, right?"

He bobbled in the air. The first real indication that she'd gotten to him. Why? Because she was the one to bring it up, acknowledge it without him pointing it out?

"Are you saying you don't hate dragon shifters anymore?"

"I'm reserving judgment about one or two of them..."

A low grunt of acknowledgment rattled around in her head, and she gave a sleepy smile. "Because deep down, I believe in you," she said. "Not the clans. There's a hell of a lot that needs fixing about the clans. But *you*... You I can get behind."

Heavy silence greeted her words. Had he even heard?

"I mean, you say things I don't like and make assumptions all the time. You're arrogant, and hard, and controlling, *and* a king. I *should* hate you."

"But you don't?"

She couldn't get a read on how he felt about that. "Not at the moment."

A dark chuckle greeted her words. *"I'll keep that in mind."*

The kind of answer she would have wanted before, when she was trying to keep a distance between them so she could leave him one day. But, damn him, not what she was looking for now. That's all he was going to say?

She shouldn't be surprised. Talking about emotions was the same for him as it was for her. Something to be avoided. Still, disappointment skittered around in her chest. Skylar had no idea what she'd been expecting him to say, but sort of brushing off her statement as nothing wasn't it. "Don't let it go to your head or anything."

"Why are you mad?"

"I'm not."

"Yes, you are. Did you expect me to say something else?"

"Of course not." Not if she had to drag it out of him. Or worse, he lied.

"I'm flattered, if it helps."

"I'm not mad," she gritted between clenched teeth.

"I can tell." Amusement laced his words, only making her more irritated.

"I'd have to let you close to be mad," she pointed out. He was already too close.

"So...you believe in me, but you don't want to let me close."

In a nutshell. "People can only hurt you if you let them close enough to do it."

"Who has ever been close enough to you to hurt you?"

Heat surged through Skylar with each word. Not a good heat, but an angry heat. If he kept going, her head might start spinning any second. How dare he? He hadn't lived her life, or even known she existed until recently. At the same time, she couldn't deny that he was right. Which only pissed her off more.

"Thanatos was my father's best friend," he said when she didn't respond. *"He had my parents killed so they couldn't challenge him for the throne Pytheios helped him claim. They disappeared, so I didn't know he was their killer, not Pytheios, until recently. He spent all those...centuries...pretending to still be a friend of my family's, almost a second father to me. I thought he was a weak king, a bad leader, and uncaring of his people. But he was a murderer and a fiend."*

His confession came out flat, emotionless, as if he'd shut off everything he felt about it like turning off a spigot. *"I killed him, this one-time friend,"* he said. *"Slit his throat and put his head on a spike in the middle of the city so no one could doubt his death."*

All the anger steaming through her lost its heat, seeping out of her in slow waves. "I'm sorry."

She wished they were both human right now, so she could see his face. The best she could do was place her hand on one of his scales. A tiny show of commiseration, of solidarity.

"I didn't tell you so that you'd pity me." He was back to the harsh man she'd first met, but she had a feeling now that the harshness was a front.

"No. You told me to make a point. Good job. Point taken."

"Yeah. What was the point?"

Skylar huffed. "Not to talk bullshit around you."

Another snorted laugh had smoke drifting back to her. *"Try again."*

She sighed. "Keeping my distance is not the answer. Neither is letting everyone in. About right?"

"About right."

"I suppose you think you should be on the list of people I let in?"

"As your mate, it makes sense."

"True. But as someone I barely know, you'll need to earn it. And, to be fair, I need to earn it with you, too."

"Damn. I was hoping that whole believing in me thing would take care of that. Now you're going to make me work for it?"

"Damn straight—"

He jerked beneath her, cutting her off. *"Fuck. Hold on!"*

Skylar barely had time to register his words let alone grasp him tighter before Ladon performed a smooth but hard backflip. One that slammed g-forces through her, pinning her to his back even if the ropes hadn't already been holding her to him.

Skylar's vision went spotty for a brief second, but as a pilot who'd experienced this before, she pushed through and searched the skies behind and around her, trying to find the source of whatever caused Ladon to do this.

She didn't see anything.

He came out of the flip only to drop his right wing, throwing them into a tight downward spiral. Again, her vision threatened to close in on her. But Skylar held on to her wits and kept searching, until finally she caught movement among the clouds. But that couldn't be right.

"Why are the clouds moving?" she yelled above the rush of air, doing her best to keep her focus on the weird phenomenon above them.

"White dragons," Ladon answered. *"Two of them."*

He leveled out suddenly, and Skylar grunted at the change in pressure against her body. However, she was too focused above her to care much. Sure enough, now that she knew what she was looking for, those fluffy white clouds developed tails, and spikes, and wings. Only flashes of them, as they moved, but still there.

"Tricky motherfuckers," she muttered to herself.

As the dragons overhead dove after Ladon, she caught the flash of ice-blue eyes, so like her own, that she gasped. These bastards were her father's clan.

My clan.

Fear took a back seat to purpose. "Get me close," she yelled over the wind.

"Why?"

"If I can touch them, I can send them to your holding cells."

"No fucking way." Ladon did a maneuver akin to a sudden dip in a rollercoaster, up and then down fast. *"You were barely keeping your eyes open until five minutes ago."*

She hated admitting that he was right about that. And the thought of trapping anyone in that soundless, sightless in-between, even enemies, made her sick. "What's your plan then?"

He changed direction sharply, almost as though he hit ground midair and launched off it to go straight up. The two white dragons jerked out of Ladon's way as he shot upward, separating them. She didn't miss the fact that he hadn't answered her question but was smart enough to stay quiet.

At speeds that boggled her mind, Ladon continued to head straight up until even the warm clothes they'd bundled her up in and the fire warming her from underneath couldn't hold back the frigid cold, and the spots dancing in front of her eyes had nothing to do with Gs and everything to do with lack of air.

"Ladon," she gasped. "Can't breathe."

Even those few words had her chest heaving. Immediately, Ladon flipped and they plummeted back toward the earth in a controlled free fall. Only this time, she couldn't keep her vision from closing in. She didn't pass out, still vaguely aware of the screaming winds and Ladon's massive form beneath her.

As fast as they dropped, he suddenly flared his wings, slowing their downward progress rapidly in a way that flattened Skylar like a bug against the windshield of a Mack truck.

Finally, momentum stopped, and she blinked her sight back into being. "You're damn lucky I don't have a weak stomach," she grumbled.

Even so, she was sweating and trembling in a way that frustrated the hell out of her. Weakness had no place in this world.

"Sorry."

Urgency had her twisting in her seat, searching for those white dragons, fighting the very bindings that probably saved her from falling off her mate. "Why'd we stop? Where are they?"

Ladon was fast, but his up and down rodeo shouldn't have lost the dragons after them.

"Look down."

She did. "All I see is blue scales. Very pretty, but—"

That grunt sounded again, and he tipped, giving her a view of the ground and two white dragons pinned down by massive nets. Each time one moved, blue electricity shimmied over the filaments, forcing them to still. On either side of them, two blue dragons stood guard—one leaning almost toward purple in color, and the other so ice-blue as to be almost white.

"Who are they?"

"Ivar and Rainier."

A warmth settled in Skylar's gut as Ladon drifted to the ground, then waited for her to untie and scoot off his back before shifting. No way would her king show weakness by having his men follow him, which meant Ivar and Rainier were there to protect *her.* Her silly heart clenched at the realization.

To cover her concerning reaction, Skylar stoked some helpful irritation. Ladon was hardly done with the shimmering reforming of his body before she gave him a pointed stare. "Some warning might have been nice."

· · ·

Once again, Ladon had to stamp out the urge to laugh, because his mate was definitely the take-no-prisoners, never-back-down type, and he had to admit that side of her was an unexpected turn-on. Even after dropping a bomb on him like the giving up her immortality thing, those walls of hers still remained impenetrable. A challenge. "I'll make it up to you later."

Dark eyebrows winged high. "Sex is not going to fix everything, you know."

Except now an unmistakable heat melted those glacial eyes of hers, and everything inside Ladon tightened and hardened… and melted…in response.

Get your head where it should be. On the immediate danger.

Ladon turned to the two dragons still pinned by the electrical nets. "Shift. Now."

Despite a hiss of frustration from the more opaque of the two, both shifters shimmered briefly, their forms reducing in size, shrinking in on themselves, joints and bones realigning in a silent slide until two men in white military gear, likely designed for snowy climates, lay beneath the nets.

Ladon nodded, and Ivar and Rainier shifted in order to release their prisoners. Then they replaced the nets with shackles made of dragonsteel around their wrists, ankles, and necks. As soon as they finished, Ivar returned to dragon form, in case one of the prisoners did something. Not that either white dragon would be shifting any time soon. If they tried it, the dragonsteel restraints would cut deep, and the cuffs around their necks would decapitate them. They wouldn't try it.

"Who sent you?" Ladon demanded.

The two men recoiled then looked at each other and remained silent. The taller of the two pulled his lip back in a sneer.

"Volos, of course," Ladon surmised. "But Pytheios is pulling your king's strings. So, I have my answer to that. Are you only on recon?" A small contingency out to determine what information they could glean? Or were these men part of a larger army on the attack?

"We answer only to our king," tall guy insisted.

"Oh?" Skylar tipped her head. "What about your rightful queen?"

Ladon slowly turned to find her glaring at the two men with a disgust she didn't bother to conceal.

"We have no queen. Volos is not mated." The white dragon shifter's voice indicated he thought her dim-witted not to know that.

Skylar raised a single eyebrow, reflecting the dimwit opinion right back at him a hundredfold. "Wrong. My father was your king and my mother your queen until Pytheios murdered them both and put his lackey on the White Throne."

She moved forward and placed a hand on each man's shoulder. To what end? To gain their confidence? To show she carried no fear of them?

Despite an immediate need to yank her back, away from possible harm, he knew his mate would not appreciate his interference. Muscles tight from the effort, Ladon held back.

This should be interesting. Ladon folded his arms and sat back to watch Skylar go to work on these two fuckers.

"Lies," the tall one hissed.

Her lips tipped up in a chilly smile that made even Ladon shiver. "You think so?"

Skylar lit her fire, loose tendrils of her hair lifting around her face in the flames. She drew herself to her full height. "I am Skylar Amon, daughter of Zilant Amon and Serefina Hanyu, rightful heir to both the Red and the White Thrones."

Both men trembled, eyes wide and focused on her. "This can't be." Tall guy was losing his confidence by the second, almost visibly shrinking. "Serefina Hanyu died with Zilant. No phoenix has existed since."

"Lies," Skylar spat. "Fed to you by the false High King, Pytheios."

She crossed to Ladon's side and held out her hand, which he took without hesitation. "I am a phoenix, and mated to Ladon Ormarr, King of the Blue Clan. Bow down now, declare your allegiance, and I'll allow you to serve me instead of executing you where you stand."

Not exactly on the list of what queens got to do in their society, but Ladon rolled with it. He'd back her up if they called her on it. If anything, her display of power only had him harder, eager to claim that body as his all over again. Put that lush mouth to work on his cock. Maybe while she was on fire, warming him both inside and out.

He adjusted his stance.

"How do we know this isn't a trick? Maybe you're a witch."

Skylar let her fire die as she lifted her gaze to the skies, appearing almost bored. "I don't really care. Choose. Die or serve."

The two men hesitated, mistrust and distaste clear in their flat lips and narrowed eyes.

Skylar pretended to check a watch she wasn't wearing then looked to Ladon, who nodded to Ivar. The bright blue dragon slithered forward in a river of motion.

"Wait!" taller of the two called out.

Ladon held up one hand. This would be the only stay of execution they'd get from him.

The two men exchanged another glance, then, together, fell to their knees before Skylar. "My queen," tall guy said, his compatriot parroting him in a hushed tone.

Skylar smiled. "For your faith, I will show you."

She turned to Ladon, giving him a significant look he shouldn't be able to interpret, and yet he instinctively knew what she wanted. "You sure?" he asked, voice low, just for her.

In answer, she turned her back to him, lifting her braid, showing the still-blank skin at the back of her neck. *His* brand would show there one day.

"Do it."

Entranced by that unmarked swath of skin, Ladon leaned forward to place a kiss right where his mark would go, not missing her shiver, holding in a satisfied grunt. Then he built the fire inside him and, with his mouth puckered, blew a concentrated stream across her neck, controlling the flames to keep from burning her.

As had happened when they mated, Skylar's skin started to glow and that feathered design appeared over any skin exposed by her tank top, flaming wings lifting around her. Unlike the first time, though, this time Skylar's markings glowed blue.

My color.

Damned if that didn't push his already hard body into

overdrive. Ladon fisted his hands to keep from wrapping them in her braid, yanking down her pants, and plunging into her. He could just hear the names she'd scream at him if he did, and a secret smile unfurled inside him at the knowledge that they'd soon be where he could, taking the worst of the edge off his need.

"We are yours to command, my queen."

Tall guy's voice pulled Ladon's attention away to find both men watching her with a fascination in their eyes nothing short of awe. And this time, their loyalty was no longer in question, conviction in every word.

"I want you to go back to your people," Skylar said.

What? Release them to let these men attack them again?

She turned to face him. "Trust me," she whispered.

Had she heard his thoughts? Mates could do that, but her voice hadn't sounded in his head yet. Regardless, Ladon waved her on.

"Go back to your false king and pretend as though nothing has changed. Report to me any and all plans the White Clan has against my king. Understood?"

"Yes, my queen," both men answered.

Again, she looked to Ladon, who nodded at his men. Their prisoners' restraints were removed, and both men shifted and flew into the skies. At the same time, Ladon dismissed Ivar, who returned to dragon form, and Rainier, and both sped in the opposite direction, heading back to Ben Nevis and leaving him alone with his mate.

"You don't know that they will stay true," Ladon murmured as they watched the dragons shrink then fade into the clouds and sky.

"Yes, I do," she said with zero doubt.

"How?"

Skylar shrugged, her gaze still on the skies. "Because I saw their faces when they saw my markings. They believe me. They'll remain loyal."

In the space of less than an hour, he'd seen all her sides— vulnerable and open, cunning and fearless, and always, arresting.

Unable to stop himself, Ladon stepped in to her, pressing

his body along hers. "Sexiest damn thing I've ever seen. You all commanding, and brilliant, and calling me your king."

"Oh?" Her lips tipped up, a siren's call, and his dick pressed against the zipper of his pants.

"I want you." Those three words came out more growl than voice.

CHAPTER FIFTEEN

S he should definitely not allow herself to be turned on by his words, or the way he was watching her with raw need, that edge to his voice that told her he was on the verge of out of control.

He nuzzled into her neck, inhaling her scent. An even bigger turn-on. "Tell me you want me."

Skylar tipped her head back, giving him more access. "Gods, you have the worst timing."

As far as she could figure, they were in the middle of the flat, lush farmlands of Denmark, far from the men who were waiting for them at the southern tip of Norway. The farthest a dragon could fly was two hundred miles, and many needed a short rest after less. The trip to Norway was beyond those ranges if they took a direct route across the water, so they'd had to take the long way around, down through England, across to the Netherlands, and now back up through Denmark.

"Tell me," he demanded. He lifted his head, pinning her with eyes lit by blue fire.

Damn her weakened state, or she would've simply teleported him. Maybe by tomorrow morning. But at this moment, she and Ladon were alone and undefended. Not a good time to be distracted. That's what the angel on her shoulder was saying. The little demon on the other shoulder, however, was thinking all sorts of naughty thoughts and reminding Skylar that she could lose

Ladon in what was coming.

A reality slowly creeping up on her. One that scared her more than she could ever have thought possible.

And I thought I'd just walk away from him when this was over.

"We have to stop for the night anyway, right?" she asked, trying to change the subject. Damn that little demon. Along with the man standing in front of her who managed to have this much of a pull on her.

His lips tipped in a smile almost cruel, the long scar down one side giving him a wicked edge, and she'd bet he knew what she was up to. She didn't want to answer that question, to give him that power over her. True or not.

Ladon dipped his head to give her a direct look. "You can be honest with everyone but yourself. Is that it?"

Skylar crossed her arms to keep from reaching out to him. "Just the opposite, actually."

He dropped his head until his lips hovered over hers. All she had to do was sway… "I'm your mate," he murmured. "It's right that you should want me, that your body needs my possession."

Possession? No way in hell, even if heat flushed through her at the word. She leaned away and tipped up her chin. "My mind made the decision without my heart involved."

Lies.

Words that had his mouth flattening, even as he raised unimpressed eyebrows. "My head and heart and body are having the same conversation. You're mouthy, headstrong, and independent to a fault."

Ouch. "In other words, with all four of us standing before you, you wouldn't have picked me for your queen?"

His face settled into the harsh lines she recognized from when she'd been watching while hidden in his mountain, that twitch kicking up. "Actually, I sort of love that about you," he said bluntly. "But it doesn't make you easy."

Skylar had to breathe through her nose several times to loosen lungs that had suddenly gone tight. "Oh." With no clue how to respond to that, she glommed onto the second part. "If you wanted easy, you shouldn't have mated me."

"I'd say the same thing to you." He cocked his head, still so close his body heat and his scent surrounded her. "Then again, you thought I was going to die in the process."

Skylar hid a grimace. "I knew I shouldn't have shared that with you."

Eyes still ablaze searched hers. "I'd rather we be honest. Wouldn't you?"

Maybe there was such a thing as too honest.

"Yes," she grudgingly agreed. "If we aren't, we'll be stepping on each other's dicks every five minutes."

Ladon dropped his forehead to hers, and she couldn't make herself pull away. "Not an image I want in my head ever again. I like you dick-free, unless it's my dick involved."

"It was a metaphor—"

"I got that." He pressed a short, sweet kiss to her lips that addled her brain and scrambled all her lady parts. She inhaled sharply, although by the time her reaction shot through her, he'd already lifted his head and stepped back. "I want you. You need to figure out what *you* want. And you're right, the time and the place suck. So, I'll wait."

Skylar remained frozen where she was, body still buzzing from that brief contact. "You'll wait," she repeated. "For what?"

"When you can tell me you want me, too."

He turned and walked away, leaving her staring after him. It hardly registered that he was shifting, until the mirage-like waves grew with his size. She blinked at the magnificent indigo creature in front of her, all power and destruction. The scar down his face was more obvious in this form. It looked as though he'd caught a tail spike in a fight. Maybe with some dragon fire to sear him from the inside. She'd mated a badass.

"Don't you think I've already shown that?"

The dragon gave a warning rumble that should've had her backing up, but instead drew her closer.

"I want to be inside you so bad I ache," Ladon's voice scraped against her. *"I want to explore and claim every inch of your body. I want to fill you up with my seed and see your belly grow with my heirs. I want you to trust me and work beside me as an equal partner."*

Holy hellfire. Even as her heart squeezed tight at everything he said, fear froze her in place at his words, every part of her paralyzed.

"I want you, Skylar."

Part of her leaned into that declaration, wanted to believe. A pang of hope rang through her, true and deep.

She closed her eyes and wondered, just for a moment, if she could go down this path he wanted her to take.

Except... Despite the trust that had grown faster than she'd ever thought possible, she couldn't see beyond the ultimate goal of taking down Pytheios so that she and her sisters could be safe. Until that happened, she couldn't be sure every decision she made wasn't made only to further that end. Including admitting she wanted him back in the way he'd described.

He deserved more. So did she.

She needed to be sure.

Skylar swallowed, then shook her head. "I can't give you that, yet."

From the way his scales rippled with the muscles underneath, she could tell how Ladon took her words. He blinked at her for a long moment, then lowered his belly to the ground. *"We'd better get going."* His voice had flattened out. *"I'd like to fly through the night. Staying in one place isn't safe."*

While irritation was a familiar sensation in Skylar's life, having that combined with sexual frustration, along with an emotional quagmire she wasn't willing to acknowledge, was new.

This sucks hairy balls.

Except that unfortunate choice of phrases, even if just in her head, got her thinking about sucking certain things, and that only upped her frustration levels. Holding back her own growl, she deliberately tried to arrange her expression to one of indifference, thrown even more off-center by Ladon's suddenly distant, business-only demeanor. In silence, she climbed up on his back and strapped back in. Exhaustion still lined her limbs with lead and dragged at her steps. Better safe than sorry.

They didn't speak again as they flew toward Norway, other than quick comments about the trip in between Skylar's catnaps.

"Several of my personal guard will be joining us."

Skylar blinked out of a half sleep at Ladon's words and readjusted her fur-lined coat for the umpteenth time. Her ass might be warm, but her face was not.

A glance around didn't tell her much about how far they'd come.

Minutes later, a group of five dragons suddenly appeared around them—above, below, behind, and to either side. Despite being on her guard, she hadn't seen them coming.

Having always wished she could join a precision flying group, like the Blue Angels, but held back by the restrictions of her life, Skylar watched in fascination at how the dragons flew together. Close enough that wings almost brushed. If she undid her ropes and stood on Ladon's back, she could touch the navy underbelly of the dragon overhead with the tips of her fingers. Asher at a guess, given how dark his scales were, except that most of them were dark in the moonless sky.

Almost as one mind, the shifters rode the currents. Over a fathomless void of water, they tipped their wings in a uniform move, like watching a flock of birds, to turn north and east toward where the rest of their forces awaited.

After drifting off several more times, Skylar jerked awake as Ladon angled downward in a steep drop, the dragons around them working as a unit. She could still discern only water below them but had to trust that their heightened sight allowed them to know where they were going. While the frigid temperatures of the Norwegian air warmed slightly as they descended, she clenched her teeth to keep them from chattering as the wind pierced her skin even through her thick jacket, all the way to the bone, making her muscles clench and ache.

She kept quiet.

None of the dragons had made a sound, likely communicating telepathically, but also to conceal their location from any enemies lurking in the shadows. They'd dive like this only if they were about to land, so she held her tongue and waited.

Sure enough, the darkness still impenetrable to her eyes, Ladon reared back, flaring his wings wide and bringing an abrupt deceleration. He beat his wings twice more, seeming to hover in the air, before rocking as he touched down.

Out of the inky black, figures emerged. *I hope those are our people.*

Immediately, Skylar uncoiled herself from the ropes with fumbling frozen fingers that didn't want to do the work for her. She climbed down, arms wrapped about herself as she waited for Ladon to shift. Then she followed behind him on stiff legs.

"Káthor." Each man nodded, respect reflecting in their eyes. No doubts about their king whatsoever, despite his absence at a crucial time.

Finally, they made their way to where Asher waited with Duncan and Wyot beside him. No doubt Reid and Arden were close by as well. Exhaustion had her tuning out Ladon's gravelly voice as he talked to his men in low rumbling tones. She was too damn freezing and tired to care what was being discussed or the fact that he wasn't including her.

I'll ask him later. When every part of her, including her mind, thawed enough to function properly.

Turning back to her, apparently done, Ladon approached. "We're staying in a system of caves hidden within these coastal rocks. Brand's father brought him here as a child. My men have already determined they are abandoned. I'll have to fly you there."

Dammit. "Let's go."

A quick shift from her mate and she was back up between those damn spikes. Centuries of fleeing during the night meant these weren't the most unpleasant conditions she'd experienced before. That didn't make it suck any less.

In seconds, Ladon flew out over what she guessed was the water, then, following another dragon whose tail she could barely make out ahead of them, they went straight at a wall of cliff only to tip sideways at the last minute, entering a narrow, tall cavern only barely big enough to accommodate a dragon of Brand's size. If that. Could Brand even get in here?

After a few seconds, Ladon leveled out, then flared his wings. Again, he rocked as he landed, and she climbed down.

After shifting back to human, he approached. Asher, who must've led them down, turned on two flashlights, handing one to his king. "This way," he said.

Ladon took her by the hand, coming into contact with the skin between her glove and jacket sleeve, and immediately jerked to a halt with a hiss. "You're fucking freezing."

Still clenching her teeth against the chatter, her jaw aching with the effort, Skylar glared at him. "No shit."

"Why didn't you say?"

"Could you have done more than you were?"

"I could've flown lower," he pointed out, his thick brows practically meeting in the middle with his glower.

Skylar shook her head. "We're safer up high. Even I know that. And it wouldn't have made much of a difference."

"So, you risked hypothermia instead?"

"I'm f-f-f-fine."

She moved past him to Asher, who'd waited in silence, only to be jerked around by a rough hand on her arm.

"There's stubborn, and then there's downright foolish," Ladon said in a clipped tone.

His eyes, glittering with blue fire, cast his face in an otherworldly glow in the darkness of the cavern. Only this time, the flames were caused by anger, not lust.

Normally she'd pop off at him about now. But somehow his anger, which deep down she could tell came from a sort of caring, slowed her own.

Skylar stepped closer, though she didn't touch him. "If I thought you could do anything, or I could do anything, I would've spoken up," she said. "This wasn't about me being stubborn, but practical."

His jaw worked for a moment as he absorbed her words, then he gave a jerky nod. "I'd still rather know."

She blew out a long breath. "Why?"

"Would you have told your mother? Or your sisters?" he asked, softer now.

Skylar scrunched up her nose. "I hate it when you have a legitimate point."

Flat lips twitched, but he held his hard stare.

"Fine," she acceded, though her words held no ire. "Brutal honesty in the form of constant communication. But expect it to take some practice. Got it?"

"Not too much practice. We don't have time."

Asher led them to a single room crudely dug into the rock, round opening and with no door leading out into the cavern, it sported a single mattress on the floor with...

"Blankets!" Skylar couldn't hold back the exclamation.

Asher glanced down when she cast a questioning glance in his direction. "We felt you and your sister would be more comfortable. Kasia's said that your fire isn't as hot as ours and doesn't keep you quite as warm."

True. But she wouldn't have expected a bunch of dragon shifters to think of that. "Thank you," she murmured softly. "Maybe I need to take back the Grumpy nickname."

She received a slow nod in return. "Maybe so."

Asher melted into the darkness, his flashlight showing his progress farther into the system of caves until the light blinked out, leaving her alone with her mate.

He waved a hand at their bed and, with a mental shrug, she climbed in. A rustle of sound behind her and the flashlight turned off, plunging them into oppressive darkness. "Thank the gods I didn't mate a bat shifter is all I can say," Skylar said.

His low voice feathered over her skin. "Don't like the dark?"

"Not like this."

Another rustle and the mattress moved as Ladon joined her. "Let's warm you up," he rumbled behind her.

She gasped as a big arm circled her waist, pulling her in tight against him. No missing the thick, hard rod of his erection, only he didn't touch her with anything other than the need to help her stop shivering.

Despite the instant tension inside her, the need to turn in his arms and fuck him to warm herself up with more than a platonic touch—a need she forced herself to ignore—she still relaxed against him as his warmth penetrated her clothing and seeped into her body.

Kasia was right that her own fire only did so much, at least when she wasn't using it. She could've warmed herself by lighting that fire but using it while on the back of a dragon, especially at night, would've been like a beacon to every creature hunting them. Which meant not an option.

After a moment, she sighed, closing her eyes, ready to let sleep that had been dragging at her finally take her into a peaceful oblivion.

Except Ladon tightened his grip, pulling her even closer into him, his lips at her ear. "I can smell your need," he whispered.

Skylar's eyes shot open, and her heart took off like she'd been running a sprint.

Ladon chuckled, and she mentally damned his senses to the darkest realms of hell.

"Sleep," he whispered, then seemed to relax into her, supposedly doing just that.

...

Ladon watched Skylar as she talked quietly with Kasia. Their forces had settled into the dilapidated caverns that clearly hadn't seen use in centuries, the secret of their existence temporarily dying with Brand's father. They'd had to go the old-fashioned way and use torches and fires to light the space sufficiently as they hadn't brought enough flashlights. Hopefully they wouldn't be here long.

His warriors had been here a day before his arrival, and they'd remained here for two days. Not hiding, but not entirely in plain sight, either. A deliberate move to draw out their enemy who was hopefully wondering where they were.

Skylar glanced up and caught his stare. Did she blush? Or smile? Or any other normal response for a mate? Nope.

Sky scowled at him. "Quit that," she mouthed, swatting her hand indicating he should stop his staring and turn away.

He crossed his arms and held her gaze.

Quiet contentment lined with something else that clenched in his gut settled over him every time he looked at his mate. A fact that should have him scared witless or pissed at himself for the weakness. She was supposed to strengthen him, not make him more vulnerable, dammit. For better, worse, or indifferent, Skylar Amon was his mate, chosen by the fates themselves.

He hadn't expected to feel anything other than a mild annoyance at being shackled when he mated. Perhaps this wasn't the adoration that he sometimes caught Brand and Kasia basking in. Yet. And maybe that wouldn't come with the same intensity they showed. But he knew, through and through, that in this woman he'd found a mirror of himself.

Dedicated, determined, obstinate, self-sacrificing. A crusader.

Not afraid to get her hands bloody if it saved the people she fought for. Add in a physical need the likes of which he'd never experienced before, and here he was.

Fucked.

Because the damn woman seemed determined to ignore instinct, fate, and need. She was going to leave him when this was over and Pytheios gone. He'd never been more sure of anything.

And he had not one bloody clue how to fix it.

Hell, he couldn't even get her to admit to wanting him. Two nights in a row he'd touched her, bringing them both to an aching precipice, then denied tumbling them over. Waiting for her submission. And two nights she'd refused to admit it, despite how her body chased his touch, leaving them both in an agony of deprived desire.

He wasn't asking for love, just an acknowledgment that there was more between them than sex or politics.

Appealing to her body, which was clearly on board, wasn't working.

Now, as he watched her studiously ignore him, it galled him to admit he needed advice. "How did you win Kasia?" he asked the man standing at his side.

Brand turned those hard gold eyes his way, eyebrows raised. "Problems with your mate?"

He'd known this man since they were boys. Known each other as young men. And Brand had been working for him in secret for decades. Still, the guy owed him his life. "I could've let you fend for yourself," Ladon grumbled.

Brand grunted, his only acknowledgment. "You don't want advice from me," he said after a lingering silence.

"But you won Kasia." Seemed obvious. Ladon hadn't even seen it coming, in the middle of wooing the red-haired phoenix himself.

"I came this close to fucking it up." Brand held up a finger and thumb with no space between them. "First, I tried to give her to another man. You."

Ladon huffed a dry chuckle. "I hadn't thought of that, but yeah. Dick move."

Brand hitched a shoulder. "But the real dick move was not telling Kasia about who I was, the heir to the Gold Throne, before we mated. She found out from a vision and decided I'd tricked her into mating to get my clan back."

Ladon gave a low whistle. "How'd you fix that?" he asked, though he suspected he already knew.

"I almost gave my life to protect her, letting Uther go when I could've killed him."

Total self-sacrifice, though Brand had still killed the gold king in the end. *Except I'm already a king. I have people depending on me.* Besides, he and Sky weren't Brand and Kasia. "Guess I'll figure out my own way," he muttered.

Brand snorted a laugh. "Good luck with that. You landed the wild one."

A low growl cut through the still morning air, one Ladon couldn't have controlled even if he wanted to, and loud enough that Sky and Kasia looked up from across the room.

"What's wrong?" Sky mouthed at him.

He shook his head at her and, with a quick frown, she turned back to Kasia.

"Like that already?" The amusement in Brand's voice only added to Ladon's irritation, like talons on a chalkboard.

"She's my mate. No one gets to call her wild except me. Not even Skylar."

That sentiment didn't faze his friend. "Won't happen again."

"Good."

"My king." Reid approached, stopping to give a quick dip of his head, the closest the captain of his guard came to a bow, since Ladon didn't allow his guard to bow to him. They were his friends and had supported his coup long before he'd become the leader of their clan.

"Yes?"

"We've gathered those you asked for."

Tension immediately strung tight through him, like animal skin being stretched over a drum. He glanced at Brand. "You ready for this?"

Brand's eyes glittered gold in his scowling face. No doubt Ladon's own eyes had set to glowing blue. The risk was worth it. Without allies he was fucked. They needed Brand on the throne.

One move.

One move to assure himself of an ally with a clan behind him.

CHAPTER SIXTEEN

Brock stood in front of a wall of screens in a dark room that served as the main communications center within the mountain. On the center screen, Pytheios's sickening visage took up most of the view. The king swallowed in a reflexive action that reminded Brock of Komodo dragons.

After I take care of this gold usurper, it's time to take out our High King.

No creature decaying like Pytheios deserved to rule anything. His skin was falling off his bones, thin enough that it might tear at any second. He had to be half blind with those milky eyes. Hell, even the insignias on his hand and the back of his neck were faded.

How did they know if he had the full use of his faculties?

"You mean to tell me, you lost an entire army of dragon shifters?" Pytheios snarled, his jowls shaking with anger.

Satisfaction thrummed through Brock, and he held onto a smug smile with effort, remaining serious. "Yes and no, my lord."

Pytheios's eyes lit red with flames, eerie in the sunken sockets of his eyes, and he stared back, saying nothing.

"Explain," a voice barked, and another face thrust forward in the view.

A young face, the man tall and broad with dark hair and the strange reddish-brown eyes of his kind. Brock could see little else, except the top of what he knew to be an expensive, custom-made suit. Obviously Merikh.

"My son asked you a question," Pytheios said quietly. "Explain."

The fact that Pytheios had a son had been a surprise when they'd come to the mountain, but not one that bothered him any. Like Brock, the Rotting King of the Red Clan must've taken a woman showing dragon sign and used her body for an heir. Except he'd obviously turned that heir into a pampered brat, scratching for scraps of respect at daddy's heels.

"One of our spies contacted me, detailing their plan." Brock studiously avoided looking at his unmarked hand.

Pytheios shook his head. "That feels too easy."

A rhythmic clicking sound that Brock had assumed to be static suddenly ceased and a man stepped forward into view. Tall and lanky, he had the appearance of a much younger, less decrepit Pytheios. Only a vague similarity to his brother told Brock who this was.

As far as Brock knew, very few people were privileged enough to see Pytheios's brother, Nathair, in person. The man, though described as idiosyncratic by rumor, certainly fit the image Brock had in his head. Rumor also held that Nathair was beyond brilliant.

Nathair did not face the screen or address Brock in any way. Instead he whispered in his brother's ear, and Pytheios slowly smiled. Even Brock couldn't hold off the shiver of dread skating over his nerves.

"What is the plan your spy unveiled?" Pytheios asked.

Brock pulled his shoulders back, aware of an undercurrent of doubt from the red king. "They plan to hold their army where they are hiding, and Brand will come here with his mate to try to convince the people to follow him."

Pytheios's eyes narrowed. "Why would he risk that?"

"Something about avoiding bloodshed." Stupidity. Astarot would never take this throne without sacrifices. "My forces are depleted after the battle for Ben Nevis, and he holds many more of my warriors in the blue traitor king's dungeons."

"He has to know you have an alliance with the Green Clan."

Brock clasped his hands behind his back. "He's under the impression that, after losing Ben Nevis, King Fraener pulled his support and returned to China."

"And he doesn't know about Volos and the White Clan?"

"Not as far as we know." Brock allowed himself that smug smile now. "However, he has pulled most of Ladon Ormarr's warriors away from the mountain to bring them here in case his bid for a peaceful takeover fails."

Pytheios steepled his fingers, milky red gaze going distant. "They'll be waiting for the attack. If you can't find them, it means they are holed up somewhere. They've had days to prepare."

"Which is why we won't attack those forces." Brock didn't wait for Pytheios to react. "Instead, we will skirt them and go to Ben Nevis, which they've left vulnerable, and secure the rest of my warriors."

"They *will* attack at that point."

"But they'll be too far behind. When they get there, we'll be gone, back here to our mountain. Hopefully, Astarot will be arrogant enough to stay. We'll take that false king and his mate and destroy them."

Pytheios pinned Brock with a look of command that he felt even through the screen and thousands of miles between them. "You'll bring them to me."

Brock frowned. "She is useless to you. Her neck bears his brand. We know the rumors of her being a phoenix are lies, which makes her, at most, a human who successfully mated, or, even less important, a female-born dragon shifter."

"Nevertheless."

An undoubted order. But also an opportunity to get close to the High King and take him off the chessboard, permanently. "As you wish, but..." Brock paused.

"Yes?" Pytheios demanded, impatience making the word cut off.

"I've heard rumor of another phoenix, my King."

"Ormarr is—"

"This one is in the colonies. With a band of rogues, from what I understand."

Pytheios stilled, eyes narrowed, except Brock got an odd impression that he'd been expecting this. "A third? What are the odds?"

Had Pytheios not known? Or was he being played? "With your permission, after this is over, I will go myself and bring her back."

"No," Pytheios said. "I'll go."

. . .

"If you look at your mate one more time," Asher grumbled, "I'm going to have to assume she's got you brainwashed, which makes her a goddamn witch."

Ladon slowly returned his gaze to his guard to pin his Beta with a hard glare for his words about Skylar. "Is that how you address your king?"

Not that his Beta was wrong. Keeping an eye on Skylar as she said goodbye to Kasia shouldn't take much, if any, of his focus. In minutes, Brand, Kasia, and a small contingency of hand-selected guards would travel to the gold mountain of Store Skagastølstind. Alone.

As far as their spies could tell, the Gold Clan had remained quiet, which hopefully meant their ploy had worked. Had Brock taken the bait?

Skylar and Kasia stood now, quiet, foreheads pressed together in that way they had. The closest to fear he'd seen his mate show reflected in the way she closed her eyes and took a deep breath.

"Seriously, Ash. You trying to get your ass handed to you?" Reid half muttered at Asher.

"You don't mess with mates, brother," Duncan added. "Am I right?" He looked to Wyot, who gave his usual noncommittal grunt.

Asher ignored them all. "Your warriors can see you. So can King Gorgon and his people."

"And?" Ladon asked, deadly quiet.

"And you look like a puppy dog, scrambling at her feet. I'm saying she could be a liability." Asher set his stance, staring Ladon down in a way that he usually respected. The fact that Asher wasn't cowed by his position or his reputation was exactly why Ladon had made the man his Beta.

This, however, was not one of the moments that made him appreciate that. "Your concern is noted."

Asher got the hint. Ladon was done with this conversation.

"You need to focus on your own ass right now," Ladon pointed out. "I don't have time to get a new Beta if this goes tits up."

Asher lifted a single eyebrow. "You definitely can't pick from your guard. That lot is useless."

"I resemble that remark," Reid joked before frowning at something over Ladon's shoulder.

Ladon glanced behind him to find Arden standing there, dressed not in her usual flashy active wear, but in a crisp black pantsuit and towering stilettos in the same blue-green as her eyes.

"What are you all dressed up for?" Reid demanded from behind him before Ladon could ask. The man slipped his butterfly knife into his boot where he hid it.

"I'm going with Kasia," Arden said.

Immediate rejection slammed through Ladon at her words. He wouldn't put Arden in that kind of peril.

"The fuck you are," Reid snapped, beating him to it. The captain of his guard stepped forward, suddenly all bristling, pissed shifter.

Arden narrowed her eyes but otherwise ignored Reid, facing Ladon instead. "I know Reid is going as a show of your support, and Samael is going as the representative for Gorgon."

The two captains of their king's guard going in the place of Ladon and Gorgon had been Brand's choice. He wanted there to be no doubt as to which king was coming for that throne.

A glance at Reid showed a man almost vibrating with the violence of his emotions, and Ladon hid a frown. Was there something there he hadn't realized before?

His sister tipped up her chin. "I would like to go as well."

Reid snarled, echoing Ladon's dragon, though he held in his own. "Why?"

"Our clan has a bigger stake in this, in Brand, than the Black Clan does. Especially with Kasia and Skylar in the mix. Having both your captain and your sister there will demonstrate that."

She had a point. One he hated to acknowledge.

"Plus, women need a voice in this world, and I'm going to be it this time around."

Ladon blinked at her words. "You don't think I give you a voice?"

Arden snorted. "You don't get to *give* me anything when it comes to having a voice. Either I have one or I don't. I plan to have one. A large percentage of your people aren't being represented, so I will be that for them."

Had he been guilty of ignoring the female portion of his clan? So few dragons were born female, and dragon mates were all human to start, not born into this world. Those circumstances naturally led to a male-driven society.

"Kasia is a woman," he pointed out.

"Kasia is a *phoenix*," Arden came back. If they would have been alone, he'd bet she'd give him one of her pats—the ones he thought of as "poor, oblivious male" pats.

He hated those damn pats.

Still, his sister had made good points. "Granted."

Reid jerked forward. "No. You can't—"

"It's done," Ladon said quietly.

His sister's smile alone told him he'd done the right thing, not that it made the concern for her churning in his gut like curdled milk any easier to stomach.

With a triumphant grin directed at Reid, she sashayed over to where Samael and Brand stood, waiting for Kasia and Skylar to say their goodbyes. Except Reid stalked after her, grabbed her by the arm, and dragged her into another smaller cavern.

Good. Maybe Reid could convince her to stay.

Ladon joined his mate, who stepped back from her sister. He struggled to keep his hands to himself, instinct tugging at him to wrap her up. Maybe Asher was right and he needed to present a different image when they were in public together.

Instead, he reached out to Brand to shake, pulling the man who'd been more like a brother to him over the years in to slap his back. "Don't fuck this up."

Brand's grin had a dark edge to it. "We're going to have a little talk with my clan's leaders. That's all. You're the one on the line here."

Enough to get either or both of them killed. "Stay safe... brother."

Brand sobered, gold eyes turning almost amber, glittering with his inner fire. "You, too."

Arden stepped up to the group, a thunderous Reid following behind. Apparently, an unsuccessful Reid, but then, Arden had always had a mind of her own.

"Ready?" Skylar asked. She would send them to a spot Brand remembered from his youth. A place they could hide before confronting Brock's Curia Regis early tomorrow.

The small band grouped together, hands on shoulders or grasping one another's wrists.

"Keep each other safe," Skylar said, mostly to Kasia, but Ladon could tell her message was to Brand and Arden, as well.

Based on the way Brand's head snapped back, he could tell, too. After a second, the big shifter gave a sharp nod.

Skylar held out her hands and flames—were they more blue today?—flowed up her arms and over her body like a rising tide. "On three," she said.

"Wait," Reid said.

Before anyone could react, he stepped in to Arden, practically pushing Samael out of the way, and took her face in his hands, claiming her lips in a hard, fast kiss. "That's why the fuck not," he snapped, then faced forward, ready to go, leaving Arden visibly dazed.

Skylar glanced at Ladon with huge eyes, but he just shrugged. Fuck if he was going to get in the middle of whatever that was. Reid could damn well come to him. Arden too, for that matter.

"Ok-ay... Let's try this again." Skylar faced her sister, her palms up. "Three... Two... One."

With a hard shove, the group soundlessly disappeared from sight. Not even a breeze stirred from their departure, as though they'd never been standing before him in the first place.

With a sharp look at Skylar, Asher stalked away. Duncan and Wyot had already taken themselves off to be with the men, in the event that Kasia returned with bad news.

"Now we wait—" Ladon turned to face his mate and froze at the sight that greeted him.

One of his warriors, one of the many men who'd supported his rebellion and his reign, had Skylar wrapped in a chokehold, a knife at her throat.

Based on her expression—blue eyes flared, her skin tight over those high cheekbones, mouth a white slash—Skylar was about as pissed as he'd ever seen her.

"You don't want to do this." Ladon kept his voice low and even, his word aimed at his impetuous mate as much as the man threatening her.

The blade in the man's hand glinted wickedly in the dim light of the torches inside these caves. A dangerously sharp blade—a trickle of blood already snaked down the side of Skylar's throat.

"If I kill her now, you won't die," the man said. "She doesn't bear your mark yet; the mating hasn't solidified. You'll be safe."

No. Ladon's dragon raged to roaring life inside him. Even the idea of losing her now had every part of him screaming. "She's important to my cause."

The warrior pulled his lips back in a sneer. "She's not really a phoenix. We've all heard the rumors. She's not a real phoenix. If she was, we wouldn't be here risking our lives. You'd be High King. You've been played falsely. The real phoenix is in the colonies."

Old information and the power of rumors. Or was more being

said than Ladon knew of?

Skylar rolled her eyes. Of course the woman wouldn't have a normal reaction of fear.

Ladon locked his gaze on the man's eyes, trying to get through to him. "She's important to *me*."

Skylar's lashes flickered at that. An emotion that might have been regret pinched her lips and darkened her eyes.

"Shut up." The blade dug deeper, more blood oozing from the cut.

Any emotion in her eyes died, and she held both her hands where the man couldn't see, and red fire edged in sparkling blue washed over her palms. Any second, she'd start glowing.

Ladon gave an imperceptible nod that he understood what she was about to do but kept talking as a distraction. "You know I'll kill you if you harm my mate."

"You mated her to help our clan. Where the hell is that help? You've been too blinded by lust to see her lies."

More of Skylar's fire spread over her, though, somehow, she was keeping it from any part that might show to the man holding her so tightly. He'd notice the added light in the room any minute, though.

"She's the mate I *choose*," Ladon said. "As your king, I command you to respect my decision. Release her. I won't warn you again."

"If I die, I die for the cause. For *your* cause. Even if you've lost sight of it."

Damn. Ladon couldn't afford to spare a man, but he had no choice now.

Shoulders dropping, he centered his will. "Now," he said to Skylar.

With an impressive move that held her neck still, she shoved her hands behind her, and his warrior disappeared, the knife clattering to the ground at her feet. In an instant, the soldier reappeared directly in front of Ladon, blinking to find himself no longer holding his quarry.

At the same time, Ladon partially shifted, turning his hand into a deadly claw of talons. He slammed his hand through the man's ribcage and yanked out his heart, which continued to beat in his grasp for a few more thuds. The warm stickiness of blood dribbled down his hand, which he shifted back to human form. The body of his warrior dropped to the ground with a thump, blood pooling beneath him from the gaping wound in his chest cavity.

Ladon dropped the heart he still grasped, stepped over the dead man, and yanked Skylar into his arms.

"Gross," she protested. However, rather than pull away, she snuggled into his embrace. Just for a second, but still, something in his chest clenched at that small act.

He buried his face in her hair. "Dammit, woman. I could've lost you."

"Nah," she dismissed lightly. "You arrogant male dragons are always underestimating what others can do—women, wolf shifters, phoenixes. It doesn't matter. Your pride is your weakness."

Only Ladon was starting to suspect that Skylar was wrong. Asher, and now this warrior willing to give his life, had both said the same thing. For different reasons, Ladon had already wrestled with similar thoughts.

This phoenix, who was his mate, his queen, was quickly becoming his greatest weakness.

And he didn't give a fuck. Not so long as she was his.

CHAPTER SEVENTEEN

"I hate waiting," Skylar muttered into her pillow.

She lay on the lumpy, thin mattress that didn't seem to protect them from the uneven floor. Without the system of lighting like the one in Ben Nevis that allowed her to know when the sun had come up, she had no clue what time it was. Early morning, at best guess.

"Me too."

She jumped a bit at the rumbled answer behind her, then turned to look over her shoulder at her mate. "I thought you were asleep."

"I don't sleep much these days."

So that hadn't just been about getting ready for this attack? "You'll wear yourself into an early grave if you keep up that pace."

Ladon reached out and wrapped a lock of her hair, which she'd left loose last night, around his finger. "Now that I have a mate, I'm guaranteed more years. I'll be fine."

"There are no guarantees in this life, Tarzan. My mother and father didn't even get months. Their bond never solidified before Pytheios killed my father. Maybe ours won't, either."

Ladon regarded her with serious eyes that appeared almost black in the dim lighting. "What was your mother like?"

Skylar hadn't talked about her much. The pain was too close to the surface. Except he lay there, waiting for an answer, and some part of her knew that he truly wanted to know. What it was about her mate that made her want to share, she had no idea. Like her, he wasn't exactly soft.

"Powerful," she said. "More powerful than me or Kasia. She could teleport us to the ends of the earth with a single thought. No touching. No having to hop along. She saved our lives with that ability in the end."

Sending Kasia to Alaska with Maul, Angelika to Spain with Bleidd and his wolf shifters, and herself to Argentina and Rune Abaddon's merry band of misfit dragon shifters. She could only imagine where her mother had sent Meira.

"Impressive." He gave the curl he still held a tug. "I mean what was she like as a mother? As a person?"

As a person? Skylar rolled to face away from Ladon, wanting to tell him, but not where he could see her face. "Kind. Patient." She gave a little snort. "Gods, she had to be, given how different we all were."

"Who gave her the most trouble?"

The question made Skylar smirk. "Who do you think?"

He huffed what passed for a rusty chuckle. "Yeah. But I bet she didn't worry about protecting you as much as the others."

Memories and his faith in her abilities to handle herself snaked around her heart, squeezing hard. How had he known that? "I think she worried about Meira the most. Maybe Angelika. They're...sweeter. More easily hurt. And Meira can't stand blood."

"So, she's not a warrior like you?"

He thought of her as a warrior? Contentment, an emotion she had little to do with typically, spread through her with a warmth that left her with a happy little glow.

"No," she answered. "Though Mom insisted Meira learn how to defend herself. She can fight if she has to. Once computers were invented, she got into those like plugging into a socket. Meira's our family hacker. Angelika is a trained nurse. But what Meira can do with computers is pretty damn amazing. We never had to worry about how to falsify our paperwork or records, or where money was coming from once that technology became prevalent. Not that we needed much, the way we lived."

Off the grid. In small towns where a dollar went a lot further but was also harder to come by.

The pain she kept at bay most of the time rode in on the coattails of the memories Ladon had opened up with his questions. Enough sharing for one day. She wiggled to get more comfortable. "What about your parents?"

The sheets rustled as he shifted positions behind her. "Soul mates from the moment they met, if you asked them. My father, obviously, was the only child of one of the oldest families of our kind. He found my mother himself. She was Greek, born right before the Ottoman Empire captured Constantinople."

That explained his darker coloring and all the hair on his chest. Skylar smiled into her pillow. "That must make me older than you."

"My parents conceived quickly after their mating. I was born in the 1490s. You?"

"I got twenty years on you, mister. Guess you better start listening to your elder."

Ladon grunted at that, not that she expected him to agree. "My parents were a team. No decision was made by just one. Every act, every path they went down, was carefully weighed and agreed on."

Would her parents have done the same had Pytheios not been successful in his murderous spree? "Did you know your grandparents?" she asked.

"No."

"Me neither." Pytheios had seen to that, too.

Ladon shifted in the bed, though he kept hold of her. "My parents were secretly organizing other families to revolt when Thanatos killed them. Somehow, he found out. But rather than confront them, he held a celebration for the Samhain festival, inviting all our people to come. Uther, Brock's father, was there. So were the other kings, except Pytheios. He didn't bother."

Skylar frowned. "Gorgon was there?"

"Yes."

Dread came over her like a blanket of thorns. Skylar turned over to face her mate who lay on his back, hands behind his head, staring with unseeing eyes at the stalactites overhead illuminated by the faint light of a camping lantern. "What happened?"

Ladon shrugged, the sheet slipping lower. "In the middle of the festivities, they disappeared. I never saw them alive again. Before I took Thanatos's life, he told me—hell, *bragged*—that he'd chained them to walls deep within the mountain and had slit my mother's throat. She'd died a slow death, and my father died, a little at a time, with her."

Skylar closed her eyes against the pain bracketing his mouth and flaring blue fire in his eyes. "Gods above," she whispered.

She forced herself to look again, just in time to see his bitter smile. "The gods had nothing to do with that night. I found their ashes...eventually."

Skylar placed her hand over Ladon's heart, which beat steady and true beneath her palm. His loss, or at least the discovery of the truth, had to be as raw as her own mother's death.

"I'm sorry," she said quietly.

They lay there in silence, in perfect understanding. These horrendous acts had made them who they were and brought them here. That didn't lessen the pain any, though.

After a while, Skylar turned back to her side with a huff. "Why haven't we heard?"

"They're waiting for Brock's Curia Regis to gather," Ladon reminded her. "It may be hours yet."

"Yeah." Skylar sighed. "Waiting still blows."

A possessive hand snaked around her waist, pulling her up against her mate's chest. "There are...better ways we could spend this time."

His warm breath stirred the air at her ear, and she had to contain a shiver. He'd been doing this to her for three days. Touching her. Taunting her. "You really are power hungry, aren't you?"

"This has nothing to do with power and everything to do with honesty. I've said it. Hell, I've shown you more than I've shown anyone."

She knew he didn't mean sex, but the way he'd let her in. Even so, he ground his hips into her backside, making it impossible to deny the hard shaft of his erection pressing in to her.

"Why can't you admit it? Say you want me."

Every nerve in her body throbbed. *Tell him. Tell him. Tell him.* That's what her body was chanting.

"I just need three little words."

Five hundred years of running from them, fearing them, hating them...and then Ladon Ormarr. Gods she wanted to say it, give in to him. But when it came right down to it, she was just plain scared. The people she loved died or were in constant danger. And admitting wanting him was only the first step. He'd want more. So would she.

What if that admission solidified their bond? The risk to her family, the risk to his people. Right now one of them could die and not take the other.

Admit it. You don't want to kill him if you go, a small voice whispered.

"Why can't we just fuck and call it a day?" she gritted. Then she pressed against him, craving the contact. "I need the distraction."

"I'm a distraction now?" Only he didn't sound offended, more amused.

"We're sitting ducks with this plan. Kasia could die. I could die... You could die."

The hand teasing little feathered touches over her belly stilled. "You're afraid for me?"

Skylar scowled her frustration and didn't answer.

Ladon was quiet for a long moment, and Skylar wished she was facing him, so she could see his eyes, try to discern his thoughts.

Suddenly he moved. Skylar gasped as he flipped her to her back, settling between her legs before she could stop him, that hard shaft pressing in a spot guaranteed to drive her wild. "One distraction coming up. Tonight only."

About damn time, both body and mind screamed.

With agonizingly slow movements, Ladon worked her shorts down her legs, levering her up as needed until she was bare beneath him. Never once did he remove that bold gaze from hers, and damned if she wasn't wet, just from being the center of his focus in such a direct way. Days of craving built up, then denied, also had her blood pumping. And he had yet to truly touch her.

With her bared to him, he pushed his own boxers down, then positioned himself. He paused at her entrance, and Skylar couldn't hold back a whimper of need.

Please don't let him stop.

His smile held a sliver of amusement. "This one is to take the edge off. Next round, we'll take our time."

"Uh-huh." Not exactly a snappy comeback, but she was too focused on the end game to bother with snappy.

"No arguments? No demands?" he teased, slipping the tip in but stopping.

Damn insufferable man. Hooking her legs around him, she surprised him with a sudden move that flipped their dynamic, putting her on top. As luck would have it, he didn't pull out of her with the movement. Taking advantage of the leverage she now had, Skylar sank down over him, working him into her with fast, shallow strokes until she'd taken every inch of his throbbing cock.

"Fuck," he groaned. He grasped her by the hips in a hard grip and ground up into her. "You feel so good."

So did he. Skylar rocked her hips, dropping her head back to revel in the sensations bombarding her body. In seconds, with hardly a touch, she was already balanced on the precipice of an orgasm. He filled her, stretching her in the most delicious way.

She rocked her hips again, loving the sound of his groan. "What was that about a quick one to take the edge off?"

She was tempted to tease him, like he'd been teasing her for days, but her body needed release more than she needed to retaliate. Undulating her hips, grinding into him, she set a pace guaranteed to help her with her problem.

That hard, deep blue gaze trained on her did the rest, more of a turn-on than she'd ever be willing to admit. His hands, traveling with such possessiveness all over her, only added to the pleasure.

Even so, the speed with which her orgasm built shocked her. She'd hardly gotten started before that telltale tingle started at the base of her spine.

"Oh gods," she moaned. Her breathing hitched, panting out of her in sharp puffs as she tried to hold it back. Just a little longer.

"Skylar."

She couldn't deny the command in that dark voice, dropping her head to look him in the eye.

"Come now." Using that bruising grip on her hips, he slammed up into her.

Her traitorous body listened, tumbling into that sweet oblivion as sensation burst through her in shuddering waves. She allowed her mind to spin away, aware of how Ladon swelled inside her before shouting out his own release, which only spurred hers to continue on.

She'd hardly floated down from that high when suddenly, Ladon whipped her top off, then rolled so that he was above her. He settled between her legs, still embedded inside her, semi-hard. Somewhere in those moments, he'd also removed his shirt.

"You move quick for such a big man," Skylar half grumbled.

"Next time we go fast and hard, I'll go at dragon speed. Sort of like your own personal vibrator." Ladon grinned.

A full-on grin, maybe the first he'd ever given her. Despite the scar down his face—which she had to admit she'd sort of stopped noticing—he suddenly turned from harsh to something rather beautiful. Skylar sucked in a sharp breath but allowed her gaze to drink him in like this. With a fascination she didn't want to quite cop to, she trailed her fingers down the ridge of scar tissue.

"What happened here?"

"Thanatos gave me that. Blew fire directly into an open wound. He should've killed me."

Thank the gods that didn't happen.

She couldn't face the way her heart clenched at the thought of never having even known this man. It meant too much. *He* was coming to mean too much.

The rare times in her life when she'd allowed herself to picture the man she'd mate, assuming stupidly, though in a vague sort of way all those times that she'd care for him, she'd pictured a guy who would be the yin to her yang. Easy where she was intense. Fun where she was too focused. Someone to force her to lighten up, to take some time, to take fewer chances.

Ladon was none of those things. If anything, he was the male version of her multiplied. Maybe that's why they seemed to understand each other—

No. She didn't want to allow her thoughts to go down paths she couldn't finish. Not until this was over.

Pushing all these serious thoughts away, she shifted beneath him, running her foot down the back of his muscled calf. "Maybe we should try that vibrator thing now?"

"Uh-uh." He shook his head. "I told you. This next one will be slow. If I don't get to claim this body for a while—seeing as you could give unicorns lessons in stubborn—I intend to savor every inch of you tonight."

A gush of warm wetness seeped from her, and Ladon grinned again. With aching slowness, he slid out then back in.

"Already?" She cocked her head, though her lips twitched.

His gaze dropped to her lips and her heart fluttered inside her. "Kiss me."

The words were a command, only before she could obey, he lowered his head and claimed her for himself.

Skylar closed her eyes and sank into the kiss, the feel of him against her, his scruff rough against her cheeks, his thickening cock growing even harder.

Ladon lifted his head and trailed the back of his hand gently down the side of her face. "You taste of cloves and smoke, like your scent. Intoxicating."

Her heart clenched in reaction to his look and touch and words.

More than that, though…

I genuinely like him.

Not exactly a revelation, like the knowledge had snuck up on her slowly. But, in general, she didn't like anyone except her sisters. And sometimes not even them.

Words trembled on the tips of her lips. She should tell him. He'd been honest with her.

After the battle. Don't risk the bond or you risk killing him.

She settled on that decision and let go, leaning into his touch. His hands were trailing over her, his lips not far behind, even as he slowly moved inside her. And she lost herself in the man who'd become her mate.

Best distraction ever.

• • •

Meira stared at the stony face of the man in front of her and allowed shock to settle in, taking up residence inside her in the form of a pit of writhing anxiety in her very core.

"Are you sure?" she asked through lips too tight, refusing to work properly.

Over a year with Carrick and she trusted no one better. She needn't have asked, but she had to. Because what he'd just said made no sense.

"I'm sure," he said in the scratchy voice all of his kind seemed to share.

The gargoyle stood resolute in front of her, currently in his human form, though his other form still showed through in a jaw and a visage that appeared etched from the very granite that he became at will. Meira would consider him handsome, in an intense sort of way, with his dark gray hair and eyes, and those chiseled features and body. However, she'd seen him in his guardian form only once… That had frightened her enough that she'd never seen him in quite the same light.

As the leader of his Chimera—which she'd originally thought

referred to his family grouping, but lately suspected it meant his kingdom or realm—Carrick had not shown surprise when she materialized in front of him the day her mother died and sent her daughters to the four corners of the planet. He'd kept her secret and safe, and only in these last months, she'd finally started to relax her guard, that coil of anxiety loosening inside her.

Until this moment.

Both Kasia and Skylar mated to dragon shifters? How? By their will? Were they forced? If the mating was successful, what did that mean? Would it work differently, since there were four of them now, and not just one? Would any shifter do? Or had her sisters found their destined mates?

"Kasia and her mate are at Store Skagastølstind now."

The royal home of the Gold Dragon Clan of shifters? "Why?"

Carrick's expression, like all gargoyles, didn't do anything. Not in a way she could see, anyway. "Her mate is apparently the rightful king. He's gone to claim his throne."

What? The blasting roar of the red bastard who'd taken her mother's life echoed through her mind, a memory so real, she almost covered her ears. How could her sister mate his kind? It couldn't be willingly.

"What of Angelika?" she asked.

"Still no sign of her."

Mama. What am I supposed to do now?

A shard of pain at that brief thought of her parent sliced through her heart with the unerring accuracy of an assassin's blade, and she stuffed that thought and the pain down deep where it couldn't get out to hurt her more.

Still, the question wouldn't quit echoing through the hollows of her mind, still empty from the shock. She wasn't brave, like Kasia, or a fighter, like Skylar. Even Angelika would probably know what to do now. But Meira had always been the more cautious of her sisters.

More afraid, she taunted herself.

"Thank you for letting me know. I...need to think about this."

Carrick dipped his head in a smooth, rather formal nod. Living here had been like going back in time, when men were chivalrous and women delicate creatures to protect. Enslave, if you asked Skylar, whose independent nature had chaffed under such a restrictive era. A time Meira's romantic heart yearned to return to. She'd liked being protected, cosseted. Did that make her weak? Or wrong?

She flicked the thought away as she turned and slowly made her way back to her room, inside the massive, gothic castle where Carrick's people lived in the Ural Mountains of western Russia. A castle magically hidden from the world, not that the world came close that often, as deep into the wilderness as this place was.

The perfect hiding place for a precious phoenix. Something Meira wished with all her heart she wasn't.

She sank into the feather mattress of her bed, pulling a silk-covered pillow into her lap and hugging it.

She pictured her sisters' faces, their eyes like hers, but otherwise little shared resemblance. The gods knew she missed them fiercely, the heart-wrenching pain of losing their mother only exponentially worsened by the fact that she'd essentially lost her siblings the same night.

What do I do? She lifted her eyes slowly to the gilded full-length mirror leaning heavily against the stone wall across from her four-poster bed.

Almost in a trance, as if drawn to the instrument she'd requested be placed in her room when she'd figured out what her power involved, Meira got up from her bed and moved to stand before the polished glass, her reflection staring back at her.

Dressed in the more formal garb of her gargoyle protectors, a floor-length dress of black velvet with soft white fur at the cuffs and collar, her long strawberry blond curls tamed into ringlets and pinned up, again harkening back to times long gone, she could already see the glow of flame in her arctic blue eyes.

Her body had decided before her mind, it seemed.

Calling on her power, she summoned the fire to the surface,

bright white flames edged with brilliant red—bloodred—skated over her body, though she felt only a pleasant warmth, something that had kept her comfortable during the colder days, and even colder, longer nights of this far north region. The castle had been snowbound for some time now.

With practiced ease, after a year of traveling first throughout the castle, and eventually farther afield, she thought of Kasia and the location Carrick had provided, willing the mirror in front of her to do her bidding.

The one gift she'd inherited from her mother had been subtle and taken her some time to discover.

Her mother had been able to teleport. Meira had stumbled on the fact that she could as well, sort of. Her version of the power was catoptric teleportation—the use of mirrored and reflective surfaces to bridge the distance between spaces. So far, she hadn't been successful stepping through, but she'd got damn good at watching. No one ever saw her.

With her heart fluttering at the thought of finally seeing Kasia, now that she knew where her sister would be, she drew on her ability.

Immediately, the mirror before her morphed from her image to a different one. Darkness.

Meira frowned. This couldn't be right. She should be seeing Kasia right now. A sliver of light lit the darkness, appearing as though a door was being opened.

"Where is everyone?" a low male voice asked.

The sliver became a blaze of white light. Meira blinked, trying to allow her vision to adjust. Several people stepped inside. Before the door closed, she caught a glimpse outside. Swirling snow and ice over what appeared to be razor-sharp mountaintops. This had to be the right place. Only the door closed, and the space was shrouded in darkness again, obscuring her vision.

She found herself leaning in, trying to peer closer.

Then the image jumped. Another mirror farther inside, this one located in a lit corridor of some sort reflected in her own now.

Meira gasped. "Kasia," she whispered.

Her sister's deep red hair was unmistakable, not that Meira got a good look, as Kasia was surrounded by a hoard of men much taller than she. They paused in front of a set of massive double doors, iron with intricate scroll work rendering them beautiful, if intimidating.

"Ready?" a massive man beside Kasia asked in the same low voice Meira had just heard.

With a nod, he yanked the doors open.

The view changed again. Meira blinked as a dozen images appeared, like a kaleidoscope, of her sister in a large room surrounded by giants of men—the image duplicated from different points of view. Luckily, Meira had experienced this multiple perspective thing before. Her power was showing her every mirror in the room.

"Someone's a bit vain," she muttered. Who needed that many mirrors?

She dipped her chin, focusing her gaze on a single image, and the view in her mirror changed, showing her only that. Much easier to discern the scene this way rather than in fractals. The room in which Kasia stood seemed to be in a cavern of some sort, arches formed of the natural cave surrounding her in a round pattern. Sure enough, between each archway, a large mirror was set into the wall. Meira's perspective was to the front and side of Kasia.

Her sister stood beside the man who'd spoken a moment ago. Now that she had more light to see him by, Meira gazed at a brute, all shoulders and muscles and a hard gaze which would've made Meira back up a step if it were turned on her. He wore a short-sleeved black T-shirt with jeans and mean-looking boots. In winter in Norway? Definitely a dragon shifter. Also, not kingly garb by any stretch of the imagination, but it suited him regardless, giving him an edge of danger that couldn't be denied. It also showed off the tattoo that covered one entire arm. She was too far back to see the details, though. Even from the safety of her room, she shivered.

Kasia mated a beast of a man.

Behind them stood several men of varying coloring and size, but all large and muscled and with that dangerous look. Most had dark hair, which would be unusual for gold dragons. Again, her distance was a problem. She couldn't see the color of the men's eyes to peg them by clan.

"What's going on here?" a decidedly pissed-off male voice demanded.

Meira adjusted the view to swing slightly behind Kasia. A group of eight men sat in chairs at the front of the room. The Curia Regis—the men making up the gold king's council? But no gold king, as far as she could tell. The way overdone throne sat empty.

Kasia and the man beside her stepped forward. "My name is Braneck Astarot Dagrun," he said. "Your king."

"By whose authority?" The man at the center of the Curia Regis got to his feet to ask, except rather than intimidating he came off more whiny.

"All authority," her sister's mate boomed.

Now that's intimidating.

Whiner guy clamped his mouth closed and sank to his seat. "Uther's son, Brock, is next in line by right of succession," he insisted. Though his pale skin turning pink rendered that statement not as confident as he'd probably hoped.

Kasia spoke for the first time. "If that were the case, then you would wear his mark on your hand, and not my mate's."

Meira sucked in a sharp breath. Kasia was defending her mate? Standing side by side with him?

Whiner man's pale eyes snapped to her sister. "And who are you to speak on such matters?"

No surprise that Kasia's hands fisted at her side. Her sister couldn't stand male chauvinism any more than Skylar could. Her mate slipped his hand into Kasia's and she tipped her head to search his face before smiling. Then she turned back to the men waiting for answers. "I am a phoenix and Brand's queen."

A murmur of protest arose from the Curia Regis. "Impossible," an older gentleman hissed. "The last phoenix has been dead these five hundred years."

Kasia did smile at that. "Says who? Your pitiful High King Pytheios? The man who murdered my father and grandparents. The man who eventually found my mother and killed her, too?"

"Lies!" The old man jumped to his feet to bellow. "We've heard the rumors. There's already one discovered with a band of rogues in South America."

"My sister Skylar," Kasia interrupted. "Who is with us now, mated to King Ladon."

"She couldn't be. She was found only recently. Besides, more than one phoenix is impossible." His gaze cut to Kasia's mate. "You and Ormarr got greedy."

Meira reached for the mirror, wanting to protect her sister somehow, ready to yank her through the reflective surface to safety with her.

Before anyone took another step, Kasia went up in flame and blinked out of sight before appearing directly in front of the man, some twenty feet away from where she'd been standing. "I've seen you in my visions," she snarled quietly, menacing all of a sudden. "Do you want to know what I saw, traitor?"

Another blink and Kasia reappeared beside Brand. Her flames extinguished, and with supreme calm, she took Brand's hand. Meira lowered her own trembling hand, hardly recognizing her sister. Had Kasia learned that evil-looking glare from her mate?

Suddenly, Brand's image wavered, as though she was witnessing a mirage in the middle of a castle, a sure sign he was shifting. Only no way could the room accommodate a full-sized dragon. Also, Kasia and the other men stayed where they stood, rather than moving back to give him space.

In an impressive display of control, Brand brought forward his wings only. Meira hadn't even known dragons could partially shift such a large piece of their body. That had to be unusual, right?

"I state this for all the gold dragons within range to hear..."

Meira knew about how dragon shifters communicated telepathically when in dragon form. Based on his choice of words, that had to be what Brand was doing now, communicating to every shifter near him.

"My name is Braneck Astarot Dagrun. Son and only living heir of King Fafnir. Slayer of the false king Uther. And the man whose mark you bear on your hands. I am the rightful King of the Gold Clan of dragon shifters, and I *will* take my throne." Brand pointed to the empty gilded chair on a raised dais behind where the men of the Curia Regis sat.

"The warriors of the Blue Clan, led by King Ladon Ormarr, represented here by the captain of his guard, Reid Herensuge, and the king's sister, Arden Ormarr"—a tall man with an unimpressed glower bowed his head as did the smaller woman beside him— "and the warriors of the Black Clan, led by King Gorgon Ejderha, represented here by the captain of his guard, Samael Veles"—an intense looking man with slightly shaggy dark hair and fathomless eyes bowed his head—"are here as proof of the support I bring with me. I can take my throne by force, but I would rather save *my people* from the bloodshed. Swear allegiance to me now and you'll live."

The previous king's viceroys paled with each word Brand uttered. Two of the men sitting before Brand covered the marks that could be seen on the fleshy part between their thumbs and forefingers.

Finished with his claim, Brand lifted his head. He listened, and the room sat in silence for a long time, tension piling on tension until it reached screaming pitch. Until one corner of his mouth lifted in a smile that sent another shiver cascading down Meira's spine.

"My people have spoken," he murmured. "Bow to your king."

One by one, each of the men stood and knelt before their king. All except the oldest of the gentlemen. Brand gave a single nod to one of the men on his left, who took that man into custody and led him out of the room.

"Brock will not sit by for this without a fight," whiny guy warned.

The fact that Brock—whom she understood to be the son of the previous ruler—wasn't there had Meira frowning. Why would he leave his people so unguarded?

"Yes. Where is the son of a murderer?" When none answered, the men still on their knees looking to each other in obvious confusion, Brand lifted a single unimpressed eyebrow. "We'll see how he does against two armies and a clan now sworn allegiance to me." He waved a hand at the door. "Please go with my men. I'll talk to each of you when I'm damn good and ready."

The men vacated the space, practically running out of it. As soon as the door closed behind them, Kasia threw her arms around Brand's neck. "You did it," she whispered.

Brand scowled, as if he didn't like that. "It's not over yet," he murmured before claiming her lips in a kiss so reverent, Meira lowered her gaze, feeling the need to give them privacy.

Brand lifted his head to stare down at her sister, possession and something more in his golden gaze—adoration, love, desire, protectiveness. Even for someone who'd never witnessed destined mates firsthand, Meira could still recognize it when she saw it.

The mass of anxiety in her belly eased, though only slightly. Her sister had found her mate and appeared happy. She was far from safe, mated to a king with a precarious throne, but she was where the fates had clearly decreed she should be.

Meira touched her sister's reflection in the mirror. "I'm happy for you," she whispered and hoped that perhaps Kasia knew, that she heard those words in her heart.

Brand and Kasia parted. "I need to talk to Ladon. Now."

Together, they led the remaining men in the room away. Meira was about to turn off her powers when one of Brand's men stepped in front of the mirror. She froze. This was the man Brand had introduced as Samael Veles, the captain of the black king's guard.

She allowed her gaze to travel over him—almost painfully handsome with a strong jaw covered by dark scruff. She could see why such a man would earn that position. He had hardened warrior stamped all over him—from the wide military stance, to a body honed for battle, and a hard light in his eyes as black as night that never stopped checking the corners of the room.

A kick of unaccustomed awareness shuddered through her only to be replaced by a cold fear as her gaze connected with those fathomless black eyes.

He was staring directly at her.

Meira held still, not even daring to breathe. He couldn't see her. No one ever saw her.

"Who are you?" he demanded.

With a gasp, she stumbled backward, dousing her flames, her mirror immediately changing to show only her reflection. Meira rubbed at her arms, both fear and the chill from the loss of her fire penetrating down to her bones in seconds.

How could I have been so careless?

. . .

Phone to his ear, Ladon listened to Brand break down the current situation. The entire time he listened, he watched Skylar, who watched him right back. She didn't pester, didn't ask questions, merely watched him, worry icing over the determination in those chilly blue eyes.

"Got it," Ladon said. "Any sign of where Brock went?"

He'd hoped against hope that Brand's gambit to go in first would stave off a fight. But Brock's absence told Ladon he'd been right all along. The gold dragon had abandoned the weakest of his people, people a man like that would regard as useless and disposable.

"No sign of him. Samael is returning to Gorgon now."

Which meant the black king's captain had realized the same thing Ladon had. "They're going for Ben Nevis."

"I agree. Next phase?"

"Next phase," Ladon confirmed. After arriving here openly with all the combined blue and black forces, he'd spent the last several days sending half the men back to the mountain. Ben

Nevis was ready.

Hopefully Skylar had rested long enough for the second part of his plan.

"You watch your back until you hear from me again," he told Brand. "A show of force never hurt anything."

A snorted laugh came down the line. "Ain't that the truth."

Ladon hung up.

"Well?" Skylar asked before he even pushed the button to end the call.

"They're in, with most of the shifters inside the mountain having sworn allegiance to their new king and the rest in cells."

She said nothing for a moment, then straightened. "When do we go?"

He crossed his arms to stare at her, taking in the purpose in shoulders drawn back, body practically vibrating with the need to get started.

"What?" she asked slowly when he didn't speak, just kept staring.

"I never put much store in the fates. But perhaps they know what they're doing after all."

Skylar raised her eyebrows. "Why?"

He wasn't ready to confess the surge of pride that had him staring, the knowledge that this strong, capable, action-first woman was his. He knew the stories about how drawn to each other mates could be, how they clicked on more than a physical level, and he'd never been interested. But he couldn't deny that Skylar worked for him on a basic level that spoke to the heart of who he was as a man.

"Let's just say that I'm not the type to handle female emotions well. The fact that your first reaction was to get shit done..." He shrugged again. "I like that about you."

As soon as the words left his mouth, Ladon gave a mental pause, rattled. Because he *liked* his mate. She was stubborn, and rash, and standoffish. She was also brave, and loyal, and determined.

He liked her. Every part of her.

A fact that should have scared the shit out of him, but somehow settled comfortably into the center of his being.

"My king," Asher's thought clanged through his head. Ladon froze and waited for the next thought he knew was coming. *"Ben Nevis is under attack now."*

Beside him Skylar gasped, and Ladon cut his gaze to her. "Did you hear that?"

"Yes."

He frowned. She shouldn't have heard. Asher had sent that thought to Ladon alone, knowing his king would prefer to decide what to do on his own. But he couldn't address that now. "Back up," he said to Skylar.

Without argument, she scooted back as he started his shift. This was one of those moments when the process took too much damn time. As soon as he was able, he continued to talk to Asher. *"How do you know?"*

"Rainier broke comms to relay it."

"Is it Brock?" It could be another clan helping him.

"Yes. He's going for the people loyal to him who we still have in our cells. Just as you predicted."

Take out the heart then attack with a bigger force. Exactly what Ladon would've done.

Immediately, Ladon started casting out his thoughts, first to Gorgon, then to the rest of his own guard. In minutes, they coordinated. Gorgon and half of both their troops still remaining would head to Brand to hold the mountain in case of attack. Ladon would take the other half to Ben Nevis.

He would've preferred to take only his blue dragons, but he didn't entirely trust Gorgon not to double-cross them and take Brand and Kasia prisoner. This was the best he could do.

Ladon lowered his head to Skylar, who he'd made sure to include in his mental conversations. *"You need to go with Gorgon."*

"I know."

Ladon rumbled his approval, unable to contain the sound. "You're not going to argue?"

"Until you see me in a fight, I'm merely a distraction. Besides,

I can't send myself without Kasia."

"You think you're recovered enough to do what we discussed?"

She put a hand on his face, her palm not even covering one scale, so tiny beside his bulk. "They won't expect you to show up that fast. This could turn the tide now. I'm ready."

Fuck, she was incredible.

Skylar smiled. "Gather the men here. I'll have to send you in human form."

Ten minutes later, his men standing behind him, Ladon stepped in to his mate, taking her face in his hands and running the backs of his fingers down one soft cheek. "Are you sure?" he asked in a low voice meant only for her ears.

Skylar nodded, her gaze steady on his. "Let me do this for you."

Now that the time had come to go, to save his people, Ladon found he didn't want to leave her. An anxiety like he'd never known ripped his soul in half, and he had to physically hold his body still against it.

Skylar's eyes widened, and she raised her hands to his wrists, not to pull away from his touch, but to latch on to him, like she was holding him steady.

A heavy hand landed on his shoulder. "Ready?" Asher asked.

"I..." She paused, then shook her head. "Go save your people." Skylar kissed the side of his mouth in a gesture that almost brought him to his knees.

Before he could respond, she ignited her fire, the flames caressing her skin, shining in her eyes, consuming her in a rush. With a hard shove, she disappeared. Everything disappeared, his sight going black, his hearing turned off, like he'd been forced into a soundproof room.

Asher's hand on his shoulder was Ladon's only connection to the black hole his mate had forced him through. This was where she'd been trapped when he'd had to pull her out of it? He could have lost her that day to *this*? Knowing that only made the idea fester. Fire would be preferable over this nothingness.

With a *whoosh* of sound and a flare of light, Ladon's senses returned as he and his men landed directly on the training platform inside his mountain.

Immediately, shouts thundered in his ears a heartbeat before his sight returned. The second fucking time his mountain had been attacked. At least this time, he was ready.

He'd make sure it was the last.

CHAPTER EIGHTEEN

In a single glance, Ladon took in the scene.

He'd used his mountain as bait, knowing full well Brock would need the warriors who remained prisoners. Knowledge that those of his people who weren't trained or able to fight were already safely hidden in the back caverns where Brand had spent much of his formative years hiding, now with wolf shifters as protection, helped. So did knowing, as much as he could, that Skylar was safely away from here.

Ladon focused on one thing only.

Taking out the fuckers who'd dared to attack his mountain twice.

The cavern swarmed with dragons of gold, black, and blue, like living gangrene, or a glittering mass of angry weirdly colored locusts. No green dragons, though, or white.

They'd helped Brock and Uther last time. Did their absence mean they'd backed out of the fight? Had the two Skylar sent back to her father's clan convinced others to stay out of it?

A quick check showed him that Ivar and Rainier had done their jobs, shutting the massive dragonsteel door that cut off the training arena from the rest of the mountain, containing the fighting to the massive opening chamber and outside, not allowing the gold dragons in the dungeons to be freed.

Hopefully not many of their attackers had made it inside the main mountain. Neither of the brothers was anywhere in sight.

Let's hope this time we've found all the fucking traitors.

In the last attack on this mountain, Chante's betrayal—letting the gold dragons in, an act that almost lost Ladon Ben Nevis—still burned deep. Whatever his spy in Pytheios's council had done with Chante was minor compared to what Ladon would've done to him.

Immediately, Ladon's men surrounded him in a formation that allowed him to shift. Blue dragons already in the fight turned to hover over him, protecting him from above. He pushed through the process, straining and stretching his body faster than he normally would.

As soon as he finished his shift, he stepped in front of his men, spewing blue-tinged fire, allowing them to complete their own shifts.

Each of his men's thoughts popped into his head, one at a time, as they completed their transitions, relaying their readiness. Ladon looked to Samael, who'd joined them with several of Gorgon's own warriors.

"Take your men. Sweep the perimeter to the right. We'll go left and meet at the top, then close in smaller circles."

Samael, his obsidian scales appearing almost wet in the light of many fires, was unusually large for a black dragon, most of whom tended to run on the lean side. He nodded his massive head and, in near silence, spread his wings to leap into the air, angling off to the right. In an impressive series of moves, he looped back over a gold dragon on the ground, smashing his tail into the beast's sides, then picked it up with the spikes that imbedded into it and spun, hurling its body with unerring accuracy to take out another gold dragon with the force of the blow.

Damn. I wouldn't mind having a warrior like that in my clan.

But Ladon didn't have time to sit and admire. Even as he noted the other dragon's fighting skills, he turned into the fray himself. With a boom that echoed off the stone walls, he clashed with a massive dragon so dark gold, he appeared more brown than yellow.

The two of them tumbled end over end, but before they hit the ground, Ladon sunk his teeth into the other dragon's jugular. A crunch of diamond-hard scales preceded the sweet, coppery taste of blood that gushed into his maw. Ladon slammed his wings down hard, jerking them both up. Another nauseating crunch sounded as he broke the dragon's neck with the force of that sudden change of motion. He spat his opponent out, allowing the carcass to fall to the ground below.

"Watch your six!" Asher, hovering directly ahead of him, shouted.

Ladon pulled in his wings, even as he spun, which dropped his body. A blindingly bright motherfucker buzzed by overhead, right into where Asher waited, navy talons outstretched.

The gold dragon flared his wings in a vain attempt to stop, unable to slow or change course enough to evade Asher, who was a fast sucker. With a twist in the air, Asher had him by the neck, leaving just enough space between his talons to get his teeth involved. Ladon's Beta dispatched him with little effort.

A quick check showed Fallon gutting some poor bastard on the floor like the armor of its scales was nothing. Samael pinned a butter-colored dragon to the wall, slamming it into the rock face over and over until the thing was a bloody pulp, almost unrecognizable. Duncan and Wyot took yet another gold dragon by the wings, pulling it apart as though they were plucking the wings off a butterfly.

Ladon growled, even as he searched the area for his next attack. This was too easy. No way could they have killed *all* Brock's best warriors. This fight should be harder.

"Ivar? Rainier?" Ladon sent the thought out. He'd yet to locate the brothers.

No answer. Not a good sign.

He didn't have time to stop and observe, however, taking on one, then another foe, working in tandem with his men as they dispatched their enemies in turn. As they moved, each gold dragon to come at them or happen into their path was either killed outright or maimed to the point of taking them out of the fight.

Ladon focused all his senses, attuned to everything around him even as he engaged and dealt with one dragon after another. The bloodlust of battle overtook him, rage fueling every move, every calculated maneuver, driven higher by the thunder of battle all around him and the metallic scent of blood and death in the air.

He battled, not stopping, until the obsidian glitter of Samael's fathomless eyes stopped him.

Pulling up short, Ladon did a quick inventory of the other black dragons with his ally, in their varying shades of blacks and grays, as well as checking for his own men. The forces waiting for them when they got here, and the addition of more fresh fighters Skylar sent with him, had given them the advantage. Like Ladon, Samael had lost only a handful of men. In a fight like this, the best a leader could hope for.

The gold assholes they fought couldn't say the same, the bodies piled high on the stone slab below, crimson blood staining the gray rock in pools and splatters. He didn't recognize any as the prisoners they'd held, which meant the plan had worked. Except where was Brock? Or Ivar and Rainier? Further review of the area showed them to have taken control of the fight.

The battle wasn't finished yet.

Beating his wings to remain airborne, Ladon craned his neck, returning his long gaze to Samael. "Let's end this."

Side by side with their men, they moved into the center of the room. With a collective roar that shook the very mountain, they charged.

Ten more minutes of frantic fighting, and the remaining gold dragons still able voluntarily dropped to the ground to shift, the haze around them almost forming a bubble as so many did at once. The ultimate sign of surrender, putting themselves into their more vulnerable human forms. Ladon took his time, allowing his men to herd all their enemies—those who still lived—into a circle in the center of the space, surrounded by dragons ready to turn them to ash at the slightest sign of rebellion.

Once he landed, Ladon took a moment to survey the men

gathered, assessing which of those might be leaders.

Before he could address them, though, Asher clapped a hand on his shoulder.

Ladon turned to his Beta with a scowl. "What can't wait—"

But he saw. Ivar, drenched in blood Ladon hoped to the gods wasn't his, stumbled under the weight of Rainier's limp form, who he held. With a look at the men holding the prisoners, needing no order to remain, Ladon ran to his friends, shifting as he moved.

Ivar gave out as he reached him, dropping to his knees, holding his brother to him. "We decided to lure them in by being the only two in the training room, the others hidden inside the town."

Fuck. A risk. One he would've taken himself.

"Get Fallon," Ladon ordered Asher.

Ivar raised his head, sweat streaking through the blood covering his face, eyes gone dull and hard. "Don't bother."

No. Ladon dropped to his knees, putting a hand to Rainer's shoulder, already turning gray and ashy under the skin. Muscles clenched so hard, Ladon shook with the force of his own responsibility.

"This is my fault." He'd chosen to use his mountain as bait. Chosen to kill Thanatos and start this war.

"Don't—" Ivar stopped and swallowed. "Don't fucking do that. Don't take that away from him. Rainier is…was…a fighter." His voice cracked on the word, and he cleared his throat with an angry grunt. "He was born to be one of your warriors. He believed in you. And he knew the danger. You don't get to take this on your shoulders, too."

Ivar spoke in a voice gone harsh, blue fire flashing in his eyes. Ladon clenched his fists. "You're right."

Ivar dropped his gaze to his brother's still face. "Go kill the fucker who brought this on us."

Brock. Then Pytheios.

With a nod, Ladon got to his feet and stalked to the dragons still held in waiting.

"Which one of you is Brock?" he demanded, deadly quiet.

A tall man with a badly broken arm, the bone jutting out in a jagged, bloody protrusion below his shoulder, stepped forward. "You snapped his neck," he accused with dead eyes. "His body lies over there."

Sure enough, the man pointed to the form of the brown-colored dragon Ladon had taken out first, his head sitting at an odd angle to his neck, grotesque. The dragon's body was already starting to change color, turning an ashy gray at the edges of its snout, the dragon fire consuming the carcass from the inside out.

Ladon looked to Samael and Asher.

"I had heard that Uther's son was a dark color," Samael offered. "I never met him."

Ladon grunted. "No way to tell now." In less than an hour, he'd be a pile of ash.

"That might be the point," Asher warned, a conclusion Ladon had already reached.

"Bring me all the survivors, including those in the dungeons," Ladon ordered. "Tend to the wounded. Search the mountain for anyone who got past our defenses."

He had the pleasure of seeing at least a few of the men before him blanch. They *should* be scared.

An hour later, Rainier was another pile of ash along with the rest of the dead. When this was all over, they'd give their people a proper sky burial, but Ladon couldn't think of that with every last living gold dragon involved in either attack kneeling before him.

"Check their hands. Put those with Brand's mark back in the dungeons," he ordered.

"What are you thinking?" Asher asked in a low voice beside him.

"That I don't give my enemies second chances."

"These are Brand's people. He should decide—"

"He's not here," Ladon said.

On his orders, a man stood behind each gold dragon bearing no mark on his hand. Rogues. Traitors to the rightful kings.

Ladon shifted before them, assuming his dragon form; the

men, massive even in human form because of the clan they hailed from, becoming smaller in his sight with each passing second.

Soon they would be nothing.

"Now," he ordered.

Without hesitation, his men slit the throats of the men before them, then stepped back. Ladon took a second to enjoy the sight of these bastards, trying to suck air through the thick liquid pouring from them.

With no remorse, he took a deep breath, igniting the fire in his belly. In a stream of blue-tipped fire, he guaranteed not a single man would survive his wounds on the off chance one of his men hadn't cut deep enough.

As soon as he was satisfied, Ladon shifted back to human. "Get me Brand. Now," he ordered.

. . .

Mental note to avoid flying through clouds when possible. Despite the dragon beneath her, warming her from below, as well as her own fire, which provided some warmth, Norway in oncoming winter was freaking freezing. Skylar shivered against the wind. They'd chosen to take advantage of lower clouds, using them as cover as they flew to Brand's mountain. Only flying through this soup was soaking her and chilling her to the bone.

Skylar tried to ignore her discomfort. They couldn't do anything about it. She'd get dry and warm when she made it to the mountain.

Flying on Gorgon's back was a different experience than flying on Ladon. His body wasn't as broad or long, leaner as she understood most of his clan to be. That difference in size made the seat between the spikes on his back a tighter squeeze. At least they didn't have too far to go.

The creepier difference was the fact that Gorgon, and all the other black dragons, flew in near silence. When she flew with Ladon, small sounds accompanied them—a slight rustle as his scales shifted with the movement of his body, the push of his wings, hell, even the wind sounded different.

"Okay," she finally gave in to curiosity. "How are you so quiet?"

Gorgon vibrated beneath her with a chuckle, and even that was silent. *"In addition to training in techniques that make us stealthy, black dragons are genetically adapted to be quieter than the others."*

"Like how?" Never let it be said that she suffered from a lack of curiosity.

"Our scales are smaller and smoother than other clans, allowing them to adjust almost noiselessly when we move."

Skylar glanced down but couldn't see a huge difference. Of course, Gorgon was a dark gray, like sitting on a swirl of dense smoke, so making out individual scales became more difficult. "That's nifty. Anything else?"

"Our wings flow from our bodies more attached, sort of like bat wings, providing a seamless flow of air over us in a way that makes us quieter fliers. Think stealth fighter jet technology. Based on a black dragon, as a matter of fact."

Now she tipped to the side, trying to get a better view. Sure enough, the shoulder joints were thicker and more part of the body, rather than a distinct shoulder. The membrane of the wing was attached down the ribcage, rather than starting at the armpit. "Does that make it harder to maneuver on land?" She'd seen Ladon and his men crawl on all fours.

"It does. We prefer to stay in the air."

Her mother, while educating them on dragon-kind, had touched on many things, but not to this level of detail. She hadn't liked talking about dragon shifters, beyond what they needed to know to evade them. "I know all dragons are different in small ways like these."

"Yes."

But no description of how the others were? *Looks like I've asked as many questions as he has patience for.*

Skylar made a mental note to ask Ladon. She frowned as that thought penetrated. Ladon. Please let the fighting be over. Let him be okay.

Before she'd sent him to war, she'd wanted to tell him something. Something important. Something unexpected, because she'd never seen it coming. But she'd worried about being a distraction. And still, the bond between them was a concern. Especially when he was going to fight.

So she'd held her tongue. She'd tell him when she knew they were all safe.

She was still mulling over that train of thought when a shout smacked into her brain. *"They're coming for you. Get away!"*

Skylar recognized the voices. The two white dragons who'd sworn allegiance.

"What the hell is that?" Gorgon demanded.

Before she could answer, he suddenly tensed beneath her. *"Hold on!"*

She didn't have time to look around for whatever danger he'd sensed before he flipped upside down. A second later, he jerked in the air. Had something hit them or was he trying to shake her off? Either way, the sudden motion had her scrambling to hold on, but she'd been warned about the tips of those spikes. Not even Fallon's blood had fully healed Kasia's wounds, leaving scars.

With nothing to grip and gravity doing its damnedest to yank her off, Skylar fell from Gorgon's back with a screech. She flailed for a second as she dropped away from him, like if she reached for him hard enough, she could get back there, but his dark gray form grew smaller by the second. Part of the clouds they'd been flying through writhed above him.

White dragons, come for her.

Shit.

Her time skydiving, something she'd decided was prudent to know as a pilot, kicked in. Skylar flipped over so that she oriented with her belly toward the earth, her legs and arms out for balance, bent at the knees and elbows, the most stable position in the air.

Usually when she jumped, she wore a full-faced helmet. Without that protection, her eyes watered and blurred with the force of the freezing wind. That had to be why the ground seemed to be wriggling beneath her. An indistinct sea of green and white, black, and blue. Throwing out one arm for balance, she wiped a sleeve across her eyes. It didn't help.

Not that she could do much about plummeting toward the ground. They'd made it over an uninhabited swath of land above the mountains. Even if she survived the impact, no one would be there to immediately help her. Her best hope was to remain calm and stable. Assuming Gorgon's maneuver was caused by an enemy attacking, preferably one of the dragons on her side would catch her.

Skylar tipped her head back, searching the skies above her. Her fuzzy vision and rapid blinking between squinting didn't help much, and what she could make out wasn't good. Dragons above her battled and grappled in a clash of titans that echoed off the mountains around her.

With no warning, something both hard and smooth wrapped around her, and Skylar grunted as her downward momentum jerked harshly sideways.

I'm in a freaking talon?

"I've got you."

Immediately, she recognized the voice of one of her loyalists. Skylar turned her head to see the other one taking up position, flying beside them.

"Thank the gods—"

Something barreled into them like a fucking freight train, and Skylar flopped in her rescuer's grip like a fucking rag doll. A screech of terrible pain pierced her ears, coming from her friend, and suddenly she found herself released, flung back into the sky.

As soon as she managed to stabilize in the air again, she couldn't find either of her white dragons. She wiped her eyes with the back of her sleeve, but it didn't help.

Then, for the second time, all the air left her in a painful whoosh as she was plucked from the sky yet again. This time, the scales of the creature that had her were so white they turned

almost translucent, giving them a purplish hue. Not one of hers.
Dammit.

"Over here!" she screamed. Maybe her two followers could find her if they were still alive. Help her. Or one of Gorgon's people. The only way they would know she was being hijacked was if she made a racket. Skylar did just that, until that talon squeezed harder, cutting off her air.

"Okay," she wheezed. Granted, she was only able to squeak the word, but the creature who had her must've caught it, because its grip loosened.

Briefly, she considered sending her captor to Ladon, but no telling how that would go. She was running on fumes after sending such a large group all the way to Ben Nevis. Besides, she hadn't teleported a creature this large before. It could drag her with it, and they'd both get stuck in that in-between. If she wasn't so drained, she would've risked it, but she couldn't.

Which meant she was along for the fucking ride for now.

She urgently searched around for any of her people following but couldn't see much above them, given the dragon's bulk being in her way, and didn't see anyone below or trailing behind.

Desperately, Skylar tried to think of something, anything she could do to get out of this, to force him to release her.

An idea occurred. A bit of a strange one, but...what if she could teleport just a piece of him?

Again, she risked sending the entire dragon and herself with it. But if she could loosen his grip, she could get away. She placed her palms against the rough leather skin of one knuckle and called on her fire. Staring at a single scale, she pictured sending only that piece, like a swirl of flame captured in a bubble. Then she shoved that imaginary bubble. In an instant, the scale disappeared, opening a raw gash beneath.

With a screech, the dragon went wild, flapping and contorting in the air as though he wanted to run away. His thrashing slammed her around so hard, she couldn't try again on a bigger piece of him. Immediately he stopped and hovered.

"Do that again, and I'll crush you until your bones turn to liquid." He squeezed to emphasize the point.

"That was...graphic." Skylar didn't doubt it, though. Exhaustion hovered at the edges of her consciousness. Even sending that small piece had drained her. No way could she do more. Shit.

With a gut-tumbling drop, the white dragon angled toward the ground, picking up speed as it tucked its wings closer in to its body. The snow-covered, jagged-edged peaks of the mountains rapidly grew larger, despite her still-watering eyes, hurtling up at her. For a blink, Skylar wondered if the dragon who'd caught her had lost its marbles and was preparing to slam into the unforgiving rock, kamikaze style, taking her out with it. At the last minute, though, it banked.

That was when she saw him.

A flash of black on a peak above her before he disappeared, rapidly showing up on a cliff just behind them.

Maul.

She and Kasia had left the blessed beast behind to help guard Ben Nevis, but she should've guessed he'd ignore that order. The animal seemed to have only one goal: watching over the Amon sisters.

Her asshole captor flew in close to the mountains, navigating a series of sharp turns as he moved them deeper into the range. Maul kept up, though barely, trailing them in quick teleportational leaps. The dragon would follow a bend or navigate an outcropping, and she'd lose sight of the hellhound only to see his black form pop up a second later. The dog could jump only short distances, and to where he could see, but still, he was there. Losing ground, but there.

Skylar considered ripping off parts of her jacket to leave as a scented trail for him to find when he fell too far back. She might die of hypothermia, but he'd at least find her. Except the white dragon holding her slowed, dropping down a ravine to the rocky bottom with an icy river flowing over rocks formed when time began.

As far as Skylar could tell, they were alone here.

Wings outstretched, sending nearby drifts of snow flying, her captor landed. The dragon had to hop a little, as it kept its hold on her, managing to touch down with only three legs. The thing stood silently, sniffing the air like a dog.

"So…you are one of Serefina's daughters?"

The charred voice reverberating through her mind had apprehension doing its damndest to seize up her nerve endings, crawling through her like spiders. She knew that voice.

Pytheios.

No way would he risk showing himself here. Not this close to his most powerful enemies. The white dragon in whose talon she still lay lifted its leg, holding her upright and presenting her to the horror that unfurled from the darkness of a cave she had not seen until this moment.

The Rotting King of the Red Clan. Her parents' murderer. The bastard they were all trying to kill.

Deep red scales caught the sunlight, even dimmed by clouds, as the dragon moved closer. A scent of putrid meat clung to him like a dense, invisible fog, a thousand times worse than Maul's, and Skylar held her breath. As he came farther into the light, she could see how the fucker's wings were disintegrating, reminding her of moth-eaten rags.

Pytheios wasn't called the Rotting King for nothing.

Skylar faced him down not with dread inside her, but with pure hatred. The emotion threatened to burn her up from the inside out. "I'm already mated, asshole. You're too late."

He slithered closer, the decaying scent of him growing stronger, reminding her of the night her mother died, that same scent wafting on the warm breeze. Skylar had to swallow down the sour bile that threatened to upchuck her breakfast all over her captor's claws.

Before Pytheios could speak, suddenly Maul appeared directly in front of her. Immediately, he flashed an image of Skylar and Kasia both teleporting together, and she knew what the hellhound had in mind.

Did she have anything left? Didn't matter, she'd have to try.

Her arms dangled loosely over the white dragon's talons. Skylar reached for her fire even as she slammed her hands into Maul's chest, digging her fingers into his fur to hold on.

And, for a heartbeat of a second, she thought it had worked as that silent void took hold of her senses. But sound and light returned too fast. As she came back to herself, still held in those damn talons, Maul disappeared with a yelp of pain that lingered in the air, even after he was gone.

More than that, without her willing it, the flames covering her skin snuffed out like a candle in a hurricane. Iron bands of panic gripped her lungs, squeezing harder than the beast who held her, her heart taking off.

What was happening to her powers?

Pytheios lowered his head to regard her silently from one blazing red eye for a long moment. *"Who said anything about mating you?"*

A woman Skylar hadn't noticed before—older but still strikingly lovely with white curls around her face—clothed in a simple black jumpsuit, climbed up Pytheios's back. Glided more like, until she stood on his shoulder facing Skylar.

"I can feel the power radiating from her." The woman gave a smile that would make a snake's skin crawl. "She'll do nicely, but not yet. She's drained right now. She also hasn't fully realized her potential."

What the hell?

Pytheios loosed a low snarl, loud enough that a few small rocks tumbled from their precarious positions on the mountainside. The woman ran a soothing hand over his scales. "Not long, my love," she murmured. "A month at most. Worth the wait."

"Not long until what?" Skylar demanded, doing her best to control the terror trying to hijack her body and her mind. She twitched in the bonds of the claws holding her still only to wince as it clamped down on her. "What do you think you're going to do to me?"

The woman shrugged. "Suck your essence from you until you die."

She said the words the same way she might've said she'd bake a cake or take a leisurely walk.

Then she reached out and tapped one finger against Skylar's forehead. She murmured a few indistinguishable words, and Skylar felt unconsciousness enveloping her like an avalanche she was helpless to run from.

Ladon.

Her mate's name flitted through her mind, her last thought of his blue eyes. At the same time, a searing pain at the back of her neck penetrated the darkness overwhelming her senses. She lolled forward in her captor's grasp, and oblivion claimed her.

· · ·

Ladon paused walking in from the perch to the comms room. He and Samael had flown up together, but midshift...

He turned to face the black dragon shifter. "Did you hear that?"

Dark eyebrows winged high. "Hear what?"

"Did someone call my name? A woman?" He didn't want to put a name to what he'd heard, but some part of him knew anyway.

"I didn't hear anything." Samael's expression remained neutral, but Ladon still got the impression the other man was questioning his sanity, or at least his hearing.

Maybe he should be, too, but the fact that Samael hadn't heard it only confirmed what he already knew in his soul to be true. He'd heard Skylar. His mate's husky, sexy-as-sin voice was unmistakable.

And he was relatively certain he wasn't losing it, hearing her voice wherever he went. So, what had that been?

A sudden, lancing pain sliced across the back of his neck. With a hiss, he grabbed at the skin there, certain he'd find the hilt of a knife plunged deep. Instead, his hand encountered his own brand, white-hot to the touch.

Skylar.

Their bond?

But what had snapped it into place? Why now?

Heart slamming against his ribs, Ladon closed his eyes, listening, waiting for her to speak again. Only silence greeted him. He reached through the darkness behind his closed lids, trying to feel the connection that he'd heard destined mates could experience. Hell, he'd seen it. Brand and Kasia in a short period of time were practically one mind.

But he couldn't feel Skylar, and her voice didn't reach him again.

However, he couldn't shake the dread that ate at him now like acid on his skin. Something was wrong with Skylar.

"Fuck."

Ladon stalked the rest of the way into the comms room. Since he'd taken over as king, this room had seen little use. Set up to communicate between their various Blue Clan mountains, other clans, and the Alliance leaders in each of the colonies, he hadn't needed it. No other clan had interest in communicating with him, and he'd lost the other mountains of his clan, pulling all his people back into one single place to defend, intending to build back up from there.

Now, he finally had a reason to use this space. He sat in one of the black high-backed chairs at a console. One full wall was filled with screens and monitors, operated by the stations built into the long desk. Pushing a series of buttons, he brought the room online. Their model hadn't been upgraded in years, thanks to Thanatos's inability to care for his people before himself and his position with Pytheios, so it took a while to get everything humming.

Finally, a face appeared on the screen before him. A woman he didn't recognize, but a gold dragon based on the glittering eyes. "My name is Ladon Ormarr. I'm the—"

"I know who you are."

He narrowed his eyes. "Then you know who I want to talk to. Don't waste my time."

His tone of barely leashed anger must've penetrated, because the woman winced and hurried to do as he'd asked. The few minutes it took grated. By the time Brand and Kasia appeared, Ladon was up and gripping the back of the chair to keep from stalking around the room.

The second Brand and Kasia appeared, Ladon was on them. "Has Gorgon not arrived yet?"

"How the fuck did you know that?" Brand demanded.

"What happened?"

Brand made a gesture and two men with pale hair and the ice-blue eyes of white dragons walked into the room. Men Ladon immediately recognized. The white shifters who'd sworn allegiance to his queen.

"Do you know these men?" Brand asked. "They just arrived yelling about needing to speak with you—"

Ladon cut him off, directing his words not to Brand but the two men behind him. "Tell me Skylar is safe."

Kasia and Brand looked at each other.

One of the white shifters stepped forward. "We tried to warn them, but our clan attacked before we could get close enough. They took her."

"Who took her?" Ladon growled. But the black hole of dread threatening to drag him in and crush him told him the answer.

"We don't know. The Green and White Clans attacked together. A white dragon got to her. We tried to save her."

Given the jagged bone protruding from one of the men's arms, Ladon believed that. He cut his gaze to Brand, hands on the table, so he could lean in closer to the console. "My bond with Skylar just solidified. Where is Gorgon? And where the fuck is my mate?"

"Shit," Brand spat.

Yeah. They got it. Skylar had to be in trouble. His stubborn mate calling to him had to be the only way that bond formed. Nothing else made sense in this moment.

"Brand." Kasia's voice shook as she grabbed his arm.

His friend took Kasia's face in his hands. "Don't make assumptions. Let's find Gorgon."

"Go," Ladon said.

For a man as big as Brand was, he moved damn fast when he wanted to. He was out of the room in an instant.

Kasia went to follow, but Ladon stopped her. "Kasia, wait."

She turned back to the screen. Though she visibly trembled, even across rooms and screens, and her face paled, she remained calm. A quality she and her sister shared.

"The first time you heard Brand in your head...what did it sound like?"

Kasia's eyes widened infinitesimally. "Like he was right there, beside me, whispering in my ear. Why?" She leaned forward, studying him. "Did you hear Skylar?"

"Yes."

"Just now?"

He ran a hand around the back of his neck. "Yeah."

"What did she say?" Her tone kicked up a notch from calm to urgent.

Ladon scrubbed the same hand down his face, running his thumb over the scar. "Just my name."

Kasia studied him intently. "But?"

"That's when our bond solidified."

Kasia jerked upright. "I have to go."

She hustled out of the room, and Ladon ended the call. He stared at the black screens in front of him, battling the helplessness trying to drag him under and drown him. "I shouldn't have left her," he muttered.

If anything happened to his mate...

"My king is with her."

Ladon stiffened, then turned. Samael had come into the room and he hadn't even noticed. Dark eyes, even darker in the dim light of this particular room, reflected the same emptiness of the wall of monitors. Just...nothing.

"Can we trust your king?" Ladon asked, quietly.

The question was more of a throwaway. Hypothetical. To his surprise, the man before him considered it for a long moment before his jaw clenched. "He doesn't confide many of his plans to me. I'm merely his captain, but I believe his intention to ally with you is true."

That was the best Ladon could hope for. However, even if Samael was correct, even if Gorgon gave his life fighting for Skylar, Ladon was the one who'd left his mate behind. Left her unprotected.

"I guess we'll find out soon enough." Eye twitching, he turned back to the screens, mocking him now with their empty, black stares.

She'd better fucking be all right.

CHAPTER NINETEEN

What the hell am I lying on?

The cave floor maybe? But why was she lying on the cave floor? Did she roll out of her bed—

Skylar gasped and jackknifed to sitting as memory bombarded her. Pytheios. Her hand flew to her neck where she could feel the slightly puckered skin at the nape. Ladon's mark upon her, the bond now permanent.

Dammit. Not now. Not when Pytheios was going to kill her. Why had it formed now? Because she'd wanted to tell him she was going to stay when this was over? That she wanted him, too? Because she'd called to him as she'd been taken?

Taken where, though?

A glance around revealed that hadn't been a horrible nightmare like the ones she'd had growing up when they'd been on the run.

The dark cell was impossible to mistake as anything except a prison. Only this place was something else. Bars surrounded her on three sides with a solid wall at her back. She was clearly inside a mountain. Her prison room faced into a larger circular chamber with what were obviously more jail cells around the perimeter. What held her attention were the walls and ceiling.

Instead of stone, the walls and a large moonhole in the ceiling appeared like night sky, the black sky crystal clear and awash in stars. In the distance below, icy peaks of mountains stretched as far as she could see.

"It's not an illusion."

At the sound of a deep male voice behind her, Skylar jumped off her rock slab bed and crouched in a defensive position.

The shadowy figure of a man stood in the next cell over, separated from her by floor-to-ceiling bars that were no doubt dragonsteel. Another prisoner?

Skylar lowered her hands, coming upright. "Who are you?"

The man, almost as tall as Brand if she had to guess, six-three or thereabouts, moved forward until he stood at the bars, light from the moon struck his face, and Skylar gasped again. Ice-blue eyes, so like those she saw every time she looked in a mirror, or at her sisters, stared back at her from a face ruggedly handsome, though gaunt. Thick black eyebrows in contrast to a shock of white hair that appeared to have been hacked at to keep it short, somehow seemed to go together in a way that made this man starkly beautiful.

And her body didn't give a damn. Neither did her heart.

Curiosity, however, had her in a firm grip.

He cleared his throat. "My name is Airk Azdaja." His voice sounded scratchy, as though from lack of use.

Airk? Why did that sound familiar, as if an echo of her mother's voice was whispering through her mind. "Are you a white dragon shifter?"

He didn't say anything for a long moment, but Skylar didn't push him. She got the feeling he was grappling with something.

"You look like your grandmother," he finally said. "And your mother."

At his words, she took a halting step forward. "Who do you think is my mother?"

"Serefina Hanyu Amon. You are her spitting image, your grandmother as well." He waved a hand at his eyes. "Except here. The color of your eyes is all King Zilant."

Her breath deserted her in a whoosh. "You knew them both?" She had to force the words out through a throat gone Sahara dry.

Airk nodded slowly.

"How?"

"I am the son of Zilant's Beta, his best friend. I was no more than a child when your parents mated. After he killed your father, Pytheios killed mine as well, before he locked me in here."

Even through the reverberations of shock still shaking her, Skylar knew he'd skipped something important. "Why put you in here rather than kill you?"

"You can thank your grandmother for that." Airk's lips pulled back in a sneer, one that balanced on the edge between amusement and fury. "Her last act as a phoenix was predicting that the man who tried to kill me, or gave any order to have me killed, would be consumed in his own fire."

That would do it. No way would Pytheios risk his rotten hide, not when he could do this. "For over five hundred years?" Incredulity snuck into her voice.

He nodded again.

Gods above. How was this man still sane? Though...maybe he wasn't. Still, he was her only ally right now. Skylar moved closer to the bars, tilting her head back to talk up at him. "Obviously you couldn't get out."

"Pytheios has a witch who suppresses the powers of anyone in this room."

Come again?

Skylar immediately called on the fire inside her, trying to ignite, but nothing happened, as though her pilot light had gone out and needed to be relit. "Son of a bitch."

Airk's lips tilted in a smile, though tinged with bitterness. "Indeed."

"My..." Skylar paused and cleared her throat. She'd almost said sisters, dammit. Inside a fucking cell where anyone could be listening. "My people will come for me."

Did they even know she was gone yet? Ladon would lose his shit when he found out. He'd tear down this entire damn mountain to get her back. A thought that sparked a deeper hope inside her.

"Do they know where you are? That you're still alive?"

Skylar gripped the bars between them. Crap. They would know only that she was gone. Not... She glanced around. "Where *are* we, exactly?"

"Everest."

"Oh." Her eyes went wide as she glanced out at the landscape again. "We're at the top?"

"Yes."

"How on earth are we still breathing?"

"Air is piped up here for us. The inside of the mountain is pressurized past a certain elevation."

A tightness lingered in her new cellmate's voice, and she returned her gaze to him. Realization dawned. "I see. The dungeons are up here so that you can see the sky but never fly."

"Exactly." Airk's gaze moved over her head, taking in the view. "Nights like this are the hardest."

How demented could you get? And for centuries. "When they come for me, we'll get you out of here, too."

A large, rough hand fell over hers on the bar. "I hope so..." He paused with a frown.

Right. She hadn't given her name. "Skylar."

He searched her eyes with an intensity that reminded her of her mate, except she didn't warm under that gaze, her blood pumping at the same steady rate.

"I truly hope that shall come to pass, Skylar Amon," he said.

Skylar blinked at the more formal use of words but reminded herself that this man had been locked in here for ages. "I suppose you haven't had much contact with the outside world?"

"This is a longer conversation than most," he said. "Let us sit." Airk sank to the ground, leaning against the rock slab that made up his bed, one knee bent, and she did the same, crossing her legs to face him.

"My contact has been primarily limited to Pytheios and his witch, whose name is Rhiamon. They have a son, Merikh." He made a face at that.

Skylar raised her eyebrows. "And the witch survived? I thought only turned dragons could survive childbirth with a dragon shifter."

He grimaced. "She is powerful."

In other words, this Rhiamon person, who held them prisoner, was going to be a formidable block to escape.

"My other contact has been with other prisoners, though that doesn't last long. Lately, most of those to join me in this place have been other kinds of creatures."

"Creatures? Like what?"

"All sorts. A griffin. A juvenile sphinx. A minotaur. Several kitsune, also juvenile. They had only one tail each."

What on earth could they be doing with that eclectic mix? Especially the Japanese shapeshifting foxes.

"The witch seems to be particularly interested in hellhounds and fire creatures."

Oh gods. Maul. Please the fates, she'd sent him far from Pytheios's grasp. "Do you know what they want with them?"

"Not definitively. However, Pytheios continues to age. He appears worse every time I see him, but, by my calculations, his deterioration should have killed him long ago."

Skylar nodded slowly, thinking back to the state he'd been in, in his dragon form with those moth-eaten wings. "So, you think it's something to do with keeping him alive?"

"Or keeping his witch alive. She has lived long past when most humans survive."

And still looked pretty damn good. Skylar frowned as a memory triggered. The witch's words before she'd knocked Skylar out. "I think she's going to drain my powers." It had to be how they'd lived this long, right?

Airk's right hand, draped casually over his knee, clenched and unclenched several times, though he didn't seem to even notice. A tic, perhaps. Or a tell? Come to think of it, she'd taken this man at his word that he was who he said. What if he was a plant, here to gain her trust and extract any secrets she might have? *Could* she trust him?

"You have an expressive face, Skylar Amon."

She raised her gaze to find him watching her with that unblinking stare. "So I've been told."

"You are wondering if you can trust me."

Rather than deny it, Skylar looked him directly in the eyes, unflinching, watching him as closely as he watched her in return.

Airk didn't even blink. "You can. Can I trust you?"

Skylar lifted a single eyebrow. "You think I wanted to be captured and dragged in here for whatever Pytheios has in store for me?"

"No." Airk chuckled, the low sound more hacking than a true laugh, like he hadn't had cause to use it in a long time. "They stopped trying to trick me over three centuries ago. Besides, you are too much your mother not to be who you are."

Skylar considered his words, thinking through the underlying truth. Despite his emaciated form, she could see Airk was around her age, a little older, which meant his story about knowing her mother as a boy lined up. For now, she'd be careful to keep her secrets well guarded. Thank heavens she hadn't revealed the existence of her sisters.

Still, she'd always been an eerie judge of character, and her gut was telling her Airk was who and what he claimed to be. Yet another person affected by Pytheios's power-hungry claim on the throne.

"So, we agree to trust each other, then?" Without any clue as to why she'd risk it, Skylar held a hand through the bars.

Airk glanced at her hand then back up to her face before wrapping her hand in a surprisingly warm and strong grip. "We are agreed."

The new mark at the back of her neck suddenly heated, the sensation closer to stinging than a comforting warmth.

"*Skylar.*" Ladon's voice sounded beside her, and inside her, as though he'd placed his lips near her ear and whispered her name.

With a sucked-in breath, she released Airk's hand and twisted to look around the space behind her. Empty.

And silent. Black hole silent. Outside, wind scattered the ice and snow off the mountainside like a veil of sheer white floating away in the moonlight. But the sound of that wind didn't penetrate this room.

Please tell me that wasn't some weird mate thing where I'm not allowed to touch another man. She considered touching Airk again, just to test the theory, but didn't want to rock the rather new trust they'd founded.

"Are you unwell?" he asked, eyeing her with concern.

A man locked away for centuries thought she was the one with problems. Terrific.

Skylar lifted a hand to feather a touch over the back of her neck, but the sensation had disappeared along with Ladon's voice. "Honestly...I don't know."

But no matter what, she couldn't sit here like a freaking lump of uselessness. Her mother's words flitted through her mind. *Always have a plan. Always be thinking several moves ahead of your opponent. If you get caught, determine what you can use to get away.*

Airk was all she had in here.

"You must have a plan," she said.

"A plan?" Wariness crept into Airk's voice.

Skylar scooted closer to the bars and lowered her voice. "To get out of here. In all this time, you can't tell me you haven't tried it."

Airk remained silent for a long moment, searching her face.

She didn't blame him for hesitating. If she'd been a prisoner as long as he, she wouldn't trust anyone else, either. "I'm a phoenix, and the man who slaughtered my parents and grandparents has me prisoner. I'm not here to harm you."

She held her breath while he considered her words, her earnest expression. "I have tried many times."

Now we're getting somewhere. "What happened?"

He gazed back with eyes flat with defeat. "I am still here, am I not?"

"Good point." She sighed, biting her lip as she thought. "Did you ever get close?"

"They always found me before I could get out of the mountain."

Damn. Except...

"Could you tell if the witch's spell to hold back powers is limited to this room?"

Airk frowned. "How could I tell?"

"The dragon half of you... When you got out, could you feel him?"

"I always feel him. He's me. I simply cannot let him out."

Dang. That left that question as a gaping hole.

"Why do you ask me these things?"

"If I can access my powers, I can teleport you to my...people." Now why was she reluctant to say mate?

Realization followed swiftly on the heels of the question. Because it hurt too much, that was why. Being parted from Ladon forcibly like this made her want to crawl out of her own skin.

Skylar buried it deep, because it didn't help anything. "Then at least they'll know where to find me. As of now, they likely think either the White or Green Clans have me. They only saw the white dragon who snatched me, not Pytheios. They'd be wrong."

If they knew yet at all. She had no idea how long she'd been here.

Maybe, if she could get out of this dungeon in the sky, she could hear Ladon again. She hated to admit how much that thought was driving her now. Just to hear that deep, gravelly voice fed her hope. If they'd had more time together before this, maybe she could even feel him inside her head...

Again, Skylar pushed her thoughts away. Wishing wouldn't make it so. As of now, she had to assume that she needed to save her own ass.

"I am fairly certain I could not feel anything different," Airk said slowly.

But something to the cadence of his voice caught her attention. She raised her gaze to find him watching her with an intensity that, despite his staring so far, still struck her as off.

He mouthed some words, and she understood. Likely Pytheios's witch had set up some way to listen or some modern surveillance of the space. No way would they be left in here together otherwise.

What? she mouthed back.

I have a plan.

Relief, like cool spring water, soothed the edge of her fear.

In the morning, he mouthed.

· · ·

Ladon sat on the edge of his bed, the stone floor cold against his bare feet. A chill ran up his body, wrapping around his heart with a viselike grip, making it hard to breathe. This was the only place he could think to come where he might feel Skylar. Maybe hear her again.

The second Brand had confirmed the attack on Gorgon and their men and the fact that Skylar couldn't be found, his first instinct had been to fly to where they'd lost her. As her mate, maybe he could feel where she'd gone.

His next thought was to burn down the fucking world to find her. But he had no damn clue where to start. They'd been attacked by the Green and White Clans. One of them had to have her. But which one? And where would they have taken her?

He had reached out to every resource he had, including witches. Everything that could be done to find her was being done, and right now he had to wait. It had only been hours, but each second felt like years.

Fuck, he hated this shit.

No one would know the way his jaw hurt from the tension riding his body. No one could tell that the dragon inside him battled to be released and wreak death and destruction until his mate was found.

He was king. He couldn't afford to fall apart, even as he quietly died inside.

He'd learned patience, building his following and waiting for his opportunity to take out Thanatos. However, that skill seemed to have fucking vanished, because every second Skylar remained missing he wanted to rip a hole in the entire goddamn world.

Clan be damned.

"My king?"

Ladon vaguely heard Asher's call, knew his Beta had entered his rooms, but didn't lift his head. The scent of his mate lingered on the sheets, though it turned fainter with each passing day.

"Ladon?" Asher tried again.

"Yes?" He didn't turn to face his Beta.

"They have arrived."

About damn time. Brand had called in a favor, Ladon didn't ask what, to send Gorgon here faster than dragons could fly. Ladon shoved shoes on his feet, then jumped off the bed to stride through his suite to where Asher stood by the door leading to the perch. "Let's go."

He didn't wait, shifting the second he hit the outcropping of rock, frustration grinding at him to wait even that long. He launched himself into the air, dropping rapidly through the mountain, other dragons clearing out of his way in a hurry.

But their new arrivals couldn't avoid him, though they might want to in a minute.

He shot through the heart of the mountain, past the lower-level city with its bustling shops and places of business, into the training chamber. A group of men waited. One man in particular stood at the center.

Ladon didn't shift as he landed.

He couldn't. His dragon—all rage and fury—was fully in control now. Part of Ladon didn't want to wrest control from the beast that he'd loosed. Wings tucked in, allowing him to walk on all fours, Ladon prowled across the room, his claws clacking against the stone flooring, his entire focus on the man who stood his ground.

Tail whipping behind him, allowing no one near him from the back or the sides, Ladon stopped short of the black dragon shifter and roared, the sound smashing off the stone walls. Inches more, and he could bite the man's head off with a single snap of his jaws.

To Gorgon's credit, he didn't move or shift himself, instead holding up a hand to his guard, staying their own actions. "I lost Sky—"

Ladon roared again, a warning this time. No way did this man get to say Skylar's name. He had the satisfaction of seeing Gorgon visibly swallow.

The black king tried again. "I lost your mate. Something I will regret to the grave. Whatever you wish to do to me, I will accept. So will my people."

Samael stepped closer. "My king—"

"They will accept it," Gorgon spoke firmly, though he didn't take his gaze off Ladon.

Samael considered his king a beat before stepping back, head bowed slightly in acknowledgment.

Fuck. Not only did Gorgon's words indicate regret, but he'd basically given Ladon permission to kill him with no retaliation from his clan.

Ladon turned his head to the side, staring at the King of the Black Clan with a single eye. *"I was hoping you would give me an excuse to take your life."*

Gorgon's shoulders dropped, though he didn't dare smile. "Had our roles been reversed, and you lost my mate…" He shrugged.

He didn't need to say more.

The hot rage subsided, oozing out of him, leaving behind only the panic. Which was way worse. His chest constricted, but Ladon covered by taking a moment to shift. By the time he finished, he had his emotions under control, easier to do when human. Dragons were intuitive creatures, driven by instinct, less able to control their reactions in their animal form.

"What the hell happened?" he demanded. Brand and Kasia had already told him, but he wanted to hear it from Gorgon directly.

"Shall we speak more privately?"

Ladon grasped for patience, barely hanging on to it with the tips of his fingers as terror for his mate tried to drag it away. He needed to be out there, searching for Skylar. "Make it fast."

Only he couldn't go to the main conference room. All he could see in that room was Skylar's face—challenging him, blaming him, accusing him. Not that she would. She'd be doing all those things to herself about now.

Instead, he led Gorgon to the comms room. Brand and Kasia should be in on this discussion.

Gorgon raised his eyebrows when he discovered where Ladon had brought him but stood in calm acceptance while Asher hailed Brand and Kasia. Yet another sign that the King of the Black Clan had not lost Skylar on purpose. A suspicion Ladon hadn't been able to shake since he'd heard.

As soon as Brand's face appeared on-screen, with Kasia beside him and Reid and Arden behind him, Ladon turned to Gorgon.

He didn't hesitate. "We were attacked by the Green Clan, coming at us from below. It took longer to realize the White Clan were coming at us from above as well."

Made sense, the white dragons attacking from the sky in daylight, blending in with the fucking clouds. The green attacking from below, hard to see against the treed land, though with snow covering the area in patches, perhaps a little easier. For now, Ladon gave the king the benefit of the doubt.

"Two came at me at once from above. My thought was to protect Skylar by flipping over, getting her away from them, but they struck, and the force of the blow knocked her off my back."

Ladon crossed his arms, leaning against the desk. Either that or release his dragon in this small room and rend Gorgon's flesh from his bones. "Did you see where she went?"

If she was still a bloody stain on the ground in Norway, he'd kill every man there.

"A white dragon caught her. He flew off with her. I didn't see where. It took another hour to end it, and never once did they leave any of us alone long enough for one of us to pursue. We tried."

Gorgon ran a hand over his face, suddenly appearing drawn

and haggard and as old as his years. "*I* tried," he said in a low voice.

Based on the carnage that Brand's people reported, Ladon believed the older man. "And after?"

He knew all this already. Brand had informed him, but he needed to see Gorgon's face, his posture as he recounted what had happened.

Gorgon dropped his hand, black eyes going flat and void. "We tried to track her, follow her scent."

That cloves, smoky scent that was fading from his sheets was unmistakable. "And?"

"We followed to a ravine not too far from where we'd been fighting but hidden from our view by the formation of the mountains. Then...she disappeared."

"Disappeared?" Ladon glanced at the monitor to find Brand listening in grim silence.

"The trail stopped."

"Do you think she teleported?" Only Skylar couldn't send herself. Had she found someone who could take her with them? That seemed incredibly unlikely. Except... "Maul."

Brand jerked upright, turning to face Kasia, who paled. "We left him at Ben Nevis," she whispered through white lips.

"I haven't seen him." He'd assumed the hellhound was off doing whatever the fuck hellhounds did.

"Did you smell him?" Ladon directed the question to Gorgon.

Already the king was frowning, deep in thought. "When her scent went cold, a smell of rotting lingered. But..." He shook his head.

"But what?" Ladon demanded.

"Not like the dog. More like something had died there. The scent was faint, hardly a whiff."

"Maybe Maul saved her?" Kasia whispered through hands she'd raised to her mouth.

"Let's make sure he's not still here, first." Ladon nodded at Asher, who immediately rose and left the room to conduct a search.

"And if he's not?" Brand asked.

Ladon clamped down on yet another surge of gut-clenching panic. "I'm going to search every corner of this planet and find her. Starting with the White Clan."

No more waiting.

Gods how he fucking hated that word. Never, even when Thanatos was bleeding his clan dry, had he felt this impotent.

"Blood," Gorgon interrupted.

"What?"

The black king shook his head. "I can't believe I didn't think of it. We assumed Skylar had tried to fight off whoever took her, or maybe they were injured before they got to her. A small amount of blood was on the ground."

Kasia grabbed Brand's arms. "I need to see it."

"No," the Gold King protested.

"I'm going." She disappeared, taking Brand with her, leaving only Reid and Arden in the empty room.

"Uh…" The captain glanced around the space, then looked to Ladon. "Anything else?"

"Let us know when they return."

Reid nodded, cutting off the call.

"I'll be in my room," Ladon told Gorgon in a low voice. "You and your men are in the same quarters as last time."

Gorgon was smart enough to keep his mouth shut, probably sensing how Ladon was windmilling on the edge of a dangerous precipice. Terror and violence warred inside him, fighting the part of him dedicated to his clan, the need to protect both them and Skylar ripping him apart.

CHAPTER TWENTY

Skylar lay on her uncomfortable stone slab and stared at the black sky. Watching the watery winter moon cross overhead had been a slow form of torture. She needed to get out of here now.

"If you will not sleep, at least try to eat," Airk murmured from his own cell.

Last night, a tray of food had been brought in by a young woman who'd scurried back out like the hounds of hell were after her. Scraps, hardly enough to sustain life. Like she could eat.

Skylar shook her head. Be damned if she did anything her captors wanted her to do. She thought of giving it to Airk. The man was skin and bones. "You want it?"

"I am fine, and you will only hurt yourself," Airk assured her. "If they want you alive, they will force nutrients into you in more unpleasant ways. Eat."

That pissed her off even more. She'd been tempted to throw the shit at the small, female-born red dragon who'd brought it here, but the poor woman, her hands shaking and her eyes wide with fear, probably wouldn't even report it. Skylar knew a cowed, broken soul when she saw one.

No one else had come in after, but what if Airk didn't get them out before Pytheios or his witch came for her?

She hadn't heard Ladon again, though she'd tried. Maul made no appearances. With every passing minute, Skylar had to battle down fear and frustration and a shit ton of impatience. Ladon had to be out of his mind. He had to know by now...

She honestly had no idea what his reaction might be. Anger most definitely. Worry for what someone might do with her, possibly against his people.

Concern for her. Mostly because a threat to her life was a threat to his now that she bore his mark. He'd told her flat out he wanted her for more than a bed partner or what she could bring as a phoenix. He liked her, respected her. Wanted her. And she hadn't said it back.

Because I'm a damn coward.

They hadn't had enough time—

"Time." The whispered word escaped her lips almost without her realizing.

"Did you speak?"

Airk shifted in his cell, sitting up. No surprise that he wasn't asleep. She'd come to wonder if he ever slept.

"Talking to myself." She threw an arm over her head, blocking out the now less-black color of the sky.

According to Airk, the atmosphere at this elevation was so thin, it no longer masked the black of space during the day. Sure enough, when the sun was at its zenith, the sky still appeared almost black directly overhead, fading to navy. The edges, hugging the curvature of the earth, showed the sky-blue color most were familiar with. Morning had barely broken; she should rest more, but she couldn't.

Any time now, right? But she couldn't ask him.

The faint *whoosh* of the door opening didn't even ping on her radar. Must be time for breakfast, although she would've guessed it was too early.

"Hello, Nathair."

Airk's greeting had Skylar dropping her head to get a look at who her fellow inmate was talking to.

A youngish man stood outside her cell, peering in at her. Dark hair with a white streak over one eye, he avoided eye contact. A soft clicking sound had her dropping her gaze to his hands. He twisted a multicolored block game, one she recognized. Was that a…? It was. A Rubik's Cube. What the heck?

When the man didn't talk, she glanced at Airk, eyebrows raised in question.

He waved her off—though she took the signal more as an indication to follow his lead. "Nathair, I would like to introduce you to Skylar Amon."

Why was Airk being so polite, kind, even?

"Skylar, you asked why my speech is not more formal than it is, given how long I have been here?" Airk asked.

She frowned. "Uh-huh."

He canted his head toward the man still not looking her in the eye. "Nathair has kindly been my source of information. He comes to play chess with me, and we talk, which allows me to practice the changes in speech patterns in multiple languages gradually. He brings me books and, in the last century or so, magazines, when he can."

"That's…nice of him." Airk had befriended one of his captors? What was this? Stockholm syndrome?

Nathair bobbed his head as if nodding in agreement.

"I consider him to be my one true friend."

The man did lift his head at that, his hands pausing on his puzzle. He cocked his head in a twitchy move, almost like a bird. Without another word, Nathair pushed his hand through the bars, offering what she could now see was a solved puzzle to Airk, all the colors perfect on each side of the cube.

"I'm done with this game." He glanced over his shoulder. "And no one is watching."

Airk rose and accepted what appeared to be a gift to help pass the time. As soon as he took it, Nathair turned and left the room.

"He seems…fun," Skylar murmured.

Airk didn't seem to hear her, already bending his head over his new toy, rapidly rotating the pieces.

What the hell? She was surrounded by people who weren't

quite balanced, it seemed. And she was putting her trust in this man to get her out? Maybe she needed to rethink her exit strategy.

"Airk—"

A soft *snick* that didn't quite fit with the sounds of his working the cube reached her. With almost frantic hands, Airk tugged at it, and it *snicked* again, coming apart to reveal a small, hollow center with a piece of paper.

"What is that?" she asked.

"The codes to get out of our cells." He handed her one slip of paper. "This is the code to mine, you can just see it from your angle, and I can see yours." Thanks to the hexagonal shape to the cells around the edges of the room. He held up another slip of paper.

"How—" But she cut herself off. Questions could come later. For now, they needed to move.

Both hurried to their doors. Quickly, having to reach, pressing painfully against the immovable bars, Skylar punched the combination of letters, numbers, and Tibetan symbols into the modern keypad on Airk's door. As soon as she hit the last button, the lock slid back with a *thunk* of metal on metal.

Only when he swung open the door did she have the thought that he might leave her here. That tug of anxiety eased when he immediately went to work on the keypad on her cell. No sound had ever been sweeter than that lock freeing her.

"We have minutes at most," Airk said. "Let us go. Stay quiet."

Skylar actually smiled at that, though it quickly disappeared as purpose rose in her faster than a cresting wave. Stealth was her specialty. If she could hide inside Ben Nevis without being discovered, she could do this. First, they'd get to where she could feel her powers. She'd get Airk out of here, send him to Ladon with instructions. Then she'd get her own tail out of here.

Nathair had left the vault door barely open, but enough that the lock on it had not clicked into place, allowing them to force it open and move through. They found a spiral staircase, reminding Skylar again of those medieval castles, except the walls, like in their dungeon tower, were glass, allowing them to see outside.

Following Airk, they ran down those stairs as quickly and silently as they could. For such a big man who'd been trapped in a small room all his life, he sure knew how to move stealthily.

The constant spinning view, with no relief of a landing or need to stop for a hallway off the stairs, had Skylar dizzy and nauseous in short order. She breathed in through her nose and out through her mouth and kept going. She could throw up later.

Finally, they came to the bottom, which emptied into a chamber with another set of stairs to the right...and an elevator.

How tall was Everest again? And how far down did they have to go to get out of here? Shit, this could take weeks.

"Please tell me we're taking the elevator," she whispered.

Airk didn't answer. Instead, he reopened the cube and pulled out another slip of paper, punching in a code to access the elevator.

Guess that answers that.

In seconds they were inside the car, which dropped in total silence. Fast, if she wasn't mistaken. "Won't they be monitoring this?"

Airk nodded.

"If you had that plan in place already, why not try to get out of here before?"

"I've already tried on my own and failed. More times than I care to remember. I have been waiting."

"For what?"

"Help." He looked her up and down. "For the fates to bring me you."

He'd been waiting for help? Maybe the reason he hadn't escaped was his plans weren't all that great. Maybe they should've taken the damn stairs. "How far did you get before you got caught last time?" she wondered as she held her nose and blew, popping her ears.

His lips hitched to one side. "Not far enough."

Right. Focus on this attempt. This time, at least, he had her to help him out. And she had him. They could do this. Skylar closed her eyes, reaching for her fire.

Nothing.

Anxiety continued to toast the edge of her emotions, threatening to paralyze her.

On a long breath, she opened her eyes to find Airk watching her. She shook her head. His jaw clenched, but he said nothing, intent on the next steps.

"When we stop, either we get lucky or we do not," he said. "I have picked a floor that I understand to be uninhabited."

"So, let's hope we get lucky." She flicked a glance upward but found no lighted indicator. "How long does it take to get down there?"

"We are stopping at 18,000 feet, roughly 11,000 feet below our dungeons."

"Any idea how fast this thing moves?"

Airk grinned at that. "Pytheios ensures every technology in this place is state-of-the-art. This one is high-speed and travels approximately seventy-two kilometers per hour."

"And how do you know that?"

He shrugged. "I have my sources."

In other words, Nathair.

Skylar did a quick translation of speed and distance and time. "Three minutes?"

He nodded.

"Handy," she mumbled.

"I am in agreement."

"We really need to work on your contractions, buddy."

He didn't pull his gaze from the door, but his eyebrows did go up.

"Instead of I am, it's 'I'm'. Or you could just say 'yeah'."

"Yeah?" He tested out the word and gave a funny frown.

"It's a casual form of *yes*."

"I understand."

Oh, my gods, I'm giving grammar lessons to a dragon shifter in a high-speed elevator in Mt. Everest while trying to escape.

Anything to take her focus off the nerves fluttering through her.

She could do this. Handle this. She'd prepared all her life for this.

Gravity pushed down on her body as the elevator car slowed, though it still took several more seconds before it came to a stop. She and Airk both tensed, half crouching into defensive positions as the doors *whoosh*ed silently open. Immediately the air here felt thicker, though still dry and cold and pretty damn thin, regardless of the pressurization they did. Or whatever.

When no one jumped them, Airk slowly stuck his head out, then waved her to follow. The mountain down here was like a gilded imitation of Ladon's mountain home, the decor decidedly... fancy. Not in a good way, either, more in an obnoxious way. The hollowed-out stone corridors, human-sized in this part, had the same thick doors, but newer, nicer, with access panels at each door. No hopping into a room to hide should someone else happen across them.

Could no one get to the dungeon tower in dragon form?

Made sense once she thought about it. No one in that way, and no one out that way. Dungeons were meant to be difficult to access.

Airk paused, waving her back, and both of them flattened against the walls as he listened for whatever he'd heard. As her mother had taught her to do, Skylar controlled her breathing, her heart rate, focusing her mind on images that calmed her, because dragons could hear fear.

Airk started forward. She reached out to put a hand on his back, to remain close. Except Airk rounded on her, his face a fearsome mask, lips pulled back over bared teeth, though he remained silent. Had not releasing his dragon all this time made him this way? Or lack of physical interaction?

Airk blinked and stepped back, still in total silence. "I am not accustomed to being touched," he whispered.

She could see the true contrition in those pale blue eyes. "I understand."

He gave a jerky nod and they resumed their halting progress down the tunnel, Skylar careful not to touch him again. With Airk focused ahead of them, she made sure to watch their backsides.

The exact moment her powers returned to her she knew it.

The process wasn't gradual, not a little at a time. Instead, everything came back more like a rubber band stretched far away then released, snapping into place.

Airk must've heard her small gasp, because he turned, a question in his eyes. In answer she called up a small amount of the fire from within her, manifesting it at the tip of one finger with a grin.

"Do not," Airk warned. "Not yet."

She'd explained how her power worked, and the man was damn smart. No surprise he guessed that she'd been about to happily apply it to him, sending him to Ben Nevis, and hopefully to Ladon.

"Why?" she whispered.

"I am not leaving you. Let us attempt to get out of here together first."

Made sense. She nodded, and they continued on.

. . .

Ladon jerked to a stop in the middle of the training floor. He'd told his men he'd give Skylar till morning to get her ass here. She hadn't. He was going to find her now.

Asher stumbled behind him at the abrupt halt. "My king?"

Ladon waved him off.

Skylar.

He could feel her. Almost as though a switch had been flipped inside him, connecting the circuits and allowing the current to flow unimpeded.

If he could feel her, could she feel him? Hear him? *"Skylar."*

No response. He focused, the same way he did when in dragon form and communicating with his people.

"Skylar."

Still nothing.

He kept his eyes closed and concentrated. When he focused,

he could feel the members of his clan. Not individuals per se, but their attachment to him through the mark each carried on their hands. He turned that awareness on his mate, picturing a string connecting her to him, much like the game of telephone human children used to play. Distance, or the fact that their mating was so new, and other obstacles, might be causing a hiccup in the sound, but the connection was there, nonetheless.

After a few deep breaths, sensation flowed through him. Emotions. Not his, but Skylar's. She was…trapped, terrified, and…

"Hopeful," he murmured, frowning.

Why hopeful?

Holding on to that sensation flowing through him, Ladon tried to send her something back. He sifted through his own roiling emotions, an act totally against his nature. He'd never spent much time or care with emotions, finding them to be more hindrance than help.

But if this was the only way to get through to his mate, he would. The only emotions she needed from him right now were ones that could keep her safe.

Ladon called upon memories. The day he'd taken the throne—resolute, determined. The way he'd dealt with his position every day since—still resolute, still determined, but also focused on the endgame. The day he'd first laid eyes on his mate—complete.

Only he'd been so focused on her as a phoenix that day, he hadn't realized it until later. *Come back to me.*

If he could find her, get her out of there, he would leave his throne in an instant to do so. He'd give it all to Asher. He wasn't whole without her.

. . .

*L*adon.

Skylar paused in the process of placing her feet quietly, slowly as they moved through the mountain step by step.

She had no damn clue where she was oriented in relation to

the mountain and getting outside now. It seemed to her Airk was moving them farther to the interior, but knowing for sure was impossible. The same lighting that mimicked sunlight inside Ben Nevis worked here. All she knew was that dawn had broken over the mountains, as the lighting grew brighter with each passing second.

Airk turned when she still didn't move. "What?" he mouthed.

How could she explain to him in a few words that she could feel her mate. She couldn't hear him, couldn't reach him tangibly, but Ladon was with her regardless. His steady presence, that ruthless determination, and something else. A quality she couldn't put her finger on.

"Ladon." She deliberately thought his name this time, sending it to him down the connection binding them together regardless of distance.

He didn't answer. She couldn't even tell if he'd heard.

However, that connection, the person he was, served only to bolster her determination to get her ass out of here. She could do this.

Skylar went to wave Airk to continue but froze midwave when the unmistakable howl of a creature in pain split the air.

"What was that?" she whispered. It had sounded like a dog.

Airk didn't answer, instead moving forward faster, not bothering to see if she followed. She did. Another howl reached them just as Airk paused at a door.

He took out another slip of paper.

Realization trickled through her as though ice water had been injected into her veins. No fucking way. He wouldn't have this code unless he'd planned to come here well in advance.

Airk wasn't getting them out of the mountain... He was here for a purpose.

He glanced over at her as he got to the last part of the code. He couldn't speak, because whatever, or whoever, was on the other side of that door would hear, but he seemed to be trying to communicate something with his eyes.

Skylar tipped her head. "Don't do it," she mouthed.

"I must."

He pushed the last button, and the panel glowed green, the bolt sliding to with a soft *snick*. In a burst of might, Airk slammed into the room, throwing the door back into the stone wall so hard it stuck there.

Both of them ran inside, and Skylar knew immediately they were up shit creek.

She took in the scene with a lightning quick glance. The incongruent scents of cinnamon and rotting filled the room as Pytheios lay prone on a rock slab, his white witch standing over him. Rhiamon's eyes were black, like a void had consumed the sockets and sent tendrils of poison through to the pale skin below, while silver irises like moons floated in the darkness.

A creature was chained to the wall, howling its pain. Whatever Rhiamon was doing—visible, see-through lines of black extended from the creature to the king, as if Rhiamon was magically pulling the soul out of the thing and forcing it into her master.

She also knew they couldn't run.

"They're weakened when they do this," Airk snarled before he sprinted at them.

So enmeshed in the spell were the two, or perhaps so dazed by the power if it, both responded slowly at the interruption. Rhiamon turned to look over her shoulder at the intruders, giving Skylar an unimpeded view of the pathetic thing they had chained to the wall.

No! The word screamed in her mind, and her heart shattered as her gaze landed on the creature they tortured. "Maul!"

Airk sprinted at the king, but Skylar knew, after how they'd knocked her out in the ravine in Norway, that if they were going to make it through this, she needed to take out the witch.

She'd better damn well be weakened.

"Do not harm him," Pytheios rasped. An order to his witch? Skylar blinked. Right. The prophecy.

Skylar reached Rhiamon just as the woman turned to face Airk, hands raised to protect her king. She opened her mouth, probably to utter another spell, but Skylar had been faster, acting on decades of training.

Using the martial arts skills her mother had insisted all her daughters master, she vaulted over her, grasping the woman's head in her hands and twisting as she cartwheeled her legs in the air. The snap of Rhiamon's neck caused her nothing but satisfaction. So did watching the woman's body drop to the floor in a contorted heap of limbs, her eyes still open, staring, unseeing.

"No one was holding me down this time, bitch," Skylar spat at her.

The roar that pierced the air wasn't one of heartbreak, but rage. She whipped her head around to connect with glowing red, flames consuming the sockets of Pytheios's eyes, even as his entire body went up in crimson flames.

Fuck. Fuck. Fuck. Run.

Except Pytheios moved oddly. Like a decrepit old man who had to concentrate to take each step. Skylar didn't give herself time to think. Airk already lay beside him. Skylar lunged at Airk's form on the ground even as she called for the fire inside her. She hoped to hell this worked. Thinking of the only place she could send him, she shoved Airk's limp body.

The white dragon shifter disappeared in an instant.

She didn't have time to appreciate that or worry. Getting to him brought her too close to Pytheios.

He backhanded her so hard the hit echoed in her head and pain exploded in her cheekbone. *Ugh*. If he'd done that while at full strength, he would've snapped her neck or broken her face.

He lunged for her, and she tried to move, get out of his path, but he managed to clamp a hand over her wrist, his grip shaky. Weak.

Skylar bit down a scream as his fire burned her skin. He was trying to kill her now, no doubt in her mind.

Panic filled her body, a sound like white noise a cacophony in her ears. But the fighter in her raged against the end. Raw heat built inside her, an inferno of fire stoking hotter, her skin starting to glow, the feather marks taking on a white-hot shine.

On the edge of out-of-control, Skylar used his grip as leverage, jumping up to get her legs between them, then let the inferno escape, blasting out of her in an explosion of rage and terror. The force slammed them apart, but she managed to send her power into the hit.

The blast sent her flying backward to slam against the stone wall before crumpling to the ground. At the same instant, Pytheios disappeared. She smacked the back of her head with enough force to make her vision go black for a long beat. Heart throbbing, arm in agony, and head pounding, she still managed to scramble up off the floor.

Holy shit. What was that?

She'd never come apart at the seams that way.

Then logic intruded, and she called herself all kinds of terrible things. She should've sent him to Ladon. Let her mate kill that fucker and end this.

You still have to get out of this mountain.

With a gasp she ran to Maul, who stood on all fours, though he trembled with the effort, still attached to the wall by the dragonsteel collar around his neck. Head hanging, he watched her with eyes dimmed by exhaustion and pain and whatever they'd been doing to him, his gaze begging her for help.

An image flashed in her head: her getting out of here without him.

"No way. I need you as much as you need me."

Lighting her fire, which had doused the second she hit the ground, she gently touched the hound. In a blink he left and returned outside the chains. He managed to keep his feet, thank the gods. Because if he hadn't, she had no hope of moving a mountain of fur and bones.

A quick visual assessment turned up nothing that she could see as an immediate cause of his weakness. Across one shoulder a white slash of already healed flesh told her he'd recently been wounded. Was that how they'd caught him? The yelp she'd heard in the ravine? But they'd allowed him to heal first, brought him back to full strength. Why? So they could do whatever they were doing?

Skylar aimed a glare at the dead witch still staring at her from glassed-over eyes. "What did they do to you?"

The images he sent her made no sense. Something to do with sucking and teleporting and strength.

They didn't have time to dissect it now. Skylar had to think. She could send him to Ladon, just as she'd done with Airk, but the likelihood of escaping this labyrinth on her own, even with her skills, before being caught were low. Especially now that Pytheios knew she was out.

No way could she hide here with Maul. His unique stench alone would bring the red dragons down on them. And, while she'd sent Pytheios far from civilization, and he was weakened, he'd still call upon his army and return. Plus, the girl who served her and Airk in the tower would discover their absence by tonight.

Oh fuck. I should've sent Pytheios to the bottom of the ocean, the center of the earth. Killed him. Even the in-between. Except she hadn't been thinking.

Too late now. Worry about that later.

They needed to get out. Fast.

"I need your help, boy."

Not to get to Ladon. They were definitely too far away, and Maul was too weak to combine their powers, like she'd done with Kasia, to get them home to Scotland. Still, maybe they could get out of this mountain.

"Have you been here before?" *Please. Please. Please.*

Flashes of the inside of the red mountain came to her, but jerky, with time between each one, like he was reaching for the ability to communicate.

"What about outside?"

Images of rock and ice and snow. Everest in oncoming winter. Terrific. At least they were at an altitude, which meant she could breathe outside, though she might freeze to death in the process.

Better than burning or whatever Pytheios had planned. She

sank her hand into Maul's spiky fur, her heart constricting as she could feel the effort behind every breath, the tension trembling in his big body. "Let's go."

Maul's teleporting was faster. A blink and then they were outside, Skylar's stomach protesting the transition. Immediately, she was blasted with icy wind, the snow stinging her exposed skin. Her body clenched in immediate, terrible cold, shivers racking her, shaking her until her teeth rattled in her head. They couldn't stay here or she'd die of exposure.

A roar trumpeted through the blast of the storm. No mistaking that sound. A dragon. "Please tell me you have a few more hops in you?" she asked through teeth clenched painfully together to stave off chattering. She needed to get to civilization and then she could send Maul to Ladon.

"Do you know this area? Is there a city close enough that you can get me to the outskirts? If I can get to humans, I can get myself home."

The words were hardly past her lips before they hopped again, three times in quick succession. The first several jumps took them farther and farther down the mountain. Each jump took longer, not instantaneous like it usually was with the hellhound. The nothing reached for them, grasping at them like the bony hands of death. In between, Maul had to rest, his sides heaving as he sucked in air.

The last time, they ended up on a ledge where she could see the glitter of lights through the snow. Maul could barely keep his eyes open by this point. Gods, she was killing her hellhound.

Skylar wrapped her arms around his neck, ignoring his smell as she buried her face in his fur. "That's far enough. I can make it down there on my own."

She couldn't. She'd die of exposure before she got near it. But at least Maul would live and Ladon would know where she was.

A shadow darkened the gray and white sky overhead, and instinctively, Skylar ducked. The dragons were risking being seen to come for her? If she ignited now, they'd see. But they'd see anyway; the ledge she and Maul were on was exposed with no place to hide, and dragons had excellent eyesight.

"I'm sending you home. To Ladon."

Maul shook his head, jowls slapping.

She'd let the red dragons find her and put her back in that dungeon. The rest would be up to Ladon at this point.

"I'm not arguing about this." Before she could ignite her fire, the hound took a shuddering breath, then they were gone.

That horrible black, soundless space wrapped around her, and Skylar had to hold back her panic, tightening her grip on Maul's fur. Like what had happened with Kasia, the pressure increased and her hold on consciousness started to slip. Like clawing her way out of a nightmare, only she was going into it.

With a whoosh, sound returned. The cracking of wood surrounded them as the kitchen table they ended up on buckled and split. For the third time, Skylar's head hit stone. That was going to be one huge goose egg when she bothered to check.

Shaking off the lethargy of the unconsciousness that had tried to overtake her in the in-between, she pushed unsteadily to her feet. A quick check told her Maul had taken them to an abandoned home of some sort. How he knew it was here, she had no idea.

The effort to get them there had taken its toll on Maul. Still lying on his side, breathing sounding like a horrible effort, the dog's eyes rolled to the back of his head as he went limp, but at least he was still breathing, the smoke and rotting scent of him coming out in ragged puffs that crystalized in the freezing air. Tears stinging the back of her eyes, Skylar wrapped her arms around his thick neck, laying her head against him. "You did good, you big lug. Now it's my turn to take care of you."

She sat back on her haunches. Maul blinked, trying to focus on her. "I saw lights that looked like an airstrip. If it is, I'm taking one of those planes and flying my ass out of here."

No way would dragons expect her to use human technology that put her directly in their territory as an escape method.

"Tell Ladon."

He gave a small whimper, not even the sound a newborn

hellhound might make, and Skylar had to control her own tears. She needed to stay strong. "I'll see you soon."

With that, she ignited her fire. "Sorry about this." She slammed her palms into his chest and sent him to her mate.

Skylar bent her head and took a moment. At least Airk and Maul were both safe. That was, if Ladon didn't kill Airk before hearing him out.

The dragons wouldn't come among the humans in dragon form but might appear here as human and search for her. By now they had no idea which way she'd gone. That shadow had not been a scout, or it would've zeroed in on her and Maul sooner.

Please don't let him have sensed us.

She couldn't hop in a plane immediately, not with the dragons in the air searching. As plans went, that would be too obvious. But if she held off a few hours before she took a plane, or snuck into a cargo hold, or perhaps tried to find enough money to get on a flight, using humans as camouflage, that could work. Which was the greatest risk—waiting or not waiting?

Regardless, she needed better clothes for this climate. Plus, if she could find a graveyard, she might have a way to camouflage her own scent.

She stood on shaky legs, bones aching from the cold.

Move.

CHAPTER TWENTY-ONE

"Let me see him." Ladon pushed through the men gathered in a circle around someone sitting on the floor of the training space. A man who appeared out of thin air, apparently beaten unconscious though apparently now awake.

"Káthor." One man stepped back. Then another repeating the same word. Only Ladon didn't acknowledge as he usually tried to.

Sure enough, a white dragon shifter, evident by his pale eyes, his shocking white hair the hallmark of an ancient lineage, sat on the floor, knees drawn up and arms draped casually over them as he warily stared back at Ladon. His face looked like he'd walked into something hard. Despite already healing, blood continued to drip from his nose, and bruises remained black across the left side, starting to turn green at the edges.

First instinct was to rip this man's guts out and hang him by them. Logic stayed Ladon's hand, and a calm settled over him. He squatted down to the man's level. "I am Ladon Ormarr, King of the Blue Clan."

The man gazed back at him in silence.

"It is customary to reciprocate an introduction with one of your own," Ladon said, his voice going quieter.

"My apologies. I was attempting to determine how to introduce myself. Airk Azdaja. I have been Pytheios's prisoner these five hundred years or more. Skylar Amon sent me."

Everything around Ladon froze, the people gathered around them faded to insignificance, as he zeroed in on the man. "What do you mean Skylar sent you?"

"I helped her escape from the tower dungeon in Everest where Pytheios was holding the both of us."

If that was true... "Then where is she?"

The words came out a low snarl. Any sane man would flinch. Not Airk Azdaja. He merely stared back, unmoved, though not uncaring, if the way a small nerve at the side of his jaw ticked. "I was knocked unconscious. I must assume she delivered me here to save my life."

Dread clutched at Ladon's insides even as his blood hardened in his veins, frozen with cold fury. "You *left* her?"

An unidentifiable emotion passed over the man's face. Irritation maybe. "I was not permitted a choice in the matter. No person regrets this situation more than I."

Ladon jerked to his feet, reaching for his dragon, prepared to summarily execute this man. Either he was a liar and a spy, or he'd left Skylar in that fucking red dragon stronghold to fend for herself.

Common sense stopped him. Of course Skylar would have done this. Damn the woman. She never worried about her own safety. Not if it meant saving someone else. If she was standing here, unharmed and with him, he'd admire the hell out of her for it. But, at this moment, with fear threatening to choke him, fury beat at him with the strength of dragon wings.

How the hell am I supposed to get to her?

Didn't matter. He was going. Now.

Before he could start his shift, Asher called out from behind them. "Ladon." Followed by several curse words. What snagged Ladon's full attention was the tone of his voice. He'd never heard his Beta sound agitated like that before.

"Watch him," Ladon told Wyot and Duncan, who bracketed Airk, still seated on the ground.

Satisfied the man couldn't get away, Ladon strode to where Asher stood. He didn't need more than a glimpse of the thing lying

on the ground at his friend's feet to break into a run. Skidding up
to the hulking form of the hellhound, he looked the animal over.

"Maul?" He laid a hand on the dog's massive chest, grateful
that his ribs moved up and down. "He's alive." He jerked his gaze
to Asher. "Get Fallon."

Ladon had no idea if the Healer's blood could do anything for
a hellhound, but it was worth a try.

"He was being tortured by Pytheios and his witch," Airk called
across the room. "Skylar must have sent him."

Of course she'd send her damn dog, too.

Airk's words sank deeper into his awareness. "My mate is
alone with the Rotting King *and* a witch?"

Ladon started across the room even as Airk mouthed the word
mate, shock freezing his expression. Had he not known?

Who the fuck cared? He was going to kill the bastard anyway.
Skylar was on her own, across the world with their enemies, and
the only man who could have helped her was standing in Ladon's
fucking mountain.

A small whimper stopped him dead in his tracks. Ladon
whipped around to return to Maul, who could barely lift his head.
"Where's Skylar?"

A series of images flashed through his mind, all a little hazy
as if he was seeing them through Maul's own pain and exhaustion.

Airk bursting into the room with Skylar on his heels. Skylar
killing the witch, before she sent both Airk and Pytheios away,
after getting slapped back by the king, who'd appeared weakened.

Ladon glanced at the white dragon shifter, the need to rip
the man's throat out and watch his blood coat the stone flooring
waning and easing into more of a blatant mistrust.

The next series of images from Maul—Skylar getting out of
the mountain and away—knocked the idea of slaughtering Airk
away. For now.

Only because she wasn't dead or back in a dungeon. Yet.

Ladon dropped his head forward to hide the depth of his relief
from those gathered around.

"She escaped," he said. Not entirely, but he knew his mate. She'd find a way to stay hidden and get out.

An audible murmur echoing his own relief passed through the gathered crowd.

"Maul got her to a nearby town."

"Lukla," Airk said. "It has to be."

Ladon barely heard the man, already mentally sifting through his options. It would be damn tricky extracting her from under Pytheios's nose. The small town most humans going to Everest flew to from Katmandu was hardly forty kilometers from the base camp on the mountain as the dragon flew.

What if he couldn't get to her in time?

Another flash of an image from the hellhound caught him midthought, and Ladon paused. "What are you telling me, Maul?"

Skylar couldn't be planning what he thought she was.

The dog grunted, a sound most definitely commiserating with Ladon.

Ladon jerked to standing. "Fuck."

He signaled his men. "Find a room to shove our new guest in. I want him guarded until Skylar returns and can tell her side of the story."

With that he strode away, muttering to himself about stubborn, risk-taking females trying to do everything by themselves. How the fuck was he going to find his mate if she was flying all over the goddamn planet?

Anger piled on like a bunch of dirty laundry as he made his way to the tech room. "Get in contact with Gorgon," he told the man currently operating the equipment.

"Yes, my lord."

The Black Dragon King was on his way back to Mt. Ararat, his stronghold in Turkey. Flying a direct path from Nepal to Scotland would take Skylar north of Turkey, if she could fly such a straight course. Regardless, Gorgon was already closer to her than any other ally. He could reroute, possibly intercept, run interference.

Something. Anything.

"He's not answering, my lord. They must be in flight."

Of course they were still in flight while dark still ruled the land over much of Western Europe, where Gorgon most likely was by now. Black dragons preferred to fly when the land was shrouded in darkness.

Ladon grabbed a piece of paper, writing out instructions. "Keep trying. Relay this message to him when he answers."

"Yes, sir."

Ladon strode toward the platform. Fuck waiting a second longer.

Asher followed. "You're not going after her."

"Yes, I am."

His Beta snagged him by the arm but released him, holding up his hands in defense as Ladon rounded on him with a snarl, fire no doubt ablaze in his eyes. "You are *king*. You can't go off, half-cocked, on some wild-goose chase."

"She is my mate. If she dies, no more king."

Asher got in his face. "And vice versa."

"You think I hadn't thought of that?" Ladon snapped. "But...I can feel her."

His Beta frowned and took a step back. "Already?"

Ladon said nothing.

Asher, jaw tight, shook his head. "I don't like it."

"No shit." He was still going. "Stay here until you hear from me."

"But—"

"That's an order." Maybe his last as king.

Leaping off the edge of the training platform and shifting as he fell, Ladon burst into his dragon form, faster than he'd ever made the transition. So fast, for the first time he felt as though he ripped his own skin off to let the beast out. The flash of pain lancing through him disappeared quickly enough that he dismissed it.

In a deliberate show for any spies watching, Ladon popped up over the top of the mountains then quickly gained more altitude. Flying during daylight hours meant staying where humans couldn't accidentally see at high altitudes. Luckily, that meant faster flying, a more direct line over the curvature of the earth.

I'm coming, Sky. He sent the thought to the woman who'd become everything to him.

No answer. Not that he'd expected one. That didn't mean he'd stop trying. Hell, he'd never give up on her.

He'd give all of it up, give the throne over to the men he trusted, walk away from everything...for her.

Skylar had morphed from being his means to an end to becoming the bright center of his life. If she died, he died, too, now that they were bonded. But even if his mark didn't grace the back of her neck, he'd follow her to the grave.

Ladon allowed his body to take over, flight the most natural thing a dragon could do. Some dragons were known to sleep in the process, even claiming they didn't have to stop to rest. Keeping half his mind attuned to senses taking in his surroundings, in case of impending attack, the other half he devoted to sending a constant signal to his mate.

Words poured through him and out of him to her, and he hoped to the gods that she heard. Even if she didn't answer.

Hours in, and already having stopped to rest for short periods, exhaustion threatened to pull him out of the sky. But he kept pushing.

A flash of white ahead and adrenaline spiked his blood, bringing him sharply back to full alert. Ladon tipped up, beating his wings to hover, focused on that spot.

"My king..."

The voice was familiar. Ladon looked around for more movement among the clouds. *"Who are you?"*

"Servants of our queen." Two white dragons dropped out of the clouds a good ten miles away.

"How the fuck did you find me?"

"Your people are trailing you, but we can fly for longer than blue dragons, so we caught up to you first." Right. Blue dragons may have the speed, but white were built for long-distance flying

and could go longer.

"My people—" Dammit. *"Hold on."* He sent the thought to the white dragons. Then he aimed a thought to one man only. *"Asher."*

"My king."

This far from Ben Nevis, no way should Asher have heard him. *"You disobeyed a direct order."*

"Actually, sir, you left me in charge. I gave myself a different order."

"If you left the mountain vulnerable—"

"You left us vulnerable taking this chance. Of course I didn't fucking leave the mountain—"

"Maybe this one…"

Ladon bobbled in the air, practically fell out of the sky at the sound of Skylar's voice.

"Skylar!" He shot the thought out, practically yelled at her.

Except Asher was still sending thoughts his way. Loud ones. *"Shut the fuck up for a minute, Asher. I heard her."*

Silence descended in his head and he waited.

"Skylar."

"Ladon?"

He dropped a good hundred feet in relief before he remembered to keep his wings moving.

"Where are you?" Why did she sound like she was whispering?

"Can't talk now. I'm stealing a plane. Headed to Rus…"

His head went quiet, like she'd disconnected a phone call, and Ladon couldn't hold back the rage of his dragon a second longer. On a roar of pain, and panic, and fury, he spewed blue flames into the air.

• • •

Skylar dragged the unconscious human she'd just knocked out over to another plane nearby, one tethered to the ground in what was obviously its permanent home. The guy was too heavy to try to stuff him into the plane out of sight, but she sort of positioned him around the wheels and prayed to the gods no one else at the airport would notice.

Then she grabbed the head of the wangliang—a malevolent spirit, this one manifested physically as a fenyang, or grave sheep. She'd slaughtered it in Lukla and brought it with her as camouflage. Not even dragons would scent her over the corpse of a creature that reeked of dung and decay. Granted, it meant she had to live with the nausea the smell caused, but it'd be worth it.

Skylar climbed into the man's plane, already fueled and primed, with a flight plan that wasn't the greatest for her, but she'd make it work initially, and, with full permission from the tower, took off into the sky. Once she was satisfied she'd gotten away without garnering attention—yet—she settled in.

She swiped at her eyes, fighting the exhaustion that wanted to drag her body into needed oblivion. She could sleep when she got to Ladon.

Of course they'd finally heard each other when she'd been in the middle of this.

"Ladon?" she tried now. And then several more times. But only silence greeted her.

She let out a huff of frustration. What good was this connection thing if it didn't work most of the time, dammit?

It had already been a long-ass day. Thanks to various human limitations—like language, guarded airspace, and the fact that she was a woman doing illegal things in aircrafts in western Asia—layered with needing to stay away from where the red dragons might look for her, she was sort of screwed no matter what direction she'd gone.

But she'd managed to stow away on a plane in Lukla, which had involved stuffing herself into a mail sack. She really should've mated a black dragon, because damn she was good at sneaking. Turned out, that plane had taken a northerly path up through China, over mostly desert. Not a direct route. Hopefully also not the way Pytheios would expect her to go.

She kept that heading now, for several reasons, crossing into

Russia in the small spot between Kazakhstan and Mongolia. Her mother had taught her Russian well, wanting her to have that part of her father's white dragon heritage. She blended in better there. While still precarious in general, the culture for human women wasn't as problematic in the region as it could be in western Asia. Also, if dragons caught her, she'd rather it be her father's clan. She could attempt to convince them, as she had the two men who'd sworn her loyalty.

What felt like eons later, now in the dark, she was still flying.

Stops for fuel had required her finding a map at the next stop that could show her small airfields she could get in and out of, sometimes stealing another plane already fueled rather than taking the time to top hers off and getting out before they caught her. She'd been going nonstop now for around forty hours, by her estimation, but who the fuck knew given time zones and the level of her exhaustion.

Not to mention hunger. She was starting to tremble with it.

Skylar gave her head a shake, widening her eyes to focus on her instruments. At least she'd made it over the border to Russia without incident. If she'd had Meira with her, they could've hacked the computer systems, making her flight legit and this trip loads easier. Instead, she'd flown low to the ground. Beyond foolish to try in the dark. Still, she'd managed to snag a skydiving rig, rather than a pilot's emergency chute, at her last stop. More uncomfortable to sit in, which she sort of hoped would keep her awake, but she'd have more control over it if she had to use it.

The panel in front of her started to blur, and Skylar sat forward, taking another deep breath, blinking rapidly. Just a little longer and she could rest.

Sleep.

Gods, the word dragged at her mind as much as the exhaustion did her body. Just a little nap. Close her eyes for a second.

Just a second.

Just a…

"Don't leave me. I'm nothing without you."

Skylar jerked awake with a snorting cough as she inhaled too hard. Adrenaline flooded her veins, giving her an extra spike of alertness. But catching herself nodding off wasn't what kicked off that little fit. Ladon's voice had done that.

She'd heard her mate again.

He'd sounded...beaten down, defeated, and almost as exhausted as her. And those weren't descriptions she expected when it came to him.

"Ladon?" She felt a tad ridiculous calling out to him like this, but she knew what she'd heard. Clearer than in the tower.

No answer.

Skylar focused, picturing her mate's face—that thick black hair, the scar making him appear so harsh, and those blue eyes that were anything but when they looked at her. *"Ladon?"* she reached out with her mind.

"Skylar?" This time disbelief edged his tones. *"Can you hear me?"*

"I can hear you." Tears of relief stung her eyes even as shock that this was happening at all pinballed through her. Was this nightmare almost over? Or was she hallucinating now?

"Thank the gods. Are you safe?" He sounded so...worried. Not like her in-control mate at all.

"For now. I'm still flying. Did Maul make it?"

"Yes. I left him with Fallon."

Another surge of relief had her breathing harder to keep her emotions in check, her hands gripping the yoke. *"What about Airk?"*

"We have him."

She couldn't quite pinpoint the emotion underlying those words. Not anger exactly, but something. *"You didn't kill him, did you?"*

"No."

Good. Airk was safe.

"Where are you?" he asked next.

"Approximately a hundred kilometers from Aleysk, Russia,

headed northwest through Russia toward Norway."

"Thank fuck for that."

"What?"

"Gorgon was already almost to Turkey, so he took the more southerly route to intercept you if you went that way."

Which put the black king too far south to help her. Her mind remained sluggish, like wading through deep mud that sucked at her, and she couldn't figure out why that was a good thing. *"Am I missing something?"*

"I went north. I'm somewhere over Nizhny, maybe 2400 kilometers from your location."

Quick math put that around 1500 miles. Skylar gripped the yoke so violently, she bobbled the plane. He was close. So much closer than she'd imagined. Almost close enough to feel him, close enough to touch. Yet still so far. What were the odds they'd reach each other before a dragon found her or humans shot her out of the sky?

They couldn't worry about that, though. *"What's the plan?"*

She could almost feel the rumble of his chuckle, the shake of his body. *"That's my mate."*

The small glow of pride at those words couldn't be helped. Not that he probably meant them as more than a pat on the back, but she'd take it.

Am I turning into one of those pathetic people whose entire identity is tied up in her partner? That was fast. Skylar rolled her eyes at herself, then realized that Ladon might have caught the thoughts, except she wasn't directing them at him.

"I'm trying for another four hours before I have to stop to rest," he said.

Her rib cage loosened up, letting her breathe again. He hadn't caught it.

His words registered. Dragons, if they pushed it, could go a max of approximately two hundred miles before needing a decent sleep. If she was right in her guess about the distance he'd come already, Ladon was already running on an empty tank. Concern for her mate poked at her like a dagger to the heart, but she managed to regain her tenuous hold of control and think. Four hours, at the speeds blue dragons could fly, put him roughly four hundred miles closer to her.

"I'll go as long as I can."

She might have to stop one more time to refuel, having already identified two private airstrips as possible locations—ones that were shared by überwealthy residents in a neighborhood at the edge of a city. The runway was accessible to each resident, all of whom had a plane hangar attached to their homes. Fly in, fly out.

The rich were the rich, no matter where you went or what you were.

"When's the last time you slept?" Ladon asked.

"I'm fine."

"Sky?" The low rumble of command was unmistakable, even through their link.

"Not since we got out of Everest."

"Shit, love. You'll kill yourself if you keep going."

She would not react to the endearment. *"I'll sleep when we're safe."*

"If you crash, I'll wring your neck."

Skylar chuckled at that. *"Back at you, Tarzan."*

"I'm not kidding." He growled this time.

Skylar playfully yawned before it dawned on her that he couldn't see. Plus, the fake yawn turned into a real one. A big one that stretched her jaw to the limit and made her eyes water.

"You need to stop."

He was right. *"Can't. Not yet."* She blew out a frustrated breath. *"Talk to me."*

"I thought I was."

"No. I mean keep it up. Keep me going."

"Uh. I'm not much of a talker."

"No shit."

"What do you want to talk about?"

"Anything." Just hearing his voice was keeping her going at

this point, giving her a second wind.

"Now that's a proposition."

Skylar laughed, then lowered her voice. *"Anything."*

"I'm holding you to that when I see you, woman."

"I'll hold you to it myself."

He was quiet a long moment, and Skylar laughed. *"Figures. I bet you were a contrary kid. The moment you have to talk you can't find anything to say—"*

"I'm glad you're my mate."

That shut her up in a damn hurry.

"And..." he continued. *"I think you feel the same way."*

Well, as topics went, this one was certainly the most interesting he could've picked. All that fatigue disappeared for a moment. *"What makes you think that?"*

"You mean besides the fact that I can feel you? Like you're inside me, part of me?"

Skylar bit her lip, her body heating up at his words, flushing at the idea. *"I can feel you, too."*

Holy cow, even her mental voice went all husky, despite having nothing to do with vocal cords. Could he hear that?

Ladon groaned. *"Don't hold back, Sky. Not anymore."*

He didn't say please, but she felt it just the same. *"What do you want from me?"* She whispered the words even as she thought them.

"Don't run from me. When all this is over. Stay."

"I never—"

"Don't lie, Sky. As soon as you thought Kasia was safe, you were going to...what do the Americans say? Jump?"

She gave a soft smile. *"Bounce."*

"Yeah. Don't do that."

Skylar shook her head with a grin. He sounded like she mattered even more than he'd already told her.

"Sky...promise me you'll stay."

"What if I can't? What if I'm not built for ruling a kingdom at your side?"

A derisive snort preceded a sensation...his emotions...

She blinked as realization struck. *"You don't want to be king?"*

"Never did."

"Then why?"

"No one else with the proper bloodlines"—he spat the last word—*"would confront Thanatos. Not that there's much royal blood in me. A few drops at best."*

He'd taken the position for his people. Skylar waited for something—shock maybe, or surprise, or something like that—but none came. Because she'd already figured that out about him. He wasn't the type to accept the restrictions his position would place on him, let alone have patience for the politics, unless the other choice was watching people he cared about suffer.

Then again, she wasn't built for politics, either. *"I'd make a horrible queen,"* she said.

"You're smart, driven, honest, and you care about others. Explain to me which part of that isn't meant to be a queen?"

"I can be too honest, and I'm stubborn."

"You don't need to tell me that."

She would've smiled at the frustration in his tone if she wasn't trying to have a moment. *"I'm serious."*

"I know." The words came through gruff. She could picture the intense light in his eyes as he watched her in that total way of his. That possessive way of his.

Skylar shivered.

"You are my mirror image, Skylar Ormarr, my match. I'm not asking you to stay queen, though it comes as a package deal. I'm asking you to stay with me. With me, Sky. Your mate."

Every part of her stilled before her heart kicked into a tripping rhythm. Her lips parted, but she closed them, having, for once in her life, no clue what to say in response. Maybe because she was too chickenshit to hope he meant what she wanted him to mean.

"Sky?"

For the first time since meeting her mate, Ladon sounded... hesitant, unsure of himself even.

Before she could reply, he broke in. *"Fuck, Sky. I hate having this conversation with you so far away. Say something."*

She smiled. *"What do you mean by stay with you?"*

"I mean I'll walk away from the throne. My people are liberated and now have allies. Asher can step up to lead. If being queen is going to make you run, then I can fix it."

Holy shit. He'd do that for her? Skylar couldn't wipe a ridiculous grin from her lips. At the same time, every part of her knew that wasn't the right choice. *"Don't do that."*

A pause greeted her comment. *"Don't do what?"*

"Don't walk away from the throne. It's part of who you are."

"You are a bigger part of who I am now."

That was the closest to a declaration of the heart she'd probably ever get from the rough man she'd mated. *"Well, Tarzan...I guess I'll have to stay."*

"What are you saying?"

Skylar smiled to herself, though she knew he couldn't see it. *"I'm saying I want you, Ladon Ormarr."*

CHAPTER TWENTY-TWO

If he hadn't been pushing himself to the very brink of his physical abilities, no way could he have slept while Skylar was still out there. Hell, he'd been reluctant to cut off the connection allowing them to communicate, even for something as basic as rest. At least the white dragons were still in the air, thanks to their longer distance abilities. They'd be taking a break about now, but he'd made sure Skylar knew to watch for them.

What if he couldn't reach her again?

They'd formed a plan, but no way was Pytheios or his lackeys not somewhere behind her. What if that bastard caught up or sent a squadron of dragon shifters after her? They'd been damn lucky so far, but what if that ran out?

Vulnerability did not sit well with Ladon.

Obnoxious beeping roused him from a dreamless slumber, and in a heartbeat, he was wide awake. He'd slept in his dragon form, curled up in the shadows of towering pine trees beside a still pond. His fire, closer to the surface in this form, kept him comfortably warm despite the freezing temperatures, though no snow or ice covered the ground.

Not bothering to uncurl, Ladon took a moment to shift, forcing himself to go slower than last time, his body receding into itself in a silent slide as the pine trees seemed to grow taller above him and the ground came up at him. Moments later, he lay in a field of dried grass crushed flat by his larger form. He'd set the alarm on his watch to wake him. He needed to turn it off, or it would be a beacon to anyone and anything tracking him.

Ladon hit the button to shut it up as he got to his feet.

"Skylar?"

No answer.

She'd flown another half hour after he'd landed to rest. Still, they'd agreed to wake at the same time. *Please don't let that connection be broken.* What if it had been a fluke?

Maybe he needed to be in dragon form.

Again, he forced himself to allow the shift to happen at its maddeningly slow pace. Lean bulk replaced his smaller form, his neck elongating, the spikes protruding, teeth and nails growing and sharpening to deadly weapons. Such a quick time between transitions, and his senses still enhanced, sharpening, the colors around him brighter, the sounds more brilliant in his ears, like he'd gone into a tunnel and emerged into the light.

Ladon waited, growling low in his throat, for the full scope of his dragon to be realized before reaching out to Skylar again.

"Talk to me, Sky."

Again, no answer, but something was different. He could feel her—the softness of her, and the hard, inside him. She was okay. Asleep maybe.

Gods he hoped he was fucking right, because who the hell knew? Feelings were not his strong suit. No one warned him that mates came with feelings.

Extending his wings out the forty feet from his body, Ladon gave a hard push, lifting into the air. Gaining speed, he barely cleared the tops of the trees, the needles slapping against his talons. Clear skies today meant he'd blend better, not having to be as careful about where he flew.

He should be so exhausted that his control over flight, his ability to shoot through the skies, was impaired. But at the end of another few hours, his mate waited for him, closing the distance between them.

Behind her, who knew what was coming, but damned if she'd

face it on her own.

Two hours in, he'd caught up with the white dragons as they roused from their own rest. They hadn't seen her, either, and panic was eating at his insides as though someone had poured acid down his throat. He searched the skies with every sense at his disposal, checking out every plane that flew into his notice. They shouldn't be close yet.

"Ladon."

He might've lost a hundred feet in a drop when her voice hit him. *"Sky, what the fuck?"*

"I overslept two hours, I'm sorry. Just getting started now."

That was so much better than every other alternative his mind had come up with, Ladon didn't care about the time lost.

"Ladon?"

"Are you on your way?"

"Yes."

"That's all that matters."

She was quiet a moment. *"You were wigging out."* Quiet delight came through in every syllable.

"I don't wig."

"Of course not." But he had no trouble interpreting the self-satisfied laughter in her voice.

Ladon grunted, then jerked his wings a bit too hard as her husky chuckle skated through him.

To conserve energy, they kept their conversation to a minimum. Flying at each other meant they were closing the gap as fast as they could. Hours later, Ladon's tension turned suffocating with every passing second he hadn't found her.

Where are you?

A flash of silver caught his eye before the buzz of an engine reached him. Fear and dread and hope blended in a nauseating mix with the fire in his belly. That had to be her.

"Flank her," he ordered the two white dragons on either side of him. Just in case.

"I can see you," he said to Skylar.

· · ·

S kylar searched the sky, but her mate was too far away, not to
mention the camouflage his belly scales provided, reflecting
whatever was below him. *"Are you sure?"*

"Dip your wings."

She tipped the yoke and righted it.

"Definitely you."

The relief in his voice was palpable, as if he were sitting beside
her already.

"We need to find a place for me to set it down." The closest
airstrip, according to the attendant's information, was another
hundred miles from here. Skylar relayed that information to Ladon.

"I'll fly beside you until we get there."

The plan was to leave the plane behind, with a note as to
where it came from originally. She'd check later to see if it had
been returned. She might be a thief when she had no other option,
but she refused to hurt other people in the process.

"Where should I look?" The level of anticipation, the need to
see him, shocked her in its urgency, tightening her insides like a
vise.

"Directly ahead. You'll see me any second."

Searching the skies in front of her, not even a blip of a dot
registered. With the sun almost directly above her, glare wasn't
the problem, though the brilliance of the early winter sky had
her blinking.

Where is he?

She'd come so damn far, and she was so damn tired. They
weren't safe yet, but they'd be together. Something she wanted so
badly, she ached with the tension of it.

I love him.

The realization came not as a sudden thought bubble over her
head, or even as a surprise, if she was honest about it. Knowing she
loved Ladon Ormarr...her mate...was already there, underneath

everything she'd done and said, every thought, so ingrained, she wasn't sure when it began. Otherwise, his appeal to stay with him would have fallen on deaf ears. She just hadn't put the words to it until this moment.

A dual sensation joined the urgent need to see him, to touch him. Flutters of excitement, like champagne fizzing through her blood, joined a deep-seated sense of belonging. With Ladon was where she was supposed to be, where she was her strongest, her most powerful, even though it also put her at her most vulnerable.

And she was okay with that. More than okay.

Who knew vulnerability would become something to embrace rather than scoff at or avoid at all costs?

A tiny movement, directly ahead and slightly above her, caught her eye. The beat of his wings maybe.

As she stared, his form grew larger, taking shape.

"I see you."

"What? You didn't believe me?" he teased.

Skylar shook her head with a goofy grin stretching her lips. Mr. Serious was teasing her now? Finding his destined mate had changed him like it had her, it seemed.

"I see you smiling. Are you laughing at me?"

Darn dragons and their overdeveloped senses. *"Maybe just a little. More like laughing with you."*

Foolish to allow herself the distraction of giddiness. They were far from finished with this perilous journey.

"I can't wait to get you out of that tin can. I need to touch you."

Gods what those words did to her. *"Me too."*

Ladon was bigger now, close enough for her to make out the glitter of the sun against his indigo scales. How could she have ever found dragon shifters abhorrent, based only on the actions of a few? He was the most beautiful thing she'd ever seen—terrifyingly powerful while gracefully controlled. Awesome.

"A soon as I get to you—"

Ladon flared his wings, halting his forward progress to hover in the air a moment, jerking his head to look at something off to her right, his left. Before she could attempt to locate what had caught his attention, he blasted a roar so thunderous, her small plane rattled with the force of it.

Ladon arrowed toward whatever threat he'd perceived, moving faster than she'd thought possible. The white dragon finally took shape in her feebler field of vision about a second before Ladon slammed into it.

It couldn't be one of her two loyal followers who'd come with him. Wherever they were, they weren't close enough to exhibit aggression and earn that reaction from Ladon yet. Which meant she'd been followed.

To her horror, he and the other dragon wrapped around each other, grappling, jaws snapping, and plummeting toward the ground.

Skylar held in her yell, deliberately shutting down her own fear. Fear could only get in both their ways right now. Ladon was a skilled fighter. She had to trust he could handle one dragon—

"Fuck," she muttered as clouds above her took ominous shapes.

She knew what that meant now.

More white dragons.

After they'd taken her to Pytheios, she would probably never trust a cloud again.

One dropped down directly in front of her, opalescent in the sunlight, wings spread wide, flapping sideways to hover in an almost upright position with its tail hanging down. It stared her down with such obvious deadly intent that Skylar had to rethink the level of danger in which she found herself.

I killed Pytheios's witch. Not only that, but she was mated. Skylar had no doubt that Pytheios intended to take her and keep her again. He was out for blood this time, and killing her would kill Ladon, too.

I don't think so, asshole.

Skylar nosed the plane into a dive, concentrating hard as she monitored her instruments, her altitude, and the fucker who dove after her.

Right about now, she would rather be in a plane built for more maneuverability, but she'd work with what she had. No matter what, she needed to survive this.

For Ladon.

The dragon after her was catching up quickly. Too damn quick. No way was she going to make it to the ground before he caught her. She considered ditching the plane and doing a low altitude pull with the chute strapped to her back, but the last time she was freefalling around dragons, she was plucked out of the sky and given to Pytheios with a fucking ribbon tied in a big red bow around her neck.

"We're right behind you," a foreign and yet familiar voice reached her. *"Turn on my signal."*

It had to be her own white dragons. Skylar focused and was ready when the order came.

"Turn hard."

With a sharp maneuver, Skylar banked right, into the creature, forcing him to avoid her in a hopping maneuver that then dropped him below her where she couldn't see. Hopefully into her new friends' clutches. About now she was wishing for a plane with firepower as well as maneuverability.

She didn't have time to think about it as yet another dragon, this one closer to silver, came directly at her. Tipping her wings, she put the plane into a spiral, which would hopefully make it harder for the next dragon after her to do much. Regardless of his impervious scales or healing abilities, she was doubtful he wanted to test crashing into her plane.

No. He just wants to crash me.

Her best hope was Ladon or her two protectors shaking the opponents they'd tangled with and getting to her in time.

But given her spinning motion, she couldn't find her mate in the air, and she didn't dare reach out to him through their mental link for fear of distracting him.

A glittering flash of movement to her right told her she'd run out of time. She had maybe ten seconds tops before this asshole took her and her little plane out.

No way was she going down without a fight, though.

Locking her focus on where she thought he'd show next, Skylar got ready to pull out of her spiral and fly right into the fucker.

Five. Four. Three. Two. One.

She pulled on the yoke, leveling out in time to see the literal whites of the dragon's eyes, satisfaction spiking through her at the shock reflected in that gaze.

Skylar reached for the door handle when, with no warning or sound, Kasia appeared in the seat beside hers.

"What the—"

Kasia clamped a hand on her wrist. "Let go of the plane."

Instinct and all the training her mother had put them through had her obeying before consciously deciding to do so.

In an instant, she was yanked through that sense-obliterating space of nothing before reappearing almost immediately on the ground below the fighting.

Her sight and hearing returning in a harsh pop, Skylar put her hands on her knees, breathing steadily. "Kasia, what the fuck?"

Her sister looked less than impressed, her lips compressed in a tight line. "I should've known you'd try to crash your plane into one of them."

Skylar ignored the accusation. "How are you here?"

"We teleported. No way was I letting Ladon rescue you alone. You'd both end up dead."

The boom of an explosion almost felt like it rocked the ground, and they jerked around to see. Behind a stand of tall pines, a ball of flame billowed up into the sky followed by thick black smoke. Not the first plane crash she'd witnessed, but damn was she glad no one was in it.

"Skylar?" Ladon's voice pierced her mind, and she grabbed for her temples. In his haste, he forgot to temper the volume of his thoughts.

"I'm safe."

"Good." That was it, though. She assumed he reengaged with

his opponent.

Kasia tipped her head back, searching the sky.

Skylar followed suit and could only just make out shapes moving above. Flashes of blue or gold or what seemed to be a cloud rolling around, which she guessed were white dragons. When the hell had so many shown up?

A hard push of wind had both of them spinning to face whatever was close to them. Kasia was reaching for her, but Skylar sidestepped as she recognized the two dragons landing beside them. "I know them," she told her sister.

"Help Ladon," she ordered. "And be careful."

One shook his head, his scales rippling with the emphatic movement. *"He ordered us to protect you."*

"*I* am your queen, not him."

Kasia's head whipped sideways as she stared from Skylar to the dragons and back. "Your what—"

Skylar waved her off. "Go."

Without a blink of hesitation, they spread their wings wide, sun turning the pale membranes translucent, and launched into the air.

"Holy shit," Kasia muttered.

Skylar turned a grim countenance her way. "I'll tell you about it later."

"Right." Kasia looked up again, this time her gaze assessing. "For now, I need to help, too."

"Wait!" Skylar flashed a hand out to hold on to her sister. She knew what Kasia meant to do. Teleport herself up there and use her skill in any way she could to help. If she got creative, she could wreak some decent havoc. So could Skylar…if she could get up there.

"Take me up there with you and drop me."

"What?" Kasia shook her head. "No way."

"I know it's dangerous, but if I can touch them, I can send them away. Far away."

Kasia paused at that. "Damn," she mumbled to herself. "What if I can't get you out of there?"

"I have a parachute." She pointed at her back. "I'll use it if you can't get to me before I hit the ground." It would have to be a very low altitude pull, but it could work.

She convinced herself that it was true, because she had to do this.

"Ladon's going to kill me," Kasia muttered. She grabbed Skylar's arm. "Ready?"

"Let's give them hell."

In a soundless, sightless blink, Skylar found herself above the fray. Immediately, the pull of the planet yanked her downward, the wind in her ears increasing as her fall went from zero to terminal velocity.

Same problem as last time, in that her eyes watered like hell, blurring. At least this time she had sunglasses she'd pulled out of the plane's small glove compartment. She could see well enough to aim and avoid, because if she smacked into one of these guys, the impact would break her.

She probably looked fucking ridiculous, but she didn't care. She could help.

The first thing she saw was her two white dragons, but they were too far away to help. Looking down, she spotted Ladon directly underneath.

Of course Kasia would pair her with her mate. About five thousand feet below her, giving her roughly thirty seconds, he faced off against two other dragons—one so brilliantly white, the sun glinted painfully off its scales. She aimed for that one.

"Push them more to your right." She sent the thought.

"What?"

"I'm above you. I can take one out as I go past."

Then she gasped, as a shadow was the only warning of another dragon coming at her. Skylar curled up in a ball, knees to her chest with her arms wrapped around them, and dropped faster through the air, then popped back out to her skydiving position.

"Are you fucking kidding me?" Ladon was yelling at her.

"Don't argue. Push them right."

Below her, Ladon performed a spinning move that slammed his barbed tail across the darker-hued white dragon. Then he jerked his head up in a flash of a move, but she knew he saw her when a low growl of frustration came through their link. *"What the hell do you think you're doing?"*

"Helping. To the right. Now!"

Ladon dipped his shoulder, sliding to his left, then moved forward, forcing both dragons more to the right, exactly where she needed them.

"Five seconds. Keep them there."

I hope I don't lose a hand trying this.

Skylar pulled her fire from where it smoldered deep within her, the flames pouring out over her skin and clothing. Luck was with her, and the white dragon backed in closer to her as she dropped by.

Surging forward, she reached out, sending him away the second she made contact. She hardly felt him before he was gone, and her hand didn't break. More like the sting felt when you slapped someone good and hard. The other white dragon jerked back, startled enough to make her laugh as she shot past him.

· · ·

Ladon gritted his teeth against the instinct to go after his mate, her laughter following her past him. His wild woman in action. Still, she was wearing a parachute, not yet deployed, and he couldn't ignore the fucker in front of him.

"You're going to kill me, woman," he called after her.

"Focus on your own ass, lover boy," came the unrepentant reply.

Then Kasia popped up beside her and the two of them disappeared, probably to drop over another dragon.

She was right.

Without his partner, the cream-colored dragon in front of him turned and dove away. Ladon shot after him. No way was that guy getting away. White dragons were longer, more willowy, which made them beautiful in the air, but slower, built for distance more than speed. Some could go twice as far as other dragons. Which was probably why, once the Americas were discovered, the clans had found a handful of rogue white dragons already living there, their ancestors likely having crossed over the Bering Strait ages before.

Quickly, Ladon gained on his enemy. Every facet of the dark rage consuming him focused on taking out the dragon in his sights. These fuckers had followed Skylar, had attacked his mate. No way were any of them leaving here alive.

As the meters between them shrank, Ladon ignited the inferno inside him, roiling in his gut, ready to spew over his opponent. He knew he'd caught the guy across the top of his head with that tail strike a moment ago, and speckles of blood flew back at Ladon, the metallic scent faint in the air.

Suddenly, the white dragon flipped over onto his back, bringing his back claws up. Ladon's momentum meant he couldn't turn away. To avoid being gutted by those razor-sharp talons, he flared his wings, curling his own back legs under him.

They struck talon to talon, the shock of the impact reverberating through him. Each gripped the other, refusing to let go. Ladon tried to go for his opponent's bared chest, doubling over to rend him with his front claws. The other dragon was smart, though, flinging his wings wide, putting them into a spiraling spin.

His mistake. *You really want to play it that way?*

Ladon locked his grip and flung his own wings out, adding to the death spiral straight down. The Gs sent their bodies outward from that link, making it impossible for either to get at the other, but that wasn't his goal. The browns and greens of the ground below spun closer and closer and he wasn't letting go. Not yet.

The trick to playing chicken was knowing when to flinch.

"What are you doing?"

Skylar. Where was she? He couldn't look for her.

"Ladon, what are you doing?"

"You worry about you." Even his thoughts sounded strained.

"Let go."

Not yet. But he couldn't spare the thought now. He needed to time this just right.

The white dragon pulled at his grasp, trying to escape, flapping his wings in more frantic jerks, but Ladon wasn't letting up.

The ground came at him, the only thing he could see now.

"Let go!" Skylar yelled inside his mind now, her fear like an electric wire snaking inside him.

He waited one beat longer, then used his wings to flip the both of them over before he released his grip. Both he and the other dragon shot away from each other with almost uncontrollable force, but flipping had guaranteed Ladon's orientation to the ground used that force to throw him more upward while his opponent hurtled toward the ground.

A *boom* resounded below him. As soon as he stabilized, pulling out of earth's gravity into the air with a roar of effort, he looked down. The white dragon lay on the ground in a twisted pile of limbs, dirt scattered on and around him like a bomb had gone off, a dark red pool of blood seeping out from beneath him.

One fucker down.

Ladon returned his gaze upward, searching for his next opponent. All around them, dragons swarmed the skies. Some paired off. Some fought two on one or ganged up with several against one. Diving, flying, dropping, gaining altitude. Roars of fury or howls of pain. Bursts of color-tinged fire. Blood raining down from the skies to cover the earth. The battle filled his view with a strange sort of beauty.

This... This was what dragons were built for. Carnage.

He zeroed in on an enemy not far away, his back turned as he also seemed to search for a dragon to engage. Using that against him, Ladon arrowed his body. Again, luck was with him. The other dragon didn't turn to face him, and the sounds and smells of the battle hid Ladon's approach.

He could discern no visible open wounds on the guy, so Ladon saved his fire. Deliberately holding in his roar of challenge, approaching in near silence, he opened his maw wide and went for the back of the neck.

The dragon turned at the last minute, not quite getting his body around where his talons could be used to rip into Ladon. Pain spiked through his own neck as Ladon hit hard, but he ignored that and clamped down roughly. He didn't get the latch just right, sort of on sideways, which meant he couldn't snap the white dragon's neck.

The fucker went berserk, bucking beneath him like a wild thing, thrashing his long neck every which way, jerking Ladon through the sky. Then the guy pulled in his wings and rolled them over. Ladon slammed into something hard with his back. The impact forced air out of his lungs and triggered a reflex that forced his jaws open.

The other dragon flipped again, backing away. Only now he wasn't alone. Two other dragons joined him. They didn't give Ladon a second to regroup, diving on him all at once.

"We're too far away," the accented voices of Skylar's two helpers hit him in stereo.

"I'm coming," Brand's voice split into his thoughts.

Ladon didn't respond, grappling with the three dragons ripping at him with talons and teeth built to penetrate dragon scale. Agony scissored through him as something penetrated on his back, near his kidney.

Brand hit the group of them with all the force of his size. The pounding collision managed to crack Ladon's neck back, a new pain splintering through him. He'd had one of their tails in his mouth when Brand hit, and he didn't let go, a portion of the spiked end ripping off. The other dragon screamed as the tin taste of blood poured into Ladon's mouth. He spit out the twitching end of the tail and aimed his fire at the gaping wound.

He might be broken, but no way was he stopping. He'd fight until every last one was ash.

• • •

Keeping tabs on her mate's fight while falling through the sky, avoiding dragons, and sending some away was no easy feat. For the third time, Kasia plucked her from freefall only to drop her from a higher altitude over a different section of the sky.

Skylar looked down and swore. Directly below her three white dragons grappled with Ladon and Brand, one of them trailing flames and smoke, except she couldn't figure out which one was burning alive. They made such a tangle of dragon parts—wings and necks and tails and talons sticking out at every odd angle and writhing around—that she couldn't tell where one began and the other ended, despite the difference in colors.

She was also coming down on them too fast to be able to clear out of the way. She was going to have to go through them and hope to hell they disappeared before she made contact and killed herself.

"I'm right above you," she called to Ladon. *"If you don't disconnect, you'll teleport with them."*

"Do what you have to."

Skylar frowned. Even in the midst of fighting, she could hear the pain in his voice. Was he injured?

Black fury tunneled her vision on the fray below her, drowning out the insanity still raging all around her.

Those assholes were going down.

A deep calm stole over her as she timed out what she had to do. She held steady in the skydiving posture that provided her the most stability.

Fire flared over her body, her reserves running low but still there. She hoped to all that was good and right in the world that she didn't splat. *"You've got five seconds to clear, or you're going to Ben Nevis with them."*

Ladon didn't answer.

She didn't alter her position or course, holding steady. Five. Four. Three. Two… Skylar thrust her arms straight out from her body. Just as she hit, Brand and Ladon both flew out of the mass of dragons, though she wasn't sure if they cleared enough, because she was focused on sending those bodies out of her way, or her momentum would crush her against their massive, diamond-hard scales.

She was through the space vacated by three of the five dragons as they disappeared before she could even cringe at the impending strike to her body. With a gasp, Skylar jerked her head up. Sure enough, they were gone, Brand and Ladon still above her. A thrilled twitter escaped her even as exhaustion flooded her system, like alcohol hitting the blood, turning her thoughts and movements sluggish.

Oops. Maybe I shouldn't have sent three at a time.

Not that she'd had any choice in the matter.

Still, that same cold calm remained with her. She probably shouldn't teleport any more dragons. Hopefully the men still guarding Ben Nevis had no trouble subduing their new prisoners, who she'd sent to a spot outside the mountain, at the bottom of the ravine.

Right now, she needed to avoid striking any more of the massive creatures battling around her and get as low as possible before pulling her chute. Harder to judge without an altimeter, but she could do it. Hopefully Kasia got to her before she had to.

Remembering how that white dragon had plucked her out of the air from above last time, Skylar kept her head on a swivel, searching all around her, tracking to the right or left, even going head down once to increase her speed and decrease surface area, shooting the gap between two dragons going at it.

Her white dragons were tag-teaming a large eggshell-colored beast. A navy blue dragon she recognized as Asher ripped the jugular out of his opponent's neck, the tendons hanging from his maw, reminding her of a turkey's gizzard. Brand and Ladon were still busy above. No help from them.

She didn't see Kasia coming until her sister smacked into her from above.

"Gotcha!" Kasia yelled, the word hardly discernible over the deafening winds.

A blink, a loss of that blasting wind, then she was on the

ground again. Skylar's legs buckled, and she dropped to her ass beside a large pond. Randomly, she appreciated how, despite the battle raging far above their heads, the stillness of the water turned it to glass, reflecting the skies above, which almost appeared to twist in a dance of dragons.

Only her vision started to constrict, going dark on her. Skylar shoved her head between her legs. "I think I used a bit too much energy." The words came out groggy, slurred.

Kasia leaned over, breathing hard. "Yeah. It's a lot harder transporting such big things. I'm out of juice. You?"

Together they managed to get Skylar's parachute off her. At least she hadn't had to deploy it. Even low to the ground, she'd been fooling herself that a dragon wouldn't have used it to snatch her right out of the air.

Skylar lifted her head to look at her sister. "How many did you get?"

"I slammed at least three into the ground before they knew what hit them."

A screech from the pits of hell had them both jerking their heads to gaze upward in horror. Directly overhead, and close enough to hear the disruption of the air as they plummeted, Ladon and Asher had a white dragon by either wing, both of which appeared deformed. Had they broken his arms, disabling his ability to fly?

Sure enough, both blue dragons released the bastard and stopped their descent as they allowed him to continue to fall. Right at her and Kasia.

"Kas..."

She looked to her sister. Kasia reached out and closed her eyes, but nothing happened. "I can't. I used the last of it to get us down here." Panic laced her words and landed in Skylar's chest, clenching hard.

They couldn't run. They'd never make it.

No. Gods no. I just found him.

They didn't have time, though. The shadow of the beast came

at them, blotting out the bright sun like a harbinger of death.

Shit. No way in hell was she letting both of them die. Searching down deep for the last spark of power inside her, Skylar reached for Kasia. "I love you."

Whatever Kasia was going to say cut off abruptly as she disappeared. Not far. Skylar didn't have enough to send her more than yards, but she got her out from under the dragon, and that was adequate.

Closing her eyes, she sent what she knew was going to be her final thought to her mate. *"I love you, Ladon Ormarr."*

As the beast's screams got louder, and the shadow under which she sat grew darker, Skylar waited for the hit.

A splash of freezing wetness smacked her in the face, and she opened her eyes in time to recognize two arms coming up out of the pond a breath before she was grabbed by the ankles and dragged under the water.

CHAPTER TWENTY-THREE

The second he heard her message, Ladon realized his mistake. He couldn't see her, but he could feel her through that connection and knew exactly where she was and that she couldn't get away.

A scream of a roar punched from him. *What have I done?*

He bolted after the white dragon, vaguely aware that Asher followed a heartbeat later, focused only on stopping it. Except he knew he couldn't.

Dirt and grass and water exploded up around the massive body as it struck with a boom that echoed through the air.

"Skylar!" He screamed her name, a roar ripping from his maw.

He flared his wings, hardly halting his own progress and hitting the ground hard. *"Get him off her,"* he yelled at Asher, who was right behind him.

Together they heaved the carcass up and threw it away from the spot where it landed. Only she wasn't there. He'd expected to find his mate's mangled body, but nothing but mud, filling quickly with dirty water from the pond, remained in the crater the dragon's impact had made.

"Where is she?"

Using his talons, he dug deep gouges into the earth, taking care, barely holding a panicked scramble at bay. She must've been forced deep, buried even as her frail body was crushed.

Asher jumped in front of him. *"Stop."*

Ladon snapped at him with a deep reverberation of warning. He'd take his own Beta's head off if he stood between him and his mate.

But Asher didn't move. *"She's not here."*

"She has to be." He pawed at the ground.

"You'd both be dead. Think." Asher slithered over the crater, stopping Ladon's digging.

"I felt her. She has to be here." Gods, what if she was dying right now.

"You'd feel it. You'd be dying with her."

Asher's logic finally penetrated. Fuck. He was right. *"Then where the hell is she?"*

Brand dropped beside them and prowled over, the outline of his jagged wings appearing as glittering edges against the blue of the sky as he moved. He paused, and Ladon caught sight of Kasia, lying on the ground.

But no Skylar.

"Where the fuck is my mate?" Ladon boomed. Every one of the dragons in the area would've heard that, and he didn't give a shit.

Shifting, Brand pulled Kasia into his arms. She wrapped around her mate, though even from this distance, Ladon could tell she was trembling with that effort. Kasia babbled something he couldn't hear. She sounded hysterical.

Brand looked up, well aware Ladon would be listening. "Something pulled Skylar into the water."

Immediately, Ladon shoved his head into the pond, but the thing was too shallow and too murky for him to get even one eye under the surface let alone see anything.

Going by touch, he methodically dragged a taloned claw through the water to the deepest point. But he encountered nothing but fish and rocks.

"She's not there."

This wasn't working. He needed to do something else.

Something…

"I'm still alive."

Pulling his control around him like donning a suit of armor, Ladon stilled and breathed. He closed his eyes and reached for his mate through a connection that had only grown stronger over the last days.

There.

He could feel her. Feel her life force. Her emotions. She wasn't afraid. No shock there. But she was…confused. Shocked, maybe? And far away. And…holy shit, she'd said she loved him. Those had been her last words.

"Skylar?"

"I'm here."

His head dropped as relief surged through his veins. *"Where are you?"*

"I…can't say. But I'm safe. Are you okay?"

"Yes." Except for the fucking heart attack this woman had caused him.

"I can meet you back at Ben Nevis."

What the fuck?

"Everything is going to be okay. Finish the fight."

Ladon raised his gaze to the skies, satisfaction slowly dripping through the adrenaline of the fight and the terror of having thought he'd lost his mate. She'd said she loved him when she thought she was going to die.

Above and around them, white dragons were either dead, about to be, or teleported elsewhere. Once he'd discovered Asher's disobedience, following with Ladon's guard, he'd spent time in flight planning. Hiding not only his men, but Brand as well, using himself as bait, had worked.

"It's already over."

The fates—because he no longer denied them—had given them this day.

. . .

Skylar let go of the connection that had allowed her to talk to her mate, her mind falling into silence, and dropped her head forward and sent a small thought of thanks to the fates, wherever they might be. The people she loved were safe.

All the people she loved...

Skylar got to her feet and yanked her sister into her arms. "Meira," she whispered, her voice breaking. "Thank the gods." She pulled back, framing Meira's face with her hands. "You're safe? You're okay?"

Tears welling in her eyes, Meira nodded. "You're mated to a dragon?"

Skylar shook her head in wonder. "How did you know?"

At that Meira smiled, almost appearing to light up from the inside like an angel. Skylar had missed her smiles.

Her sister's strawberry blond curls framed her dear face in such a familiar way, the breath punched from Skylar's lungs for the second time. The first being when her sister had pulled her through the pond, through a mirror, and somehow into this room, dumping her on the floor beside a stony-looking man.

She'd thought another creature was dragging her under that water to drown her. Though, in hindsight and without the great, hulking form of a dragon bearing down on her, why would they? Fighting for all she was worth, she'd been pulled into what appeared to be a bedroom in a castle. A really, really old bedroom in a really, really old castle—all velvets, massive four-poster bed, antique furniture, gray stone walls, and frigid air.

What was this? The Stone Age?

But then she'd locked her gaze onto her sister. "Meira? What the hell?"

Meira stepped back. "I'd like to introduce you to Carrick. He is the leader of his chimera of gargoyles."

Gargoyles. Damned if that didn't just make sense. Known to be secretive, mild when at peace, and fierce fighters when roused, Serefina Amon had chosen true guardians for the gentlest of her daughters.

The man before her looked like both man and living statue—all hard angles, flinty eyes, and dark skin with a gray hue to it.

Eyeing him with wary confusion, Skylar hoped like hell she wasn't about to trap herself in yet another prison.

But Meira was there, calm and steady, and so she trusted that.

"Thank you for keeping my sister safe."

Carrick nodded. "I owed your mother a great debt."

Skylar exchanged a glance with Meira, who gave a subtle shrug. "It seems many owed our mother a great debt."

How or when those debts had been drawn, what her mother had done to earn the loyalty of creatures like wolf shifters and gargoyles, was a damn mystery.

Situation explained—as best as it could be—Skylar's natural need to get shit done reasserted itself. There was still a battle raging. "Can you get me back to my mate?"

Meira wrinkled her nose. "The water is too disturbed, but I can return you to your mate's mountain. They have mirrors there."

Stone man said nothing.

"Okay, so what happens now?" Skylar asked.

Meira glanced at Carrick, whose stoic expression didn't change one iota. "I guess that depends on you. When do you want to go?"

Good question. "It will take Ladon several days to get back to Ben Nevis, so I guess I have a little time."

Meira's sweet smile returned. "Good. Then we can catch up."

Was it horrible that she felt divided at this moment? She wanted to spend time with her sister. It had been over a year now since their mother had separated them. At the same time, she needed to be with her mate, like a compulsion manifesting as trouble breathing, concentrating, or any other damn verb.

Everything—first the attack on Gorgon's people, then her imprisonment, the never-ending trip to get to him, and the battle—had kept them apart. The need to be with him clawed at her, almost painful in its intensity.

But logic had to override desire. She'd be safer going back to the mountain via whatever method her sister used. She could wait and fill that time catching up with Meira.

She stepped closer, putting her forehead to her sister's. "I want to hear everything."

. . .

Pytheios leaned his hands on the raised stone slab, trailing his gaze over the body laid out there.

Rhiamon.

The cold had preserved her nicely over the days it had taken him to get home from where that bitch, Skylar Amon, had sent him. His witch lay there, eyes closed as if only in repose, hands folded over her belly. Her pale skin had turned almost translucent with deep purple under her eyes and no doubt pooling along her back, and her neck lay at a contorted angle.

Hopefully that could be fixed.

"Father." Merikh entered the room. His only son. The son his witch had whelped him. One who'd taken on Pytheios's dragon nature, rather than his mother's magical gifts.

But magic and his mother's blood still cascaded through the man's veins. Pytheios was counting on it.

Merikh moved to his side. "The phoenix will pay for what she's done," he promised.

Yes. The phoenix would pay. He'd take her and her sisters, and he'd make her watch as they siphoned off each of her sisters' power, draining them of their life force until they withered and fell away like dead leaves. After the dark-haired phoenix witnessed that, he'd take her life as well. Slowly maybe. Over eons.

But first, he needed his witch back. An act that would take great sacrifice.

A knock thumped against the heavy door.

"Enter," Pytheios called.

Jakkobah, his faithful councilor, came in dragging a woman with him. One gagged, to silence any unwanted magical spell from slipping from those lips. Jakkobah dragged her around the slab to the wall where a heavy iron chain already hung, irons for her wrists and ankles dangling at the ends.

As soon as she saw them, the witch increased her struggles, screaming around her gag and flailing in Jakkobah's arms. But the puny human was no match for a dragon shifter, even a physically weaker one. A thinker, not a fighter.

In short order, the woman was chained to the wall. Warded, of course, to prevent her escape, and to force the witch to do his will. Those chains were a gift, many ages ago, from his own witch.

"What is this?" a man asked.

Pytheios turned to find Brock Hagan standing just inside the door. Jakkobah had brought him, as requested. "I heard you were dead," Pytheios said.

Brock glanced from the woman in chains to the woman on the slab before moving his gaze to his High King. "I escaped under the cover of the battle. The shifter my men claimed to be me was someone else of like coloring."

Pytheios glanced to Jakkobah. The man had ears in every clan, every colony. "They believe he's dead?"

Jakkobah dipped his head in that birdlike way of his. "Yes, my lord."

With a pained grunt, Brock dropped to his knees before Pytheios. "I lost. I should have done better. For you, my king."

True. "Normally, I'd execute you where you kneel."

Brock paused, as if considering those words, then lifted his head. "But you won't?"

"I won't."

"Father—"

Pytheios silenced Merikh's interruption with a venomous glance, and his son choked back his protest.

Brock slowly rose to his feet. "If I may ask, why not?"

"You shall see in a moment."

With that, he turned his back on the man and nodded at Jakkobah, who removed the witch's gag.

Immediately pagan words tumbled from her lips in a spell

most likely intended to end his life.

"Silence," Pytheios thundered.

The warding on her chains turned them red and glowing in an instant, the flesh at the witch's ankles and wrists sizzling with the heat, her screams of agony piercing air now filled heavily with the scent of burning flesh.

Almost as quickly as it started, the iron-cast shackles cooled, and she glared at him through a tangle of hair almost as white as Rhiamon's, her chest heaving and tears streaking her cheeks. "I knew my grandmother should never have trusted you," she spat.

Most likely true. "Bring her back."

"Is that possible?" Merikh demanded. Pytheios ignored his son.

The witch's eyes widened, her gaze dropping to the woman on the slab. "I will not."

Pytheios sighed. "Jakkobah."

Immediately the man pulled out a small device, showing the witch the image on the screen. Pytheios didn't need to look to see it. He knew what she'd find. A dozen men, women, and children surrounded by bloodred dragons. Her coven.

"No," she begged. But he heard what he needed in her voice. Defeat.

"Your grandmother was the only thing keeping your coven alive. You want your people to live? You do as I ask."

The witch closed her eyes, more tears seeping from the seams. "You don't know what you're asking."

"I do."

"She may not come back as herself. She could be...an abomination."

"I'll take my chances."

Rhiamon's grandchild, from a line of children started before she'd met him, shook her head. "Do you know the blood sacrifice that must be made?"

"Yes."

"It can't be me," she warned. "I must finish the spell."

"A blood sacrifice?" Brock spoke up behind him. "Is that why

I am here?"

Pytheios did not deign to answer.

The witch swallowed convulsively. "Still you wish me to do this thing?"

Pytheios nodded.

She shook her head for a long minute, as though silently arguing with herself. One more glance at the screen Jakkobah held before her convinced her, though. He could see it in the way her shoulders came back. "I have your word. My people will live. You'll leave them alone in peace?"

He dipped his head. "You have my word."

The witch swallowed again, then started murmuring words. Words that made no sense, even to his own ears, familiar with many tongues. Words that seemed to wend their way around the room, filling the chilled space with whisperings.

A pressure started to build, tension thrumming through the room. Then Rhiamon's body began to glow with a blinding inner light that hurt to look at directly. The younger witch's mutterings grew louder as she wove the spell over her ancestor, pouring her magic into the woman Pytheios desperately needed if he was to continue.

Rhiamon's body began to twitch. A terrible crack sounded as her head jerked to the side, the broken bones of her neck realigning. The blood pooling under her skin dispersed, flowing back into her veins.

She was close. He could almost feel his witch's presence, though he had yet to hear the beat of her heart.

Pytheios raised his gaze to her granddaughter, still chanting, filling the room now with a thunder of words. Magic flowed from her into Rhiamon in a glittering, cresting wave of white-gold light.

She lifted her gaze to him, her eyes pleading with him one last time to give this up.

But he could not. This sacrifice was one he'd gladly make.

Seeing his resolve, the witch's expression fell, even as she continued her chanting. He watched her for the sign that the time had come.

Finally, she nodded.

Without hesitation, Pytheios whipped out the blade he kept hidden in his sleeve at all times, stepped behind Merikh, and sliced open his son's neck with a clean, sharp stroke, the blade hitting bone, he cut so deeply.

Merikh's cry was a bloody gurgle, his life's essence pouring from him over his mother's body, where it glowed and twitched within the power of the spell.

Pytheios held his dying, flailing son there, emptying his blood over Rhiamon until Merikh went limp, then he allowed his son's body to slip to the floor. Merikh stared at his father with wide eyes, his blood-soaked hands held to his neck, mouth opening and closing around words that would not form.

Then Merikh sucked in one last rattling, spluttering breath before everything about him went still.

At the moment of her son's death, Rhiamon sat straight up, gasping in air, her heart thundering back to life. "Pytheios?" she croaked. "What happened?"

Then her eyes rolled back in her head as she dropped back to the slab, out cold. However, the steady beat of her heart told Pytheios everything he needed to know.

The spell had worked.

In the silence after the storm, darkness stole back into the room as the glow of magic receded.

He looked to where the witch hung limply from her chains. Still alive. Barely. "Take care of that thing," he said to Jakkobah. "And have my witch moved to her rooms and tended to. I'll be there shortly."

Jakkobah nodded.

As he turned to leave the room, Pytheios didn't bother to glance at Merikh's body, already turning to ash where he'd fallen. He stopped at where Brock still stood, revulsion in his eyes, his gaze snared by the woman raised from the dead and Merikh's pile of ashes on the floor.

Pytheios clapped a hand on the man's shoulder. "You are my son and heir now."

Slowly, Brock turned his head to stare back with glittering golden eyes. "You're insane."

"I assure you, I am not."

Brock scoffed. "Why kill your son and not me?"

"Because the sacrifice had to be someone of Rhiamon's blood."

Brock shook his head. "I'm dead, as far as anyone not in this room is aware." He held up his hand, which bore no mark. "Rogue. Without a clan."

In a move akin to a striking snake, Pytheios snatched Brock's hand and raised the dagger still clutched in his hand. Brock didn't even have time to take a breath before Pytheios slashed a deep cut across the man's palm, then across his own before clamping their hands together.

After a second of stunned silence, Brock hissed, his face contorting in pain. Still clasping the man's hand, Pytheios flipped it so they could see the new, white-hot mark etching into Brock's skin between his thumb and forefinger.

"My blood. My mark. My clan... My son."

Brock's eyes grew wide, then his lips drew back in a cold smile. "How will we take Ormarr, Astarot, and their phoenixes down... Father?"

Pytheios chuckled. "We'll bring our own phoenix to the fight."

That pulled a frown from his new heir. "How?"

"You don't rule for centuries without learning a few tricks." Pytheios dropped his hands and turned to look at Rhiamon. The color was coming back to her face. "We made our own phoenix. Like a Trojan horse, she sits among our enemies now. A poison gift, waiting to be opened."

· · ·

Ladon flew at speeds even his own guard could hardly keep up with as he navigated the twists and turns of the canyons leading to the entrance of his home. He'd left them behind along with white dragons who'd joined their cause, including the two who'd sworn loyalty to Skylar. He had two allied kings, and soon Ben Nevis would look like the colonies with their integrated groups of dragons from each clan. More came to their cause daily, and he'd be grateful later.

Right this second, with Skylar close but not close enough, he didn't give a shit. Every kilometer between when the fight had ended and this moment had dragged, the need to be with his mate eating at him.

"I'll be there in two minutes. Have them open the door." He shot the thought ahead of him to Skylar.

"Already open and waiting."

She was waiting for him. The realization sank deep, tugging at both the primitive satisfaction that came with knowing she needed him as much as he did her, as well as the need to hold her, confirm for himself she was unharmed, then bury himself in her sweet body. Maybe for weeks.

Fuck, he needed her. Needed to touch her, hold her, assure himself she was okay.

Despite being a man of few words, he'd been in constant contact with her throughout his journey, needing that invisible connection like he needed air.

She'd filled him in, confidentially, on her location with a Chimera of gargoyles located deep in the Ural Mountains. How her sister had been staying there, and how Meira returned her to Ben Nevis using a form of teleportation that used reflective surfaces like mirrors…and apparently ponds. The notoriously cautious gargoyles had not deigned to come to Ben Nevis with Meira, too wary of the danger, despite Ladon's request to thank them for saving his mate's life face-to-face.

Again, that bone deep ache to hold her and claim her at the same time pulsed through him. No way should they have any audience for this reunion. *"Meet me in our chambers."*

"But everyone has gathered to greet their returning king."

Amusement tinged the words.

"I don't give a shit. I need to see my mate. The clan can greet their king later."

"Impatient much?" she teased.

"Yes." He was in no mood to laugh. The journey to get here and having her separated from him time after time drove him almost to a frenzy now. *"Have Kasia teleport you to our room and then tell her to get the hell out."*

He bulleted straight through the entrance, over those gathered on the training room floor. They raised a shout that quickly died as he kept going through into the main cavern, tipping straight up and flying fast until he landed on his perch.

Even his shift took too long, that now-familiar sting itching at him as he forced it, but he didn't care. He had to see her.

Ladon burst through the doorway and into the living area. "Skylar?" He was calling her name before he cleared the door.

She didn't have to answer, because there she was. Launching across the room in two hurried strides he lifted her off her feet, wrapping his arms around her and burying his face in her hair. He breathed in her smoke and cloves scent, his body tense with the rush of finally being able to hold her.

"You're here," he murmured into her hair.

"So are you," she teased.

He didn't lift his head. "You're safe."

"I'm safe." She feathered a kiss over the side of his neck.

Ladon pulled back, drinking in the sight of her, memorizing every feature, then ran the back of his hand softly down her cheek. "You're mine."

The words came out harsh, but he didn't pull them back or apologize. He slammed his mouth over hers, claiming those lush lips in a possessive kiss. He relished her sweet taste, both familiar and new, with every sweep of his tongue as he hungrily claimed her for his own.

He drew back only slightly. "Say it," he demanded.

"Say what?" she panted, peppering his face with kisses.

"Say you're mine."

Skylar drew back and grinned, her eyes dancing even as she shook her head at him. "Dragon shifters can be so alpha."

"Skylar," he urged and warned in the same breath. He needed this, needed to hear this with her in his arms and not thousands of miles away.

Skylar placed her hands on either side of his face. "I'm yours and you are mine."

"You love me." Say it. He'd never known he would need to hear those words so much, crave to see her lips form them and know they were true.

Her eyebrows went up, though the grin stayed. "Oh? Who says?"

"You said."

She cocked her head. "When?"

"When you disappeared under that dragon and I thought you were dead."

She blinked at him, as if trying to remember, then her eyes went wide.

"Say it."

Only this wasn't her dominant king talking, or even the hardened warrior. The man addressing her now *needed* to hear those words. She had to be able to tell in the way he held himself so rigidly against her, his arms a tad tighter, his eyes focused on her face.

She swallowed. "I never wanted to believe in the fates, because if I did, that would mean giving myself to another person."

Ladon nodded, waiting.

"But it's not like that. Is it?"

Now he slowly shook his head, still searching her expression.

"I don't have to give myself to you, because I'm already yours… and somehow always have been."

His arms tightened another hair. "You have my heart and my soul, woman. I love you so much, these days without you hurt like the fires of hell."

Skylar smiled, and he felt her ease in his arms, as though everything released inside her. Through their connection, he could almost touch a sensation, relief maybe, pouring through her, cool and serene and yet fizzy with anticipation. He'd known she needed to hear it first.

She lowered her head until her lips hovered over his, close enough to feel his warmth. "I love you, and I want you, too."

She didn't need to close that gap. He did it for her, claiming her lips as though he was laying claim to all of her—body, mind, heart, and soul.

With her still wrapped around him, and their lips fused together, he moved, striding confidently across the room in the direction of their bed. She giggled as he tumbled her to the mattress, following in a flash, covering her with his weight and heat.

He went to kiss her, but Skylar held a finger to his lips, then traced them over the cleft in his chin. "You should know that I'm not some sappy, holding hands, says I love you every time she leaves the room, mushy sort of person."

Ladon captured her finger in his mouth, sucking on it in a way that shot arrows of pleasure straight to his cock, before releasing her with a wicked grin. "You think *I* am?"

Skylar grinned right back. "As long as we have that straight... I'm all yours."

"About fucking time," he growled.

EPILOGUE

Samael followed his master, the shifter who'd taken on a paternal role when Samael had been a young man and had lost his own father to his mother's death. Cancer, it seemed, was not only a human affliction. With a dragon's accelerated healing, few succumbed to the disease…but some did.

Gorgon had given a man with no royal lineage—a commoner—a chance. Samael had worked damn hard to prove himself a true warrior, earning his post as captain of the king's guard. A role he took seriously.

He watched his king, Gorgon, out of the corner of his eye as they flew up the inside of the mountain to a perch belonging to another king.

"What is it?" Gorgon's voice echoed through his mind, both familiar and commanding.

"I don't like that we are still here." They had their own clan to protect, and given their location in Turkey, closer to Pytheios, they, more than the Blue or Gold Clans, were exposed.

"We are here at King Ladon and Queen Skylar's insistence."

"I know this."

"We leave tomorrow."

"I know this as well."

The black dragon beside him sighed, his chest visibly heaving. *"What bothers you, then?"*

"Our people are exposed, like an open wound, and yet we sit here."

"At our allies' request."

"Right. Allies that don't entirely trust us after we lost their phoenix."

Gorgon gave a low snarl of warning, given that he was the one who lost Skylar, but Samael wasn't worried.

Their relationship was one of mutual trust, and his king expected his honesty. *"I'm just saying what the hell are they making us wait for?"*

They reached their destination, and Gorgon flared his wings wide to land on the outcropping of stone. Samael hovered, waiting for his king to shift and move away, then landed and shifted himself. Deliberately, he preceded his king into the room.

But no hailstorm of fire or bullets greeted them. Instead, gathered inside were both their allies—Brand Astarot and Ladon Ormarr—along with their phoenix mates.

"I didn't know you'd arrived," Gorgon said, skirting Samael to shake hands with all four.

He directed the comment to Brand and Kasia, who exchanged a glance. Kasia merely offered a pleasant smile. "We wanted to thank you for your help, not only with the Gold Clan, but with my sister as well."

Skylar stepped forward. "I wanted to add my thanks."

Gorgon dipped his head in a nod of acceptance, but Samael kept his own council, watching all four closely for any signs of suspicion, blame, or otherwise. The Black Clan had helped hide all evidence of the fight in Russia. Afterward, half of Gorgon's people had headed home, taking some of the prisoners with them. Brand and Kasia's people had taken another group of prisoners back to Norway. Meanwhile, the other half of Gorgon's people had escorted Ladon and his clan back to Scotland...at the Blood King's request.

The question was...why?

"I know you must be wondering why we asked you here," Ladon

said. "I apologize that it took us a little longer to get organized."

Gorgon and Samael both said nothing, waiting.

"As our closest allies, we have information that we'd like to share with you," Brand said. "This is something no one else in either of our clans knows yet. Not even our Betas."

What next?

Both kings looked to their queens. Kasia stepped forward. "Skylar and I are not the only ones."

Samael stiffened as shock tore through him. He glanced at Gorgon, noting the small tic at the edge of one eye, a sure sign of his king's own shock.

"Not the only phoenixes?" Gorgon asked slowly.

Both women nodded. "Our mother gave birth to quadruplets, and all four of us survived."

Fuck. *Four* phoenixes? How was that even possible and what did it mean? Samael narrowed his eyes. Or was this a lie to—

Two women stepped out from the bedroom. One he'd seen around the mountain with a bunch of wolves, which would take some explaining. But he didn't focus on her. Instead, his gaze sought the other. She had the same big eyes, wide and wary. The same color as her sisters', though he could've sworn they were darker the first time he'd seen her. The same stubborn chin, too.

The woman from the mirror.

As soon as her gaze landed on him, the phoenix hesitated. Only a fraction of a beat, but he still caught it. She definitely recognized him, if the slight widening of her eyes was any indication before she jerked her gaze away, focusing on Gorgon.

Holy shit. He hadn't been seeing things that day. She *had* been in that reflection at the Gold Clan's mountain...watching them.

Tormenting him in his dreams every night since.

"I'd like to introduce you to our sisters—Meira and Angelika."

Meira. Hebrew for "one who illuminates." The name suited her unusual beauty.

Meira stepped forward and addressed Gorgon directly. "As the only other king allied with my sisters and their mates..." She paused to swallow, then tipped up her chin. "I would like to…offer myself to you as a mate."

No.

Everything inside Samael clenched in rejection before cold logic shut him down hard. He had no choice in this matter.

Mine.

The thought clanged through his mind, and he had to clench his fists to keep from stepping forward and claiming her. Thoughts bombarded him even as his dragon pushed to be released.

He wasn't royal. The clans would never allow him to mate her. Fated mates was more for humans, and she wasn't human. A phoenix had to choose, and she'd made her choice. Only kings could mate a phoenix. He'd have to challenge his king for her. A man who'd given him everything.

His dragon roared inside his head, a wail of longing and loss that he'd experienced only once in his lifetime—and had vowed never again. With all the strength of will of the warrior inside him, he contained the beast within. Shut it down. Shut *himself* down.

Meira turned her gaze his way. A gaze now more blue than white, darker. Almost as though imploring him to understand, which she couldn't be. Wishful thinking on his part. Samael hardened his soul and looked away.

He could never have her.

EXCLUSIVE

BONUS CONTENT

Ladon

"There is *one* area in which I wouldn't mind trying that whole obedience thing out."

Skylar lowered her lashes so Ladon couldn't discern her thoughts. Lips tilting slightly, she raised a hand and drew a pattern across his chest with the tip of her finger, her touch branding him, leaving a trail of fire in its wake, even through his clothing.

The animal inside him roared his approval. "Is that so?"

Already he was thinking of all the decadent, dirty things he wanted to do to and with her.

She flirted outrageously with those eyes. "I'm not saying that our mating has been on my mind way too much these last few days, or that I've had to take care of myself more than a couple times just to alleviate the tension."

"You're not saying that, huh?" Ladon put his hands in his pockets, faking any sort of relaxed pose while tension gripped him. "I have definitely not been constantly hard since then, either."

Her chuckle, full of sin in that husky voice of hers, shot straight to his dick, already straining against his zipper.

The timing was shit, but if he was about to send her on a mission, then dammit...

"Strip for me."

Skylar's eyes went wide, her cheeks flushing with an answering heat already threatening to consume him.

To his shock, she didn't snap off a snarky comeback or make him work for her obedience. Instead, she backed slowly away, a sway to her movements that was hypnotic. That icy-hot gaze unwaveringly on him, she slowly pulled her top over her head, followed by her sports bra, her luscious breasts falling free, dusky pink–tipped, and nipples already hard for him.

Ladon unzipped his combat pants and pulled out his pulsing cock, fisting it.

She glanced from him to the door to the conference room and back. "Someone could walk in."

"Then they're going to get a show." He had no problem with that. "Keep going."

With agonizing slowness, she slipped her black pants down those lean, muscled legs.

Ladon yanked his shirt over his head and shucked his own pants.

"Oh," she murmured, eyes on what his hand was doing to his cock. "You're a commando guy?"

He ignored the comment. "Panties off. Now."

Functional nude panties already showing a damp spot at the crotch slid down next. Gods, his mate was perfectly made.

He'd been too impatient to find all the ways to make her orgasm to have gotten to this yet. But damned if he hadn't been fantasizing.

"I want to see those gorgeous lips wrapped around my cock."

With the grace of a jungle cat, she dropped to her hands and knees and slunk across the floor to kneel in front of him. Her warm breath blew against his shaft, teasing. Ladon fisted his hands at his sides to keep from thrusting at her.

Taking him in one hand, she didn't immediately suck him. Instead, she licked from his balls to the tip in one long stroke. Ladon buried his hands in her hair as she slowly drew him into the hot, wet recess of her mouth, so slowly he was shaking with the effort of holding back. He was too big for her to take him all the way, but he didn't give a shit, because she felt so damn amazing.

He kept expecting this thing with her to get less intense somehow. If anything, each time with her only added another level to his need.

Skylar set up a rhythm, sliding her mouth up and down his cock, using her tongue on the underside, and Ladon grunted with each thrust. Only this wasn't nearly enough. "I need to taste you, too."

He scooped her up off the floor, crossed to the conference table, and laid her across it with her ass at the edge. Hooking her legs over his shoulders, Ladon grasped her by the hips and speared his tongue into her slit, the now familiar, glorious flavor of her, along with how she moaned around his dick, driving him higher, faster. Hell, she tasted like sex and woman, already so wet. Ladon licked his way to her clit, sucking the little nub into his mouth, teasing it. Skylar arched, tossing her head, panting.

Ladon would've gladly continued this for a while, but neither of them was in a position to go slow. Maybe next he'd take his time. "I'm going to take you from behind."

Skylar stilled, only her panting breaths filling the silence, mingling with his own harsh breathing.

He gave her ass a light smack. "Rethinking that obedience thing already?"

She shook her head, her long, loose hair spread out over the table. With his help, she soon had her feet on the floor, bent over the table ass positioned perfectly, pussy lips glistening and ready. Just for him.

He'd wanted to claim her this way since the first moment he'd seen her. Bend her over the conference table exactly like this and fuck her hard. Even—or maybe especially—with his dragons watching so there was no doubt who she belonged to.

He barely gave her time to get ready, grabbing her hips hard and slamming, balls deep, into her. Her pussy gripped him, clamping down tight, dragging at him as he pulled all the way out to the tip then slammed home again.

Skylar moaned, long and low, her pleasure turning him on even more.

But the next moan she tried to hush.

"Uh-uh. Let me hear you," he demanded.

"Kasia and Brand are—"

"I don't give a fuck."

Ladon set up a punishing pace, driving into his mate with frantic thrusts on the edge of out of control—needing to mark her, needing to brand her.

He wrapped his fist in her hair, not to the point of pain, but holding her for him as he pounded into her. "That's it, Sky. Take everything I have to give."

"Then give it to me hard," she demanded.

He released her hair to take her by the hips again in a bruising grip. Ladon increased the pace, and Skylar went wild beneath him. Slamming back into him, begging him to go harder, faster. Pressure gathered in his balls, and Ladon held on to his control with everything he had, white-knuckling the woman underneath him.

She started to shake in his grip, and he knew she was close. "That's it, Sky. Fuck."

With a jerk, Skylar screamed into her fist as her body clamped down hard on his.

The pressure in his balls slammed outward as he came in long, hot spurts, filling his mate with his seed. Marking her with his essence. Every godsdamned time they claimed each other this way called to something primitive, something dangerous inside him.

Skylar was *his*.

Ridiculous to want to mark her over and over. They were mated. He shouldn't need that. But he did.

Gradually, the pace slowed until he collapsed over her, panting.

"Fuck me," she groaned.

Ladon chuckled as he hooked a chair closer, keeping her close, still buried in her as he sunk them down into it. She lay her head back on his shoulder, replete.

Skylar hummed her contentment. "Next time, I'm on top."

He brushed her wild tangle of hair back from her face. "What happened to obedience?"

She grinned. "Only when we fuck, Tarzan. And sometimes, I'd like to be in charge."

"Yeah?" He had to admit to being curious. "And what would you order me to do?"

Skylar pursed her lips in thought. "I'd tie you up and ride you until you came so hard you saw stars," she murmured sleepily.

That mental image seared into his mind, his cock responded.

Her lush lips curved. "I think you like the sound of that."

"I could be into it."

She chuckled. "Good."

He nuzzled her neck wondering how she'd managed to take him from boiling fury to agreeable to needing to fuck her hard in such a short period of time.

One thing was for sure. He'd never be bored with Skylar as his mate.

ACKNOWLEDGMENTS

I get to do what I love surrounded by the people I love—a blessing that I thank God for every single day. Writing and publishing a book doesn't happen without the support and help from a host of incredible people.

To my fantastic, equally dragon-obsessed readers... Thanks for going on these journeys with me, for your kindness, your support, and generally being awesome. Ladon and Skylar took me on quite a ride. I mean talk about the epitome of rock meeting hard place. Stubborn versus more stubborn. But they somehow just fit. I think their equal strength put them on an equal footing, and that's the only way they could be with a mate. I hope you fell in love with these characters and their story as much as I did. If you have a free sec, please think about leaving a review. Also, I love to connect with my readers, so I hope you'll drop a line and say "Howdy" on any of my social media!

To my editor, Heather Howland... This series is as much yours as it is mine. Your support is something I will always cherish, and the way you fight for my dragons makes you one of them. And we really should try to avoid the phone, because we only get each other deeper in trouble. Lol.

To my Entangled team...I don't know how you guys do it, but you're awesome. From the various stages of editing, to production and packaging, to marketing and my publicists, I've had nothing but support and help along the way. (And the most gorgeous, drool-worthy covers! I stare at them daily. Seriously.) Y'all rock!

To my agent, Evan Marshall... Thank you for your belief in me and guiding me through every crazy idea and new opportunity and my inability to say no to any project because I want to do all the things. You are a delight to work with!

To my writing partner and BFF, Nicole Flockton... You keep me sane and worry over me and help me brainstorm and edit things for me and rein me in when I'm getting too crazy. Love you!

To my support team of beta readers, critique partners, writing buddies, reviewers, RWA chapters, writer's guild, friends, and family (you know who you are)... I know I say this every time, but I mean it...my stories wouldn't come alive the way they do if I didn't have the wonderful experiences and support that I do. And that's all because of you.

Finally, to my own Fated Mate...I love you so much. No woman has ever been loved the way you love me, and that's what I try to give every heroine who crosses my path. A hero who lifts her up and inspires her every day to be the best version of who she is. To our awesome kids, I don't know how it's possible, but I love you more every day. I can't wait to see the stories of your own lives.

talk about it

Let's talk about books.

Join the conversation:

f @harlequinaustralia

♪ @hqanz

○ @harlequinaus

harpercollins.com.au/hq

If you love reading and want to know about our
authors and titles, then let's talk about it.